Sinners, Rage & Pain

The Brixton Trilogy

Heidi Stark

This is a work of fiction. Any resemblance to real people, living or dead, organizations, places, events or locals, are entirely coincidental.

Foreword

Sinners, Rage and Pain is a Dark Reverse Harem (Why Choose) Romance trilogy comprised of *Sea of Sinners, Sea of Rage* and *Sea of Pain.*

18+.

Warning: this book includes graphic violence and sex scenes, and references of abuse/assault that some readers may experience as triggering.

Sign up for Heidi's newsletter herefor the latest on new releases, promos, giveaways and events!

Join Heidi on social media:

Facebook: @heidistarkauthor

Instagram: @heidistarkauthor

TikTok: @heidistark_author

Website

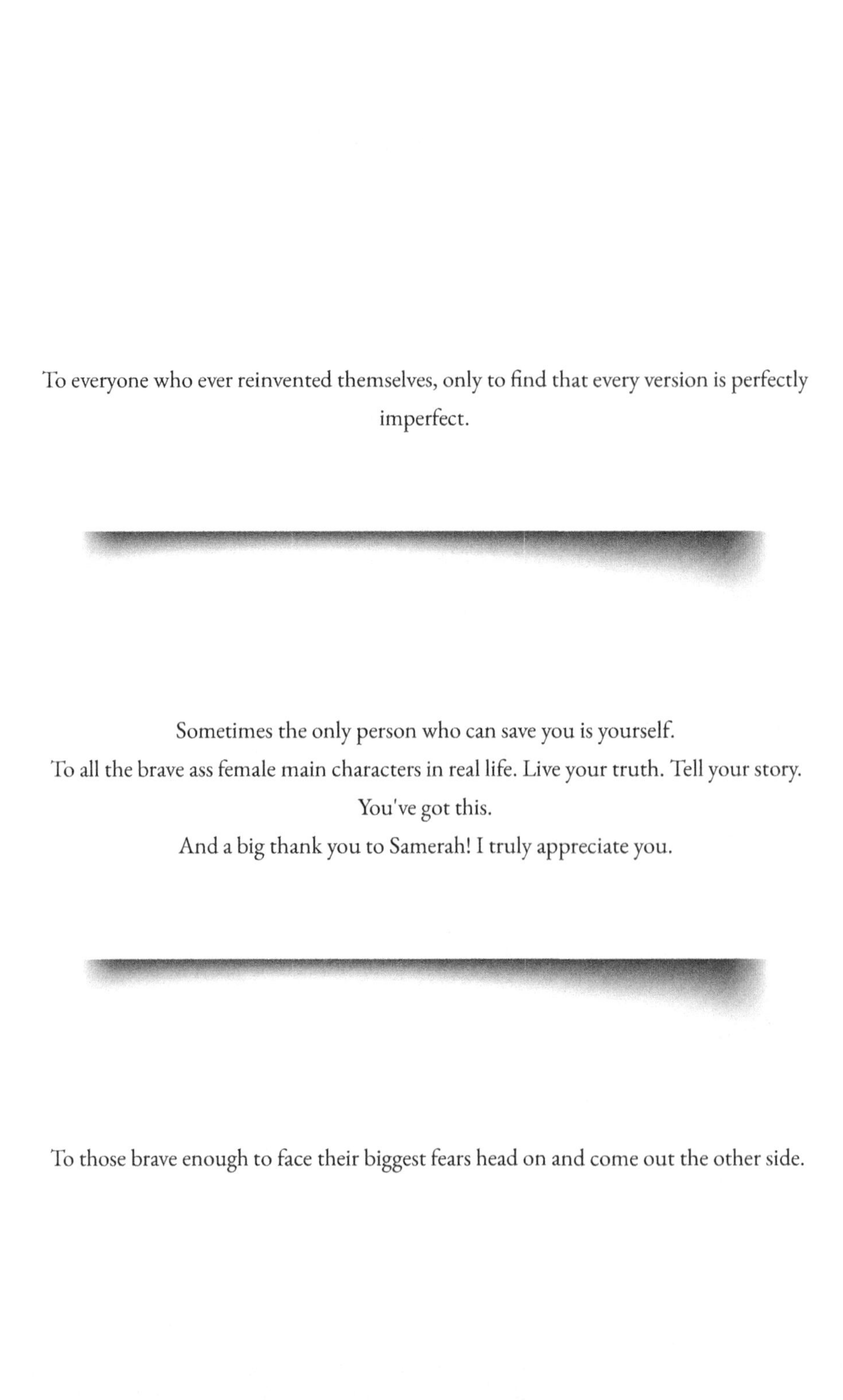

To everyone who ever reinvented themselves, only to find that every version is perfectly imperfect.

Sometimes the only person who can save you is yourself.
To all the brave ass female main characters in real life. Live your truth. Tell your story.
You've got this.
And a big thank you to Samerah! I truly appreciate you.

To those brave enough to face their biggest fears head on and come out the other side.

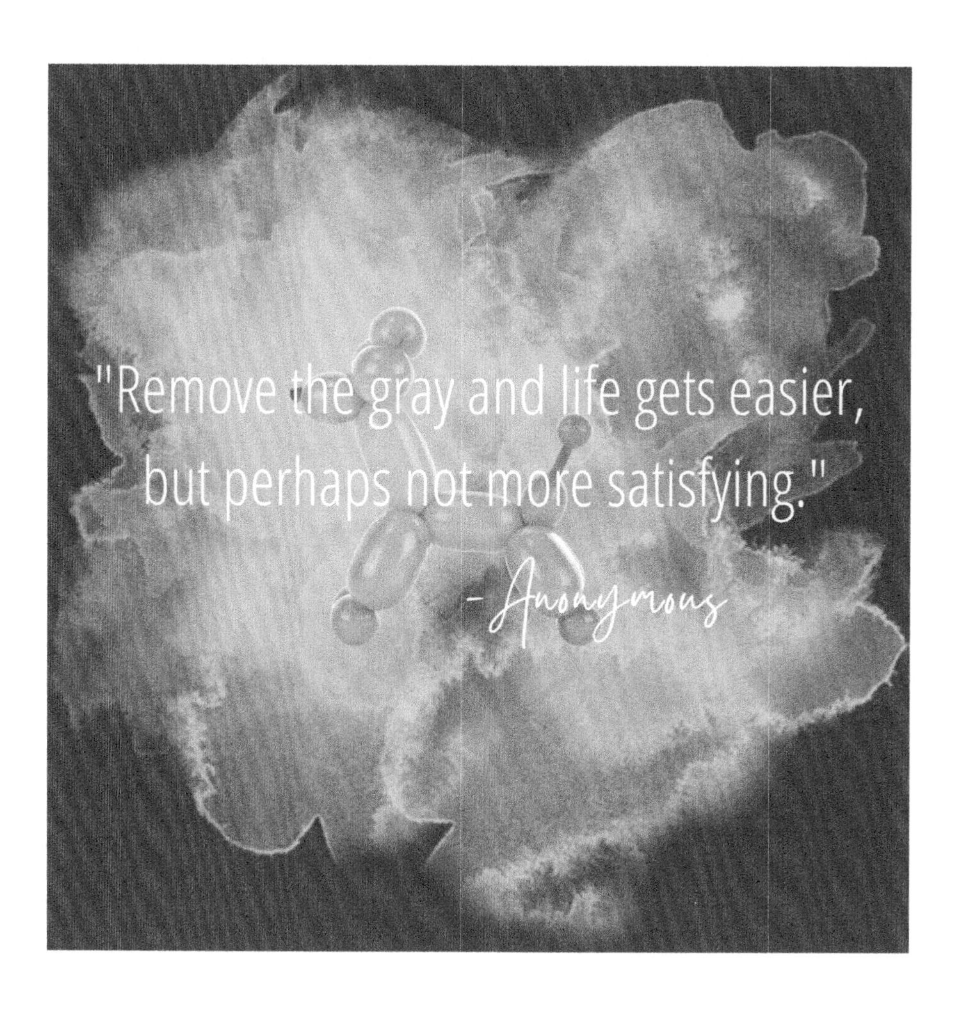
"Remove the gray and life gets easier,
but perhaps not more satisfying."
- Anonymous

Chapter One

Angel

The front door jingles as someone enters the salon, and for a moment I take my eyes off my client and glance over to see who it is. It's a guy I haven't seen before, but he strolls in with confidence, as if he's been here many times.

And he is *hot*. Not just kind of good-looking. He's scalding, a clear twelve on a ten-point scale.

Closing the door behind him, his eyes skim the salon and, seeming to pass his invisible standards, he nods almost imperceptibly before making his way further inside.

I wonder what most people's first impressions are when they enter this place. It has everything it needs to give clients what they're looking for, but it's pretty bare bones.

It's a small space, big enough for one hairstylist, two at max, and every surface is cluttered with hair products and equipment and cleaning supplies.

The furniture is secondhand, every table and chair slightly nicked or peeling or getting threadbare if you take a closer look, but people come here for a great haircut, not for a comfortable place to hang out.

And while the salon may not be the height of interior design, I pride myself on making sure everything is clean and sterilized and follows proper health and safety guidelines.

Jars of blue barbicide solution line the walls, reminiscent of the specimen containers you see in biology classrooms where preserved organisms sit suspended in formalin. But in this case, they're filled with combs and scissors and other items that are better off cleansed of human grossness.

The first thing I notice about the hot stranger is his dark hair, longer at the top and swept away from his face, and shorter on the sides and back. Hair that requires taking a fair bit of maintenance, not just a regular short style like most guys want when they come in. He takes care of his hair, and it's clearly important to him. I'm a hairstylist and I notice these things.

His eyes are a striking gray-green, like olive and fog swirled together, and they twinkle as he looks around the salon, his gaze eventually settling on me. Combined with his sexy lopsided smirk, it's almost as if he's in on a joke that nobody else is. He exudes confidence and comfort in his own skin.

He's taller than average, maybe around six-two, and he wears a fitted T-shirt that shows off his well-developed pecs and shoulders. Tattoos cover his muscular arms, which I find sexy as hell. And despite the island heat, he wears dark blue jeans and leather shoes. Not many guys dress this well around here, with everything fitted to his body like it was made for him.

The client I'm working on looks up as well, and her eyebrows involuntarily raise ever so slightly in a sign she thinks he's hot, too. She grins at me in the mirror, and I wink back at her.

I smile and nod in his direction, and call out, "Welcome! I'll be right with you!"

"Good with a pair of scissors, are you?" His eyes roam my body and settle on the shears I'm holding in my left hand.

It's like he doesn't even care I'm working on someone else. Like he expects to have my undivided attention the moment he enters the store.

The way he looks, he probably doesn't have to work for female attention, and he's probably used to getting what he wants when he wants it. Jerk.

"I might be a little while. We still have a bit to do here before we finish up," I say, gesturing toward my client. "Feel free to look at the products on display in the meantime, or you're welcome to take a seat."

I point my shears at the display case beside the cash register to the left of where he's standing, as well as the slightly threadbare couch off to the right side of the front entrance.

I'm not apologetic about making him wait. Whoever he is, I know he doesn't have an appointment, because this is my last booking for the day. I do accept walk-ins, though, and I'd be happy to take a look at his hair once I'm done with my current client.

We don't get a ton of foot traffic here. The salon is located on the second story of a strip mall in a suburb tucked away behind the highway, about a mile from the beach. So if people end up here, it's generally because they've found the salon online or through word of mouth.

I hardly doubt this guy just happened to be strolling through the neighborhood, judging from the way he looks. Someone must have referred him here, although I don't see him being BFFs with any of my regular clients, or he's done his own research. He definitely looks more like a city guy, from a proper bigger city on the mainland rather than the small and low-key one we have here. But he also bears the signature tan of someone who lives here and spends a lot of time in the ocean.

I wonder if he surfs. From the way his muscles ripple under his T-shirt when he moves, it wouldn't surprise me.

He glances over at the glass shelving stacked with gels and waxes, but his gaze quickly returns to me.

"No rush," he says, continuing to survey me. "I'll just watch you work."

As his eyes linger on my ass, a strange look passes over his face, almost like a half-grimace, half-smile, and he suddenly plunks himself down into the couch in the waiting area. A weird, jerky movement that seems to come from out of nowhere, a contrast from the confidence and poise he's exhibited so far.

Unlike most of my other customers, he doesn't pick up a fashion or hairstyle magazine from the pile stacked neatly on the coffee table in front of him, or scroll mindlessly through his phone as he waits. Instead, he continues to watch me, his eyes roaming over my body as I work on my client's hair.

I feel a flush creeping up my chest and neck and onto my face, my body feeling tingly under his gaze. I'm not used to people watching me work.

"It's rude to stare," I say, narrowing my eyes at him. "Can you read a magazine or something?"

"I like what I'm looking at more." His eyes blatantly continue to explore my every angle, and my face grows hotter, the flush intensifying.

"I'm not sure whether that's meant to be flattering or creepy. Can't you see I'm working on my client here?" I roll my eyes at him.

I meet my client's eyes in the mirror as I continue to cut her hair, and she smirks.

"If you'd like me to leave you two alone, I can," she says. I feel myself flush further and my reflection confirms my face has reached tomato-level redness.

"No, of course I don't want you to leave," I quickly reply. "Sorry for this... distraction." My eyes flit to the insanely good-looking man observing me from the couch and then back to my client. "My focus is entirely on you. You're my top priority."

The hot guy smirks and picks up a magazine. He flips the pages and occasionally glances down at a picture or an article, but in the mirror I can see his eyes always quickly return to rest on me. If he wasn't so hot, it might creep me out, but his gaze isn't unwanted.

Because I can be slightly petty, I make sure to give my client the VIP treatment, taking my time on the finishing touches, and giving her a thorough rundown of all the products I used on her today.

I notice that the hot guy wriggles his ankle a little and checks his watch now and then, but he doesn't leave or complain about the wait.

Interesting. I wonder what makes him want to stick around. It's not like this is the only salon in the area.

By the time I'm done with my client, she looks fantastic, and I can tell by her glow and the way she's beaming that the hair revamp has given her a confidence boost.

It's amazing what a few layers, highlights, or even just a conversation with someone who listens for an hour or two, can do to a person's energy. It's the main reason I do this job, my personal avenue for artistic expression.

There have been so many times I've been down on myself and my life circumstances. I know what it feels like to desperately need a little pick-me-up.

Helping other people feel good about themselves is one of the few things within my control. I get to work alone and do things on my terms, with nobody telling me what to do except for the odd bossy client. And I can fire clients if they get to be too much.

Plus, I'm exceptionally skilled with scissors. That helps, too.

Chapter Two

Roman

Against my better judgement, I'm biting the bullet and trying out a new hair salon today. Despite my apprehension, the moment I enter the space, I'm glad I did. Because even if I end up leaving here with a buzz cut, this hairdresser is hot as hell. At least the view will be enjoyable for an hour or so.

I've been a little stressed the past few weeks, ever since the hairstylist I've trusted for years broke the news that she was moving away. She was one of the few humans I trusted, aside from my business partners, my brotherhood.

It might sound like I'm laying it on a little thick by saying that, but it's the truth. A haircut can make or break someone. She or he who holds the shears and razor blades rules the world, or at least dictates whether I'm going to have a good time for the next few weeks.

My former hairstylist was so worried about telling me she was leaving that she insisted I meet her for coffee away from the salon when she broke the news. I think she was maybe concerned I'd have a temper tantrum and destroy her place. But I'm not a monster. I just have a vested interest in her work, and I liked the consistency of knowing I could rely on her when I needed her, which was often.

I recall how she trembled as she told me she was heading out of town, and seemed relieved when I didn't try to talk her out of it. She looked surprised as I handed her a generous roll of bills to thank her for holding me down for the past eighteen months or so.

So now I'm a free agent with my hair, which is an uncomfortable place to be.

After extensive online research, I found people had lots of good things to say about this place, so here I am. Nobody mentioned that the hairdresser is a fucking smoke show.

It might sound vain, but I take my face and my hair very seriously. They, and my body which I also keep very much in shape, are what help me get the ladies. And ladies are my primary hobby. Lots of them, all the time. Sometimes several at the same time. I rarely meet one I don't like.

I move in circles where attractive women are plentiful, a mixture of tourists and wealthy folks who live on the island. Owning several upscale clubs and bars gives me access to an endless supply of gorgeous women who take phenomenal care of themselves. They're easy pickings at the venue we own, consistently dressed up and manicured and looking to let loose and have a good time.

Being a club and bar owner is like having a magnet stuck to me that draws women in whenever I'm near. They're attracted to the power and the celebrity of it all, basically dripping and creaming themselves at the chance to be seen on my arm, maybe seeking the heady thrill of being given a complimentary bottle of champagne courtesy of the owner.

It's an all-you-can-eat buffet and I like to feast often.

Having fantastic hair only sweetens the deal. Self-maintenance is worth the investment, and I can afford it, so why not?

As soon as I see the hairstylist in this new salon, I can't keep my eyes off her. I know it's rude to stare, but I'm attracted to beautiful things. And she is really fucking gorgeous.

Her hair is a vibrant purple that contrasts vividly with her creamy complexion. She wears bright red lipstick that showcases her plump lips. She beams a wide, bright megawatt smile at me in a friendly welcome, her teeth straight and white. Long lashes frame her large green eyes, and her high cheekbones are stunning.

As she works on her client's hair, I can see her from the side, as well as her reflection in the mirror. She makes conversation with her client, smiling frequently, and I notice she has a dimple on one of her cheeks. Adorable and sexy.

She's wearing a short green denim shirtdress that hugs her curves and has a slightly military look to it. Her reflection shows a hint of cleavage, and it looks like she maybe has a tattoo chest piece hiding under there that I want to see more of.

She has a nose and lip piercing, as well as countless piercings in her ears, some of them connected by small chains. And while I love a lot of things about women, I'm a particular sucker for tattoos and piercings.

The more I look at her, the more things I notice that I like, and the more she captivates my attention.

Blood rushes to my cock and makes me hard, and my heart beats faster, just at the sight of her. She's having a stronger effect on me than most women, just being in her presence. I wonder if she smells like citrus or vanilla or bergamot or rose. I wonder if her hands are delicate and gentle or strong and purposeful.

Hopefully, she finishes up with this client soon, because I want to be near her, to see her up close, and to learn more about her.

To see why I'm reacting to her in this way. She's sexy, but she's a stranger, and we haven't even spoken yet. I need to know more.

Because as much as I like women, I'm always in control. I'm the one making their pulse race, making them aroused when I choose to. Taking my time to tease, or just grab what I want with no preamble, depending on my mood.

I dictate the pace, what happens, when it happens, and how it happens. Everything that takes place is because I make it so, and I decide how my body responds in every situation.

But one look at this woman and I'm a mess with a throbbing cock, practically salivating on the floor. I can't tear my eyes away from her.

She's a masterpiece. And I want her.

Chapter Three

Angel

I check my happy client out at the cash register, and she beams as she hands me a generous tip for my work with her today, insisting we get her next appointment locked into the calendar.

As soon as she leaves the salon, I pick up the broom and start sweeping the locks and hair fragments discarded during the haircut into a pile in the middle of the floor. I sweep the pile up with a dustpan and brush, and start to reset my station for the next client.

As I wipe the counter down and hang the hairdryer back up on its hook, I turn to Hot Guy, who's still on the couch observing me while poorly pretending to read a magazine. "So you want your hair cut, or do you just like to stare at strangers while they're working?"

Without being invited, he strolls over to my hairdressing chair and plonks himself down right in front of me while I'm still setting up. "You made me wait long enough. I'm invested now. And it's not my fault you're pretty to look at. Beautiful, even."

Oh, so he's one of those. A charmer. Knows all the smooth things to say to the ladies. I know his type, and have him pegged a mile away. I bet he gets away with it too, with his egregiously good looks.

I lower the chair by pumping the lever with my foot. He's a lot taller than my last client.

Wrapping a hairdressing cape around him and securing it carefully at the back, I run my hands through his hair to see what I'll be working with. It's soft, and I vaguely recognize the masculine, unique scent of his pomade as cognac and Cuban cigars.

I face him in the mirror and he maintains eye contact while I try to get a sense of what he wants today. "What are you looking for? Sticking with the taper fade with slick back?"

I run my fingers through the lengths of his hair, my nails gently scratching his scalp as I get a feel for its thickness and the direction it grows.

"That feels good," he says. "And is that what it's called? Taper something or other? I just call it my hair." He shrugs and smirks at me in the mirror.

"You keep it in good condition for someone who doesn't know much about it," I smirk back at him. "I think you know more about your hair than you say you do. In fact, based on its current condition I'd venture to say you're quite particular."

"What can I say? I need to make sure I look good for the ladies." He winks at me and grins.

"I'm sure there are a lot of ladies that are interested in your, uh... hair."

My eyes travel over his muscular body and my words trail off as my gaze reaches his crotch. I feel myself blush when I realize he's watching my eyes roam all over him.

He smirks. "Are you interested... what did you say your name was?"

"I didn't. But my name is Angel." I can't resist giving him a hard time. "It's why the salon is called Angel's Hair Salon."

"Clever," he smirks. "And are you an angel, Angel?"

"It's a somewhat ironic name, but I didn't choose it." I shrug. It's a lie. I totally chose it, but he doesn't need to know that. Nobody needs to know that except me. As far as anyone else is concerned, it's been my name since birth.

"Oh, so you think you're a badass?" He raises an eyebrow.

"True badasses never talk about it." I grin.

He smirks again.

I make eye contact with him in the mirror. "So what happened to your last hairdresser? Clearly, you haven't been cutting your own hair at home. Are you new to the island? Or did they fire you because you kept staring at them while they worked on other clients?"

"She moved away, actually," he frowns. "It was traumatic. It happened recently and I'm still grieving a little. I had to scour the internet to find this place. It better live up to all the hype." He says it like he's joking, but I sense some truth to it.

I snort. "It's a salon in a strip mall, not a Beverly Hills boutique. A step up from Great Clips. So maybe set your expectations accordingly."

He smirks. "As long as you don't have a buy nine haircuts get one free coupon, I'm good."

I shake my head to indicate we don't have coupons, and he looks relieved.

"If you fuck up my hair, I'm coming for you, though," he laughs, but it sounds hollow and I shiver at the coldness in his voice.

"Well, that sounds ominous. I'll make sure I do a good job. You just need to be clear about what you want."

He just laughs the hollow laugh again. Weirdo.

"So, help me out here. Do you want the same again, just a little trim?"

"Yeah, this hairstyle seems to be doing the trick. Just a trim will do. We can mix things up a little once we've established a trusting relationship. It's very important to me that I trust my stylist implicitly."

The way he says it sounds like he's picking a neurosurgeon to conduct delicate brain surgery, not just trim the ends of his hair, but whatever.

"We'll do the trust fall exercise at the end of the appointment," I roll my eyes.

He smirks at me in the mirror.

"Alright, let's get you over to the hair washing station." I gesture to the wall of sinks with reclining chairs lined up in front of them. "Second one down."

He gets up and walks to the chair next to the one I pointed to. "I prefer this one. Three's my lucky number."

"Sure," I roll my eyes. "Whatever one you like, snowflake." What a picky asshole. Superstitious too, it seems.

He sits in the recliner, leans back and places his neck in the basin's divot, and I turn on the water.

After testing it on my forearm, I wet his hair, making sure to saturate every lock. "Is the temperature okay?"

"It's a little hot, like you. But I like that," he says, looking up at me, his head still reclined in the sink. He's hot upside-down as well. Jesus.

I massage a blob of shampoo into his scalp, making it lather up into a rich foam, and then rinse it carefully until the water flows clear. I repeat the same with some hydrating conditioner, making sure it coats his hair from the roots to the tips.

"This needs to sit for a few minutes. Would you like a scalp massage while you wait?"

"Is that something you ask all your clients? Or am I getting the VIP treatment?" he smiles.

"I definitely offer it to all my clients. Don't flatter yourself," I say, but I wink at him.

"I thought I was special," he pouts. "But I'd still like to see what you can do with your hands," he grins his upside-down grin and winks back at me.

I massage his scalp, using my finger and thumbs to knead the top of his head and his neck, and he closes his eyes and leans into my fingers. I gently swirl my nails across his scalp, well aware of the tingly sensation this creates, and he sinks his head into my touch.

When I massage just above his ears, making firm circles with two fingers on each side, he lets out a soft groan.

"Fucking hell, Angel," he says. "You're very good at this. Your hands are amazing. I almost fell asleep when you used your nails. I love the way you're scratching my scalp."

"Just doing my job," I shrug, but his words generate a brief flutter in my chest that travels down to my core. There's definitely a little electricity each time my hands touch him.

I carefully rinse the conditioner out of his hair and then towel-dry it, pressing the towel firmly onto his head to gather the excess moisture.

"Right, we're all set." I discard the towel, then guide him back to the hairdressing chair where he sits down again.

I pick up my shears and take another look at his hair, mapping out my approach to his cut.

"So, tell me about yourself, Angel." He eyes me in the mirror. "What do you do other than look drop-dead gorgeous?"

He's back again with the flattery. But this time his words flow a little too easily, and it's clear he's using a line he's spun before. It's something he could say to absolutely any woman to get their heart racing. Gross.

I narrow my eyes at him. "Stop distracting me, or I might accidentally chop off one of your ears."

"I'd be okay with that, as long as you're the one who did the chopping. I don't mind a little knife play." He winks at me.

Jesus, this guy has no boundaries. I've barely known him for thirty minutes and he's whipping out knife play talk. Still, it's kinda hot even if it's a bit unusual for a first-time conversation.

We chit-chat about life on the island. By the sounds of it, he's been here a little under two years.

While the island is relatively small, I'm not surprised we haven't crossed paths, even though we've been here around the same amount of time. Judging from his appearance, he and I run in very different circles. And to be fair, I spend most of my time here at the salon and at my apartment, and occasionally in the ocean when I go surfing. There's limited opportunity to bump into someone new.

As I snip away at his hair, preserving his existing style, my body occasionally presses into his for leverage. Each time it does, his eyes get a little darker, and my body feels a little tingly at the connection.

He mentions owning a couple of clubs in the city and over in the tourist area. I'm past the time in my life when I frequented clubs and bars every weekend, and that phase was long gone by the time I moved here. I only visit the congested tourist area when I have to, or for a special occasion of some sort.

I stick to myself for the most part, and I live in the same suburb as the salon. It's a sleepy area, with pockets of lively cafes and neighborhood restaurants. We have a grocery store and a pharmacy and a hardware store, so there's not really a need to venture much further afield.

Especially when you value alone time as much as I do. And especially when you're trying to keep a low profile, and stay off the radar of someone who might be trying to find out where you are.

The one thing I seem to have in common with Hot Guy, other than a love for good hairstyles, is surfing.

He mentions having grown up on the coastal mainland, and having worked as a surf lifesaver in some fairly treacherous waters when he was a teenager. It sounds like he's enjoying being able to do it every day, living here.

I didn't really get into surfing until I moved here. I'd tried it a couple of times when I was growing up, but it was more a case of splashing around with a surfboard for fun and I didn't really know what I was doing.

Here, I've taken a few lessons from locals. It's so casual on the island that people will trade haircuts for surfing lessons, plumbing repairs, home-cooked meals, and pretty much anything else you can think of.

I've made a small group of surfing acquaintances who I head out with a couple of days each week, after I've locked up for the day and headed home from the salon. We like to sit out in the water and watch the sunset while we casually chat about our days, much of the time spent in silence just listening to the gentle voice of the ocean lapping at our boards.

My surfing buddies are very low-key and don't ask a ton of questions. They just want companionship out on the water, which works well for me. I can choose what I want to share, and so I share very little. It's better that way for everyone. And I also enjoy the quiet camaraderie that comes with sitting out in the ocean with a group that will have your back if you need it.

I'm about halfway through Hot Guy's haircut when the door jingles again and another man enters the salon. I've never seen him before, either.

His figure is large and imposing, he's maybe six-foot-four and made of solid muscle, and he breathes heavily underneath his puffy coat.

He has long light-brown hair pulled back in a ponytail, bushy eyebrows and brown eyes that flit around as if he's constantly assessing his environment for threats. I know that look from people who work in security, as well as in restaurant managers. They're always scanning for trouble, having difficulty maintaining focus because they're keeping track of a million little things.

The new arrival has thin lips, and his nose has a prominent bump in it like it's been broken and reset one too many times. An angry red scar protrudes from his jaw and extends down his neck. Whoever he is, this man has been through some things.

He's definitely not one of my usual clients, and I'm not sure why everyone is dressing so warmly today. We're on a tropical island, for goodness' sake.

The man stops for a moment, glancing around the salon. After establishing the three of us are the only ones in the space, his gaze settles on Hot Guy and his eyes narrow.

"You fucking Brixton scum," he growls, fumbling inside his coat.

"Excuse me? To whom do I owe the pleasure?" Hot Guy cocks his eyebrow.

"You don't need to know who I am," the big guy snarls.

"Well, you clearly know who I am," says Hot Guy. "It's only fair that you introduce yourself as well."

"I'm not here for pleasantries, you piece of shit," he growls. "I'm here to give you and your brothers a message. Except in this case, you'll be the message."

I gasp as he finishes unzipping his coat, pulls a gun from his waistband, and aims it at Hot Guy.

Without flinching, Hot Guy looks over at him through the reflection in the mirror, his back to the man. "Asshole, whoever you are, you're making a big mistake. Put the gun down." His voice is calm and steady.

My heart feels like it's going to beat out of my chest as I glance between the men. I don't dare make a move, and instead, I stand glued to the floor, willing my muscles not to twitch and remind either man I'm here.

"Look, there's no need to be pointing a gun at us, man," says Hot Guy. "You seem like a reasonable guy. Let's just have a conversation. How about you tell me why you're here?"

The Asshole shakes his head. "We don't need to do any talking. My gun will do that just fine."

Hot Guy shrugs. "Sure, that's an option. But how about you tell me more about what's going on, and we can figure things out together? There must be more than one option here. We can work it out. I might be able to help you in some way. Let's just talk about it."

There's a man literally pointing a deadly weapon at us and Hot Guy is unflappable, talking to The Asshole like he's soothing a toddler, trying to reason with him so he'll put the weapon down.

But it doesn't seem to work. The Asshole doesn't answer, and keeps the gun aimed at us. He takes a step closer to Hot Guy. In this cramped space, it's feeling claustrophobic.

"Who sent you?" Hot Guy asks again, his body tensing a little as he sees his efforts to use logic aren't working. The energy is shifting, and Hot Guy's demeanor is quickly transitioning from congenial and helpful to frustrated.

"I work alone." The Asshole's eyes flicker downward. The way he says it doesn't sound convincing. But he juts his chin out as if to double down on his comment.

Hot Guy smirks at the man. "I find that hard to believe."

The Asshole growls and steadies the gun as Hot Guy pivots from trying to reason with him to being straight-up condescending.

"Fuck you, Brixton. You all think you're fucking better than everyone else. Trying to take over the business that we worked so hard to build up over years and years."

"Look, I don't know who you are. But my brothers and I are doing well because we are the best at what we do. We work hard and we get to reap the rewards for our efforts," he shrugs. "I'm not sorry for being strong and powerful, so I will not apologize. I don't care what weapons you have pointed at me."

"You don't just get to come here and take what's ours," The Asshole growls.

"I'm not sure what you're referring to exactly, but if we took something from you, I guess that makes it ours now. That's how things work around here. Again, not sorry."

"You fucking mainland fucks! Coming here and trying to tell us how things are meant to work!" The Asshole raises his voice and clicks off the safety of his gun.

Hot Guy snatches the hairdressing shears from my hand and spins in the chair to face The Asshole. "Come on, Asshole," sighs Hot Guy. "Put the fucking gun down or things won't end well for you."

The Asshole cocks the hammer of his gun, keeping it trained on Hot Guy.

At that moment, Hot Guy flits to where The Asshole stands, and suddenly my hairdressing shears are embedded deep in the side of The Asshole's neck. His eyes bulge and he groans, his hands flying to the handles of the shears as blood runs from his mouth in a dark red rivulet, trailing down his chin and dripping onto the floor.

"I told you to put the gun down, asshole," hisses Hot Guy. "You really should have listened to me. Your failure to do so is going to be your undoing."

The Asshole lurches forward, arms raised to shoulder height as if he means to attack Hot Guy, and bubbles of blood pop and splutter as they exit his mouth. He makes a terrible gurgling sound that I'm probably never going to be able to fully rinse from my brain.

Hot Guy yanks the knife out of The Asshole's neck, and blood erupts from his carotid in waves of crimson, reflecting the rhythm of his heartbeat.

Jesus. Hot Guy knew exactly where to stab for maximum damage.

Hot Guy circles The Asshole until he's behind him, then grabs him by the ponytail and yanks his head back. The Asshole's eyes grow large and he tries to reach back and free himself of Hot Guy's grasp as Hot Guy raises the shears high in the air and off to one side of The Asshole.

I cry out, "No!" as Hot Guy slices The Asshole's throat from ear to ear. After a moment, while his body catches up to what just happened, blood pools at the gash and then pours forth a violent scarlet waterfall, splattering all over the floor and the Asshole's shoes, some splashing onto Hot Guy's face and clothing.

The Asshole gurgles, "Fuck!" as he falls to the floor, his gun slipping from his grip and clattering to the ground. His body topples and he lands on his front, one of his legs bent and splayed out to the side, an arm stretched upward, prone like a perfect chalk outline at a police crime scene. A pool of crimson forms beneath him.

I stand, hand across my open mouth, as blood continues to drain from his body onto the floor.

I glance around and it's now just me, the Hot Guy, and The Asshole's dead body, squeezed into the cramped salon. The salon is silent except for the tick-tock of a vintage cat clock, its tail and eyes darting from side to side each second. There's no traffic noise, no hustle and bustle of commuters making their way to or from work. Just the tick-tock of the clock and the heavy weight of death hanging in the air.

Hot Guy picks up The Asshole's gun from where he dropped it when he crumpled to the ground, clicks on the safety and slides it into his back pocket.

He then calmly walks over to one of the hair-washing basins on the far wall of the salon and rinses my shears under the running water. He dries them on a towel and casually walks back to where I'm standing.

I'm tempted to reach out and try to grab the shears back from him, but as I try to extend my arm, I realize my hands are shaking violently. Hot Guy just used my beloved work tool to kill someone right in front of me.

He was so calm and controlled, dominating the situation even in the face of death. The way he looked at The Asshole, not flinching while he pointed a deadly weapon at him, was impressive and kinda hot.

But who the fuck is this guy, and why did The Asshole come after him with a gun? I know Hot Guy acted in self-defense, but did the altercation really have to end in murder?

And who's going to clean up the body and the big puddle of blood in the middle of my salon floor?

Hot Guy glances around the salon, and then at me, and he sighs.

He walks to the front entrance, locks the door and pulls down the blinds on the door and the window so nobody can see inside.

"What are you doing? The salon is still open."

I stare at him as he tries to take control of what happens in my salon. This is my turf, not his. I don't even know this guy and he's wandering around and trying to dictate my business hours like he owns the place.

He shakes his head. "Not anymore, it isn't."

"What do you mean? I have a business to run. I can't just close the place whenever I feel like it. Clients expect me to be open when I'm meant to be."

"Too bad," he shrugs. "You're coming with me."

"No, I'm not. I have to work."

"You're planning on cutting hair while there's a body and a huge puddle of blood just sitting there?" He gestures at the dead guy and the mess. "And you think you can concentrate on work right now?"

"Well, I figured you would clean that up," I say. "Besides, I've seen worse." I shrug.

He glances at me sideways, as if he's trying to see if I'm joking or not. Unfortunately, I'm not, but I'm not going to elaborate on that with him right now.

"Well, the salon is closed for the day. That's going to take a bit to clean," he says, indicating the puddle on the floor.

"Fine." I cross my arms over my chest. "But you need to figure... that... out." I gesture at the body. "I'll wait here while you do."

"We won't be able to move the body until it gets dark," he says, as if he does this all the time and already knows the drill.

"Okay, well I'll stay here and you come back when it's nighttime then. I'll be here waiting. There's plenty of cleaning and admin paperwork to do between now and when you come back."

"No, not happening. I can't just leave you here," he says, shaking his head. "You might run away or call the cops or something. Plus, you've heard my name and you've seen my face. You could identify me in a lineup or whatever, and have one of those drawings made that they put on the news. I can't let that happen."

He does have a fairly unique hairstyle for the island, and that alone would make it easier to track him down. But there's no way I'm sharing that with him. That would just add to his insistence that I can't stay here by myself.

"Listen, I have a vested interest in letting you remove this body and clean up the blood without incident. Do you really think there's a wide audience who like the idea of coming to a murder salon? I'm sure there are some kooks out there who'd get off on it, but not enough to keep a small business afloat and thriving. I need this cleaned up, too, just as much as you do."

He frowns and shakes his head. "No. I mean it. You just watched me murder someone. I'm not going to head out without you and hope for the best."

I roll my eyes.

"Besides," he adds, "you might be tempted to do something stupid like service clients while I'm gone, and then we'll be in trouble."

"Is that what I just did? 'Service' you?" His use of the word makes me feel a little funny, and I feel the need to mention it. Jesus, I just watched him murder someone, there's a body on the floor of my salon, and yet I still have the urge to flirt with him. What is wrong with me?

I feel like maybe what just happened hasn't sunk in. That I'm infusing humor and flirtation rather than facing what just happened head-on. It wouldn't be the first time I've found ways to distract myself from things I don't want to think about.

Hot Guy peers at me for a moment, as if he's trying to read my mind, and then winks. "No, but I'd like it if you did. Any time you want, Angel, you can service me any way you like. Or any way that I tell you to."

His gaze explores my body, lingering on my chest, and he bites his lower lip.

"You know, we have a little time to kill before it gets dark," he says.

I feel a crackle of electricity and my cheeks flush. I'm tempted to see what he has in mind. But after a moment of gazing back at him, and a dull ache starting in my core, I wrench my eyes away from his gorgeous face.

Instead, I now look at The Asshole's dead mouth, curled up in a scream, blood running from it as well as his gaping neck and throat wounds.

A shiver runs through my entire body as I recognize the air in the salon has taken on the all too familiar sweet and metallic scent of blood. I've been around far too much blood in my lifetime, primarily my own, and it's still a bit of a trigger. I have a little flashback to all the times I've seen it pouring, trickling, oozing from places it shouldn't, both on me and other people.

I watch Hot Guy as he stalks around the body like he's mentally mapping how he's going to dispose of it. His eyes are cold and clinical, and gone is the twinkly, flirtatious, warm guy I was chatting with before The Asshole entered the salon.

Hot Guy's abrupt change in demeanor snaps me out of my trance. This is not the time to flirt, this is not the time to perv at hot men. This is the time to protect myself and get out of a potentially very dangerous situation.

I've just become a witness to a murder. I know who did it, I know what he looks like, his last name, and what he does for work. This knowledge compromises my safety.

The hairs rise on the nape of my neck and my hands grow clammy.

I just watched him kill a man.

I can't let on that I'm scared, so I clear my throat and try to keep my voice calm. "So what, then? Are you going to kill me, too?" I may as well be direct, to know where I stand. To let him know I know he might consider ending my life.

As he shifts his gaze from the dead body to me, I shiver under his stare. His warmth has definitely disappeared. It feels like he's assessing me and my value, both alive and dead. The way he'd maybe assess accepting or turning down a business opportunity.

"I guess we'll have to wait and see," he says, pressing his lips into a firm line, his eyes boring into mine. "And the decision won't be mine alone."

Fuck. I don't even know what that means, but it doesn't sound good. I need to tread carefully here while I figure a way out.

He may be incredibly hot, but he's clearly fucking psychotic.

And he's just killed someone.

If I'm not careful, I'll be next.

Chapter Four

Aidan

The living room TV murmurs quietly in the background, and occasionally pots and pans clatter in the nearby kitchen. Other than that, the place is quiet.

Our compound is a recent acquisition. Business has been doing very well here on the island, and having top-notch security has only become more important.

Success brings a target on your back. We're well aware that several rival groups envy the wealth and power we've accumulated in a very short time here, and we're only getting started.

My business partners and I had visited the island several times over the past decade or so, mainly for pleasure, but we'd also dabbled in the odd business deal and found it worth our while.

It was only around eighteen months ago that we moved from the mainland to make this our home base. We saw an opportunity here to muscle in and stake our claim to some lucrative opportunities that weren't being leveraged by others as well as they could have been.

For whatever reason, this island attracts subpar criminals with a misplaced sense of right and wrong, their potential to be the best smothered by their arbitrary moral code.

That's the thing about us Brixtons and moral codes. We don't have one and we never will. That's a big reason we're so strong, why we're amassing power here at an exponential rate while others flounder or just stay stagnant.

The compound sits in an industrial neighborhood surrounded by warehouses, factories and storage facilities. On the ground floor is a warehouse that imports items used by restaurants, a cover for the more profitable items we move to and from the island. It's a massive industrial space, full of crates and forklifts and workers scurrying around to get things where they need to go.

We don't just move restaurant equipment and food. We'll move anything, as long as the price is right. Guns, drugs, organs. Even entire people. It's all the same to us, a means to an end. We mainly focus on guns and drugs at the moment, but nothing is off the table and we make that abundantly clear to whoever does business with us. We're a one-stop-shop, and people value our ruthlessness and our commitment to execution.

The top floor of the compound is where the actual business happens. It's a far cry from downstairs, not that anyone who works down there would have the slightest idea.

Up here it's sleek and modern, a soundproof luxury apartment with the best technology. There are high ceilings dangling with elaborate light fixtures, and modern art adorns the walls. A large living room with an oversized U-shaped modular couch and a massive TV with all the latest features. A state-of-the-art kitchen with a massive kitchen island and breakfast in the middle, and a dining room table off to the side. Several bedrooms and bathrooms, an entertainment room, a library, multiple offices and a state-of-the-art fitness center.

And on the other side of the top floor, there are commercial premises that we use as our corporate headquarters. That side of the building features a huge reception desk with a chandelier hanging above it. Sleek office setups with glass desks boast views of the mountains at the back and the ocean in front.

We haven't exactly followed the island motif here. It's cosmopolitan, sophisticated luxury, like we've transported what we were accustomed to on the mainland right into this tropical paradise. Sometimes it's nice to have creature comforts that remind you of home.

In terms of business, besides our import, export and transportation dealings, it helps to have some front-facing operations on the island as well. Being able to get in front of people makes it easier to connect sellers with viable buyers and keep a pulse on the island's activities.

We own three strip clubs in the city and tourist districts, a couple of bars and clubs, and a restaurant with an underground gambling den tucked away in the back. Some of them are more lucrative than others, but all serve a purpose.

I glance over at Brick. He's slouching against the corner of the overstuffed couch across from me, looking deep in thought as he chews on a toothpick. He's wearing his usual black leather jacket and a black and red plaid shirt with dark jeans and red lace-up Converse shoes.

Brick didn't get the memo that we moved to an island. I guess none of us did. It was warm at first, but we've acclimated and stuck with our mainland style. None of us can get down with the idea of wearing shorts, tank tops and flip-flops every day like most other people here do, even when they're working. We're much more comfortable dressing for business. Except for when we're surfing, of course.

When we're in the ocean, it's one of the few times we ever see Brick without his leather jacket. You wouldn't know it to look at it, but it's made of vegan leather. One of the weirdest things about Brick, and there are many, is that he's vegan. Not that being vegan is weird, but being Brick and vegan certainly is. He tortures and kills people for work, getting off on disemboweling and shooting and stabbing. Becoming elated after administering electric shocks and burns and removing fingernails. He enjoys every moment that he gets to torture and maim and kill, and wouldn't trade his job for the world. But apparently, he won't eat an animal.

"Do you think we can trust Tane and his men?" Brick emerges from his daydream, glances up at me and then over to the kitchen where our business partner Slade is cooking.

While they're my business associates, sometimes I'll refer to these guys as my brothers, because we are a brotherhood of sorts, although technically we're not related. We may as well be, having grown up together and now living under the same roof and running an empire.

Besides, we're the closest family any of us have anymore.

"That's like asking if we can trust a vegan with a paint can around a fur coat," calls out Slade from the kitchen, not missing a beat.

He rarely says much, he's just not a big talker for the sake of it. But when he does, it's usually acidic, zinging his target without pause. The topic of Brick being vegan is accepted as fair game for teasing, even by Brick himself.

Slade flicks a saute pan in his right hand and I hear a sizzling sound as the pungent aroma of garlic fills the room. He's a skilled cook, and the kitchen is his refuge, which works for the rest of us in the apartment who can barely boil water.

Brick stares at him, confused. "What the fuck does that mean, bro? And is there meat in that?" He gestures toward the pan Slade is expertly flicking with his wrist.

I smirk. "I believe it means no, Brick, Slade and I don't trust Tane at all. But it's not like we have a choice at the moment. He has too much power over the island chain for us to do much about it. For now, anyway."

"Yeah, that is what it means," Slade nods, "and I'm making you a separate meal, like usual, you picky tree-hugging psychopath."

I snort. That's a pretty accurate description of Brick. He's a psycho with a soft heart when it comes to nature and wildlife. One moment he's strangling a man and threatening to chop off his dick, the next he's patting a bunny and making a wheatgrass smoothie. A real mind fuck, that one.

Brick forms his hands into a heart shape and holds them up to Slade. I snort and roll my eyes. I'm trying to take over an island and two of my key counterparts are over here acting like complete goofballs.

I hate Tane Brown more than just about anyone I've ever met. He essentially rules the islands, controlling who and what comes and goes. He funnels the most profitable opportunities to those he favors, and his connections run deep. Thankfully, his own compound is based on a different island from ours, and he rarely visits, but he still controls things here remotely.

He's an evil man, very strong when it comes to his networks, with a large team of loyal followers who will risk their lives to protect him so they can share in his power. Several groups have tried to overthrow him over the years, but none have succeeded.

"We need to bide our time and strike when the conditions are perfect," I explain. "It's like when you know the waves are going to do exactly what you need them to do. If you rush out an hour beforehand, the waves are going to be too big and crush you. But if you wait until things are just right, until the conditions set you up for success, you can get exactly what you want. You can use them to your advantage and take what's yours."

"I'm getting sick of waiting, though," huffs Brick. "His rules and limitations on us are frustrating. We could be doing so much more. There are better ways to do things here."

"I know, man. But it hasn't been that long, only about eighteen months. We're growing stronger every day. I'm hopeful that we'll reach a point in the next couple of years when we can take him on and have a chance at winning."

"Hope is for the weak, and years are long." Brick juts out his jaw and taps his foot. He cracks his knuckles, his nostrils flared, like he's ready to go and overthrow the islands' primary mafia boss single-handedly. He isn't the most patient person, and sometimes he makes rash decisions. His enthusiasm can have a run-on effect on the rest of the guys. Part of my role is to make sure he and the others don't do anything stupid.

"I will not die at the hands of Tane fucking Brown because we didn't plan things out because you got impatient," I say, glaring at him because I've already explained this many times. "Right now, we would stand no chance unless we formed an alliance, maybe multiple, with other groups here. We'd have to make compromises to partner with them and then find a way to go after him together. And I don't want to weaken our position. We need to be the alpha group if we do end up joining forces, which I really don't want to do. We might be scaling our operations quickly, but it's still early days and we need time to prepare."

Brick takes a deep breath and then lets it out heavily, dropping his shoulders in resignation. He's always champing at the bit to rush in and start a fight. Or in this case, what would almost certainly be a full-blown, bloody war.

Slade's a little more restrained, more cautious and less of an instigator on his own behalf, but he'll jump in and do anything to help us when any of us need him. If Brick jumps into a situation preemptively, he can end up dragging Slade into unnecessary danger.

Roman, who's out getting yet another haircut, is down for anything that won't mess up his physical appearance. And he's a decently good fighter for a pretty boy.

Besides enjoying women, he also enjoys breaking the odd skull, of dominating others physically and having them submit to his will.

It's on me to pull them all back, having them operate on logic and rationality over instinct and the thrill of the chase. Making sure that our moves are purposeful and thoughtful.

It's on me to keep my brothers alive.

And to make sure we always come out on top.

Chapter Five

Roman

While the hottie was very flirty immediately after I killed The Asshole, which made my cock twitch, something in the air has shifted now.

I get the sense that she initially blocked out the death part, diverting attention to me while her brain raced to process what had just happened. I'm sure witnessing a murder wasn't what she was expecting during her shift today.

Neither was I, but here we are.

She's panting a little, her ample chest visibly rising and falling and her plush lips parted slightly in a way that makes me want to plunge my tongue deep inside her mouth. Her gorgeous green eyes are wide now as she glances from me to The Asshole's bloody body.

Her face is slightly flushed and coated in a gentle sheen, the way I can imagine she looks after she's just been fucked. In fact, everything about her looks like she's turned on by the thrill of what just happened, the sight of this man's blood pooling on the floor. But I also know she's scared.

I must seem like a massive threat to her, and I am, so she'd be right to think that. She doesn't know anything about me other than that I'm more than prepared to kill, to use deadly violence.

She turns as if she's going to walk away from me.

I grab her arm just above her elbow.

She tries to wrench it free, but I increase my grip.

"Let go of me!" she hisses, narrowing her eyes at me through her long, thick lashes, her lower lip jutting out in an angry pout.

Jesus, she's sexy when she's pissed.

She can see I don't have any plans to let her go, so she kicks her leg out at me, aiming for my nutsack. I narrowly manage to avoid her foot and I twist her closer to me so she has less leverage to try to kick me again.

With my hand still on her forearm, I grab her other wrist and pull her close to me.

She hisses in my face and tries to stamp on my foot, but she's too close to get decent leverage and she misses, her leg twisting awkwardly in the air until she places it back on the ground.

I move my hand from her arm to her throat, and I squeeze, cutting off her air supply for a moment, her face just inches from mine. Fear flashes in her eyes, but she immediately regroups and her eyes narrow.

I loosen my grip on her throat, and she hungrily gulps air into her starving lungs.

"Let *go* of me!" She tries to wrestle out of my grip, but I just pull her closer, moving my hand from her wrist and clamping it down just above her elbow.

I squeeze her throat more firmly again, and she fights for breath, but she can't get any air. Her face flushes and her eyes bulge slightly, her face breaking out into a panicked sheen.

She needs to calm down and realize I'm the one in control here, of everything. That I'll let her go if and when I feel like it. That there's no point in trying to run.

I release my grip on her throat, and she gulps in more air.

She glares at me, her chest rapidly rising and falling.

"Are you done now?" I ask her.

She narrows her eyes further.

"If you're going to kill me, just fucking do it. Double the body count," she snarls, glancing over my shoulder at The Asshole's prone corpse. "You're either going to or you're not. There's no need for this little dance, of you cutting off my air supply every five seconds. So if I'm going to die today, do us both a favor and get it out of the way." Her voice rises as she speaks, her agitation growing.

She tries again to yank her arm away from my tight grip, and instead of letting her go, I shove her in her shoulder, spinning her around so her back is to me.

Still firmly gripping her arm, I twist it behind her and push her up against the floor-to-ceiling mirror. The side of her face presses into the glass, and her breath puffs steam against her reflection.

I press my body up against her and dip my head so my mouth is right beside her ear.

"Stop fighting," I growl, my breath whispering across her face, "and lower your voice, because there's a dead body in here and I really don't want anybody to call the cops right now because they heard a hysterical person screaming from the nearby salon."

"Let go of me then," she rasps, her face still pressed against the mirrored wall. "I don't like being held down like this. It makes me panic, and I shout when I'm panicked. So if you want me to be quiet, let me go."

She wriggles in an attempt to get away, and I press closer, my body melding into hers from behind, holding her in position.

"I'll let you go when I want to let you go," I hiss in her ear. "Remember, I'm the one in control here." The back of her ear proves too much to resist, and I run my tongue up the hard piece of cartilage that joins it with her skull.

She jerks her head away and yells, "Fuck you, asshole!"

With all her might, she rears back, smacking the back of her head into my chin and elbowing me in the abdomen. Startled, I jump back and lose my grip on the hand that I've been pressing behind her. She wrenches it free and wheels around to face me. Lowering her center of gravity by bending herself into a squat, she lifts her forearms up in defense and balls up her fists. She tries to dart to my right, but I block her, moving my body into the space.

Panting, she darts to her left and ducks, almost slipping through the gap at my side, but I manage to wrap my arms around her waist from behind and pull her to me. I spin both of us around and move toward the mirrored wall directly in front of us.

My own heart is racing now. I really had to work to get her under my control. She almost slipped through my grasp. For someone her size, for a girl, she's a pretty scrappy fighter. She was never going to win, but fuck, she gave it a good go.

I turn her around so that her back is up against the wall, and my body presses in close to hers so there's no chance she can slip past again. I'm acutely aware of her breasts squeezing against my abdomen.

She emanates anger and heat, her chest rising and falling rapidly as her eyes flit around looking for any options to escape.

"Don't make me hurt you," I growl. "Because I'll need to if you don't cooperate."

"You'd really hurt a girl?" Still breathing heavily, she looks at me through her thick eyelashes and raises her voice to a higher pitch. I know exactly what she's doing, but I'm immune to her manipulation.

She's given me a taste of who she is, and I want more. But I also don't trust her as far as I can throw her. I have the feeling she'd escape in an instant, given a fraction of a chance. She's proven herself wily. Feisty. I like it, but I will not let her get away.

"The way you fight, you give me no choice." I shrug, maintaining eye contact.

She narrows her eyes again.

I let my eyes trail down her face and chest, enjoying the way my body feels pressed into her curves.

"You really are drop-dead gorgeous, by the way." I tilt her chin up with my finger, and her gaze meets mine.

I feel myself getting hard as I take her all in, my erection poking into her stomach. "And the way you fight is hot as fuck."

Her eyes darken, and she bites her bottom lip while she continues to meet my gaze. She doesn't respond verbally, but she doesn't need to. I can tell she's attracted to me, too.

A long moment passes while we just stand here, looking at each other. Not to mention my throbbing hard-on that's digging into the front of her body, wanting to be inside her.

"Let me go," she eventually says, her voice husky. But she makes no move to get away from me.

I dip my face closer to hers, our mouths nearly touching, and know that she can feel my breath on her face. "You don't have a say in this. But I might never want to let you go."

Her chest rises and falls more rapidly now, and her face flushes, her mouth parting slightly, her gaze lowering to my lips. She wants me to kiss her.

I consider it for a moment, but instead of indulging my lips on the kissable pillows that frame her smart mouth, I abruptly pull away.

For a moment, she looks surprised and almost disappointed. But then she glances around the salon, presumably still looking for an escape route. She sighs, clearly not seeing any options.

"Now, are you going to be compliant, or do I need to knock you out?" I ask, my eyes locked on hers. "I can tell you're still looking for ways to get out of here, and that needs to stop."

She glares at me. "Wouldn't you be doing the same if you were in my situation?"

"Yes, but I wouldn't be in your situation." I shrug.

She clenches her jaw and narrows her eyes further. I guess what I said might have been a little condescending.

"Is there a door leading into a back alley here?" I ask, looking around.

"No," she says, but she hesitates for a fraction too long and her eyes involuntarily flicker toward the rear of the salon.

"You just lied to me," I frown at her. "I don't like liars."

"What the fuck do you expect from me right now?" Her voice is shrill, and it echoes around the room's thin walls. I'm increasingly worried she's going to draw attention to the salon and therefore the body of the man I just murdered.

"Be *quiet*," I hiss, glaring at her. I'm getting annoyed now, because she's really starting to put us at risk.

The last thing I need is to be hauled away in handcuffs for dropping the loser whose body lies prone in the middle of the salon. My brothers would work their magic to get me out and any charges dropped, but it would slow down our progress on the business, which we really can't afford.

"Okay, okay," she says, lowering her voice and putting her hands up in mock surrender. "No need to hiss at me."

"I expect you to tell me the truth, Angel," I say, my voice low. I carefully enunciate every syllable because I want no room for misunderstanding. "But you chose to lie to me just now. I asked you to be quiet, but instead, you are choosing to yell. I'm going to make you pay for both of these things. You can trust me on that. You're coming with me, whether you like it or not. And now you've eliminated all of my other options."

I yank The Asshole's gun from my back pocket and raise it high above my head. Her eyes grow large as she looks up at it, and I bring it down forcefully, butt-first, smashing her in the top of her skull.

She crashes to the ground, her head narrowly avoiding the hard edge of a hair-washing basin during her descent. Oops. It looks like it's made of some pretty hard material, and if she hit it hard enough, it could have killed her or at least done some serious damage.

That would have been the last thing I needed. Two dead bodies on my hands, both unexpected.

And in her case, it would have been a real waste. Because she really is gorgeous.

Glancing at her unconscious body crumpled on the ground, I clench my jaw. This could be a really bad idea, but for whatever reason, I've decided not to kill her. I'm taking her with me, back to the house.

I shake my head. Today has been unbelievable. I've murdered some guy with a poor attitude and a trigger finger. Now I've knocked out a hot girl and am going to take her captive because I can't figure out what else to do with her.

And all I wanted was a fucking haircut.

I grab my cell phone out of my pocket and call Aidan and, as usual, he answers on the first ring. Reliable and predictable, no messing around from him. "What?" he says. Also not the height of hospitality when he's on the phone.

"I need your help with something. Bring the others. Now."

"You need help to get your hair cut?" he snorts down the line.

"Stop fucking around. This is serious," I frown. "No questions. Just get here and bring a tarp. I'll text you the details."

He must realize I'm not my usual jokey self. If anything, I'm acting more like him, all business. So he stops with the quips and questions. "Alright man, we'll be right there. Send us the details."

I message them the address and tell them to meet me out in the back alley.

While I wait, I take the opportunity to make sure the blinds are fully closed and double-check the front door is securely locked. I don't want to take any chances with the body just laying there. We don't need some grandma coming in for a blue rinse and a perm right now.

They only take about ten minutes to arrive, announcing their arrival by knocking on the door to the back alley. All three of them come—Aidan, Slade and Brick. Aidan must have recognized the serious tone in my voice when I said to bring everyone. This isn't a two-person job.

Letting them in through the back entrance, they give me strange looks as they pass through the small staff kitchen and enter the main salon. They glance at the bodies and the pool of blood spreading out underneath the man.

"I thought you were just getting a haircut," says Brick, assessing the scene. "But it looks like you had a lot of fun without us."

I shrug. "That was the plan, but I guess he followed me here," I gesture at the body.

Slade walks toward it to take a closer look. "Looks like one of Zero's guys. I've seen him around," he says. I envy his photographic memory, particularly when it comes to assholes trying to take over our business.

"We need to get rid of him, obviously," I say. "I was hoping you guys could help with that."

"And what about her?" Aidan asks, gesturing toward Angel. "You knocked her out?" He inspects her from a distance. "She's not dead?"

"She's alive, and she's coming back with us," I say, as if I've made the executive decision on behalf of all four of us, mentally crossing my fingers that they'll all just go along with it. Even though we've never taken someone captive before and it's kind of a big deal now that I'm thinking about it.

"Like you think we should kidnap her?" Aidan raises an eyebrow. "I don't know if we have time to deal with a prisoner."

"Yeah, that sounds like an awful idea," Slade scowls. "We don't need females getting in the middle of our business."

"Could be fun, though, having a woman around." Brick wiggles his eyebrows.

I might have a reputation as the ladies' man of the group, but the rest of them like women a lot, too. Except for Slade, who's just different. Lots of baggage with that one when it comes to females. Of course, Brick is excited at the prospect of having one in our house to play with.

"Listen. She's got some fight in her," I shrug. "She could be useful to have around."

"So she's not only a prisoner, but a stroppy one who will try to fight us?" Aidan raises an eyebrow.

"Bad idea," says Slade, furrowing his brow. "I'm telling you."

"I can think of some things we could use her for." Brick grins and wiggles his eyebrows again.

Slade rolls his eyes. "Can we think with our brains and not our dicks? *Please*."

"It feels like we're going around in circles here," I say. "But either way, we need to clean up and get this dead body the fuck out of this salon. And we can't just leave her here."

"Alright, look. I agree we can't just leave her here," says Aidan. "We need to remove her from the scene. Let's bring her with us and then we'll figure out what to do."

"Sounds like a plan," I nod. "We're four powerful guys and she's just one woman. What could possibly go wrong?"

Chapter Six

Aidan

"Ro, go get your car and drive it around back. And then you two dispose of that," I say to Roman and Slade, gesturing at The Asshole's body. "Brick, you and I will deal with the girl."

"Sure, I'll help to clean up Roman's mess as usual," says Slade, rolling his eyes. He might be protesting at my instructions, but I know he'll still follow them.

After Roman retrieves his vehicle from the front of the strip mall and drives it around the back of the building, I pick the girl up from the ground and haul her over my shoulder.

Brick follows me, grabbing her purse from a hook on a coat stand in the break area.

I carry her outside, and he closes up, locking the back exit.

He opens the door to the back seat of the car and I place her inside so that she's lying down on her back.

The other guys wrap The Asshole's body in a tarp, and then silently carry it over to their car and throw him in the trunk. They know what to do. Even though today's events were unexpected, it's not entirely out of the ordinary having someone coming to fuck with us, and us needing to teach them a permanent lesson. It's just how it is around here. It's just business.

While I drive, Brick digs around in the girl's purse and retrieves an ID.

"Angel Benson," he reads aloud. "248 White Oak St, Apt 3."

I nod and type it into the GPS.

"Also, I've never seen so many box cutter knives and pepper spray canisters outside of a hardware store," he says, rummaging around in her purse and pulling some out to show me. "We should watch out when she wakes up." He grins as he extends the sharp blade on a box cutter and inspects it. "I like a girl who knows her way around a knife."

I shake my head and roll my eyes. Brick is obsessed with weapons and women separately, but together they're his kryptonite. If they have tattoos and piercings, even better.

Glancing at the sharp blade in his hand, maybe he's right. We *should* watch out when she wakes up. For all we know, she's a complete lunatic. Who knows what she's capable of?

After driving for about half an hour, the GPS signals that we've reached our destination. We pull up at a dilapidated apartment building on the outskirts of the city.

Without going in, I already know a lot about this place. I grew up somewhere just like this. It's not a good part of town, with lots of sketchy activity going on at all hours of the day.

An air of hopelessness and decay emanates from the grungy gray building that would probably never look clean even if someone water-blasted it for days. It's like the human despair hiding inside is leaching out into the architecture, exposing it for the world to see.

Or maybe I'm just projecting.

By the look of the building, it's going to be easy for Brick to get in without a key, and there's guaranteed not to be any high level of security, maybe none at all. Not that it would matter. Brick is talented at getting into most structures when he wants to, the slippery fuck.

From what I know of buildings like this, it's probably unsafe for a woman to live here by herself with its flimsy locks, questionable onsite activities and lack of security. Although judging by Roman's tousled appearance earlier, which for once didn't come about because he just fucked someone, it looks like she gave him a run for his money, and that she's fairly capable of defending herself.

"You go in," I say to Brick. "I'll stay here with the girl."

"You going to have some fun with her while she's knocked out?" Brick grins at me and wiggles his eyebrows, pretending to squeeze his pecs as though they were breasts.

"No, of course I'm fucking not." I narrow my eyes at him. "Jesus. Just go get a bunch of her clothes and whatever other shit she might need. Makeup and shoes. Underwear. Tampons. Hair ties. Whatever it is that women need."

"How long is she going to stay with us, man?"

"I don't know. Just get a bunch of stuff and put it in a bag. It's not as if we planned today in advance, so I haven't really thought about how long she might stay. I'm not sure what Roman was even thinking, getting us to take her with us. But we needed to get rid of the body and couldn't just leave her there. Seemed a bit rash to kill her on the spot."

"I would have," smirks Brick. He glances at the girl. "Even though she's really pretty."

"Yeah, well, you're a fucking psycho."

"Samesies," he says, pointing at me, grinning as he slams the passenger door closed. He spins around on the ball of his foot and walks away from the vehicle. He slips into the darkness and heads toward the apartment listed on her ID.

I wait for five, then ten, then fifteen minutes and Brick still hasn't come back. I sigh and roll my eyes. He's probably busy sniffing her panties and jerking off.

There's a soft moan from the back seat. Shit. She's starting to wake up already. Roman mustn't have hit her hard enough.

It's always a delicate balance, bashing someone in the head forcefully enough so that they're rendered unconscious, without permanently damaging their brain. I've seen Brick blow through that threshold a few times with people that deserved it.

I turn some music on, loud enough to create some cover, but also not so loudly that it draws undue attention to the vehicle.

She groans again, louder this time, and her arms reach up to rub her groggy eyes. Poor thing, she's going to have a splitting headache soon if she doesn't already.

"Wh—where the fuck am I?" She narrows her eyes at me as they adjust to the moonlight. "And who the fuck are you?"

"Hi there, Angel," I say, letting a small smile play across my face. "Nice to meet you."

She sits up and groans, looking around. She tries the door handle on her left side, but of course, it's locked. Tugging at it some more, she glares at me. "Let me the fuck out!"

"That's not going to happen, Angel," I shrug.

"How do you know my name?"

"Magic." I grin, and she narrows her eyes at me.

She peers out the window and her eyes light up as she recognizes the building. "We're at my apartment! Let me out!" She tugs at the door again.

"Angel, the door isn't going to open. You're not going to your apartment. You're coming with us. My buddy is just getting some of your things, so you can be more comfortable."

"To go where?" She stops talking for a moment, as if she's trying to process what I just said. "Wait, seriously though. Who the fuck are you? Where's the guy from the salon?"

"He's... tending to an errand."

She peers at me, and then recognition dawns in her eyes. "Fuck, is he getting rid of The Asshole's body?"

I laugh. "If you mean the guy he killed back there, then yes. That's what he's doing."

"Thank goodness for that. It's really off-putting for customers to have a corpse just laying there while their hair gets cut. I was worried he was just going to leave it there." She winces and grabs the side of her head. "By the way, I have a really nasty headache and it hurts like hell. Is that courtesy of your friend, too?"

"Yeah. Sounds like you deserved it though." I grab a small bottle of water and a travel pack of over-the-counter pain relief and pass them back to her. "Here you go."

She snatches the items out of my hands and unscrews the water bottle. For a moment, I think she's going to throw its contents all over me, but she seems to change her mind. She opens the pain relief packet and uses the water to wash the two tablets down.

"So, are you going to tell me where you're taking me?" She glares at me in the rear-view mirror.

"You'll find out in good time. Be patient."

"You try being fucking patient when you wake up in the back seat of a car with a stranger outside your apartment. After witnessing a fucking murder in your workplace!" Her voice is rising, and I need her to shut up. Not that I think the people who live in this apartment building are necessarily the types that would call the cops for any type of help.

"I need you to calm down, Angel. Stop yelling, please." I keep my voice calm, hoping it will rub off on her.

"Or what?"

"Or there'll be a repeat of what happened to you earlier."

"What? You're saying you'll knock me out, too?"

"If I have to, yes," I shrug.

"Fuck you!" she yells. "Let me out of this car!"

I'm not worried about anybody seeing what's happening inside the vehicle, because the windows are heavily tinted and it's dark outside. But I am a little concerned about someone hearing her yell. I turn up the music a little more.

"So, Angel, what do you do when you're not waking up in cars with strange men?"

She crosses her arms across her chest. "I eat guys like you for breakfast," she fumes. "You're making a big mistake holding me like this."

"Oh really? What are you going to do about it? Because so far, from what I know, things haven't been going so well for you."

She reaches over and bops me on the head with the empty water bottle. It makes a hollow sound and bounces off my head and out of her hand, landing on the passenger seat.

I snort at her. "That all you've got?"

She tries to reach around the seat and punch my arm.

"I really wouldn't try that, sweetheart." I smile at her as condescension drips from my tongue. "You remember what happened when you tried that with my brother last time, don't you?"

Her eyes narrow. "He got so turned on his dick pressed against my stomach, from what I recall," she snarls. "And then he fucking *knocked me out* apparently, and then *kidnapped* me! Who the fuck are you guys anyway, except obvious assholes?"

"According to my brother, the guy he killed at your salon was an asshole. Is that right, Angel? Didn't you just call him that, too?"

"Fine. Yes, he was an asshole. The Asshole. That's what I called him. I'll call you something else instead. What's your name, anyway?"

I smirk. "My name is Aidan."

"Alright, then, *Aidan," she narrows her eyes and glares at me in the rear-view mirror.* "You're a bad person, I can tell. I know you do bad things. You're like an evil demon."

I smirk and look her dead in the eye. "I can live with being called a demon. You'll come to learn that I'm much worse than that. And before long, I'll have you doing whatever I say. You're under my control now, Angel."

Her eyes grow dark and narrow, her pupils transforming into tiny pinpoints.

I watch in the mirror as she rears her hand back and balls it into a fist, then attempts to crash it through the space between the seats and hit me in the head. Reaching my opposite arm over, I block her with ease, even though the power of her punch is impressive for someone her size, especially given the cramped confines of the vehicle. I laugh as I deflect her fist, and she narrows her eyes further.

She punches at me again with her other arm this time. I dodge her with my body and reach out a hand to stop her. It's tricky to maneuver in the small space and while I deflect her wild blow from my face, I feel a sting as momentum crashes her hand down on me and her sharp nails scratch me through my shirt.

"Putting your nails on me already, baby?" I grin at her. "I like that. Maybe one day you'll rake them over my back and make me bleed while I fuck you senseless."

"More like I'll fucking scratch your eyes out with them," she hisses. "I'll fucking kill you."

She grabs hold of each of the front seats and tries to launch her whole body through the gap, and I laugh, grabbing her by the throat and holding her steady in limbo between the front and back of the vehicle. She tries to gulp in air as my fingers clamp down, cutting off her supply, but it comes out like a dry croak.

"I'm stronger than you, Angel. You might be beautiful, but I'm physically much superior. And I'm a killer. Just like my brothers. We're all capable of that. You've seen it for yourself. Just remember that." I pause and lock eyes with her in the rear-view mirror again. "Now forgive me for what I'm about to do."

Using my free hand, I remove my gun from my pocket and raise it up high. Her eyes grow wide as she watches me smash the butt of it down on the top of her head, and she crumples between the seats, knocked out for the second time today.

Some people never learn. But then again, I haven't had a chance to train her yet.

As I inspect her crumpled form, Brick knocks on the passenger door and I let him in. He hops in and sees her slumped over the middle console. "Having some fun while I was up there in her apartment, were you?" he grins.

"The fun is just getting started, brother," I smirk. "What the fuck took you so long, anyway? Did you try on all of her clothes or something? Jerk off in her bed?"

"The place was a mess, man. She had shit everywhere. Had to make sure I grabbed a bit of everything."

He looks slightly suspicious to me, avoiding eye contact like he's hiding something, but I'll let it go for now. We need to get her back to the compound before she wakes up again. We've already knocked her out twice today and a third could be bad for her gorgeous skull.

We silently move her so that she's lying across the back seat again rather than dangling partway into the front of the vehicle.

As we drive back to our compound, I consider her fate.

While the eventual outcome might be us killing her, because she is a murder witness after all, we've gone through all this effort to bring her with us.

Killing or damaging her too badly right now would seem like a waste. A sunk cost. We need some type of return on investment.

She's lucky I'm stubborn like that.

Chapter Seven

Angel

I wake with a start and immediately know I'm somewhere I've never been before. It's not entirely unusual for me to wake up in a strange location, but this time I know it's different.

For one, I glance to either side and there's no random guy snoring next to me. I have a feeling there's nobody in the kitchen making me coffee or breakfast in bed, either, like in a romantic movie.

My skull is also thumping and my mouth is bone-dry, and I'm sitting up with my back against the wall.

It's dark in this room, but the eyelashes on one of my eyes are crusted together and by the familiar metallic smell I assume that it's blood. I try to lift my hand so I can assess the damage by touch, but my arms are restrained behind me somehow. Whatever's holding them feels cold against my wrists rather than something like a rope. It doesn't feel like I'm on a bed, either. The surface I'm on is a little springy, but it seems thin, and like I'm only slightly elevated from the floor.

An image flashes into my head of being in a vehicle and trying to fight someone. I vaguely recall my vision receding until everything went black. And now apparently I'm here, wherever this is.

It wasn't that fucker from the salon, though. Not the Hot Guy who killed The Asshole. I remember him and what happened there.

The person in the car was another guy, also hot, but different. Aidan, I think he said his name was. He must have brought me here.

I'm assuming that the Aidan guy and Hot Guy know each other, but I'm not sure what I'm basing that on. Just a hunch. Or maybe I'm just linking them together because they're both good-looking, like all good-looking guys are part of some secret gang. Sounds like a gang I'd like to get to know. *Focus, Angel.* Jesus.

My eyes are adjusting to the darkness of this chilly space. The room I'm in is a concrete rectangle with wooden steps ascending to an unknown destination. The floor is hard cement, with a floor drain in the corner. Bare beams and insulation are exposed where a ceiling would normally be. It doesn't take a rocket scientist to guess this is probably a basement.

Lining one wall is a row of lockable cabinets. One has been left open, its double doors spread wide, leaving its contents on display. Various tools are hung neatly on hooks, and the more details I notice, the more I get the sense these guys aren't just into home decorating. Hooks and blades, some that appear to be very sharp and others serrated, everything with a sinister quality that doesn't spell casual weekend wallpapering. I shiver as my eyes rest on something that looks like a branding iron.

Looking down, I can now see I'm sitting on a thin mattress with some strange stains on it. I prefer not to think about what they might be, but there's a definite possibility they're bodily fluids. I fight the urge to wretch. There's no need to add vomit to the existing mess.

I try to squeeze my wrists out of the shackles that keep me attached to the wall, but there's no wiggle room. I'm firmly stuck in place, helpless, with a ton of questions racing through my mind.

Who the fuck are the men that brought me to this room?

Why was The Asshole after Hot Guy at my salon?

Who is Aidan from the car and how does he know Hot Guy?

Why do they keep knocking me out, and why am I here?

Chapter Eight

Slade

"Did you dispose of everything okay?" Aidan asks, glancing from me to Roman. We just got back to the compound after leaving the hair salon and taking a long drive out west with the body in the trunk.

"Yeah, we broke it down, bagged it up and buried it in the woods. Found a good deserted spot far from where we left the other ones. We should be good."

We have a few 'regular' spots to leave bodies. There are many untouched locations on the island—forests, rivers, and lakes. It's safer to mix things up rather than create a mass burial site that someone might stumble upon.

"Good," Aidan nods, steepling his fingers under his chin. "Now we just have to figure out what to do with the girl."

"Where'd you put her?" I glance around but don't see any signs of her, which is a relief. I'm half-surprised the guys don't have her laying on a sun lounger while they fan her and feed her grapes, the horny fucks.

"She's down in my special room," grins Brick.

"We're just going to keep her shackled down in the basement?" Roman raises an eyebrow.

"It's out of the way. She'll be less of a distraction down there," I reply.

"But that's no fun." Roman narrows his eyes at me. "And it's not like you're distracted by women."

"I'm not, but the rest of you are. Especially you." I glare back at him.

"We didn't bring her here for fun, Roman," says Aidan. "If you recall, you chose to bring her here because she saw you murder someone."

"The two don't have to be mutually exclusive, you know," Roman wiggles his eyebrows. "Murder witness. Sexy concubine. She could be both."

"She is really sexy," nods Brick. "Such a pretty wee captive."

"I have a feeling she'll end up being more like a succubus," I sigh at him. "Look, you really need to learn to stop thinking with your dick. It's going to get us in trouble one of these days. It already almost has on countless occasions."

"I've always wanted to bang a succubus," says Brick, grinning. "Sounds like a good time!"

"Fuck you're weird, man!" I roll my eyes, and Aidan snorts.

Despite our differences, we're all in agreement with one thing, and that's that Brick is a weird dude. We love him, but he's got some strange ideas.

"I'm okay with her being down in my special room, though," says Brick. "It's almost like she's my pet, waiting for me there. I want to show her all the things I can do with my tools. Maybe I'll find some prey and bring it back just to show her my skills."

"She's not yours. Not your pet," snaps Roman, narrowing his eyes at Brick. "I found her."

"See?" I say to Aidan, gesturing toward Roman and Brick. "She's been here for five minutes and she's already causing conflict, even when she's shackled to the wall in the fucking basement. This is an awful idea, and it's going to rip us apart." I glare at Roman. "There are easier ways to get pussy. I don't know why you're so pressed on her."

"It didn't feel right, killing her there in the salon," he shrugs. "Does it help that she's fucking hot? Sure. But I still wouldn't have snuffed her out there, even if she wasn't."

I'm skeptical about what Roman would have done if she didn't look the way they say she does, but there's no point pressing this now.

My main concern is what having a gorgeous woman under our roof is going to do to our business and our brotherhood.

We have a lot to do if we're going to continue to scale. Rivals are constantly popping up on the island, trying to take over our turf.

Recently, we did a deal with a group of guys who have some type of protection role on this island. Before we came to an arrangement, they'd been a thorn in our side, slowing our profits because of their stupid rules. But we were able to help them free their girl from Tane Brown and his men, and now they owe us. Now they have a window of time to pay off their debt to us, and during that timeframe, they can't fuck with our business the way they usually do.

It's more important than ever that all four of us are laser-focused so that we can ramp and scale before the window closes again and things go back to normal.

The protector guys, I think they're loosely called snakes, are a case in point. In their case, a woman was a distraction, and now their business is suffering greatly as a result. We're benefiting from their weakness and their poor decisions. They're hemorrhaging money because they chose to prioritize her and save her life. They chose love over profit, and look where it's got them.

I just hope this woman we kidnapped today doesn't end up being our downfall, too.

Chapter Nine

Angel

I hear footsteps descending the steps toward me. Out of the darkness, a burly man enters the room where I'm shackled to the wall. He's tall and extremely muscular. He wears a red and black shirt rolled up to his elbows, revealing tattooed forearms, and long dark pants with Chuck Taylors that make me want to go back to the eighties when they were originally on trend.

His hair is a dirty blonde, tied back in a ponytail, and he has a scruffy beard.

His eyes are a piercing blue-gray, like the ocean during a windstorm, and his skin is tanned golden. Like his buddy from the salon, I get the feeling he spends a lot of time in the ocean. He's like a sexy tattooed lumberjack surfer, and I am here for it.

I rip my eyes away. *Pull yourself together. You're shackled to the wall in some random basement full of torture implements, not at a restaurant for a first date. He's obviously insane.*

Trying to come out swinging and to put him on the back foot, figuratively at least, I narrow my eyes at him. "Who the fuck are you?" I ask, my raised voice bouncing off the basement walls.

He glances at me, a half-smirk on his face. "Hey pretty lady," he says. "Nice to meet you. They call me Brick."

"Brick?" I raise an eyebrow.

"Yep, like the thing you build houses with." He shrugs.

"Why? Did your parents not like you?"

He smirks at me. "If I tell you, I'll have to kill you."

My eyes involuntarily dart toward the open locker with all the torture implements neatly displayed on hooks. He could definitely kill me with several of the items. A shiver runs down my spine as I look at some of the sharp blades.

"It's okay. Just don't ask me why my nickname is what it is and you'll be fine." He winks at me and then follows my gaze to the open locker. "Oh, don't worry about those, for now at least. I save them for people who insist on understanding the reason for my nickname."

I'm not sure whether to laugh at his torture jokes or stay completely still, so I freeze in some type of half-smile.

"It's okay, Angel is it? I'm not going to bite, today anyway. I'm going to give you some time to settle in. But after today, all bets are off."

This time I smirk.

"Why am I here?" I ask. "Why am I shackled to a fucking wall in the middle of a basement, sitting on a thin-ass mattress that appears to be coated in some combination of vomit and blood and piss and shit and probably semen and god knows what else?"

His eyes flit to the mattress and he pulls a face as if he's realizing how filthy it is for ht first time.

"Oh, Angel. Don't play dumb. You witnessed a murder. And we can't have you running around telling everyone, can we? And now that you mention it, you've seen a bit more of my basement than I intended you to. I should have kept those lockers closed. Now there are two reasons we can't just let you go."

I feel the color drain from my face, and my lip trembles involuntarily. I jut my jaw out to steady it, and blink hard to hold back the tears that are trying to free themselves from my tear ducts.

Brick glances again at the filthy mattress I'm sitting on and its many stains, and then he looks at me. "There's no semen down here, by the way. I get turned on by the things I do down here, but I haven't jerked off on any of my victims. Then again, I have had no one nearly as attractive as you down here before."

His eyes devour me, trailing over my body and taking me all in, but in a way that makes me feel pretty despite the dingy surroundings. It's like he's admiring my every angle, memorizing my lines. Except I get the funny feeling that instead of analyzing my anatomical contours for a painting or sculpture, he's thinking about where he'd slice me with his scalpel.

As he gazes at me, he steps back, crossing his arms and putting one hand up to his mouth as if he's deep in thought. "Shackling you to the wall and making you sit in this filth, in my house of horrors, doesn't seem fitting, especially for someone as beautiful as you. I want to spend time with you down here, don't get me wrong. There are so many fun activities we could do together, so many things I want to show you. But not right now, not like this."

Removing a key from his pants pocket, he moves toward me and kneels sideways between me and the fixture attaching the shackles to the wall.

As he gets within inches of my body, I flinch and look down at the floor. His figure is imposing, and I can't wrench myself free from my restraints. I'm completely at his mercy.

"Relax, Angel," he says softly, tipping my chin with his hand so I have no choice but to look right at him, our faces so close I can feel his warm breath. "You deserve somewhere nicer than my torture basement."

He unlocks the clasps that bind me, and as he frees my wrists are I lower my hands, shaking them to get the circulation going again.

He reaches out and clasps one of my forearms in his large, powerful hand. He pulls me to my feet and tugs me across the basement and up the stairs. "Come on, my beautiful Valkyrie. We're getting you a proper room."

"What did you call me?"

"My Valkyrie. You're my little angel of death."

What a weirdo.

"Are you meant to be doing this? Letting me out of here?" As he leads me away from the disgusting mattress, I raise an eyebrow. I feel like I need a thousand showers after sitting on that, and my skin crawls at the thought of what might have been living on it. I really hope wherever he's taking me is better than this, or at least clean.

"I prefer to ask for forgiveness than permission." He grins. "Besides, you're hardly going to be able to roam free. You're still our captive, after all."

He motions for me to be quiet as we reach the top of the basement stairs and emerge into what seems to be an apartment. We briefly pop out into an open-plan kitchen and dining area with hardwood floors, and he leads me through a short corridor and then up some stairs. We walk along another longer carpeted hallway lined with rooms until we get to a door near the back of the house.

He opens the door and leads me inside. It's a spacious bedroom, and I'm assuming it's a guest room because it doesn't look lived in. It's more like a display you'd find in a model home, sleek and modern, the sheets and walls sparkling white. The bed looks freshly made, and there isn't much personality in here, just some generic modern art. Two nightstands flank the bed, and there's a large dresser on the wall opposite the bed.

At the back of the room are two doors. Brick shows me that one is an ensuite with a shower bath and a basin, and the other is a spacious walk-in closet. Not that I have anything to put in there.

After showing me around, Brick turns to me. "I need to go now, but this suits you much better than my basement. We'll spend some time down there together later, though. I want to show you all the things I can do. You might like it so much you want to join me, try out a few tools yourself."

I shiver as I recall the contents of the closet he'd left open down there.

"Thank you?" I say, my voice tipping up at the end like a question, because I'm not sure why he's doing this for me and I'm still confused about why I'm here at all. But this is a damn sight better than being shackled in the chilly basement full of torture implements.

"I'll see you later," says Brick. He pats my hand and then slips out of the room, closing the door behind him. I hear a lock click into place and his footsteps retreat down the hallway.

Waiting a minute or so, I tiptoe over to the door and turn the handle just in case, but, as expected, it's locked.

I try the window that faces the backyard, but that's locked, too. Through the large glass pane, I can see a small yard below. Tall trees line the yard, blocking out the view of any neighbors.

Although this is better than being in the basement, I still feel claustrophobic. I was trapped down there, and now I'm trapped up here. Still a captive, just more comfortable with a real mattress and pillows.

I flop onto the bed, alone with my thoughts, wondering what's next.

Chapter Ten

Aidan

"You did *what*?" Slade glares at Brick. "That's not good. What were you thinking?"

"Slade was right about this whole thing. This doesn't seem like a good idea," I sigh, resting my elbow on the countertop and running my fingers through my hair. Three of us are sitting on chrome high-top chairs at the marble breakfast bar while Slade cooks a meal.

The other guys tease me for being overly cautious, but I prefer dead ends to loose ones.

"At the very least, she's going to be a distraction. And we definitely don't need those right now, with what's going on in the business. This is a critical time for us."

"Listen, like I said, I think we should keep her around for a while," shrugs Roman. "See if she can be of any use to us. Sometimes having a female around could come in handy, especially one that knows how to fight. And besides, you helped bring her here."

I narrow my eyes at him. "Yeah, because I didn't trust you boneheads to handle it. She would have almost certainly run away if you'd been in charge of transporting her, and then we'd have a witness to hunt down."

Roman glares at me. He hates it when I point out his incompetence. But he's the reason we have some feisty lunatic woman under our roof.

"How the hell could she be useful to us, Ro? Is she going to kick us in the nuts? Slit our throats while we're sleeping?" Slade glares at Roman. "It's great that she's good at fighting, but that means she's just as likely to fight *us*. That's the last thing we need to be worrying about."

"I wouldn't mind if she kicked me in the nuts," grins Brick, his eyes twinkling.

"Is that why you freed her from the basement and gave her a proper bedroom?" Slade crosses his arms over his chest. "In hopes that she'd think you were her hero and indulge in all your kinks as a thank you?"

"No. That's not the only reason why," huffs Brick.

"I still think we can have at least a little fun with her before we decide she's more trouble than not," says Roman, shrugging and turning to lock eyes with me. "Maybe she can help relieve some of your pent-up stress, Aidan. Because clearly, you need someone to loosen you up."

I cross my arms and roll my eyes at him, my lip curling slightly at his words.

He glances at Slade. "I'd say the same for you, but we all know you're a lost cause."

Slades eyes narrow at Roman while he chops meat with a sharp cleaver and throws the chunks into a large pot.

"Slade's managing the situation just fine. You're the one who seems to be obsessed with fucking her," I say, looking at Roman. "So do you, Brick." I turn my attention to the bearded vegan psycho. "By the way, I saw you stuffing those panties in your pocket when you brought her bags of clothing and stuff into the house."

Brick shrugs but doesn't offer any defense against the allegation because it's true. "The only one who doesn't want to fuck her is Slade, because he never wants to fuck anyone anymore," he says, gesturing at Slade whose face remains expressionless. We all know that he isn't completely abstinent, still has a bit of fun now and then. But he just hasn't been the same since his ex betrayed him in the worst way.

"So I don't want her here. Brick and Roman clearly do." Slade stops what he's doing in the kitchen and crosses his arms over his chest. "Where do you stand on this, Aidan?"

I'm not quite ready to throw her out yet, or worse. I'm usually so careful that I wouldn't risk something like this, having a captive in our home, especially someone who has information that could hurt us. But there's something about her I can't quite put my finger on. I need to know more before I can decide.

"Listen, I'll try to break her down a bit and we can go from there," I say, and I can't help a hungry smile from forming on my lips. "I owe her a little talking to for her behavior in the car earlier. Trying to attack me and whatnot."

"Oh, so *you* get to play with the girl and then we'll decide what happens to her? Potentially like a catch and release?" Brick frowns.

"No, it's not like that. I have plans to show her that her behavior hasn't been acceptable. She'll hopefully get in line after what I have planned for her. Although with what I'm planning on doing to her, she might act up just so that I do it again." My cock twitches in anticipation of her punishment. I'm going to take it slowly and enjoy every moment.

"Not fair, I want to play with her too," Brick pouts and crosses his arms tightly over his muscular chest. He looks ridiculous, like some muscly bearded man-child, and I shake my head and laugh.

"I found her first, bro," Roman snaps at Brick. He glares at me. "You always take over everything. If anyone gets to play with her, it should be me."

"Hey, I cleaned up your mess and now I get to enjoy the spoils of my labor," I grin back at him.

Slade says nothing. He just continues to clean the kitchen, but his wiping of the counters becomes more aggressive, his face set into even more of a scowl than usual.

It's clear he doesn't want her here, and he doesn't have the same carnal interest in her that the rest of us do. But that's just how Slade is these days, ever since he lost his love. None of us push him to get over it and move on. He'll change when he's ready and if he wants to, and it has no negative impact on our business. He just rarely gets his dick wet, and he hates all females. No biggie.

I, on the other hand, have a punishment to dish out to our sexy little captive. And I can't wait to see how far I can get her to go until she breaks. Until she submits to me and admits that I'm the one in control.

By the end of our little session, she's going to be screaming my name.

By the end of our little session, I'm going to have a better idea of whether she's someone we'll risk keeping around for a bit longer.

But first, I'm going to lay a trap so the punishment can be even more brutal.

Chapter Eleven

Angel

I wake to a sound, a loud click, or maybe I'm imagining things. It seems I dozed off on the bed.

I'm lying on my stomach, my face squished into the pillow. It's a comfortable mattress and the pillows are heavenly. Much better than that mess in the basement.

Hopping off the bed, stripped down to the tank top and hot pants I wore underneath my shirtdress, I pad over to the door and try turning the handle. I'm not sure why I'm bothering, given they say the definition of insanity is doing the same thing over and over and expecting a different result. But here I am, insane, expecting the door to be locked but trying it, anyway.

I press down on the handle, waiting to feel resistance, but surprisingly, it keeps turning until the latch pops open with a satisfying ping.

I push the door open, bracing myself for it to squeak and alert everyone that I'm escaping the confines of this room, but the hinges are well-oiled and it silently swings outward.

Peering out into the hallway, I don't see anybody, so I exit the room and tiptoe across the carpet, careful to stick to the edges in case a floorboard creaks. The foundations in this place seem more sturdy than the ones back at my apartment, or anywhere I've ever lived, but it's still a habit to try to slip by silently, to not draw unnecessary attention to myself from people who might hurt me.

Tiptoeing down the stairs, I eye the front door through the kitchen and living room and down an entrance hallway. As I reach the bottom of the stairs, I suddenly feel eight eyes on me.

There's Hot Guy from the salon and the one I have memories of in the car, Aidan. And then Brick, the burly guy who brought me up from the basement to the new room. And another guy, tall and muscular, who seems to be cooking something in the kitchen.

From where I'm standing, I glance at each of them. They're all ridiculously attractive. Four hot, tall, muscular men, their attention focused entirely on me. I still don't know what I'm doing here, but I don't mind the scenery.

"Well, well, well. If it isn't Sleeping Beauty," grins Hot Guy from the salon. The hot murderer that I saw kill someone. That probably has a lot to do with why I'm here, now that I think about it. In fact, it's kind of shocking that I'm still alive after what I saw yesterday.

"Well, well, well. If it isn't Mr. Come Into Your Workplace and Kill Someone and Kidnap You Guy," I reply, deadpan.

The others glance at each other and laugh.

"Who said you could leave your room, Angel?" Aidan arches an eyebrow at me.

"Nobody said I couldn't," I reply, placing my hand on my hip. "Last I looked, I was a grown-ass woman who could make decisions about where to go in this world."

"That was before you became a witness to a murder," Aidan shrugs. "That carries responsibilities. You've become a liability, and you have to do what we say now."

"The door was also unlocked, so I walked out of it," I shrug.

"It shouldn't matter if we have removed the door from its hinges and there's just air keeping you between the room and the hallway, Angel. You're under our control, and you need to do exactly as we say. If you're told to stay in your room, you need to stay there."

"Because you said so? I'm not under your control." I glare at him. He's treating me like a dog who's being trained to sit and stay when there's a treat sitting right in front of it. But in this case, the treat is my freedom. "Why are you such a jerk, anyway? You're so controlling. I remember how you behaved in the car, and now this. Fuck you, asshole!"

"Oh, you're going to regret talking to me that way, sweetheart," Aidan's voice is calm, but it drips with condescension.

"I am *not* your sweetheart!" I narrow my eyes at him. What a prick.

"Keep going, and watch the punishment get more severe," shrugs Aidan, his eyes glimmering at me as if he's planning something truly cruel.

"A punishment? Really? How innovative of you." I roll my eyes.

"Watch it," he says, his tone changing from amusement to a warning.

"Or what?" I raise an eyebrow.

"Or I will make you ride the line between pleasure and pain so hard you'll never think about another man again."

Okay. This changes things. My pussy clenches. I wonder what he has in mind and I can't wait to see. "Is that a threat or a promise?"

"Can't it be both?"

"I dare you to punish me." I jut my chin out in what I hope comes across as defiance. He clearly wants control, and I will not let him just take it. If he wants to punish me, I'm going to make him really punish me.

He shakes his head. "I don't think you could take it."

"I bet you I can." I've never been able to resist a dare or a bet.

"Fine. But you need to tell me you're sure that you want everything I'm going to dish out to you," he says, his eyes locked with mine, his expression serious. "Because this will be painful. Your body is going to be screaming and spent by the end."

"Even better." I maintain eye contact, my body tingling in anticipation at his words.

"Oh, you like pain?" His eyes grow dark and he once again lets them trail over me as if he's planning my punishment out in his mind.

"It all depends on the circumstances, the setting, and whether there's pleasure involved, too."

"Alright, well you're literally asking for it," he smirks, his gaze unwavering, "so I'm going to give it to you as requested." He diverts his gaze to the kitchen, where the guy I haven't spoken with is standing. "But let's have dinner first. Slade made us a nice meal, didn't you, Slade?"

I glance over at the guy in the kitchen. Slade, I guess. He's scowling at me.

"Oh, you've both realized you're not the only two people in the room?" he smirks and shakes his head. "I told you she'd be a distraction. You were so focused on her you almost forgot to eat, Aidan."

Aidan glares at Slade.

I can tell that Slade dislikes me and doesn't want me to be here. It's palpable.

"Why are you glaring at me like that? You don't even know me. I have done nothing to you and I didn't ask to be here." I narrow my eyes at him.

"Don't take it personally," says Brick. "Slade hates all women."

"Yeah," says Slade, his eyes narrowing at me in what appears to be disgust. "You're nothing special."

Chapter Twelve

Angel

The five of us seat ourselves around the dinner table.

Ordinarily, I'd describe the table as large. It's sleek and modern, like the rest of the furniture in this place, made up of solid woodgrain planks, and looks like it would seat about six normal people. But with this group, it's a tight squeeze. Four tall and muscular guys and me, crowded around the slab of wood. It's cozy, but we make do.

I'm sitting between Slade and Roman, each of us in our own plush black boucle chairs. The seats are comfortable with curved backs, and I lean into the backrest, sinking into the softness. I don't know that any of these guys have an eye for interior design, but if someone picked the furniture out, I think it would have been Aidan or Roman.

Aidan, because he likes to control everything down to the last detail.

Roman because he'd want everything to look perfect in his den of seduction.

Maybe I'm wrong. Maybe Slade has an eye for design, and his grumpiness just overshadows his artistic side. He is pretty creative with his cooking, judging by the attention he seemed to be putting into cooking dinner.

It's definitely not Brick who picked out the furniture, though. That's for sure. I've only known him for a moment, but can tell he largely reserves his creativity for torture. That's what lights him up, gets his juices flowing. And, if he was to dabble in interior design, his aesthetic would be much more gothic, with skulls and crosses and lots of red and black detailing.

Aidan sits across from me and Brick is over to the left of Slade, at the end of the table. It would have made more sense for Roman to sit at the other end, across from Brick, but when I sat down, he picked his chair up and carried it next to mine, creating the Angel sandwich that I'm now in the middle of.

Slade seems annoyed to have to sit in such close proximity to me, but he doesn't move. For a moment I thought he might take his plate over to the breakfast bar just so he doesn't have to be near me, but for whatever reason, he's decided to stay where he is.

As if he's standing his ground and enduring my presence. As if moving away might give the others the idea that I had displaced him, that I had more right to be there than he did.

Maybe I'm overthinking this. He just seems so angry that I'm here. I have a knack for being acutely aware when I'm not wanted somewhere.

To add insult to injury, I'm left-handed and Slade is right-handed, so our forearms keep crashing into each other as we try to eat. He glares at me each time it happens, as if I'm doing it on purpose just to annoy him.

Despite his grumpiness, every time the hairs on his arm connect with my forearm, I feel a little zip of electricity between us, a little tingle that radiates up my arm and then feathers out into my body.

Maybe it's his hatred emanating from him and shocking my pores, but each time it happens, there's a little crackle, a brief connection. Maybe like a moth to a flame, I'm drawn to the thing that might ultimately kill me.

Slade made meat lasagne for dinner, and it's fantastic. Saucy and cheesy and perfect, the various layers all made by hand. The kitchen has been emitting mouth-watering aromas for a while now. I have had little to eat in the last twenty-four hours, so my bar is set extra low, but even if I wasn't starving, I'd savor this meal.

In addition to the meat lasagne, Slade made Brick a special vegan version of the dish, and the guys tease him about his fake cheese and his large side salad.

He smirks. "Want a bite?" he asks me, gesturing at his plate.

"Sorry, what?"

"Want a bite of my vegan lasagne? See what you're missing?"

"Sure," I grin. "I went through a vegan phase a while back, actually. There's some pretty decent stuff available these days. They just need to work on the cheese."

"Yeah, it's the one thing they don't seem to be able to nail. I might get Slade to try his hand at it, see what he can come up with."

Slade rolls his eyes. "Yeah, just how I want to be spending my time. Making even more vegan crap for you."

Brick carefully prepares a forkful of his meal and feeds it to me.

The flavors are fresh and savory and citrusy. "Oh wow! This is amazing!" I exclaim, and Brick smiles proudly, even though he didn't make the dish.

I glance at Slade. "This is almost better than the meat version. In fact, it might be my favorite!"

From the way he's beaming at me now, I may as well just have announced that Brick is my favorite.

Aidan clears his throat, interrupting the flow of conversation. "Don't forget what's happening later." He gazes at me intently, as if he's playing out what's going to happen later in his mind. "You're not off the hook, Angel. You owe me."

"For now, I'm going to enjoy my dinner and I'll worry about that later, thank you." I dismiss him with a flick of my wrist.

He narrows his eyes at me.

I don't think he liked that, being dismissed. I think he's used to doing the dismissing.

As I work my way through my lasagne, and wash it down with a can of sparkling water, the guys make chitchat about some business deals they're contemplating. I don't recognize any of the names or places they mention, and it feels almost like they're speaking in code, their own language.

Every time I get the sense they're using certain words in place of others, I file away the things they're saying. There seems to be some talk about gambling, maybe some bars or clubs, which would make sense given what Roman shared back at the salon. And lots of talk about moving kitchen equipment and supplies.

I sit and listen to them talk, more chatter about the incoming 'kitchen equipment'. I'm still not buying it. These four incredibly hot men are not making their money selling overhead vents and top-of-the-line stovetops to the restaurants around here.

I want to decipher their code to see just how criminal their activities really are, and what they're prepared to move through the islands to turn a profit.

Glancing around their opulent apartment, it's only logical that whatever they're involved in can't be legal. Nobody makes this much money unless they're involved in something shady. And innocent people don't have armed killers hunting them down in hair salons.

I'm thinking maybe they're involved with guns or drugs. Hopefully, it's not kidneys or humans or worse. I shiver as I think about the types of activities they might be involved in.

But what do I know? I'm not sure what their backstories are, or why they do the things they do. I'm not here to judge them for how they keep afloat in this uncertain world. It's not like I'm Ms. Morals doing everything the way society tells us to.

It's not like we all haven't found a way to get by, found a life that we can justify, even if others might judge it as morally gray. After all, we only have ourselves to answer to in the end.

I look around the table, letting my gaze rest for a moment on each of them. They're all so incredibly good-looking, and they're clearly very close, bantering back and forth as if they can read each other's minds.

It's confusing being here with them, sitting around the table as if I'm a special guest in their home rather than someone who's been kidnapped and brought here against my will. They treat me as one of them throughout the meal, passing me bread and salad and making sure I have enough lasagne. I'm a prisoner, but sitting here I feel for once like I belong, like I'm meant to be here.

Generally, I prefer to be by myself, a solo act. It's not often I get invited to spend time with others, and I've intentionally pushed everybody away to ensure that's the case. But there's an odd comfort in sitting with others at dinner and feeling like everyone accepts me having a seat at the table.

Well, everyone except Slade, who has glared at me the entire time and is continuing to do so right now. I can see him in my peripheral vision, sitting right beside me and scowling at me.

I want to call him out, but I'm scared that if I do, if I draw attention to myself, they might suddenly all decide they don't want me here and either lock me in my room or worse.

My mind flashes back to the last time I sat around a family table for a meal with my parents and my brother.

It must be the holidays, because otherwise my parents are rarely home at the same time. They're ships passing in the night with their multiple jobs and, in my dad's case, extracurricular activities.

We're sitting around the table that Mom has intricately decorated with festive napkin holders and candles and paper decorations. She always goes over the top, finding something new to add to the already busy decorations.

The center of the table is full of delicious holiday items. Carved, roasted turkey with cranberry sauce. Roasted Brussels sprouts. Herb stuffing. Mashed potatoes and gravy. Parker house rolls.

The aroma of each dish co-mingles into a cacophony of festive flavors, butter and roast turkey skin and garlic the most prominent tones.

The dining table is alive with the sounds of chatter and laughter, the clinking of silverware against ceramic plates, and the chewing noises of children trying to use their best table manners.

My mother looks tired, but she's smiling. I know the holidays are important to her, giving her a brief reprieve from the jobs that work her to the bone.

My father, taking a moment for once to spend time with his wife and children rather than taking on jobs he can't speak about that barely pay the bills, and chasing skirts all over the country under the guise he's 'traveling for work'.

It feels like we're in some Hallmark movie, frozen in time, where we're doing something families are meant to do, and actually enjoying it.

If anyone saw us here like this, they'd likely assume it was like this all the time. That my parents enjoyed each other's company, our company, and that our lives were light and fun and joyful. It's a lie, but one I'll happily take part in until it's over and things will go back to normal.

We're all laughing as my baby brother tells a story about school. He's so cute with his missing front tooth and a smattering of freckles across his nose.

I add to his joke, embellishing it to make it even more ridiculous. He giggles with joy, and everyone around the table laughs with us.

But then my brother looks directly at me, his eyes locking onto mine.

His lips thin and curl into a tight grimace as his pupils turn into tiny black pinpoints. His entire face changes, his cuteness fading as his flesh melts away to reveal a decomposing skull crawling with worms and other hungry insects.

Transformation complete, his rotting lips curve up in an evil smile and he bares tiny pointed teeth in my direction.

His mouth opens wider than it should, tilting back like a cap from a toothpaste tube, and he lets out a bloodcurdling scream.

Suddenly, there's blood everywhere, and my brother is covered in gaping stab wounds. He grins at me, his expression unhinged, and starts walking toward me with jagged, limping steps. As he advances on me, his flesh flays itself from his body, peeling away to reveal the muscles and tendons underneath.

My dead brother has almost caught up to me, his corpse disintegrating but still holding him together enough for him to keep limping toward me.

He wants to take me with him, to drag me into hell.

He cackles as he gets closer and pulls a scythe from behind his back, raising it above his head and preparing to slash it across my body. He wants me to be as disfigured and ruined as him.

I need to get out of here.

I hear screaming, and male voices saying, 'Angel, Angel.'

I tap my clavicle bone. Tap, tap, tap. Just the way my therapist showed me. Tap, tap, tap. You are safe. You are present. He can't hurt you. You are safe. You are present. He can't hurt you.

The screaming is me. The screaming is me. Stop screaming, Angel. He can't get you. Stop screaming.

I snap back to reality as a hand touches my shoulder.

For an instant I think about slapping it away, but the tapping worked, reminding me I'm not watching my brother as he's stabbed to death. That some sick, evil version of him doesn't exist, and he's not really after me.

He's gone, but it was a long time ago. I'm not here with him, and it was just another flashback trapped in a nightmare.

I glance around the table, eight eyes studying me with a combination of confusion and surprise. I'm here with my kidnappers who grabbed me because I witnessed one of them murder someone. Fuck. I'm glad my brother's decomposing corpse isn't about to annihilate me, but my current situation is hardly ideal, either. Talk about a rollercoaster of emotions.

There's not much worse than being in a nightmare, realizing you are, so you wake yourself up, feeling relief you're not in that nightmare anymore, but then quickly realizing your real life is worse.

A wave of grief washes over me, and I blink back tears as I think about how I lost everyone from my mind's dinner table scene at the hands of a complete psycho. And not just them, either. He went much further than that, working his way through everybody I cared about until there was nobody left who could give a flying fuck about Angel Benson. Although that wasn't my name back then. I will never speak that name again. She's dead.

He says he did it for me.

Intuitively, I know I can't blame myself, that his justification is just part of his psychopathy, but it's much easier said than done.

I'm the one he was after, that he's still after.

I'm his reason.

I can never get my family or friends back, and they live on only in my memory. I'm scared because some of my memories are already fading, and one day I fear that all I'll have is a couple of photos with no context.

I don't want the day to arrive when I don't remember the sound of my brother's innocent laugh or the way he would giggle when I'd pick him up for a hug. My parents were far from perfect, but I miss them, too.

I miss my good friends who were like rocks when going through all the things that life threw at us. The frantic text messages I sent to them, warning them, going unread since the night they died. Their Facebook profiles are deafeningly quiet, just an odd tribute post or memory from a relative or friend now and then.

Luckily, the crazed lunatic who killed them all is securely locked up facing life in a maximum security prison thousands of miles from here, but I've always known it may not always stay that way.

So these guys I'm sitting with, breaking bread, might be bad guys.

They might do really fucked up things.

But if they do try anything crazy, there's a good chance they'll regret it.

Because what they don't know is that I have nothing left to lose.

And I'm a pro at saving myself.

"Angel, are you okay? You were just really out of it." Roman looks at me with concern.

"Did I fall asleep?"

"No, you just looked... like you were here, but you weren't inside anymore. And then you made this noise like you were trying to scream with your mouth closed."

"Ugh, sometimes I wake up from a nightmare doing that."

"You've done that before?" Aidan asks.

"Not while sitting at the dinner table. Maybe you gave me a severe concussion when you knocked me out twice in one day," I glare at Aidan and Roman. "I'm going to call you the Knockout Crew."

Aidan smirks. "We've been called worse."

"I gave you so much opportunity to spend the day fully conscious," says Roman, "but you just couldn't behave yourself."

"Yeah, you had a chance to be a good girl, Angel," says Aidan, his eyes on my lips. My pussy clenches when he uses those words, reminding me he's got a punishment to dish out to me later. "But you couldn't just do what Roman said at the salon. And then you tried to attack me in the car several times. You really brought everything on yourself. Well, everything after the murder. That wasn't your fault. You were just collateral damage."

"Okay, sure Aidan. You're the boss," I say, rolling my eyes.

He gives me a warning look, but then goes back to talking to the guys.

I take a deep breath, trying to push the flashback from my mind as I finish my lasagne.

My attention floats back to the conversation at the table, and once again I listen as the guys cryptically allude to business pursuits.

I look at each of them again.

Aidan and Slade seem like the more serious of the four, planning and anticipating different courses of action they might need to take, and assessing the risks involved. Aidan seems to approach things from a neutral perspective, while Slade seems to assume the worst in everything.

Brick and Roman seem more low-key, like they still very much care about the business but are more willing to go with the flow than needing to be the ones setting the direction. I also get the sense they might be the more impulsive ones in the group, that Aidan and Slade might need to pull them back from danger now and then. They seem to elaborate on Aidan and Slade's ideas with suggestions involving a lot of violence and risk-taking. Brick, in particular, seems to want everything to happen right now. Roman's sense of urgency seems to depend on what works with his calendar.

What the four clearly have in common is that they're all hot as fuck. I really don't mind being here, around this table with them. Whatever happens later on, I'll worry about it later. For now, I'm content watching and listening to them.

After a few minutes of conversation, I feel something brush against me, touching my knees. Trying not to react too obviously or draw attention to myself, I lean back slightly in my seat and try to get a look underneath the table, but I can't see what's happening from my current position.

I refocus on their conversation but then I feel it again, and this time whatever it is tries to press my knees apart. I squeeze them together and look around the table. That's when I see Aidan's eyes locked on me, his eyes twinkling and his mouth turned up in a smirk.

He nods at me, almost imperceptibly. Oh my god, it's his foot, and he's trying to wedge my legs apart. He bites his lower lip as he gazes at me and pushes his foot toward me again, wedging it between my knees.

I let his food spread my knees apart slightly, and he brushes his foot further up my inner thighs, causing them to tingle. He keeps moving his foot closer to my core until it rubs against my pussy through my shorts. I stare at him, my eyes growing large as I realize what he's doing.

He uses his foot to stroke me while he engages in conversation with the rest of the guys. My pussy throbs at his touch, little ripples emanating out from where his foot makes contact.

I know this is a test. He wants to see if I'll let on what's happening, if I'll let him continue doing what he's doing without saying anything.

The truth is, his foot feels fucking good rubbing against me while I sit here, and I don't want him to stop. My body has been on edge with everything happening, and Aidan is hot as hell. It's a turn-on that he's doing this while the other guys sit there, oblivious, scarfing down their lasagne while he manipulates my body.

Locking my eyes with his, I spread my thighs wider to give him more access. My pussy throbs intensely, and I feel myself getting increasingly wet as he flicks his foot up and down my slit through my pants. As he narrows in on my clit and rubs against it rhythmically, I feel my arousal dripping from me, soaking my panties.

I raise my gaze to meet his and bite my lower lip. I need his touch directly on my skin. My body is craving more of him. His fingers, his mouth, all of him.

My mind drifts to what my supposed punishment is going to be after dinner. Clearly, his foot is intended to be foreplay. My entire skin feels tingly, like it's lit up in anticipation of what's coming.

He flicks at my clit with his toe, grinding it against me, and I ball my hands into fists at my side, taking a deep breath to avoid crying out.

I resist the urge to reciprocate by grinding my hips against his foot to further increase the friction because everyone would see. I'm surprised they haven't noticed anything by now, and I'm really struggling to keep my breath slow and my face neutral.

He's zeroed in on my clit now, caressing it through my shorts and panties, increasing the pressure.

I'm getting close now, even through the layers of fabric. I can feel a white-hot coil tightening in my lower abdomen.

I press my lips into a thin line and take a deep breath, and they all glance at me.

"Are you okay?" Bricks asks, peering at me. "You have a funny look on your face and you're breathing funny."

"Uh—yes, fine. I'm fine," I say quickly, consciously slowing down my breath and forcing my face into a neutral position.

He shrugs. Everyone has finished eating, and he stands up to clear plates from the table.

Aidan removes his foot from between my legs and smirks at me as he stands up to help him.

My clit is aching, throbbing for more. I can't believe he stopped. I was getting really close. Then again, it would have been hard to not cry out at the dinner table and let on that Aidan was pleasuring me with his foot throughout our meal. I'm not sure what the other guys would think about that, although it's fairly safe to assume that Slade would not be impressed.

I leave dinner feeling very worked up, and hungry for my punishment.

As the other guys wash up, Aidan comes over and leans down behind me, his neck over my shoulder and his head parallel to mine. "Did you enjoy dinner?" he growls in my ear. A shiver of pleasure runs down my neck and makes my hairs stand on end as he tugs my earlobe gently with his teeth.

"Yeah, especially where some asshole reached out his leg and rubbed my pussy with his foot. That was unexpected," I hiss at him in a whisper.

"Are you complaining?" he asks, nipping me playfully on the curve of my neck.

"Not at all," I say, biting my lower lip. "It made dinner even more delicious. But I'd really like for you to finish what you started. I'm aching for you."

"Are you saying your cunt is aching for me, Angel? That you want me to bury my cock deep inside you? To rail you until your legs are like jello? You want me to make you fall apart over and over again until you can't remember your own name?" he growls.

I nod at him, my eyes pleading. I need him to give me a release.

"Which one?" he asks.

"All of them," I reply, my breath rapid as I picture him on me, in me, manipulating my body with his cock and his fingers and his tongue.

"Well, I'm glad you liked that, because I'm not sure how you're going to feel about what happens next. It's time for you to pay for how badly you've behaved today." He smacks me on my ass. "It's time to finally get what you've been asking for. Come with me."

Chapter Thirteen

Angel

"Turn your ass around and face the table." Aidan looks truly annoyed, his eyes boring into mine and then trailing their way over my body. This time his gaze isn't just a general check-out, it's predatory. Like he's assessing which part of me he wants to eat first.

We're in an office with a large desk on one side of the room. It's located off to the side of the dining area where we just had dinner. I hadn't noticed this room before, and even if I had, I wouldn't have considered it a sex room.

Its walls are lined with wooden floor-to-ceiling shelves stuffed with books about business and economics, but also what appears to be an extensive fiction collection. They give this room that rich old book smell and I inhale deeply because it's one of my favorite scents in the world.

Okay, this room is more appealing than I realized at first glance. These guys are so hot they could make any room sexy. Books are sexy, and this space has lots of them. This room is blowing my mind.

As with the rest of the house, it's sleek and modern, with grand light fixtures and streamlined furniture. The desk is sturdy and metallic, the perfect height to be bent over and fucked against. But I'm not sure what he has in mind for me today.

I comply, placing my hands on the desk, and I hear the sound of him sliding the leather belt out of his belt loops. He cracks it loudly on the table next to me. I flinch at the startling sound and the vibration the belt creates on the table. I'm excited about what's coming, and a little shiver of anticipation runs through me.

He walks to the side, just out of view, and I turn to look at him over my shoulder.

"Don't you fucking turn around unless I tell you to," he growls. "You're really going to get it now."

My breath catches and I obediently follow his instructions, turning my neck back to neutral and focusing my eyes on the desk in front of me.

I hear him moving something, and then suddenly he's behind me again. I gasp as I feel cold metal pressing into the skin at the bottom of my shorts, skimming my butt and moving towards my inner thigh.

I shiver as the cool metal rises to the hem of my shorts, and instantly recognize the distinctive noise as he snips away at my clothing. He removes my shorts first, and then cuts off my panties, leaving my lower half completely bare. Too scared to look anywhere else but down, I see a flash of metal. I recognize what's in his hand. He's using my hairdressing shears to cut off my clothing.

"Where did you get those? They're my shears from the salon."

"Ro gave them to me as a souvenir of our special day."

I think better of telling him you're not meant to use them on anything but hair because it blunts the blades.

I shiver as he glides the sharp tip along my ass cheeks, moving towards the center where he finds the cleft that marks the center of my butt.

"Bend over," he says, tracing the hairdressing shears down between my cheeks, letting them drag slightly against my very delicate flesh. He slowly slides the blade downward, keeping his pressure very light.

I gasp as the point of the shears skims over my back entrance. My breath grows faster as I wonder what's coming next, realizing his brother used the shears to kill someone in cold blood only hours ago.

These shears are extremely sharp, he's using them in a very sensitive area, and he's clearly unhinged just like the other guys in this house.

He continues to trail the points of the shears across my body, and just as he gets to my entrance, he pulls his hand away.

"No more unacceptable behavior or I won't stop there," he leans over and growls into my air, his breath hot against my earlobe.

He places the scissors over to the side of the room on the top of some drawers. I begin to straighten, as if to stand. "Did I tell you to move?" he growls.

I stay silent, my body tingling with goosebumps as I anticipate his next move.

"Answer me when I speak to you, brat," he snarls, and I jump.

Fuck. I keep making him madder, whatever I do. Probably not a good idea seeing he and everyone else in this house seems to be in a kill-y mood. Especially with my shears so close by. There's a fine line here between what might be fun and what might be deadly, and I don't know any of these guys well enough to tell the difference.

He presses me down with one firm hand on my upper back, and I feel the sensation of cold leather as he places the belt across my lower back, laying it flat on me and letting it sit there for a moment.

I shiver as I feel it lifting off me. There's a soft whoosh as leather cuts through the air before lashing the fullest part of my ass cheek with a loud thwack.

It stings like fuck and I try not to jump or cry out, but it's easier said than done and I feel myself flinch. My eyes water, but I squeeze them together as hard as I can and somehow hold in a gasp.

"You've been a very bad girl over the past twenty-four hours, Angel," he growls, "and this is what you get as your punishment. You need to learn what happens when your behavior is unacceptable."

I place more pressure on my forearms, flat on the table, and tense myself in anticipation of the next lashing.

He whips me again, harder this time. The area he made contact with stings and tingles, and I imagine the welts that are forming across my cheeks.

"Are you sorry for your behavior, brat?" he growls.

"Yes!" I cry out as he whips me again, no doubt adding another stripe to my cheeks.

"What are you sorry for?" he asks, revisiting the same spot as the first lash, the belt flogging me even harder than before. The smell of leather fills the air, and the sheer masculinity makes my pussy clench.

"Lying to Roman," I grimace as the belt thwacks against me again. My eyes are watering more now, but I'm determined for him not to see me cry.

"That's right. He told me all about that. And when you lie to one of us, you lie to all of us," he says. "You were a bad girl, not sharing important information with him." He pauses, and I flinch in anticipation, not being able to see what he's doing behind me. "What else do you have to apologize for, Angel?".

"Not following instructions." I brace for more impact, but it doesn't come. He steps back and I can feel his eyes on me.

"That's right. Good girl. You should see your gorgeous ass right now," he growls, his voice husky. "It's an artwork. I'm quite proud of it, actually. Flushed, with several areas of pretty, raised flesh. I enjoy putting my mark on you."

He runs a finger over one of the welts as if fascinated by it, admiring his handiwork. His touch adds to the heat that swarms the locations where he's lashed me, my skin tingling further at his touch.

"What else am I punishing you for, brat?"

He strikes me again, and I hold my ass as still and tense as possible as the belt cracks down on my flesh. It hits the very edge of my folds, causing a stinging situation to radiate into my core and generate a little ripple of pleasure. My arousal hangs thick in the air.

"Leaving my bedroom without your permission!" I grind out, reeling from the sting of the latest lash of the belt.

"That's right," he says. "I let you know when you can come and go from the bedroom. Do you understand me? I control you and your activities in and out of the bedroom."

He cracks the belt down on my cheek again, and I grit my teeth and squeeze my hands flat against the table in a mostly successful attempt not to cry out.

My ass stings like hell, the welts tingling as my body's response kicks in, rushing to heal the swollen skin. Even though it's painful, there's an intense throbbing between my thighs. He can probably see my arousal from his vantage point.

"Let me look at you," he says, taking a step back. He groans as he examines me. "It looks like you enjoyed your punishment. Your cunt is gushing."

I can't explain it. I need this type of pain.

I moan as he extends a long finger and slides it inside me. It glides in smoothly, through my arousal, with absolutely no resistance, and I buck against it. He growls and slides it out, wiping my juices on my ass.

He moves to the counter and I hear him pick up the shears again. I shiver as I wonder what he's going to do now, but this time it's a shiver of anticipation and desire. He might kill me at the end of this, but I'm enjoying the process.

A gasp leaves my lips as once again I feel the cold metal against my skin, but this time he gently presses it through my folds and collects some of my wet heat. Using his free hand, he grabs my arm to pull me up to standing and turn me around.

"Open your mouth and taste yourself, like a good girl," he growls, extending the shears toward my face.

I do what he says. I'm really hoping I still have a tongue after he's done with me. As I lick my juices off the shears, I maintain eye contact with him.

The same shears that took a man's life earlier.

Holy fuck. This is insane.

He gently twists the blade of the shears against my tongue and I feel a sharp prick, and then warm blood begins to flow gently into my mouth. He removes the shears and grabs me by the throat, pulling my mouth to his.

I tremble, my skin prickling as he swipes his tongue through my lips and explores my tongue with his, tasting a combination of my blood and my wet heat and sucking it into his mouth. He groans as he savors me. "Fuck, you taste so good, Angel."

I moan as he gently sucks on my tongue.

He suddenly yanks his head away and walks to the other side of the room.

"Get back into position, hands on the desk and bend over," he barks.

I do what he says, but I'm uncertain I can handle too many more lashes with the belt right now. My body is still stinging, on edge from earlier.

I brace myself for impact, but I hear him get down on his knees behind me.

His hot breath fans across my pussy and his hand part my slick folds from behind. I gasp as he tilts his face underneath me sucks my clit into his mouth, massaging it with his tongue before licking his way along my slit and to my entrance.

He laps at my soaking cunt, drinking in my arousal.

"Oh my god, your pussy is perfect. You taste so fucking sweet," he says, humming against me and sending vibrations throughout my cunt.

He swirls his tongue around my clit and then strokes it with one of his long fingers. He moves his tongue back down to my entrance and slides it into me, exploring my walls and coaxing more arousal from me, drinking it all in as he continues to massage my clit.

I grind my hips back against his face as he devours me. He cups my ass cheeks for leverage as he feasts on me, sliding his tongue in and out of my hole and over my folds, lapping at my clit, tasting every part of me he can access.

"Mmm, you're going to come for me now, baby, aren't you? I want you to come all over my face."

He spins himself around underneath me so that his front is facing mine and focuses his tongue solely on my clit. I feel two of his fingers sliding into my wetness until his knuckles are flush with my entrance.

His other hand holds me still so that all I can do is bend over and take it while his tongue lashes at me.

He fucks me with his fingers, spearing them into me as his tongue suctions onto my clit. I moan as he bites down gently and continues to unravel me stroke by stroke.

The room is quiet except for the sound as he works my wetness with his powerful hands. My eyes roll back in my head and my pussy clenches around his fingers, my hips bucking and writhing under his skilled touch as I start to get close.

"You're going to come for me soon, aren't you, baby? I can feel you getting close."

He slams his fingers inside me as far as they can go and sucks and slurps on my swollen clit as I buck and shudder against his hand and face, my body completely under his spell. An orgasm crashes through me and I see stars on the back of my eyelids as he continues to eat me while I squirm. I clamp my thighs together as firmly as I can around his face, and he groans and continues to lap at me while my whole body shudders with pleasure.

As my body stops twitching, he pulls his mouth away from my pussy, sliding his fingers out of me and standing up. I turn around to face him and he narrows his eyes as he stands there, both of us panting, his face slick with my arousal.

His eyes trail over me, dark with desire, and his cock stretches tight against his pants.

"Back in your room, Angel. Now!" He suddenly says, his voice raised, and points toward the stairs, dismissing me.

I look at him, questions in my eyes, but he just glares and continues to point.

I walk out of the office and toward the room, bottomless, my only shorts and panties snipped to pieces with my own shears. Glancing back over my shoulder, I see he's putting on his belt, his cock still straining against his pants.

I don't know quite what to make of what just happened. I'm surprised he didn't try to fuck me. His body clearly wanted to, maybe it's his mind that wasn't so sure for some reason.

But there are two things I know.

That I've never been as turned on in my entire life.

And that Aidan is a giant tease. And he's also a psycho. Just like his brother.

Chapter Fourteen

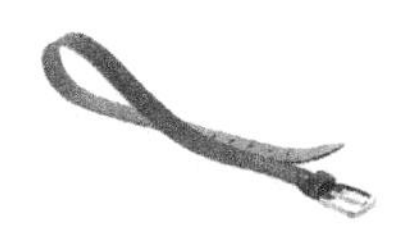

Aidan

Fuck, that was hot. It's been a while since I've spanked a hot piece of ass. And it wasn't just any ass. It's certainly up there on my list of the nicest ones I've ever laid eyes on.

Angel was so sexy, the way she was clearly enjoying that pain as it melded with her pleasure. Her gorgeous rounded cheeks growing pinker and redder each time I brought the belt down hard on her creamy flesh. Marking her and making sure she'll feel me for days every time she sits down.

She's open-minded and sex-positive, I can tell. Two things that are really important if you want to succeed around here.

Besides her gorgeous tattoos, I noticed that her body was also covered in scars. Like, smothered in them. Some were raised like they were more recent or from a more serious injury, some little silver spidery lines that seemed to have been there for a while or are just more superficial. They vary in their angles and depths, making me think more than one tool or weapon was responsible for inflicting them.

I wonder how she got them, of course, but I didn't ask her because I had other things on my mind. Like spanking her hot ass and plunging my tongue into her soaking cunt.

I'm still worked up from earlier and I get hard again thinking about all the things I want to do to her, and how sweet she tastes. I want to trace my fingers and my mouth along each scar, and learn the angles and little details of her body that I haven't yet had the chance to acquaint myself with.

By the time I was done with Angel's punishment, her ass was a palate of reds and pinks and creams, like I'd turned her into an even more beautiful creation than she already was. I didn't think it was possible. I should have taken a photo so I can relive our little encounter. Although maybe not having one gives me reason to do it all over again.

As I whipped her, I couldn't help but notice how her creamy thighs opened slightly for me, giving me a better view of her pussy, glistening with her arousal by the time I was done with my belt. I could smell her arousal in the air, and she was so sweet I couldn't resist having a taste. Seeing how wet she was, tasting her, it took everything I had not to come in my pants.

I could hear her breath quicken as I went, and she did a good job not crying out several times when I deliberately lashed her in the same spot to amplify the pain. She's definitely brave, even leaning into the agony of the belt. Trying so hard to hide the fact it hurt, even though I could see the aftermath on her body.

Her skin was flushed and covered in a slight sheen by the time I was done, emanating heat. She was so fucking hot, she had me as hard as an iron bar.

The way she took the lashing, it's like spanking her with my belt gave her life, like it filled a void deep inside of her, just for that moment. It's almost like she was craving, desperate for this kind of release.

She was soaking wet by the time I was done whipping her, and I'm going to jerk off to memories of the sounds her pussy made as I finger fucked her, and the way her arousal released onto my hands and my face.

I could have fucked her if I'd wanted to. I know she wanted my cock buried inside her sweet cunt. But I'm going to make her wait a moment.

She doesn't need to know I had to come straight to my room to relieve myself. That I'm picturing her curvy ass and the way her cunt dripped for me, pleading for my cock. But I will not give it to her that easily.

I want her to crave it.

I want her to beg for me.

And soon she'll be screaming my name.

Chapter Fifteen

Angel

A while after I retreat to my room, the door opens and Brick comes strolling in. He stands just inside the entrance, clearly inside 'my' space, and turns to me.

Maybe he feels like he has carte blanche to come in whenever he wants now because he freed me from his torture basement. But there's no announcement, no knocking on the door to see if I'm decent. He just walks in like he owns the place, which technically, I suppose, he does along with the other guys.

It's fine, though. I've just been sitting on the bed bored out of my brain so I don't mind the interruption, if you can even call it that. My back is propped against the pillow with my head tilted back, because there's literally nothing to do except stare at the ceiling. I turn my head to look at him.

His gaze travels over my body and lingers on my bare lower area and I feel myself flush.

"Jesus, he didn't waste any time getting to know you, did he?" he chuckles. "That's our Aidan, although it's more of a Roman move, if I'm honest."

There's a burning sensation in my stomach at the thought of Aidan doing what he just did to me, to anyone else. It felt special between us, not something that he does regularly with new women he meets. But it's probably naïve of me to think that way. We just met, and who knows how he operates? Slade says I'm nothing special, and maybe Aidan thinks that, too.

Aidan is interesting. He's clearly so used to leading the group, so dominant, and it definitely extends into the bedroom with him. He's fixated on making people submit to him.

I've barely met the guy, and he's already comfortable whipping me with his leather belt, marking me with welts. And then what he did with my hairdressing shears. And his fingers and his tongue. Just remembering it is enough to send a shiver of pleasure shooting through me.

I'm never going to be able to work, to hold the shears in my hand, without thinking about what he did with them. My clients are all going to wonder why I'm blushing and have hard nipples while I'm giving them a shag cut with curtain bangs.

I grab a pillow from the head of the bed and modestly place it over my pussy because Brick is still staring at it.

"Oh, you're shy now, are you?"

"Not shy," I shrug. "Just wasn't expecting you to wander in here while my pussy's out."

"I'm not complaining. Totally fine about seeing your pussy, clothed or unclothed. I don't believe you've formally introduced us, though. Just give me the word and I'd be happy to say hello."

I smirk. "She's shy. And she's had enough visitors for the day. Needs time to recharge."

Brick laughs. "Fair enough. Speaking of which," he extends his hand to me, "here, these are for you."

I cautiously take what appears to be a ball of bunched-up black fabric.

Unfurling it, I see it's a pair of familiar-looking underwear.

"Hey, these are mine! Where did you get these?"

"We got some of your stuff from your apartment so that you'd be comfortable," he explains. "I'll bring the rest up later. These were just, uh, for safekeeping."

"You *stole* my underwear from my apartment?"

"More like borrowed," he shrugs. "See, I'm returning them now. It's a bit like a library, you see. Took them for a spin."

"You'd better not have jerked off on these," I say, narrowing my eyes as I inspect them.

"Oh, I didn't jerk off *on* them," he grins. Jesus.

All of them are unhinged.

Roman, Aidan and Brick most certainly are.

I haven't interacted much with the one who was cooking earlier except to know he strongly dislikes me.

But if three out of four are complete psychopaths, then chances are good the fourth one is as well.

Chapter Sixteen

Angel

It's the morning, and I slept surprisingly okay for someone who's been kidnapped by a bunch of hot psychopaths. The bed was comfortable, and I'm sure my body and mind desperately needed to recharge after everything that's happened over the last couple of days.

Brick did as he promised last night and dropped off a bunch of my stuff, all shoved haphazardly into a duffel bag, and left it outside the door to my room.

I tip the contents of the bag onto the bed. There are tank tops and shorts and T-shirts and dresses and leggings. Underwear and some toiletries.

Brick did a good job throwing this together in a rush, especially considering the state I left my apartment in. What can I say? I keep my salon immaculately clean, but the same can't be said about the space where I live. It's just not a priority and I've never been that good at cleaning or organizing my own stuff. You win some, you lose some.

I pore through the items and pick out a clean outfit. Fresh panties and a sports bra, shorts and a racer-back shirt. Dressing for the island weather. I'll no doubt look more casual than The Brothers Fancypants downstairs, but this casual beach style works for me.

Hopping into the shower, I let the hot water run over me, cleansing me from the craziness of the past forty-eight or so hours and my interaction with Aidan that left arousal dripping down my thighs. The guys were thoughtful, remembering makeup and hair products, and I emerge from my bedroom looking relatively well put together in the circumstances. I tie my hair into a topknot and secure it with a bandana.

There's a knock on my door. "Angel, can I come in?"

It's Roman.

"Yep! I'm decent," I call out.

"That's no fun! I don't want to come in then," he jokes, as he opens the door.

He's so fucking handsome, and he's also had a shower and changed by the looks of it. He's wearing a fitted polo shirt that shows off his muscular body, and dress shorts. It's a step more casual than I've seen him so far, but still very smart, like he could attend a business meeting in this outfit and nobody would blink an eye. I'm sure all of his clothing is designer, and that a tailor was involved in getting everything to fit the way it does.

He smells great, too. His cologne today is a refreshing, masculine scent I want to say is a pleasing combo of yuzu, sage and cardamom.

"You look cute," he says, appraising me. "I like your shorts."

"Oh yeah? They're just shorts."

"That's an understatement. I like them because they're so short that you don't even have to bend over and I can see the curve of your gorgeous ass. It's sexy as hell, and I'm going to be staring at your butt for the rest of the day."

I grin mischievously. "Slade will be mad if he sees me distracting you with my ass."

Roman laughs. "I'm sure he'll get over it when he sees why I'm distracted. He may not like to fuck anymore, but he can appreciate the beauty of the female form."

I grin. I don't mind these compliments one little bit. Especially from a man as gorgeous as Roman.

"Anyway, I've officially come here to collect you. You've earned some time out of your room because of your good behavior. We'd like to reward you with some chill-out time. The downside is you have to spend time with all four of us, not just me."

Oh my god, yes. Finally. I can get out of this room and do something more interesting than just wait and stare at the ceiling. I can get out of my own thoughts. Also, I want more time around these guys to see what makes them tick. I haven't quite untangled their interpersonal dynamics.

On the face of it, I think Brick would probably be the easiest to manipulate, or maybe Roman.

Brick is a bit like a puppy dog around me, his eyes growing big whenever he sees me. An underwear-stealing puppy. If he had a tail, it would wag like crazy as he tried to come up with more and more ways to impress me.

Roman is clearly used to manipulating women to get pussy. I don't think he's used to his wiles being turned around on him and that makes him vulnerable.

Slade and Aidan will be harder nuts to crack.

They're both on the lookout for any hint of risk, and even though Aidan doesn't seem to automatically assume the worst like Slade does, both seem highly attuned to someone trying to pull one over on them.

This is all speculation at this point. I don't have a ton of data points and a lot is based on my gut and my understanding of human motivations. I need more information, and to know all of them better so I can figure out the best way to take them down so I can escape.

"Really? You're saying I get to... not be locked in a room? That's so exciting!" I clap my hands together. "Don't tease me with bodily autonomy. I might get used to it."

He smirks. "It's just for a little while, Angel. Think of it as a test. If you don't fuck up too bad, and if you're a good girl, you might get to do it again."

The way he says good girl, his voice a husky growl, does things to me. My pussy clenches hard. I'm going to have dreams about him calling me that while he buries his cock deep inside me. I hold in a moan as I think about Aidan saying the same thing yesterday when he gave me my punishment.

"I promise to be a good girl this time," I wink, and his eyes darken with lust, the words clearly affecting him, too.

He clears his throat and speaks quickly, as if slowing down might make him change his mind, as if instead of taking me to hang out with the other guys, he might throw me onto the bed and bury himself inside me. "We have to go downstairs right now. The others are expecting you and they'll get pissed if we don't come down soon."

He pauses. "And if you keep talking dirty to me, I'm going to lock myself in here with you instead and spend the entire night fucking you until I break your pussy. So let's get the fuck out of here before there's no going back."

He grabs me by my wrist and pulls me out of the room, shutting the door behind us, part of me wanting to yank him back in there and spend hours doing all the things he just mentioned.

We head to the living room to join the other guys, my pussy throbbing, and I take a seat in the middle of the sectional couch, next to Aidan. Roman squeezes in next to me on my other side. Slade sits on the furthest end, on the other side of Aidan.

Brick is perched on the arm of an armchair across from us because there's no way we could all fit on the couch at once. They're all so big and tall and muscular, and it makes me feel tiny being sandwiched between them. They might be scary guys, but I kind of like this feeling, like any of them could crush me with one hand. It might be playing with fire, thinking that way, but I like what I like.

On my way to the living room, I got more of a sense of just how huge this place is. The living room alone is many times the size of my shithole of an apartment, with high ceilings and a couch that could probably fit six to eight regular people, but only three of these guys and me. They're just all so big.

The entertainment system is state-of-the-art, with a massive screen with surround sound and a variety of remote controls that probably take a PhD to figure out how to operate. Thank goodness for voice-controlled technology.

They talk amongst themselves about an upcoming delivery. On the surface, it's about some type of kitchen equipment, but once again I get the feeling they're speaking in code. Whatever it is, it's clear that something's coming to the island that's most likely very illegal, and they're making plans to receive it and transport it onward to the next location.

I try to act like I'm not listening, that I'm focusing on the TV that plays quietly in the background. I even pretend to doze off now and then. That has to be believable after they knocked me out twice in one day. There have to be some residual side effects of being smacked unconscious, hopefully not permanent ones.

I figure I may as well try to get as much information as I can just by listening to these guys. Once they're more comfortable with me around, I might even casually ask a few questions. It might be the only way I can get out of here. Information might be as useful as having a key to the lock on my bedroom door.

At least I know I'm good at escaping.

I've run from scarier than this.

I look around the room at each of the guys.

Aidan carries himself and speaks like he's the clear leader of their group. He seems serious, thoughtful, intentional and methodical. Responsible, reliable, and consistent. All of these dad-like adjectives, but he looks nothing like my dad. He's fucking sexy. Close-cropped dark hair that he often runs his hand through when he's thinking. Piercing hazel eyes that simmer when he makes eye contact with me.

Plush lips, his lower one slightly moreso, that I just want to tug at with my teeth. That he used to rub against my folds while he was feasting on my pussy.

The gentle throbbing continues between my legs at the memory of how skilled he is with his tongue and his fingers. And what he did with my shears that I'll never look at the same way again. He's given me a hairdressing shears fetish. My heart flutters and my pussy clenches hard, and I want nothing more than to feel him dragging the cold metal against the most sensitive parts of my body, breaking my flesh and tasting my blood.

The others seem to defer to Aidan, waiting for him to make decisions and answer questions that are anything more than straightforward. Like he's always the one who knows what to do.

I imagine that must get overwhelming at times, having other grown men relying on you when you're probably just trying to figure things out like everyone else.

I'll file that away, and see if it comes in useful later on. Maybe I can drive a wedge between the guys and make a run from it while they work through the conflict.

While Aidan's calm, he's not devoid of human emotion. He was clearly pissed at me before, after I attacked him in the car, but he seems to have calmed down since he took his feelings and emotions out on me with his belt.

A shiver runs through me, but it's not unpleasant. The thwack of the leather still feels very close to my body, my ass is still a little tingly and some of the red marks are still very visible.

I got a little thrill earlier when I saw them in the mirror after my shower. I wish I had my phone so I could take a picture and remember the way he marked me forever. So I could send it to him as a reminder if he was having a bad day, or if I wanted to jump his bones the moment he got home from a job. But I'm getting ahead of myself. It's not like I'm going to be here forever.

He was just so sexy with the belt, so in control, making me ride the fine, fine line between pleasure and pain. He knew exactly how to mark me like I was his pretty picture, and how to make me feel something, anything, for the first time in a very long time.

He was sexy. It was raw. It was just what I like.

Because I like a little punishment now and then. I like to feel.

Brick is quite different from Aidan. He seems to be the enforcer for the group.

He's brutish and clearly very strong, not opposed to a little torture.

I've noticed that except for the first time I saw him in the basement, he seems to always be wearing a leather jacket. It seems to be his signature look, even though I've only seen him a few times.

He seems quirky, but caring, like when he didn't want me to have to stay on the piss- and shit-stained, grimy mattress in his torture chamber, shackled to his wall. How he insisted on begging for forgiveness rather than asking for permission when he snuck me out of his torture basement and into a spacious, clean spare bedroom.

Despite his obvious quirks, his basement is incredibly well-organized. I don't know if he forces himself to be that way because it's his pride and joy, or whether it comes naturally to him when it comes to his work.

Based on something primal I can sense about him, besides just being an incredibly large and strong human being, I imagine he's into some filthy, nasty sex, but that's a hunch I still need to verify.

I haven't figured out Slade yet. He's quiet, brooding. He spends a lot of his time in the kitchen, and it seems to be by choice. It's like he wants to be around the group, but from a distance.

He's part of the pack but tends to physically position himself away from it, listening, and thinking, quietly observing.

I almost smack myself in the side of the head as a light bulb goes off. Slade is a fucking cat. In human form.

And like a housecat that doesn't like visitors, by the way he's been scowling and glaring at me ever since I arrived at this house, it's not hard to figure out he doesn't want me here.

Well, the feeling's mutual, buddy. I don't want to be here, either.

And then Roman, of course, is a big flirt. He's good at it, too. A true player, a master fuck boy. Charming and charismatic, able to boost your confidence to the highest high so that your inhibitions and your panties disappear.

Maybe there's more to him, but that's all he's shown me so far.

Well, and that he's a violent murderer who will knock me out without a second thought.

I shiver, goosebumps forming on my arms. He could have killed me at the salon too, and it would have been easier for them to clean up than having me here at their house.

I wonder what stopped him, and then what stopped the larger group, because they don't seem like nice guys that would dish out a softer punishment just because I'm a woman.

I have a feeling they're all pretty ruthless, and that they'll do what they need to do to come out on top.

The scope of their business dealings seems broad. From what Roman shared at the salon and what I've been able to piece together while here, they have a diverse set of interests here on the island. And some people in those industries don't fuck around—bars, clubs, strip clubs, underground gambling dens. Not one of those businesses is for the fainthearted.

And if the kitchen supply warehouse really is a front for trafficking guns and drugs and god knows what else, they have to be pretty hard guys themselves.

Clearly, not one of them is originally from this island. As usual, all four of them are well-dressed, not in the casual clothing that most guys wear around here. Roman's outfit from the salon yesterday seems to be par for the course. Nobody dresses like this here, the only uniforms being at hotels and fast food places. Their style makes no sense in this tropical climate. They stick out like sore thumbs, transplants from the mainland just like me, although I do a better job of trying to fit in.

Instead of tank tops and board shorts, they wear tailored suits, and designer T-shirts and polos. The most casual their pants get seem to be jeans and dress shorts. This place is air-conditioned perfectly, so I'm sure they feel just fine in here. But when they exit into the island's thick humidity, I can't imagine they could be comfortable.

Instead of colorful flip-flops, they wear monochrome leather shoes that look like they must have cost a fortune. Brick is the exception with his retro sneakers. I'm a bit of a sneakerhead myself, so I appreciate his style. He generally looks one step more casual than the others with his tight-fitting polo shirt which wraps around his impressive torso, showing off his bulging pecs and biceps, and today he's wearing shorts that reveal muscular, tattooed calves.

They might be bad boys, and their style might be fussier than I've gotten accustomed to living in a tropical paradise, but they are also all hot as hell. At least I have four hot men to look at while I'm here.

I just have to hope that they don't kill me.

Or on second thought, maybe that would give me some peace at last.

I could finally stop running and looking over my shoulder. Of waiting for the rug to get pulled out and finding my way backsliding into terror when *he* finds me.

Not that I'm planning on telling these guys about any of that. About *him*.

After talking business for a while and figuring out that Brick and Slade will be the ones who will actually go pick up the shipment, they seem to remember I'm here and they all turn to face me. None of them says a word, but their eyes track over my body like they're seeing me for the first time.

"Um, hi?" My voice squeaks.

Aidan smirks. "Sorry, were we ignoring you, princess? Apologies for the lack of hospitality. Are you having fun yet?"

"Yes, so much fun," I roll my eyes. "Trapped here with the four of you. You're lucky you're all good-looking or I'd be trying harder to get out of here."

I may as well make this time as entertaining as possible. That way, they might not keep me locked in my room while they plot my death. I wouldn't mind another round of punishment with Aidan, and I'd like to get to know the others better as well.

"Oh really?" Roman looks at me and narrows his eyes. "You think all of us are good-looking?"

I nod. "Sure do. All four of you are hot as fuck. I thought it was a dream when I first saw you all together."

They glance at each other. I can't tell if they're amused or what, but they seem to be non-verbally communicating, and then all eight eyes turn back to me.

"I thought I was your favorite, seeing I'm the one that found you," Roman pouts.

"The jury's out," I say. "I don't know any of you yet, really. All I know about you, Roman, is that your hair smells nice, that you murder people and leave big puddles of blood all over the floor, and that you knock women out stone cold in their workplaces if they dare to stick up for themselves and try to escape while you're trying to kidnap them."

"That was a first for me, too," he says, putting his hands up in defense. "It's not my fault you're good at your job, and that's how I ended up at your salon. And I hardly knew that lunatic was going to run in there and point a gun at me."

I smirk, secretly pleased his extensive hair salon research led him to me. Even though this whole situation on the back end is less than ideal, it still feels nice to know I'm good at something and even a picky motherfucker like Roman is willing to give me a shot.

"So, do I get a house tour?" I ask the group, peering at them through my eyelashes. May as well try to act cute and see who seems most vulnerable to it. "You brought me here while I was unconscious and I've only seen a few rooms. The basement and the kitchen and dining area. This living room and..." I feel myself blushing and I glance at Aidan, "the office."

Aidan smirks and winks at me. "I've given you a deep dive tour in there."

I flush as I remember his tongue delving into my folds and piercing my entrance. Talk about a deep dive.

I realize I'm being held prisoner, but I figure if I act as confident as possible, as if I belong here, maybe they'll let me have a little more leeway while I figure out how to escape. Knowing the layout of the house might give me some ideas and some options.

"What do you think this is? An open home?" Slade narrows his eyes at me. "Would you like me to bake some cookies and leave them out on the counter for your tour?"

"Yeah, that sounds lovely. Could you avoid baking your salty personality into them, though, please?" I smile sweetly at him with the fakest smile I can muster.

His eyes narrow further, but Brick laughs. "She's got you all figured out already, bro."

Relief washes over me as Slade transfers his glare from me to Brick.

"Sure, we can take you on a tour," says Brick, grinning. "It sounds like fun."

Roman glares at him. "I'll come, too," he says.

"I'll keep an eye on you both," says Aidan.

"For fuck's sake, let's make it a family trip." Slade rolls his eyes. "I'll make sure none of you does anything stupid."

I don't know what his deal is, and I need to watch out for him.

They take me through the apartment to show me the many rooms I haven't seen yet, all four guys and me padding around the giant compound.

Brick decides to play host, putting on a funny voice and announcing each room as we pass by.

"This is the powder room, where Aidan powders his nose," Brick makes flamboyant hand gestures at each doorframe as he gives us the rundown. "And here's the nursery where Roman wears duck-print onesies."

"Shut the fuck up, Brick," Roman and Aidan say in unison.

I laugh and Slade snorts but then stops himself when he glances over at me and sees me laughing, too.

I guess he hates me so much we're not allowed to find the same things funny.

I shiver under his icy gaze.

The property is expansive, with a bunch of extra spare bedrooms in addition to mine.

There's a game room with a pool table and shuffleboard, as well as every video game console you could think of. Vintage pinball machines and arcade games line one side of the room, and there's a fully stocked bar on the other side.

"You've seen my torture basement," says Brick, proudly gesturing down the stairs as we walk by. I shiver again, remembering the cupboard full of sinister equipment.

He points out a high-tech gym with a bunch of free weights and machines and cardio equipment, and large screens attached to the walls. No wonder they're all so fucking built. They have a state-of-the-art fitness center right in their home.

"What else is there to show you? I won't show you Roman's bedroom," says Brick, his eyes glimmering. "You can be the one woman on the island who hasn't seen it."

"I'm not that bad, Brick. Jesus!" Roman looks pissed, like I haven't picked up on the fact he's clearly a fuck boy.

"I thought you were a virgin when we met," I say to Roman. "I figured you'd have major problems getting laid."

Roman smirks. "Clearly, you need glasses."

I snort. "Humility's a noble trait. You should look it up."

"I'm not familiar," says Roman, winking at me.

"We won't show you the office, because you've already experienced that," Aidan taps my ass as he walks past me. My face flushes as I'm once again reminded of his tongue and his belt and my shears. All of it.

The throbbing continues in my core. The perpetual throbbing I've experienced in this house is driving me insane. Being around four drop-dead gorgeous men, as scary as they may be, it's like every look, every word they say in their sexy voices, every time they stretch or move near me, triggers more intense throbbing. And it's only getting worse. I desperately need a release before I explode into a puddle on the floor.

We make our way back to the living room, and everyone remains standing.

"And that," Brick gestures theatrically, "concludes our grand tour!"

"I have an idea," I say, suddenly. I'm worried if I don't speak up they'll just lock me in my room again. "Let's make a bet." I haven't thought this through at all, but I need to keep their attention away from me being a captive who should be shut away again.

"On what?" Brick raises an eyebrow.

"On who wins a contest."

"Pretty sure we can smoke you at just about any contest," snorts Slade.

"What kind of contest are you thinking?" Aidan asks, peering at me.

I think about it and then smile as an idea comes to me. "A hot dog eating contest."

The guys glance at each other.

"Well, this is going to be easy. It's your funeral," says Slade. "Have you seen how much food Brick can pack away? All of us, really, compared to you. Look at how much bigger we are!"

"And what do you want if you win?" Aidan raises an eyebrow. "You must have something in mind. I don't think you woke up this morning and said 'hey, know what I want to do today? Stick all the hot dogs in my mouth and take them down as quickly as I can'."

"Imagine if that's what she really thought about when she woke up, though," grins Brick mischievously. "I would have lent her mine as practice."

"I don't want you to lock me in the bedroom anymore," I shrug, changing the subject back to what I want to win as a prize. The reason I came up with this random challenge in the first place. Freedom. "I want to be free to roam around the house whenever I want."

"What would stop you from escaping out the front door, never to be seen again? What if you stab us in our sleep?" Slade narrows his eyes at me.

"Both are tempting." I narrow my eyes back at him. "But in case you don't remember, you took my phone and all my belongings. We appear to be in some type of industrial area, and our closest neighbors are probably miles away, judging from the little I've seen."

"Okay, that covers off an immediate escape plan, kind of," says Aidan. "I'm still skeptical, though. What about the stabbing in our sleep part?"

"I guess that's just a risk you'll have to take. I am good with a pair of shears... just like you are, Aidan."

His eyes flick to mine and he bites his bottom lip, no doubt also remembering our time together in the office and what he did with my shears.

My tongue tingles as I remember him piercing it so that it bled, of him sucking my bloody tongue as if it were my clit. My pussy clenches hard. I want a round two. I want him buried inside me this time.

"Okay," he says, looking around at the group and then back at me. "If you win the bet, you can have privileges for twenty-four hours. Not forever."

"I guess that's a start, better than nothing," I shrug. "But, if I'm good for twenty-four hours, will you reconsider?"

"Maybe," he says, "if you're a good girl, anything is possible. But there's a very high bar."

Slade shakes his head and sighs. "This is yet another terrible idea."

"And what do you get if you win?" I raise an eyebrow and look at each of them. "Not that it's going to happen, but we should set the wager up front, so we're all clear about what's at stake."

They glance at each other without speaking, and the weirdest thing happens. After several exchanges of eye contact, they nod at each other as if they just had a detailed conversation out loud.

"We each get an hour with you, naked, to do whatever we want with you," says Roman, biting his bottom lip, "and I get to go first."

The other guys nod. I'm uncertain that they'd agreed to the Roman going first part in their silent conversation. He probably added that on in the moment, but they seem totally down with the naked hour idea.

I feel a deep twinge between my legs and the throbbing intensifies. Not that I'd let on, but Roman's idea of a prize for the guys seems like a reward for me, too. They're all so fucking hot.

The thought of spending an hour with each of them, getting to know their bodies and the way they like to be touched, and the way they like to touch me, makes my pulse race and my body heat. I'm tempted to let them win, but as much as I want to explore their gorgeous bodies, I want my freedom more.

"Good enough. Let's do it," I grin at the guys and, as usual, they all look at Aidan for the final decision.

Aidan nods. "Alright then, the bet is on. Let's go!"

We enter the kitchen, and Slade gets things ready. He lines up a row of hot dog buns and expertly slices each of them down the middle, placing a hot dog in each.

"Ketchup, mustard and relish or no?" He raises an eyebrow and glances at each of us.

"Nope! We have to do this by the book, guys," I say. "Official rules prohibit the use of condiments. It's considered cheating."

"What the fuck is by the book with a hot dog contest?" scoffs Slade. "The whole thing sounds juvenile, like something you'd do at a kid's party."

"It's a whole industry, Slade. People do this for a career. You can make a lot of money in the hot dog-guzzling biz." I shrug. "Don't ask me how I know this, but you have to eat the whole thing—bun and hot dog—to count. No utensils, no condiments. You can have water or any other liquid. You can only dip your hot dog and bun into your beverage for up to five seconds at a time."

"Sounds like an average Friday night for Brick," Roman cracks up laughing, and I snort. Brick's so weird I can picture him dipping his dick into random cups of soda while he watches vegan documentaries on the big screen.

Brick narrows his eyes at Roman. "Are you trying to say I don't last long, *player*?"

Aidan shakes his head and laughs as well. Slade rolls his eyes.

"Okay, now that we're done talking about Brick's sexual prowess and proclivities, are we ready for this contest?"

"Yep, I'm ready," says Brick. "My beverage of choice is whiskey!"

"Are you sure?" I raise an eyebrow. "I don't think that's a good idea. It's meant to help you get the bun down, not to get you drunk."

He grins. "It sounds way more fun my way."

"Okay, whatever you say," I shrug. It's his funeral.

While Brick prepares himself a generous pour of whiskey, the rest of us equip ourselves with glasses of water.

Aidan sets up a timer on his phone. "Alright, whoever eats the most hot dogs in five minutes is the winner!"

We all nod, poised over our respective plates.

"Three, two, one, and... go!"

Out of the corner of my eye, I see Slade ripping his hot dog in half before devouring each. He's a fast eater, practically inhaling the meat and bun.

Next to him, I see Aidan grab the protein first, swallowing it down in big bites. He dunks the bun in water and then chews quickly, rocking his body back and forth slightly to ease the contents down.

Roman rolls his bun into a small ball and takes large bites to get it down.

Brick dunks his hot dog in whiskey and bites off a giant chunk, slamming it into his mouth. "Fuck yeah, drunk dogs!" he yells with his mouth full of food. I want to laugh, but that takes time, so I choke it back and keep going.

My style is like Aidan's, but more advanced. I grab my hot dog and snap it in half. Each time I take a bite, I dunk the bun in water, take another bite, and then do it all over again. I'm methodical, laser-focused, and I need to win.

Everyone is so engrossed in what they're doing. The kitchen is silent except for the sounds of chewing and sipping and slurping, everyone deeply focused on shoving bits of meat and bread into their mouths and choking them down.

Slade reaches for a second dog, and Brick tries to hold his hand back. Aidan's on to his second as well. Brick is taking sips of whiskey in between bites which slows him down, pieces of hot dog bun becoming tangled in his beard.

Suddenly, the timer goes off and everyone stops mid-chew. We look around. Brick has half a hot dog sticking out of his mouth, and everyone else holds a fraction of a bun in their hand.

Looking at each of our stashes in front of us, mine is the most depleted.

"Holy shit, Angel. You ate five hot dogs?"

"Well, four-and-three-quarters if you want to get technical," I say, holding up my remaining fragment of bun, the tip of the hot dog poking out the end.

I glance at the counter in front of the others.

"Two and a half for me, but if you count the whiskey, I think I win!" exclaims Brick. "It was like a whiskey pairing, meaning I needed to take it slower to savor all the delicious tastes."

I snort and count the hot dogs on the other plates.

The others ate four each. Which means...

"And the winner is... Angel!" Brick holds my hand up high in the air like I just won a boxing match. "Weighing in way less than any of us, Angel has smoked the competition, stuffing her mouth with hot dogs and guzzling them down her throat in an attempt to avoid having each of us stuff her with ours!"

Slade glares at me, but there's a hint of something in his eyes, like he's a tiny bit impressed by my hot dog-eating skills.

"Twenty-four hours," says Aidan, glancing at his watch. "Starting... now."

"Yeah, make the most of it," says Slade, his eyes narrowing. "While you can."

Chapter Seventeen

Slade

Picking up our latest delivery gives me some alone time with Brick, which is good because I need to get him on side. This whole situation with Angel is getting out of control.

As he drives us toward the pickup spot, he glances over at me a few times, as if he knows I have something to say. But he, like the other guys, knows I'll talk when I'm ready. I like that they don't try to force me, to pry the words out when they're not fully formed. I prefer to think things through and make sure I'm precise before I start blabbering like other people do.

"I don't like her being at our house," I say, frowning.

"Angel? You've made that pretty clear," nods Brick, glancing over at me, and then he grins. "She's pretty, though. Nice to look at."

"Yeah, that's an understatement," I sigh. "It's part of the problem. The three of you are all running around at half-mast in her presence, not thinking about work. All obsessed with shoving your dicks into her. I'm worried she's a massive distraction, and she's going to come between us and our business."

There's no way I'm telling Brick that even though my dick hasn't worked quite right for years, even though sex is usually the last thing on my mind, she's caught my attention.

It twinges at the sight of her when she bends over to put something in the dishwasher, or when I get a glimpse of her nipples hard under her thin tank top. It twitches now just at the thought of seeing her in those vulnerable moments, when her body speaks to me and mine responds.

Nobody has made my body respond like this in a really long time, and it's got me on high alert. If she's got me like this, no wonder the other guys are sniffing around like crazy, unable to focus on the work at hand.

"We don't have to keep her around forever," shrugs Brick, as he turns down a side street towards where the drop point for our most recent imports. "But I'd really like to have some fun with her before we decide how we're going to dispose of her."

I sigh. "We're going to end up regretting this, man. I don't care how round her ass is or how good she probably is at sucking dick."

Brick laughs. "Hey, she might be a bit of a firecracker, but how much harm could she do? She's tiny compared to us, and there's only one of her." He shrugs. "And do you really think she's that big of a distraction? It's not like Roman isn't constantly distracted by pussy, anyway. Maybe it's better to have one for him to obsess over in the house rather than having him go out chasing it all over town. Gives him something to focus on at home. At least we know where he is at all times, stalking Angel around and trying to get into her pants."

I snort. He brings up a good point. "Fair. Although I can't say the same for you and Aidan. You like women and all, but you're usually not this distracted."

I glance at the GPS. "We're two miles away. Can you go a bit faster? I want to make sure nobody gets there first. I know the snakes aren't actively trying to stop us anymore, but that seems to have emboldened Zero and his guys."

Brick steps on the accelerator, and within a couple of minutes we're outside a warehouse that's dark except for a grimy exterior light pointed at a side door.

"Stay here," he says, unbuckling his seatbelt. It always amuses me that Brick is so set on wearing his seatbelt. This big guy who enjoys torturing and murdering people, who doesn't mind the shit getting beaten out of him and occasionally inflicts injuries on himself just to ride the pain, and he's fixated on passenger safety. Won't even start the car unless everyone's buckled up.

Yet another of his many quirks, I guess.

"Are you sure, man? Last time we did a pickup there were like six guys waiting for us, all armed."

Brick gives me a withering look. "Please. I've got this."

I shake my head and smirk as he checks his guns and closes the car door.

Brick's recklessness can be his downfall, but I've seen him take on more than six guys and come out grinning, plumes of smoke and destruction billowing in his wake.

These guys aren't anything like Tane's foot soldiers, so I'm not super worried about them, although of course it only takes one stray bullet to ruin your night or life.

He walks to the dimly lit door. He tugs on the door and it opens, and he slips inside the fortified building to pick up our items.

And now I wait.

Chapter Eighteen

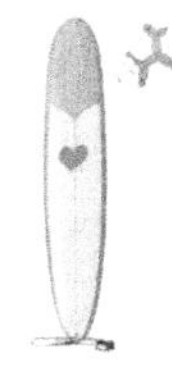

Brick

It was cute when Slade offered to come into the warehouse with me. Fretting like he was a first-time dad, dropping his kid off on the first day of elementary school. Like he was mildly concerned I wouldn't be able to take on six guys.

Come on. I snort to myself as I open the warehouse door. It's dark inside at first, but then my eyes adjust, revealing a mostly empty warehouse with some dilapidated equipment sitting in the middle of the room.

I can tell straight away that the interior of the building is empty, which is a good start to this pickup.

It's not this part of the job that I'm most concerned about. None of what I do scares me. The more fucked up, the more twisted, the better, in my opinion. That's why I prefer torture to pickups like this.

But pickups have to be done, especially as we're quickly becoming this island's premiere transporter of illicit items. Most lowlifes are too scared to come to this neighborhood, because they know these compounds are usually heavily armed. They know we know what we're doing, and that we have intensive security protocols in place. It would be guaranteed suicide for all but the best.

It's when I leave the building shortly, and when Slade and I make it onto the road with our haul, that we'll need to be on our highest alert. We've been followed many times, picking stuff up from here and other drop points. The goods we transport are worth a lot of money, and people either want them to on-sell and profit from or to keep for themselves.

Scanning the room, I see the packages are exactly where they're meant to be. One is a long, hard-cased container, a bit like a narrow suitcase. The other is a large canvas duffel that's almost bursting at the seams.

I hoist the canvas bag over my shoulder and lift the case with my left hand, leaving my right hand free for my gun.

I don't think I'll need it today, but you never know.

As I emerge from the building, I look around as my eyes once again adjust to the night.

Approaching halfway between the building and the vehicle, I sense movement in my peripheral vision to my left. A glint of metal reflects the moonlight. One-handed, I turn and swing in that direction, shooting just beyond where I saw the metallic flash. I hear a groan and a figure dressed in black crumples to the ground.

Slade jumps out of the car, his gun drawn.

We do a perimeter check, our backs to each other, our weapons pointed. These guys never come alone. There has to be at least one more guy out here, maybe two.

The audacity of these lazy fuckers, having us negotiate and arrange the entire purchase and drop-off, and then trying to pick us off when we collect the goods.

The crackle of gunfire rings out, followed by a flash of light off in the distance, and we dive to the ground, scrambling to use the vehicle as a shield to protect us from the direction the shot was fired from.

"You go left," Slade whispers and I nod. We split off in opposite directions.

Creeping around the vehicle, we listen intently for any sign of men advancing toward us.

A bullet whistles past us and we smash ourselves into the ground. That was too close. But it told us all we needed to know.

From the direction the shot came from, two men run out of the trees and race for the bag and the case. I raise my gun, shooting them from where I'm laying down on my stomach, and drop both of them with ease. My silencer keeps things polite, my gun hardly making a noise as it ejects two deadly bullets. We listen for a while, but there are no further sounds except for nature.

We get up, and I grab the case and the bag and load them into the car. I grin at Slade. "Guns and drugs, baby. Guns and drugs!" We buckle our seatbelts and head out.

We drive back in silence, and after a while, I flick on the radio. I can't stand silence. It messes with my head and allows me to have thoughts that aren't healthy.

I know that Slade's the exact opposite. He needs silence and solitude. He craves it and when he doesn't get it for a while, his energy saps out of him.

It's ironic that he lives in a house with so many people, but we've done it for so long and we're so close that he seems to have found a way to tune us out, and it's almost like we don't count toward the noise that he avoids.

Despite his probably not wanting to listen to the radio, he doesn't try to touch it at first. Partway to the house, he can't take it anymore and clicks it off. The silence returns, just the sound of the car as it bounces along the highway. I glance at him. "You okay, man?"

"Yeah... well, no. I just don't know how we're going to deal with this girl in our space, even if it's just for a few days. We talk about sensitive stuff. We can't have her running off telling people our business."

"Yeah. And I mean, she also saw Roman murder someone. That's why she's with us in the first place. I've gotten used to her being around, even though it hasn't been that long. But you're right, she could overhear a lot of confidential information and then weaponize it against us."

"Look, I get you wanting to keep her around for a bit. It sounds like maybe you'll have your fun and then we'll have no choice. We shouldn't let it just drag on forever. The more she knows, the more dangerous she is."

I sigh and then nod in resignation. She might be pretty, but I have a feeling this isn't going to end that way. For her, or for any of us.

Chapter Nineteen

Roman

The sun slowly sets until it's finally dark outside, which means it's time to think about tying up loose ends.

Aidan's mantra repeats on a loop in my mind, 'Dead ends, not loose ends. Dead ends, not loose ends.'

I don't know when he became my personal Jiminy Cricket. Level-headed and wise, sitting on my shoulder and guiding my decisions even when he's not actually there.

But unlike Jiminy, who focused on guiding Pinocchio down some over-hyped 'righteous path', Aidan's just here to make sure we don't screw anything up too badly. That we don't do anything that prevents us from amassing the wealth and power that we've worked so hard for. Whether we break a law or hurt somebody, or generally act in a way that some people would consider immoral, is of no consequence to him.

"I guess one of us should go and clean up the mess we left in the hair salon," says Aidan, as if reading my mind. Or maybe, seeing it's his voice I heard rattling around my brain, it was me reading his.

"Oh yeah. The huge puddle of blood and everything," says Brick. "Not that I personally mind a splash of blood as an interior design aesthetic." He gets a dreamy look in his eyes, and his tongue flicks across his bottom lip. "When it splatters across the basement, sometimes I leave it there for a little bit. It helps to foreshadow events for the next person I bring in there for a party. Plus, did you know that blood's distinctive metallic smell is because of the oxidation of the hemoglobin's iron molecules? That they react with fat lipids in the skin?"

His outburst doesn't raise an eyebrow from any of us. We know Brick is like a walking encyclopedia when it comes to blood.

"Yeah, yeah, we get it, Brick," Aidan smirks. "If you could wear blood as an aftershave, you would. You'd bathe in it every day if you could."

"I wouldn't go that far," pouts Brick. "But I think it gets a bad rap. It's a versatile and fascinating substance that works well in a variety of artistic mediums."

"Okay, out of Brick's science and imagination emporium and back to reality," I clear my throat. If I don't stop him now, he'll continue like this for hours. "I closed the blinds up front at the salon," I remind them. "Still, we don't need anybody peeking in and asking questions. We should probably get rid of the mess now, in case someone somehow stumbles upon it and calls the cops. There's a lot of blood, too much blood to plausibly explain away."

"Shit, do we need to change the locks as well?" Aidan's face falls. He looks like he missed a beat for a moment, like he didn't check off every potential risk, which is unusual for him. "Does she have employees?"

"It's okay, Aidan. I've checked all this. She works alone," I say. "She told me."

"Somehow I get the feeling that doesn't just apply to her at the salon," snorts Slade.

"No cleaning contractors or anything like that to worry about, either?" Aidan raises an eyebrow.

"No, she's a lone wolf when it comes to that place. Does all the cleaning and other stuff herself."

"It sounds like she's stubborn and refuses to accept any help," says Brick.

"We're talking about cleaning a blood puddle, not analyzing her inbuilt psychological trauma," says Aidan, giving Brick a sideways glance. He turns his gaze to me. "Roman, you made the mess, so you should go take care of it."

"Since when has that been a rule? Don't we help each other out and not assign blame?" I prefer making messes to cleaning them up. Especially blood. It's so stubborn to clean because it sinks into everything.

"Since now," sighs Aidan. "It's been a rule since now. Slade's clearly pissed you brought her here in the first place. I have business to take care of here. If you can get Brick to go along with you, great. Otherwise, figure it out on your own. We won't always be around to help you clean up your problems."

"I could take *her* with me," I shrug.

"Who, Angel?" He squints at me like he thinks I'm an absolute lunatic. "No, nice try, Ro. You are *not* taking *her* with you. Jesus, Roman. She's not a little chihuahua that you can carry around in a dog bag. She's a fucking murder witness. You've brought her here, and now we have to figure out what to do with her. But we're not going to be parading her around everywhere we go, hoping she doesn't sing like a bird. It defeats the purpose of bringing her with us in the first place. People ask too many questions, and we need to keep her away from people."

Brick's eyes grow dreamy again. "Because she's feisty and violent and unpredictable, and she puts up a hell of a struggle when she wants to."

"Yes," says Aidan, "and we *don't fucking know her*." He punctuates the last words, exasperated by how quickly we've incorporated her into our house. Reminding us that it's been twenty-four hours, if that. "Listen. I know some of you are fine with her hanging out with us as if she's our roommate," he glances from Brick to me. "But Slade is right to be cautious. She has the makings of someone who can stand up for herself and who doesn't take any shit. But we don't know what she's actually like. What information she's trying to get from us. How badly she wants to escape and the lengths she'll go to. Whether, if we ever let her go, she feels the need to turn us in and tell the authorities all about our business."

Slade scowls. "It's a real problem. I'm glad you're taking it seriously, Aid. I can think of one solution that would bring things to a permanent close."

"We're not killing her, Slade." Brick's eyes flash. "Not yet, anyway. I want to play with her first. She seems fun."

"Fine. I'll go take care of it alone." I roll my eyes. "I'm sure Brick has more important things to do and the rest of you are occupied. It's not like I need help to clean blood, anyway."

I've been hoping to spend more time with Angel, but the opportunities have been few and far between so far. I figured taking her with me to clean up the salon would give us some alone time together, and the opportunity for her to warm up to me some more. When I came up with the idea, there didn't seem to be much downside to having her accompany me on an otherwise boring job. But, as usual, Aidan comes and rains on my parade. Picking the safest option, the most conservative course of action. 'Protecting the brotherhood' as he would say.

Slade is, of course, egging him on, instigating all this talk of risk and distractions.

I'm frustrated as hell, but I need to get over it.

I'll just go knock this job out alone and then figure out another way to spend more time with her.

I'll ignore the fact I'm a grown-ass man who is being told I can't make a simple decision to take her on a low-risk job with me.

Aidan's probably right, as usual, but it doesn't mean I like it.

I drive north, leaving the industrial neighborhood to transition onto the freeway and then down into the residential area where her salon is located.

The roads are fairly quiet, the commuter traffic having long since trickled people back to their neighborhoods.

Island life, outside of a couple of hours in the mornings and afternoons, is relatively sleepy and predictable. You could live your life in a place like this completely oblivious to the seedy underbelly of criminal activity that goes on here.

You could live your life on this island without worrying that folks like me and my brothers exist.

But when you do want trouble, when you scratch under the surface of the sunshine and the lush green vegetation, the tourist artifice and the high-end retail and front-facing restaurant culture, we're back here doing our thing.

And it's just as dark and gritty here as what you might find in any city back on the mainland.

Everything might seem curated, beautiful, magical.

But put a foot wrong around here with the wrong people, and danger and death become imminent.

It's no different from anywhere else. And in some cases, it's much worse.

When I reach the salon, I pull around back and park the vehicle. Getting out of the car, my body tenses and the little hairs stand up on the back of my neck.

Something is off. My instincts are pretty good about this kind of thing.

Unholstering my gun, I approach the salon and enter through the back door. It's dark inside, but my eyes quickly adjust.

I am alone in here, but things are not at all as we left them.

Far from it.

The entire place has been ransacked, and I thought I'd made a mess yesterday, but now my efforts look like child's play.

Instead of the blood puddle being the center of attention in the middle of the salon, the entire place has been torn to pieces.

Cabinets have been thrown over, their contents sprawling over the ground. Files of documents and cleaning supplies spill out onto the floor, ripped and torn.

Tubes of brown and red hair dye have been squirted and smeared over just about every surface—walls, the floor, even the ceiling. It looks like someone has covered the place in blood and shit, like in some gruesome horror movie. I can't show this to Brick or he might try to decorate his room like this.

Sharp scissors have been violently stabbed into the wall, with only their handles protruding. It reminds me a little bit of what I did to The Asshole's neck.

Angel's hairstyling and business diplomas and certificates have been ripped from their frames, the glass smashed and the documents torn into pieces and sprinkled over the floor.

Looking around at the destruction, my immediate thought is that this must be some type of warning from whoever sent The Asshole to find me. They must have come looking for him when he didn't report back.

But then I see the message that's been left by whoever did this. Sprayed across the long salon mirror is *'Die Slut Bitch! I'll Finish What I Started. I'm Coming For You.'*

This note doesn't seem meant for me. The timing seems coincidental as I read that. I mean, technically the 'finishing what they started' piece could ring true for my little murder situation, but the die slut bitch piece doesn't compute. I've been called many things by many people, but that would be a new one.

This can't be about what happened here earlier. This seems to be more about... her. About Angel. But who would destroy her salon like this?

I survey the scene one more time, from the lens that whoever did this was trying to get to Angel rather than send me a message.

It makes the room feel different when the destruction is aimed at her. More personal somehow.

A chill creeps up my back. My chest and back muscles tighten involuntarily, and I clench my jaw.

I text the guys on our group chat:

Me:Get here now. I need you to see this for yourselves.

Brick:Jeez, bro. Can't you visit the hair salon without needing us to hold your hand? That'll be the second time.

Me:Not the time for jokes. Get here now.

Aidan:We can't just leave her here by herself.

Me:Bring her then.

Aidan:No way. She's not leaving the house.

Me:Well, two of you come here then and someone can stay behind to look after her.

Slade:I'll stay here and keep an eye on her.

Aidan:Alright. Be there shortly.

Me:Don't you lay a finger on her, Slade. (glaring emoji)

Slade:If she doesn't do anything to deserve it, I won't. (shrug emoji)

Brick:Don't touch her, man. (swearing emoji)

Slade:Whatever. See how she's making you behave? Distracting AF. (eye roll emoji)

Aidan:Enough. See you soon, Roman.

I use my phone to snap some photos of the scene in front of me.

Whoever did this is clearly unhinged. Full of rage when they carried out this overwhelming destruction.

Not that any of us can talk. It takes an unhinged person to truly recognize another. But it's like whoever did this completely lost their mind in this room. As if they entered an alternate reality where their sole focus was to erase her, to annihilate everything she's worked so hard for. To inflict maximum damage.

This wasn't a crime of opportunity or a petty act by someone who was mildly pissed. This wasn't done by a client not happy with their hair treatment, someone whose bangs were cut too short or whose trim was uneven. The perpetrator, whoever did this, has some type of emotional attachment to Angel. I wonder if it's a scorned ex, or maybe an estranged family member.

Within about ten minutes there's a knock at the back door, and part of me hopes it's whatever psycho did this coming back for round two. I'd really like to take care of him, show him a good time at the end of my gun for what they've done to the salon that Angel has worked so hard for. Fucking hell, I might even need to find another hair salon to go to because of this. Not again.

But then again, I wouldn't expect whoever did this to knock if they did return, and it's not like they could cause more destruction here than they already have.

I head to the back and let Brick and Roman in, like I did the first time I called them here. We're just missing Slade this time around. Which is fine, because he'd just spend the entire time reminding us that he thinks we should have knocked Angel off and buried her in the woods next to The Asshole.

If Aidan is my conscience on my shoulder, Slade is an enneagram six with a five-wing dancing around on my deltoid, always thinking several steps ahead to anticipate what could go wrong. On a constant tightrope of perceiving threats, imaginary and real, and withdrawing completely within his own thoughts.

We don't need his energy right now.

I gesture to the main part of the salon and they head on through.

Brick lets out a low whistle as he surveys the damage. "Jesus, someone really went to town on this place. I was expecting another dead body and maybe hoping for another unconscious hot chick, but this is something else." He glances around, taking it all in. "Retribution for what you did to their guy, do you think?"

Aidan shakes his head. "Definitely not. That's not what this is about."

"How do you figure?" asks Brick.

"There are two reasons why not." Aidan holds up two fingers.

"Oh, yeah?" I'm curious. I could only think of one.

"There's no dead body here. No obvious evidence tying the dead guy to this salon. It's not like anyone came in here and took DNA that leads back to you. If someone did see the blood, it's not like they know who it belonged to. He followed you in yesterday. It's not like you had a longstanding appointment, right?"

I nod. He has a point.

"This... whatever this is," says Aidan, gesturing around at the mess, "it wasn't intended to spook you, Roman. I don't think you crossed the mind of whoever did this. I'd guess that you're not even on their radar."

I nod. "You don't think I'm the slut to which the note is referring?" I grin, pointing at the scrawled writing sprayed on the smashed mirror.

"Don't get me wrong, Roman, you are a complete and utter slut so if the message was about you it would be accurate," shrugs Aidan, missing the humor in my question. "But I don't think someone would come and spray paint that about you at this place you've had no prior ties to."

"So what then?"

"Clearly, this person is fixated on whoever runs this place, or at least someone who works here."

"And she works by herself. She made that abundantly clear. Which means..." my voice trails off, the implications settling in.

"Someone wants to hurt Angel. Someone is this angry at her about something?" Brick scowls and crossed his arms tightly over his muscular chest. "I mean, it's one thing if we want to hurt her for fun, but this pisses me off. There's hate in these actions."

A thought strikes me. "We should check on her apartment. Make sure it's secure. Maybe this isn't the only place he visited."

The other guys nod.

"First let's clean up the blood puddle though, man," says Aidan. "Someone could still come in. And who knows how much noise was made while whoever it was destroyed this place. We should probably hurry in case the cops have already been called."

He's so logical, pragmatic, always noticing the details that would otherwise trip us up. If you'd left it to me and Brick, we would have up and left the salon in a race to get to her apartment.

We'd be lost without him. He keeps us focused. We need him.

I head outside and retrieve the bleach and rags from the car and bring them back inside, making sure to lock the car. We don't need to recreate some slasher flick where we're driving and a lunatic with a knife appears in the back of the vehicle.

We get to work removing the bloodstain, and I'm glad the other two guys have joined me because it takes more elbow grease than I anticipated. The blood has settled into cracks in the linoleum and splattered onto some cabinets nearby, and it takes a while to get all the dark red stains out.

For good measure, Aidan has Brick 'decorate' the freshly cleaned area with the same type of crazy artwork that adorns the rest of the salon's surfaces. He surveys the rest of the destruction like he's an aficionado at a fine art museum, and then he picks up various tubes and spray bottles and gets to work. He swirls and smears, festooning the area in a cacophony of artful lines and swishes and strokes. By the time he's done, Brick has managed to replicate someone else's unadulterated chaos, and it blends in seamlessly. Nobody would ever guess that a man died in this particular spot, or that it hadn't been created by the same person who 'decorated' the rest of the space.

We're pleased with the finished outcome, even though it's like the reverse of a TV show where some celebrity host comes and turns your business around for the better. Angel won't be having any clients here any time soon, and I'd hazard a guess that this place is not insured.

After locking up, we hop into our vehicles and ride to Angel's address.

I pull into the apartment complex moments before Aidan and Brick. Wasting no time, we leap out of the vehicles and clamber up the stairs to her apartment two at a time, following Brick's lead. As we approach the entrance, it's immediately clear that all is not okay here, either. The door has been kicked open and is dangling from its hinges.

From here, the inside of the apartment looks just as bad as the salon, but with different stuff strewn around. The detritus of an apartment versus a workplace, turned inside out for all to see.

"Well, shit. You said she was messy, but this is another level," I smirk as I glance around the disaster zone.

"What I saw before was a two out of ten on this scale," Brick says, shaking his head. "She's messy, but she's not dirty, from what I could tell."

"Oh, she's dirty," smirks Aidan. "You're reading her wrong."

"That's not what I'm talking about, Aidan," huffs Brick. "You're lucky Slade isn't here to hear you joke like that. He would have gone off."

"I know. I'm just giving you shit while I try to process what this means. Two locations hit in one day. Let's go in and assess the extent of the damage. See if we can find out anything about who might have done this."

We make our way inside, our feet crunching on various items that have been smashed into the floor.

In the living room, pictures and art have been ripped off the wall, the glass smashed, and the artwork torn just like her diplomas back at the salon.

She has a photo wall that celebrates happier times with what appears to be family and friends, and someone has gone to the trouble of scratching out her eyes in every single photo. A violent erasure of her gorgeous eyes that seem to have seen so much.

Her TV has been shattered, the screen smashed and the entire appliance thrown onto the floor. Her clothes have been pulled from her dresser and strewn about.

Brick picks up a couple of items. "Jesus, whoever did this took the time to chop up her clothing with something sharp."

Sure enough, the items he's holding have been slashed in multiple places.

In her bedroom, her bed has been stabbed repeatedly, tufts of filler floating out of the ravaged mattress.

Her floor-length mirror has been smashed into hundreds of shards, some larger pieces embedded in the mattress and pillows.

We move down the hallway into the kitchen, where knives have been stabbed through the walls with the same rage as the scissors in the salon.

What is with this stabbing of walls? Who does this? Clearly someone with a lot of rage directed at Angel.

Contents from her fridge and pantry have been poured and squirted out, leaving a nasty, sticky mess on just about every surface. We have to walk carefully so that we don't slip on the slick coating left behind by sauces and liquids and condiments.

Ants have discovered the sticky mess and started to tell their ant friends, a thin line of thousands of them marching back and forth between the goo and presumably a crack in the wall that connects them with their nest on the outside.

On the other side of the hall, the bathroom is no better. And just like at the salon, it has a message spray-painted on the mirror.

"You can't escape me. I'm coming for you, bitch. I have been waiting for this."

"Jesus," says Brick, letting out another low whistle. "Someone really has it in for her."

"We have to go home. We have to tell her," I say.

Aidan looks around one more time and nods. "Let's go. We have to figure out what this is all about. We need to talk to Angel. She has to know who hates her this much."

Chapter Twenty

Angel

They've left me with Slade, the quiet one who seems to do all the cooking. The one who knows me least but hates me most, judging by the way he constantly scowls at me.

I'm torn, though, because he's so hot when he scowls. There's something about the way his eyes darken and his lip curls that's primal, and it does things to me.

"You shouldn't be here, you know." I know he's talking to me, but he doesn't make eye contact, instead cleaning imaginary debris off the counter.

Being in the kitchen seems to be a security blanket for him, giving him something to do, something to focus on, without having to sit down next to everyone else.

"You think I want to be here? If you recall, it wasn't exactly my choice," I remind him. He acts as if I forced myself upon them, somehow sneaking my way under their roof, instead of being brought here while unconscious, against my will.

"We should have killed you back at the salon," he says, matter-of-factly, like he's not talking about whether he and the other guys should have murdered me just because I was in the wrong place at the wrong time. "It would have been cleaner. Everyone would have been better off."

Charming.

I can't help but let out a hollow laugh.

"You're probably right," I shrug. "The world probably would be better off without me. So kill me if you want. I don't care. Just hurry up and do it. Part of me already died a long time ago."

He stops wiping the counter and peers at me. "You really mean that?"

"Yeah, sure," I shrug again. "If you don't, somebody else probably will soon, anyway."

"Wait, what do you mean?" He's standing up straight now, confused.

"It's nothing." I close my eyes and sigh.

I don't want to think about it. I shouldn't have said what I did. It was obviously going to lead to questions.

"Tell me," he says, hanging the dishtowel up on the handle of the oven.

"Tell you what?"

He sighs. "Why you're sad or scared or whatever you are. And why you think somebody is going to kill you." He peers at me. "Other than us, I mean."

"I'm not sad or scared." It's a lie on both counts, but he doesn't need to know how I'm feeling inside. It'll just give him more reason to hate me.

"Then why did you just look like you were holding back tears? Why do you think you're going to die soon?"

"I had something in my eye," I say weakly. "Stop pushing me. Leave it."

"Look. You clearly have stuff you don't want to tell me, and that's fine. But I recognize the way you're looking around, trying to pretend nothing's wrong while your mind is racing to fix whatever it is. You're clearly full of pain. I recognize it in you."

"Oh yeah? And how the fuck would you recognize that?" I snap, and I know my eyes are flashing.

But instead of pulling away like most people do when I lash out, Slade walks up to me.

He grabs me by my upper arms and pushes me further into the kitchen until my back presses up against the refrigerator. He takes hold of both of my wrists, placing them against the fridge on either side of my head, and gazes into my eyes.

My pulse leaps as I feel his body press into mine and I feel the same crackle of electricity as when we sat next to each other for dinner, but our proximity makes it more intense now as the full lengths of our bodies touch. He's solid muscle, and I like the way he melds into my curves.

"Maybe I recognize it in you because it's like I'm holding up a mirror when I look at you," he growls. "Maybe you look the way I feel inside."

"You don't know the first thing about me. You're a fucking kidnapper." I narrow my eyes at him, but my voice stays eerily calm.

How dare he think he can read me, that he can possibly understand how I'm feeling? He hasn't even tried to get to know me. He's clearly assumed the worst about me and doesn't want me to be here.

"You'd be surprised what I know, Angel," he says, his eyes growing dark, a twinge of what might be sadness clouding them for a moment. "Sometimes it's not words that tell you the most about someone."

He removes a hand from one of my wrists and traces the line of my jaw with a long finger. His hand is rough, but he's gentle, and it sends a little bolt of electricity down my neck, leaving me tingling.

"Oh, really?" I roll my eyes, but I can't help my body arching into his, my softness blending with his hardness, seeking him out, hungry for him to press further into me.

He bites his lip and groans softly. "Yes, really," he rasps, and he crushes his lips down on mine, hard. I know they'll be bruised later, but I mash mine into his right back.

I feel a twinge between my legs as he swipes his tongue through my lips and explores my mouth. I reciprocate, my tongue wrapping around his, and I involuntarily let out a moan as he twirls his tongue against mine.

I feel wet heat pooling at my entrance as he continues pressing his strong body against me, as if my body is craving him, craving more of this unique connection we have.

Through our clothes, I can tell he's hard and that he's big. It's like an iron bar is pressing firmly into my stomach. For someone that hates me, I've sure got his attention.

Continuing to hold one of my wrists above my head, he reaches down with his other strong hand and cups my heat. I let out another soft moan, longing for him to touch my bare skin and to be inside me.

If he could channel his palpable hatred for me into the bedroom, his intense emotional distress at my presence, that could really be something. In this moment, I want nothing more than for him to fuck me with the energy of the scowls he constantly sends my way.

Suddenly, he pulls away, and the hand he was holding against the refrigerator drops to my side. He backs off, moving toward the counter.

Fucking hell.

I glare at him.

"Why'd you stop?" I ask. "Am I not good enough for you?" I don't handle rejection well. "I don't make you hard enough? Were the other guys right that you can't get it up?"

Slade's scowl has returned. He glares at me. "Fuck you, Angel. I told you that you shouldn't be here."

He stomps off into the other room.

A moment later he returns, probably remembering he's meant to be keeping an eye on me and he can't leave me with access to the front door.

Before I can say anything else to offend him, he picks me up, hauls me over his shoulder and carries me up the stairs. I ball my hands into fists and pummel him on the back and try to kick him, but he doesn't say anything. He just continues to carry me, silently, in his strong arms, as if I'm an annoying object rather than a person.

He brings me up the stairs and down the hallway to my room, lowers me onto the bed and immediately leaves as if he doesn't want to be in there alone with me.

The lock in the door clicks, and I hear his footsteps retreating back down the stairs.

So here I am again, alone in my room.

Turned on by Slade.

Frustrated that I'm turned on by Slade.

Confused by why he got me all worked up and then abruptly pulled away.

Confused by why he hates me so much when he barely knows me.

Thrown off by his words right before he kissed me.

What is his fucking deal?

CHAPTER TWENTY-ONE

Roman

On the ride home, I keep thinking about the destruction we just saw.

There's no question that the person who did this is extremely unhinged and obsessed with Angel.

The way they destroyed her salon and her apartment, the two spaces that are uniquely hers, was very methodical even in its chaos. And all of it was deeply, deeply personal.

The messages, the way they went to great lengths to leave a stain on nearly every surface. Scratching her eyes out in photographs. Stabbing the walls in both locations.

This is no petty crime of opportunity. This is intentional. This is about Angel, specifically. And this person wants to destroy her, to erase her, to inflict maximum pain.

I might not know Angel well, but this makes me feel protective of her. She doesn't deserve to have someone invade her most private of places. The way they'd rifled through her drawers and broken things just because they could. Basically tipped her life all over the floor and ripped it apart. Everything she's worked hard for, based on what I know.

I shudder as I think about what might have happened if she'd been at home or at work when they stopped by. It seems obvious that they were displacing the anger they felt toward her onto both properties in her absence.

When we get home, I let her out of her bedroom. Slade apparently didn't know what to do with her, so locked her back in there.

Telling her we need to talk with her about something serious, I lead her downstairs to the living room and sit her down on the couch, and plop down next to her.

Without saying a word, I show her the photos of the salon on my phone.

Her face turns ashen and her eyes grow large, but it only lasts a second. Just as quickly, her eyes narrow and become flinty, and she clenches her jaw, grinding her teeth.

She clearly knows who did this, and she's in a visible tug-of-war between fear and anger.

"There's more," I say softly, showing her the photos of the apartment. "They were there, too."

Her face pales further, and she swallows hard, blinking back tears as she squints at the photos.

"My *place*. My apartment?" Her voice cracks and her chest rises and falls with urgency. She takes my phone and zooms in for a closer look. "He was there as well?" she whispers.

"I'm afraid so," I say, my voice gentle.

"No, no, no," she whispers. "He can't be out. He can't know where I am. How did he find me?"

"Who's he?" I ask.

"You know who did this, don't you, Angel?" Aidan asks, peering at her.

She doesn't reply, and her face is stony. Her eyes seem to focus on a random spot halfway across the room while her mind races, processing what she's just seen and what it means.

"Angel. Who did this?" Aidan repeats.

She adjusts her shoulders, pushing them back proudly, but her voice is still low and it wavers as she speaks. "It doesn't matter. Nobody important. It's nothing I can't handle."

Despite her attempt at bravery, I detect a slight tremble in her chin. I look down and notice that her hands are also shaking. She sees me looking and balls them into fists so she can hold them still. I wonder if she's pressing her fingernails into her palms the way I do when I try to distract myself with pain.

She blinks rapidly, her eyes watering, and she flattens her lips together into a thin line. She crosses her arms tightly over her chest like a shield. Her body language is betraying her lack of verbal cues, and while she isn't putting it into words, I can literally see her turmoil.

A little piece of me melts seeing her like this, a little of vulnerability peeking out. She's shown us that she's capable of being so strong and feisty, and yet the acts of this person have clearly shaken her to her core.

"Angel, we can help you," I say, lightly touching her shoulder.

She shrugs me off and turns away so that I can't see her face. She sighs and her shoulders drop, and she stills for a moment.

Suddenly, her shoulders rear back and she swivels around to face me, her breathing quick and shallow and her eyes wide.

"*You* can help me? The same people who kidnapped me? Especially the guy who came into my workplace and *murdered* someone while I stood there?" She glares at me, her eyes wild.

"If you thought that was bad for business, it's got nothing on what whoever this person is went and did to your salon. Or to your place."

Her face falls further.

"Who are they, Angel?" asks Aidan. "I'm assuming it's a he. Is he the same person who gave you those scars?"

She flinches at the mention of the marks on her body, as if whatever was done to cause her scars is being done to her all over again.

"It doesn't matter who he is," she says softly, blinking back tears.

"Tell us, Angel," I say, putting a hand on hers and holding it still. "Tell us what you know so we can help you."

"He's a ghost," she whispers, her voice barely audible.

Her body quakes with a held-in sob as she rushes from the room.

Chapter Twenty-Two

Angel

An intense flood of nausea sweeps through my body. I run in the direction of the bathroom, but don't make it all the way to the toilet or sink in time.

Dropping to all fours, I heave the contents of my stomach onto the cold tile floor, and I wretch and shudder as the contents of my stomach are violently expelled.

Gasping for breath, my throat coils into a tight and scratchy little tube, causing me to gag. My eyes water and my chest pounds, both from my racing heart and the exertion of vomiting.

Panting, I stay where I am for a moment, fighting to regain my breath, looking at the mess in front of me. My body feels cold and clammy, the cold tiles like ice against my splayed fingers that tremble under my weight, barely holding me up.

I can't believe he's out. He was meant to be locked up for a lot longer. Decades.

I'm not surprised he managed to find a way out earlier than anticipated. It was a given that he'd find some way to buck the system, to turn things to his advantage.

But this? This is unimaginably early. It feels like it was just yesterday that he went in, and I always assumed I'd have a lot more time.

I'm sure that he used the same manipulative techniques he used on me, found all the loopholes the justice system provided, and took advantage.

That's how he operates.

Part of me always knew he would find me one day, that he would track me down no matter how far I ran or how careful I was. And I've lived with the idea that one unexpected day in the future I'd probably die at his hands.

Right before he was sentenced for his unspeakable crimes, and he got to say a few words in the courtroom, he didn't spend it communicating his remorse for his evil doings. He didn't pretend that he was sorry for the pain that he caused so many people, including me. He didn't try to say just the right things to minimize his sentence, either.

Instead, he locked eyes on me and told the entire courtroom that he and I were destined to be together, that he would spend every moment in prison thinking about me, and that the moment he got out of prison he would do nothing except focus on hunting me down.

He started going into detail about what he'd already done to me and what he would do to me when he got out, resulting in gasps from the courtroom as he detailed the horrific acts he had obsessed over and written about.

He delighted in detailing the joy that he experienced when he marked my body with a roadmap of scars, vividly describing each of the implements and techniques he used to craft each one, and the meaning behind them.

One person fainted as he talked about his plans for me once he got out.

In the end, he was dragged out by several wardens, his words too evil and lengthy for the room to bear. He was supposed to use the moment to gain sympathy, and some mercy from the judge and the jury, but he used the moment as a soliloquy on his obsession with me and his dark plans for my torturous death.

As they dragged him out of the courtroom, he turned his head to look behind him, locking eyes with me once more. His face had twisted into an icy smirk as he passed through the doors leading back to the jail, because he always knew he would find me again, no matter how hard I tried to hide.

"See you soon," he yelled, calling me by the name I grew up with.

Not Angel. Angel is a new development that he wasn't meant to ever find out about. But it's clearly too late to worry about that now. That ship has well and truly sailed.

He's seen the salon named after me. He's been in my home and no doubt seen letters addressed to me. He must have found out my new name long before to even track me down here. So much for being undercover.

So it's not a surprise that he's managed to find me. It's just happened much sooner than I thought it would.

I thought I'd done a good job of burning the remnants of my prior life. No attachments to my family, because he killed them all, so that part was 'easy', relatively speaking.

The same goes for close friends back on the mainland. He eliminated anyone I cared about. Some he took from the earth, the ones who insisted on remaining in my life no matter how difficult it might have been to be my friend. The ones who would send me messages and invite me out for coffee even when I said no for the hundredth time.

The others, the more fair-weather friends, he surgically isolated me from until they decided our friendship took too much effort and they naturally floated away to greener pastures, to friends who would give them the attention they so desperately craved.

Now he's eliminated everyone in his path, and he's after the grand finale. Me.

I took precautions so that he wouldn't find me, or at least so that it would take him extra time. I changed my name, and I drastically changed my appearance. New ID, new phone, new bank accounts, new wardrobe, everything new. A self-made version of a witness protection identity change.

I don't tell people very much about me. I don't chat with people online. My life here on this island has consisted of work at the salon, quiet time at my apartment, and making the odd friend who lives a quiet life here.

And surfing a few times a week, which is about as off the grid as you can get. No phones, no cameras. Just the ocean, my board, and me.

There's no way a normal human being could have tracked me down here. This has to have taken considerable focus and resources. Then again, as he's proven time and time again, he's far from normal and incredibly resourceful. Regular barriers don't stand in his way.

Unfortunately, obsession and evil sometimes find a path when it doesn't seem possible.

And I am the object of his fixation. He won't rest until he kills me, and he's made it clear it will be a torturous and excruciating death.

I hear a noise behind me and flinch at the sensation of a hand pressing against my back.

My mental box of dark thoughts snaps closed and I'm suddenly back to reality, on all fours in the bathroom, hovering over a disgusting pile of vomit.

"Angel," a voice says softly. It's Aidan, his hand on my back. "Let me help you up."

He extends his hand and I grab it. He pulls me to my feet and glances at the puddle of vomit on the floor as he helps me out of the room.

"Yo, Brick!" he calls out down the hallway. "Cleanup on Aisle Three!"

"Got you, boss!" Brick's voice carries back down the hallway and I hear him get up to go get supplies.

I glance at myself in the mirror. My complexion is paler than usual, and my eyes are still watery and bloodshot. My face is puffy. I'm a mess on the outside, but none of it compares to how I'm feeling on the inside.

I don't know how I'm going to make it through this. If I even want to make it through. I'm just so very tired of it all, and feeling incredibly beaten down and unprepared for what's yet to come.

"Let's go sit down," says Aidan, his arm around me, concern in his eyes.

He leads me to the living room and takes a seat beside me on the couch. Slade and Roman are sitting down as well, also observing me with concern.

"What's happening, Angel?" asks Roman, his eyes exploring mine for clues.

"Tell us so we can figure out what to do," says Slade. His tone isn't what sympathetic sounds like for most people, but it probably is for him. His version of care and concern, at least.

He's probably equally worried about how whatever this situation is might affect him and his brotherhood, but I can't blame him for that. None of them asked me to bring my problems into their lives. And I have some deep, dark problems including a sadistic madman hellbent on ending my existence.

"You only need to tell us as much as you're comfortable with, Angel," says Aidan, putting his hand on top of mine. "Take your time. We're here for you."

I take a deep breath. I've been burned before, telling this story, and I'm not going to risk going into all the details again.

But I'm ready to share more with them than I've shared with anyone in a very long time.

Chapter Twenty-Three

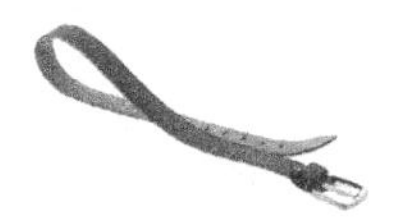

Aidan

"He was someone that I used to know," she says, her voice soft and low. "He used to do really bad things to hurt me, and to hurt others." Her voice trembles slightly, and she speaks slowly as if she's testing the waters with her words.

She pauses, deep in thought, and I wait for her to continue. She seems hollow, spooked. Like if I make a slight move the wrong way she might jump out of her skin or shatter into delicate pieces. Her face is pale and her eyes seem haunted as she bubbles up memories that clearly were shoved down somewhere deep inside her mind.

"He must be out of prison now, obviously, although he wasn't meant to be released for a long time. I always worried that would happen. He's so manipulative, I knew he'd trick the justice system and get an early release. I just didn't realize it would be this soon."

She takes a deep breath, steeling herself to continue, and I squeeze her hand, keeping it on top of hers for comfort.

Slade's eyes narrow, his eyebrows furrowing in concentration as he listens. For once, it seems like he's scowling at the story rather than at her.

Roman leans forward intently, sitting on the edge of his seat, taking in every last word.

Brick returns, having completed his vomit cleanup duty. He silently takes a seat on the arm of the chair across from the couch, his gaze exploring the tense, anguished expression on Angel's face.

"He always said he'd track me down. I thought I'd found the perfect place to escape, that he'd never find me once I abandoned my old life and created a new one here on the island. It seemed like it was far enough away that there wouldn't be any loose ends, any breadcrumbs for him to follow."

She sighs, her haunted and bloodshot eyes meeting mine.

"But I guess he has found me here after all. He's clever and resourceful and he's never going to give up. I'm never going to be able to escape him, except through death. Even in death, there are things he said he'd do to my human form."

Her face screws into a grimace and she half-gags, as if she's visualizing him doing what she just described. She clutches at herself with both arms, as if she's trying to hold herself together. As if she might fall apart the moment she stopped squeezing.

I have the urge to reach out to her and pull her closer to me, to tell her she doesn't need to say any more. But part of me needs her to keep going, to tell the parts of her story that she feels able to tell right in this moment.

Roman opens his mouth as if to speak, but then closes it again, letting her continue to have the floor.

Slade and Brick's eyes stay fixed on her, their body language still.

"I always knew it would end this way, but I really thought I had a lot more time." She squeezes her eyes shut as if she's holding in tears. Her skin is flushed and coated in a soft sheen. "I just can't believe he's out and that he's already found me."

Brick's jaw is taut and I can almost hear his teeth grinding all the way from the armchair.

My chest tightens as she tells her story, even though I sense we're getting the abbreviated version.

My takeaway is that a crazed lunatic stalked her back on the mainland and said he'd find her again one day and kill her. And now he's here ready to follow through on his promise.

No wonder she's terrified. He sounds like a psycho. Which is a little ironic given who she's been staying with under the same roof.

We've seen the type of destruction he's capable of at both her salon and apartment.

She stops talking and looks down at the ground, twisting her fingers around each other. I wait, giving her space to continue, but no more words come.

That's all she will share for now.

We sit in silence. I'm processing what she just told us and what it means, and I'm sure the other guys are, too.

Brick puts a hand to his face, rubbing his lips, and I can almost see the wheels turning in his head.

She was concise as she described what happened, but I know that beneath the condensed story are no doubt many layers of trauma, many more details she's not yet ready to share. Maybe she never will be. The fear of being hunted by someone who will follow her to the ends of the earth. The length of time that this person has had such a hold over her.

She doesn't need to say it, but it's pretty clear this person is the reason behind most, if not all, of the scars that lace themselves across her entire body.

Even though she offers limited details about what she's been dealing with, it would be a lot for anybody to deal with.

She looks up, almost flinching as if she's expecting to see us staring at her with judgement. Her shoulders settle slightly when all that gazes back at her is concern and care, even from Slade.

She goes to speak but then stops. I can sense her working herself back up to the somewhat hysterical state she was just in. Her chest rises and falls rapidly, and she starts to clench and unclench her fists again as if forcing herself to speak.

"It's okay, Angel," I say, gently, in an attempt to soothe her. "You don't have to tell us everything right now."

I rub her back with a firm hand, and she gently presses herself into my palm.

Roman reaches over me and puts his hand on her knee, and gives it a light squeeze.

"It's okay, Angel, it's okay," he says softly. "You're safe here with us. We'll protect you."

I wrap my arm around her and pull her close to me, and feel her body trembling against mine.

Slade's eyes are fixed on her, a strange look on his face. It's not the usual anger I see directed her way by him. It's almost like he's seeing her for the first time, the way the rest of us have from the beginning.

"Am I really safe here with you?" she whispers, her eyes large and vacant, her body tense.

It's a loaded question. I don't know if she's asking if we'll keep her safe from her stalker, or if she's safe from us. In either case, it's a fair question.

She didn't choose to come here, didn't choose to watch Roman murder a man. Didn't choose for this stalker to fall into a deadly obsession with her and follow her to the ends of the earth vowing to destroy her.

Telling her we'll protect her probably rings a bit hollow in either case.

Despite the unusual circumstances, I mean every word I say.

I will protect her, at all costs.

I've seen so many emotions in Angel already. I've seen fear, anger, confusion, and even a little lust.

But now I just see her terror, and I'm determined to make it go away.

Chapter Twenty-Four

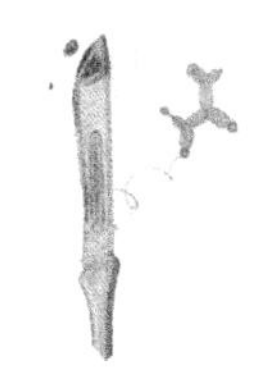

Brick

"What are we going to do now?" My heart is racing, and my nostrils flare uncontrollably, my deep exhales sending flickers of cool air across my beard.

I crack my knuckles in an attempt to calm myself, but it only makes me more agitated. I want to use them now, for my knuckles to shatter the skull of the psycho that's hunting our Angel.

Angel has left the living room, leaving the four of us reeling from what she just shared. She said she wasn't feeling well and wanted to lie down. Nobody can blame her after both what she told us and the effort it took to share it.

She was visibly drained by the time she gave us a high-level overview, as if she was beaten down by having to relive her dark memories. All I want is to heal her pain, but all I could do at that moment was listen as she bared her soul.

Roman walked her up to her room with a glass of water, and apparently, she just climbed into the bed and pulled the covers over her entire body including her face. I can't blame her for wanting to hide, for wanting to shut this all out until it's over.

It's been a wild few days for our houseguest, through no fault of her own, and with the unanticipated arrival of a psycho stalker on the island, it seems things are only getting started.

I'm so fucking furious that someone would destroy her property the way he did. Destroying every little thing that meant anything to her, shredding and slashing and carving and snapping until everything was gone. Useless. Damaged. Dead.

I shiver as I imagine what might have happened if she'd been at home or work by herself when that monster swung by. I'm pretty sure the scissors and the knives would have ended up embedded in her flesh instead of the wall. The wall was just a proxy to absorb a tiny sliver of the hate this monster harbors toward her.

I want to take whoever this guy is down into my basement and spend hours alone with him. Days even, maybe entire weeks if I can work slowly and precisely enough, inflicting maximum pain with minimum damage as I mimic his every shred and slash and carve and snap all over his body.

There will be no mercy shown. I'll sear his eyeballs in his skull while he shrieks in terror, removing his ability to look at Angel, to come after her anymore. So that he quakes in terror as he sightlessly wonders what tool I'll use to torture him next.

I will not let him rest, even when his body and mind try to give up and let him escape into a world of unconsciousness.

I will keep him awake until every last drop of blood trickles from his body, until he is nothing but a flaccid pile of gored flesh and shattered bones.

I'll string his tendons across the ceiling beams like they're streetlights.

And I will do it while she watches.

My Angel, my Valkyrie. Watching me as I bring her tormentor to his knees, to his own merciless, torturous death. Nothing could be too dark, too depraved, for him to deserve. The things I plan on doing to him will be the first time my monster is truly unleashed. Everyone around here thinks they know me, but they haven't seen the true depths of my darkness, where I'm truly willing to go.

"Come back to us, Brick," I hear Slade's voice. "Brick," he says again.

I feel a hand on my shoulder, shaking me. I snap back to the present, my eyes darting to the person connected to the arm on my shoulder.

It's Slade.

That was a risky move on his part, bringing me back to reality when I'm in the middle of a torture daydream, the rush of blood ringing in my ears, my bloodlust settling in.

I've been told I growl when I'm like that, that it's animalistic. From the way my throat feels a bit raw I'm guessing I just did it again, too.

My chest is tight, my heart is racing and my jaw is stiff from grinding my teeth as I listened to Angel share her demons.

"Thanks for bringing me back, man," I say, shaking my head. "I went somewhere."

"You sure did," Slade nods and returns to his seat.

Aidan runs a hand through his close-cropped dark hair, a sure sign that he's thinking intently. Knowing him, he's considered about five scenarios already and narrowed them down to the optimal plan to deal with the situation."There's only one thing I think we can do," he says with a sigh.

I feel a bit sick when I hear him say that, a knot the size of a large fist appearing in my stomach. I think I know what he's going to suggest. "You want to kill her first, before the psycho does? Save her the pain that he has planned for her?" I exhale, my shoulders slumping in defeat. I don't want to hurt Angel like that, but if it saves her from suffering at the hands of a psycho I'll do what needs to be done.

I'll show her mercy, make it quick and painless, the opposite of how I usually treat people who end up in my basement for one reason or another.

"I think that's a good idea," Slade nods enthusiastically, more engaged in this conversation than most. "Then we can go back to normal and the psycho can slither off and find someone else to obsess over. Or we could kill him for sport once she's gone. From what she's shared, it sounds like he deserves it." He shrugs and looks at Aidan as if he's expecting him to be in full agreement.

"No, that's not what I meant!" Aidan shakes his head and furrows his brow. "I wasn't suggesting we kill her. Far from it. What's wrong with you two? Jesus."

"Yeah, what the fuck, guys? You're both fucking psychos," says Roman, frowning at me and then Slade. "I vote we need to keep her and protect her and find the son of a bitch who did this and flay his skin from his body and feed it to crocodiles or pigs or something."

"Now you're talking," I grin at Roman. His idea sounds like a few hours of fun, and retribution for our Angel is my idea of a good time. Plus, I really don't want to kill her and won't on purpose if I don't absolutely need to. "I do enjoy a good flaying, and I have all the tools to make it perfect."

My mind flashes back to the last time I carefully peeled the skin from a piece of shit who was abusing women on the island. It was a pro bono job, and I enjoyed every moment of it. I can still hear his screams as I used a scalpel to detach his flesh from his muscle, to pull it apart from his ligaments and stretch it out on a clothes-drying rack while he watched in horror. It helps that I recorded the experience, and play it back now and then, reliving it. Having that memento keeps me refreshed and focused, and reminds me of what truly brings me joy.

"This sounds overly complicated with lots of risks involved," Slade snarls at Roman. "I think you just want to keep her here so you can put your dick inside her."

"Fuck you, Slade," Roman frowns and raises his voice. "Of course, I wouldn't be opposed to doing that, but it's not why she's here."

"Why is she here then, man? Why is she still alive, creating all sorts of problems that we don't really need right now? It seems like incredibly poor decision-making by all involved." He glares at Roman and then at Aidan who officially 'signed off' on her being here. "I'm honestly shocked by how blasé you're being about this, Aidan, considering the damage she's already doing."

"Listen, I didn't mean to bring her into our bullshit, you know?" shrugs Roman. "She was an innocent bystander. And I still think she could be useful to us somehow."

We all turn to look at Aidan because he hasn't shared his plan yet. Of course, we all know he's going to make a reasonable suggestion, something less polarizing than what Slade and Roman have suggested.

I'm guessing he'll probably say that we should just leave her on the streets and be done with her. Put her out on the side of the road somewhere and tell her never to come back. Let the psycho come after her, and she can fend for herself.

That she's not our problem.

That she's ridiculously pretty, but that's not reason enough to compromise all of us and everything we've worked so hard for.

Putting her on the street makes more sense than putting us at risk.

He hates risk.

Imaginary Aidan is on a roll in my mind, pointing out all the reasons why it's bad for her to stay here and why the right thing to do is to kick her out immediately.

But the actual Aidan takes a deep breath and presses his lips together in a grimace. "I know I was against her coming here in the first place, but I think we have to let her stay."

I do a double-take because it seems like Aidan might be malfunctioning.

"Um, what? Did I mishear you?" Slade's jaw practically unhinges as he raises an eyebrow, clearly also confused. "I thought you agreed on the risk she poses to us."

"No, you didn't mishear me," says Aidan, shaking his head. "She does pose a risk, you're right. I've agreed with that from the start and I still stand by that. But, like Roman said, she didn't start this. She didn't insert herself into our lives. We came flying into hers with murder and carnage and kidnapping. And now it turns out she has a psychopath who's followed her all the way here and is trying to hunt her down. We've inadvertently saved her once, twice even depending on how you think about it, and now I think we need to save her intentionally."

"Why? Because it's the 'good' or 'right' thing to do? Since when did we have a moral code? I thought the whole point was that we didn't." Slade crosses his arms over his chest. "Are you going soft on us now, after years of drumming it into our brains that we didn't come equipped with the misplaced sense of right and wrong that is the main downfall of our greatest rivals? Of reminding us that we should do what serves us, no matter what the implications are for other people? Brotherhood first and all that? Don't tell me you're changing your words to live by now over a piece of ass."

"We still don't have a moral code, Slade. Don't get things twisted. But, like I said, it's not her fault that Roman here went and murdered someone in her workplace. Or that we brought her here." He rubs at his bottom lip with his finger, a pensive expression on his face. "And we can hardly send her back to the salon or her apartment with this lunatic ready to skin her alive and wear her as a suit."

"But she's a risk. You hate risk," I peer at Aidan as I speak up.

He visually appears normal even though he might not sound like it right now. His pupils seem okay. His speech is clear. He doesn't appear to be under the influence of anything.

For once, I agree with Slade about something. Aidan saying Angel should stay with us is such a weird suggestion by him. All he does is talk about risk this, risk that, and now he's suddenly changing his tune.

I'm not sure what his deal is today, but his risk tolerance has apparently just skyrocketed to new heights. For Angel. Like being around her is shifting our DNA or something.

And Aidan doesn't just change like that. At least, he hasn't before.

Maybe Slade is right. Maybe she is weakening us from the center out.

"Sounds like someone's growing soft, forgetting where they came from and what they're all about," growls Slade, his eyes narrowing at Aidan. "I knew she would weaken us. Roman might think with his dick," he glares at Roman, "but I didn't expect you to be the one to fold so quickly, Aidan."

"Fucking chill out, Slade. Clearly, you disagree with me, but I'm not changing my mind. Having her here is the best thing for us collectively. It's what we need to do, so get on board, man." Aidan rarely makes threats, and I'm not sure quite what he's inferring will happen if Slade chooses not to.

"I didn't realize this was a dictatorship." The cords on Slade's neck are pulled taut and his face growing red, his pulse visible in his temples as he clenches his jaw.

He narrows his eyes at Aidan and shifts forward as if he's about to stand, and for a moment I think he's going to take a swing at him.

Aidan meets his glare, not backing down.

"Guys, stop it," I say. "All I care about is that we get to keep the girl. Angel can stay in my room if she wants protection," I add.

The other guys all turn and glare at me, momentarily distracted by my suggestion and slight change of subject.

"What?" I shrug. "Just making the offer."

Roman rolls his eyes. "Whatever, man. Anyway, I'm glad you have a reasonable perspective on this, as usual, Aidan. Even if not all of us can comprehend your wisdom right now." He narrows his eyes at Slade. "And I get to tell her about this, seeing I found her."

His demeanor changes at the mention of getting to speak with her. He beams at the prospect of saving his damsel in distress, of sharing the news that she gets to stay and that we'll do everything in our power to protect her.

"Hoping she'll run to you and put her arms around you and suck your dick because you're the one that told her?" I ask.

Roman juts his chin out at me, knowing it's the truth. "You're just jealous. You want to tell her so she'll suck *your* dick."

"Maybe," I say, crossing my arms over my chest.

Of course, I want to be the one that tells her she gets to stay with us, and that we're going to protect her. Because I want to see her smile. Because I want to be the reason that she smiles. A little bit of dick-sucking wouldn't go astray, either, but that's not expected.

There's something about this woman. I just want to make her happy, no matter what it takes.

"Listen, let's just give her a minute to settle. To process this information. I don't think anyone needs to run and tell her today," says Aidan. "Give her a while to cool down, maybe even a day or two."

"Won't she run if she thinks we don't want her here?" I ask. "What if she panics and finds a way to escape in the middle of the night because she's so afraid of what might happen to her here, of what we might decide? And then what if the psycho tracks her down and chops her to pieces, just because we didn't communicate right away?"

"Wow, you're really going on a mental journey there, Brick. To be honest, I think she's far more likely to run if she thinks we *do* want her here. She's spooked. She doesn't trust us yet, which is fair. Just give her some time and don't promise anything one way or another. Let her settle in a little."

Roman and I both glare at Aidan. He's always holding us back, trying to time things perfectly. Usually, he's right to do so. He's the voice of reason in our chaos, and that's frustrating sometimes. Like now.

I sigh. "Fine, I won't say shit until you give the word. But I will be there for her if she wants to talk or just needs company in the meantime."

"So will I," nods Roman. "But I still get to tell her first when the time is right."

"Jesus, Roman. You're like a child. 'I get to tell her, I get to tell her first." I mimic him in a baby voice because that's what he fucking sounds like. Besides, I want to tell her and if she asks me I have every intention of doing so. Roman can fuck right off, he doesn't get special privileges just because he was the first one to lay eyes on her beautiful face.

"See? I told you this would happen," says Slade to Aidan, sighing heavily. "She's causing conflict between us. She's weakening our brotherhood. She's a massive distraction, even when she's on the other side of the house. She just might be the worst thing to ever happen to us."

Chapter Twenty-Five

Angel

It's been a relatively quiet couple of days. The guys check in on me from time to time but mainly give me a wide berth. I think they're trying to be respectful and give me space after I shared what I did with them, but it's a bit lonely rattling around in this giant house by myself. I still don't have a phone, so I can't even scroll mindlessly through news feeds or play games while I watch reality shows.

I thought about cooking something, just for something to do to take my mind off things, but after taking a closer look at the kitchen and peeking in a few cupboards and drawers, I decide not to. Judging by how immaculate Slade keeps the kitchen, and how it seems to be his pride and joy, I assume any attempt to move things out of their correct positions would just turn into an argument. I'm really not in the mood for his judgmental looks and critical observations.

My mental and physical energy has been drained, and as I wander aimlessly from room to room, my limbs feel inexplicably heavy, like they're weighed down by my darkest thoughts. I feel like I'm sinking, like I'm drowning and I can't save myself. Nobody can save me now. I'm a dead woman walking.

Finally, I just give up and get onto my side on the couch in the living room and curl up into the fetal position while I watch more bad TV. It's not as much of a distraction as I need to truly take my mind off things, but it will have to do. It's the only option I have.

I'm a little out of sorts right now, and it's not just because I've found out my stalker is on the loose and trying to track me down and kill me. That's happened so often at this point I'm almost resigned to it as part of my life. The way some people learn to deal with chronic pain or an abusive parent, you just learn to endure it at the time and one day it becomes less noticeable, less intrusive on your everyday life. It's still terrifying but in a manageable way. I've gotten pretty good at compartmentalizing that type of stuff.

The thing I'm struggling with more, my acute issue, is what Roman has planned for this evening.

Because Roman is going on a date tonight.

It's with some woman he apparently met at one of the bars the guys own. He casually mentioned it earlier in the day, just brought it up in casual conversation, and it's all I've been able to think about ever since.

As he leaves to go and pick up his date, I feel a twinge in the pit of my stomach. I don't know why, though. It's not like I have any claim to him, or that I'd even want to claim him given the chance.

Hell, he's the one who came traipsing into my life and fucked it all up within less than an hour of being at the salon. He's the reason I'm here, kidnapped, captive in this house with these four men.

I should be furious with him, not pining over him because he's taking some woman out in the hopes she'll suck his dick at the end of the night.

Not that he needs to buy a woman a meal for her to be begging to do that, I'm sure. I wish I hadn't trimmed his hair so neatly before The Asshole came in, and that I'd left it uneven and sticking up at weird angles. But even if his hair wasn't picture-perfect, I'm pretty sure he'd still have to beat women off with a stick. Damn Roman and his stupid hot face and murderous tendencies.

Realistically, it's just been a coincidence that not one of the guys has left my side, except to work, since I've been at the house. It was only a matter of time before they resumed everyday activities. They all probably regularly go on dates. For all I know, they might all have serious girlfriends.

Well, I take that back. When it comes to Roman, I doubt it, actually. He seems committed to non-commitment from what I've seen.

Many women would definitely try to ship Aidan, with his handsome looks, his muscular body, and his natural leadership qualities. He seems like a sexy but reliable choice. And with the whole belt incident I got the opportunity to see another side of him simmering just beneath the surface, one that I don't think many other people know exists. He's got that two-point-five-kids-white-picket-fence-potential vibe crossed with *Fifty Shades* meets *Sons of Anarchy*. And all of this makes him insanely hot.

Women probably go crazy over Brick for his wild unpredictability, his humor and his many quirks. He is fun and hot, a sexy and crazy ball of energy. I haven't seen his cock yet, but I already know it's huge. Brick has massive BDE.

I could see him pairing up with a cute vegan one day. They could wear matching faux leather jackets and spoon-feed each other quinoa in the park in the mornings, and torture evil people in the basement in the evenings. A match made in heaven.

And then there's Slade. He's probably best-suited to someone as cynical about life as him. A Pollyanna type would drive him nuts, and he definitely needs somebody with some depth.

Someone snarky and assertive who wouldn't put up with all his shit. Someone who gives back as good as he dishes it out. On second thought, that sounds way too much like me and it's obvious that we would be wildly incompatible. We're like oil and water.

Maybe what he really wants is someone who's sweet and submissive, who'll kiss the scowl right off his lips and whisper in his ear about how wonderful and special he is. Who'll cream herself when he cooks for her. Someone who will break down his walls layer by layer until he's actually capable of showing any feelings or engaging in a two-way conversation.

Maybe he deserves a bit of tenderness. Maybe that would mix with his own prickly personality and make him into a tolerable human being.

It's fun thinking about shipping the guys with imaginary women. But at the same time, the thought of it seems to have led to a burning sensation deep in my gut and my jaw is aching from me clenching it repeatedly.

Great, I'm getting jealous about imaginary scenarios that I'm creating in my mind. Jealous of the imaginary relationship lives of the *men who kidnapped me*. That's totally normal.

I guess it makes sense that I'm feeling this way. Despite the craziness of the circumstances, I've enjoyed how many things have been so far. I'm getting used to being around all four of the guys, and being the only female in this house.

They've all been attentive in their own ways, even if in Slade's case his way is being an asshole. He's lucky he's so sexy when he scowls. I feel a bit possessive of all of them, even though I haven't known them for long.

Even so, why am I so twisted up about Roman and this date?

Why do I care who he dates, or fucks, or whatever?

I've never been a jealous person, so why would I start now?

Still, I can't help but watch out the window as he leaves to go pick her up. He's dressed nicely, in one of his custom-tailored suits that fits him perfectly. Looking dashingly handsome as always.

He smelled good, too, as he walked out the door. The same pomade I remember from the salon, cognac and tobacco, melding with an aftershave with notes of cedar wood and geranium. He seems to have a different scent for every occasion, so maybe this is his 'date a hottie and bang her brains out' fragrance of choice. I wanted to run over to him and bury my face in his neck and just inhale his deliciousness, but instead, I just sat there, frozen, as he left.

When he glanced at me on his way out the door, I almost melted onto the floor, but then I remembered he made himself look and smell this good for *her*, not for me. So, instead, I looked away and pretended not to be interested.

To make things worse, to make me really stew on things, he showed me a picture of his date earlier. She looked pretty in the photo, wearing a cute black dress, with a slim waist and perky tits, and her makeup and hair were done really nicely. Of course she's pretty. Roman can get any girl he wants. He probably doesn't have to slip below a ten a nine on a rough day. I don't know why he showed the photo to me, but if it was to make me jealous, it worked.

I guess that's something a guy would do to a female friend, show them a picture of their date. Maybe that's why he hasn't tried to fuck me yet. He doesn't see me that way. I've heard of being friend-zoned, but being kidnapped and friend-zoned is new territory. I guess it could happen. Anything is possible.

Conjured images of them making out flood my mind. A montage of their hands and mouths and fingers and bodies mashing against each other.

I imagine them at a fancy restaurant, his hand sliding into her panties under the table while she smiles at him and pretends his fingers aren't buried deep inside her while she subtly bucks against his touch.

I imagine her stroking his hard shaft while he devours a steak, his precum leaking onto the leather booth and leaving his mark.

I imagine him bending her over the dining table and ramming himself deep inside her cunt as the entire restaurant watches and applauses while he rails her, plates and glasses flying off the table and clattering to the ground, smashing everywhere as they orgasm together.

These scenarios are where my warped mind is taking me, and my heartburn is getting worse.

I exhale deeply and realize I've been gritting and grinding my teeth ever since I watched them leave, glaring out the window and waiting for his return so I can berate him like a jealous shrew. My jaw is clenched so tightly that one of my teeth does a weird thing, moving in a direction it's not meant to or something. I take a deep breath and consciously try to relax my body.

What is wrong with me? He's just a guy. A guy that would never be satisfied with just one woman, at that. From the moment I saw him, I knew he was a player. Dashing and charismatic and ready for the smooth lines to spin off his tongue like silk. So it shouldn't be a surprise that he's going on a date. That he's going to do what he was made to do, charm women and then fuck them senseless.

It doesn't stop me from being incredibly frustrated.

It's difficult to concentrate for the next few hours.

In an effort to make time go by faster, I mindlessly click between TV channels, scrolling through screen after screen of infomercials. Skincare products, exercise equipment, signal-blocking wallets, debt consolidation, ambulance-chasing lawyers. All of the jingles and accusations and authoritative tones melding into a swirl in my brain, making me want to scream. Finally, I change the channel to a reality TV marathon. People are screaming at each other but in a way that I can tune out. It helps that I've seen this episode before.

I try sitting on the couch, lying on my back, then my side, with and without a cushion. Nothing is comfortable right now. I can't relax. My body is tense.

I know I should go to my room and sleep, both because I'm exhausted and because staying up and waiting for Roman is pointless. No good can come of it.

There's a saying that people shouldn't stay out all night, that if you go out you should get yourself home at a decent hour because nothing good happens after midnight. Well, I'm guessing that nothing good happens after hours of waiting for a fuck boy to get home after a date with a woman that's not you.

Despite my better judgement, despite knowing that I'm probably only going to get myself into more of a state as time ticks by, I find myself edging along the couch until I'm as close as possible to the front door so I there's no chance I'll miss him when he comes in.

Finally, after what seems like many hours, I hear the front door open, followed by Roman's deep voice and then the tinkling laugh of a woman. I glance toward the front door, and of course, the laugh is attached to the pretty woman he showed me a photo of earlier.

They're too distracted to notice me all the way over in the living room. Plus, they're probably not assuming someone would be up this late waiting to observe them when they come in.

He has his arm around her and they're both giddy, laughing about some secret joke they have between them. She looks to be as pretty in real life as she is in her pictures, all smiles and sparkling eyes and full lips that Roman keeps looking at like he wants to kiss and lick and bite.

She's touching his arm, clearly comfortable around him. Comfortable touching him. I wish I was touching him. She doesn't need to be here, in this house. I'm enough for Roman. He doesn't need her.

He only needs me.

But he refuses to have me.

Roman's body language noticeably adjusts, and I recognize it immediately. He's going in for the kill. I can see the hunger in his eyes as they roam over her body, making my stomach churn and my chest burn.

But I also feel a twinge between my legs at the intensity of the look he's giving her. His eyes are dark pinpoints, and they're smoldering. He emanates pure, hot lust like he wants to devour her completely. Like nobody else is in the universe, let alone the room.

Given the way he's visually feasting on her, there's little risk of him glancing over and seeing me. If he did happen to look over, I don't think he'd even notice I'm here. Everything seems to be invisible to him right now, except for her.

Who doesn't want to be looked at in that way by someone they're attracted to? Like you're the most delicious, amazing thing they've ever seen and they can't get enough of you? Like all they want to do is rip your clothes off and devour every part of you?

They walk through the dining area and head up the stairs, his arm wrapped around her waist, and they disappear into his room. The pit in my stomach multiplies, sending acidic ribbons up my esophagus.

I sit for a moment, unmoving, not sure what to do. But I can't just stay here.

Making sure to be very quiet, I head through the kitchen area and up the stairs, and tiptoe along the hallway. A trail of women's perfume, not mine, marks the path. Definitely not something I would wear. But maybe something he prefers. I'm learning all sorts of things about Roman today.

I'm slightly relieved to see his bedroom door is open a crack, because I don't know what I would have done if it was closed. I'm not sure if I could have handled not knowing what was going in there between Roman and *her*. I walk a little further down the hall and peek through the gap from a distance.

They haven't wasted any time. Roman is standing up and his date is on her knees in front of him. She reaches up to unbuckle his belt and he lets her. She slides it out of his belt loops and places it to the side.

He's facing the door, so he sees me watching almost immediately, and he smirks as his gaze settles on me. He continues watching me as she undoes his pants and frees his erection. He's hard as iron, his impressive cock ready to be inside her. Or inside me, but she'll have to do for now.

She grasps him in her palm and takes his cock between her plump lips. I stand there, watching, as she uses her hand to milk his shaft while she slides his cock down her throat, gliding it in and out of her red-rimmed mouth. She fondles his balls with her other hand and I almost want to call out 'good girl' because she's trying so hard to please him.

His eyes locked on mine, he grips the back of her head so he can fuck her mouth, and begins to roll his hips so that she has to take his cock at his pace. She gags briefly at the change of intensity but soon gets right back to it.

I can see her lipsticked lips and her tongue as they caress his hardness, and my pussy clenches at the thought of my own lips and tongue and hands being on him.

He closes his eyes for a moment as he shoves his cock down her throat and holds it there, her throat impaled by his hardness. His eyes flick open toward me as he continues to hold her mouth on him, his entire cock sitting down her throat. Her body stills, and she has no choice but to just stay there, unmoving, while he drains her of her air supply.

After several seconds, he gently lets her mouth off of his cock.

She pulls back and gasps for air, saliva dripping from his cock and her mouth onto the floor. She glances to the side briefly and her eyes are watering.

He helps her up and guides her around to the side of the bed and pushes her onto her back so she lays across the width of the mattress, her head closest to me, and he kisses her on the mouth. Her arm wraps around his neck, pulling him to her. I see his tongue swipe through her lips, meeting with hers.

He looks up at me, his head above her field of vision, and he winks at me. I realize that he's had her lie at this angle so he can continue to make eye contact with me while they fuck.

His hand trails down the side of one of her breasts, along the orb-like curve, and she moans at his touch as he pulls her dress down to fully expose her chest. He cups one of her breasts with his hand and she moans, arching her back toward him.

Her nipples are hard, and he glances down and dips his head toward one of them. He kisses it and then looks back up at me. A small smirk forms on his lips.

He dips his head again, gently tugging on her nipple with his teeth this time, causing her to moan loudly. His eyes are locked on me as he twirls his tongue around her pebbled nipple and she arches her back.

He leans down and bites it, grazing it between his teeth, and she cries out as he clamps down on it, harder this time judging by her agitated cries.

He turns her around so that her head is toward the foot of the bed, her face out of my sight because of the angle of the door. I can still see all of him though, as well as her body from the shoulders down, but now I can see the entire length of his erect cock from the side. He trails his hand down her dress and hikes it up so that it's over her hips, exposing her panties, her feet flat on the bed, and her knees in the air.

Hooking his finger inside the thin material, he moves her panties to the side and rubs at her glistening slit. My pussy clenches as I watch his fingers slide into her. As he glides them in and out of her, I can hear that she's soaking wet, the slick coating glazing his fingers.

I imagine what his long fingers feel like, how they expertly caress and flick and rub in all the right places. I wonder how his cock feels when it's this hard, when he's this aroused. As if it's my throbbing pussy that he's about to pound himself into. Not this stupid bitch, whoever she is.

Anyway, what do I care? I'm not sure why I'm feeling so territorial, or why I'm watching him fuck her.

I haven't even kissed the guy.

He's clearly into this woman, he clearly wants nothing more than to spend the night railing her.

I guess it doesn't mean I can't watch, though. Because whether I'm jealous or not, watching this is hot.

I cup one of my breasts in my hand and begin to play with my nipple through my shirt, and I bite my lip while he watches my fingers.

My other hand slides down over my shorts and I begin to rub myself through my pants and let out a silent moan. I slide my hand inside my panties, trailing a finger down my slit. I'm even wetter than I realized.

He climbs over her, mounting her, while his eyes stay locked with mine. My pussy clenches as he reaches down to line his rock-hard cock up with her entrance.

Eyes still on me, he glides into her with one thrust and she cries out his name. I feel my arousal begin to pool as I watch him bury himself inside her wet cunt. I'm craving him, I want so badly for him to be inside me instead. It should be my pussy that he's buried deep inside, not hers.

She cries out, louder now, as he begins to slam into her with increased force. There's no gentleness, just raw lust, as he begins impaling her on his cock.

I watch as he rhythmically grinds his hips against her, sinking himself deep into her wet cunt and pulling his cock slowly back out almost all the way, only to slam it in again even harder each time.

I like the way his strong hands grab her hips so tightly that she can barely move, controlling her so that his cock can take her exactly how it wants. She'll almost definitely have bruises in the morning.

I feel a twinge between my legs at the thought of him holding me like that and marking me, giving me something to remember him by that would last for days. I want him to cover me in bruises that remind me of him and our sex every time I look in the mirror.

Spreading my legs further apart as I stand there, my fingers skim over my clit and down to my entrance to collect some of my arousal. I gently roll my hips in rhythm with his thrusting as I work my fingers over my clit, letting out another silent moan at how good it feels to touch myself with his eyes on me.

He bites his lower lip as his gaze drops to my fingers as I work myself over, and his thrusts intensify.

His date's tits bounce around as he holds her hips steady, rolling his own so that he slides almost all the way out and then slams in again, hard, burying his cock completely inside her. I flick my clit faster to match his pace with my fingers.

It's like he's using her body for my benefit. She's just a vessel that he's working over to demonstrate what he wants to do to me. I feel pity for her, not having any idea that he's using her body to fuck my mind.

I feel someone press up behind me and nip me on my neck.

Startled, I pause my fingers.

"Want some help, Angel?" a voice whispers from behind me.

It's Aidan.

I turn my head to face him, and he leans down and kisses me, his tongue sliding into my mouth and searching for mine.

He reaches around and his hand joins mine inside my panties, and he silently groans as he feels how wet I am.

"Jesus, Angel," he whispers, as he begins to massage my clit with his finger. "You're dripping. Are you enjoying watching Roman fuck his date?"

He bites on his lower lip and I can feel a bulge in his pants as he presses his body into my back.

I nod.

"You're a naughty girl, watching them fuck," he whispers. "I like it."

I continue to roll my hips in time with Roman's cock thrusting into his date's pussy, Aidan's fingers rubbing my clit in rhythm. I grind my ass into him and he occasionally slides one or two long fingers inside me and then returns to focus his attention on my clit.

Roman's eyes are still locked on me, but his gaze has lowered and is now fixated on Aidan's fingers working over my clit.

Roman begins to thrust faster as he watches Aidan finger-fucking me, his cock slamming forcefully into his date, and Aidan matches his pace with his fingers.

I moan and he presses his body against me from behind. I can feel his hardness, his erection pressing firmly into my back as he unravels me with his fingers.

Biting his lower lip as he watches me, Roman reaches down with one of his hands and begins to stroke his date's clit.

She moans and begins to rock and grind her hips to get more traction against his hand.

"You're close now, baby, aren't you? I can tell," he growls, and she replies that she is but his eyes are looking at me when he speaks. "I want you to come all over my cock," he grinds out, his eyes still locked on me. "I want to hear you scream my name while I bury myself deep inside your sweet cunt."

Her body tenses, and she screams his name as she comes, arching her back and writhing on his cock.

Aidan presses on my clit with extra pressure, pinching it, sending me over the edge as well, my knees buckling and almost giving out underneath me.

My eyes roll back but then flick straight to Roman, and seeing me come sends him over the edge as well. His body stutters as he expels his release, and he buries himself to his hilt, his head tilting back as he groans.

She moans loudly, having no idea what's going on beside her.

Poor, naïve woman. He just came for me. It was seeing me come that took him over the edge. She may as well not even have been there.

He slowly slides himself out of her and snaps off his condom, discarding it on the nightstand.

Aidan pulls his hands out of my pants and nips me on my neck again. I grin and squeal. Roman's date glances over at the noise and she sees us standing at the doorway, Aidan removing his hand from my panties.

We shrug and grin, and I grab Aidan's hand as we run up the hallway laughing.

This was just the distraction I needed.

Done with spying on Roman and his date, I clean up and head back to the living room. When I walk down the hallway past Roman's room I don't look in. I don't need to see the aftermath of what just happened in there.

If I'm honest, I don't want to see them snuggling or having gentle post-coital moments together. It's one thing to watch him plow his cock into her like she was just a hole, but anything intimate would send me over the edge, and not in a good way.

I'm kind of hoping that seeing Aidan and me standing there watching was enough to start a fight between them, to piss the woman off so she just leaves. There's nothing I'd rather see right now than her running out of his room and out the front door in hysterical tears. I don't like her being here at all. I feel territorial, having another woman here rubs me the wrong way. But I haven't heard any raised voices or yelling, so I'm not sure how he explained away our being there. Some clever fuck boy excuse, most likely.

As these cluttered thoughts rush through my brain, I try to analyze them clinically.

I'm quite aware that I'm being ridiculous.

I've known these guys for a couple of days and they took me against my will.

It's not like I'm the queen of their fucking family who has any say in how they live their lives. I've barely been let out of a locked room, for goodness' sake.

My interest in the sex lives of my captors is probably far from healthy.

I really need to chill.

I take a seat on the couch. It's late, but Brick and Slade just got back from a job and Aidan obviously just got done finger-fucking me, so we're all awake. They're all night owls, anyway, I've found.

They're half-watching some show on TV and chatting about business. I pay partial attention to what they're saying, but the rest of me is focused on any sounds or signs of life coming from Roman's room.

I need his date to be over, and then I'll hopefully be able to relax.

Finally, his date leaves, her hair still tousled from being dicked down by Roman. She glances at us awkwardly, putting her hand up in a half-wave as she hurries past the living room, and he sees her out the front door.

Thank goodness he didn't let her stay the night. That would have ruined me.

As he turns away from the entrance, he turns toward the living room and sees me there observing him with the rest of the guys.

He walks over and sits on the armchair opposite the couch.

He nods in greeting to each of the other guys, then his gaze meets mine and he smirks.

I roll my eyes at him, but feel a flush creeping up my neck and spreading across my cheeks, exposing me.

"I learned something interesting today," he says to the other guys. "Angel, as it turns out, is a bit of a voyeur. Got off watching me burying my cock inside my hot date."

He winks at me, and I narrow my eyes at him.

"Like you can talk," smirks Brick. "You like to watch, too, Roman. I can't count the number of times we've been fucking someone and have looked over and you were there."

Roman shrugs.

Brick laughs. "And remember when you tried that free trial of the porn subscription and then it kept auto-renewing and so you kept it streaming 24/7 for a while?"

Slade snorts. "That was a moment to remember, for sure."

"That's all fair," Roman shrugs and grins, and then looks over at Aidan. "And I already knew you were a voyeur, bro."

He laughs in Aidan's direction, and Aidan shrugs as well. "It would have been rude not to join in with Angel here. She was having fun by herself, but I wanted to help her." He turns to me and winks. "Not that it looked like you needed any help."

"Thanks for your assistance," I snort. My pussy clenches as I think about the way his fingers felt as he caressed me. It was like he knew exactly how I like to be touched.

And having Roman's eyes locked onto mine as he buried himself in someone else... it was sensory overload, sending me over the edge as I watched his engorged cock slam in and out of her. Making me come apart without even touching me. But only because the whole time I was imagining she was me, that I was her.

Making me want Roman, more than ever, to give me the one thing he's refused to do so far.

It's another distraction from my pain. I want to be railed by Roman. I want him to control my body and do whatever he wants with it. But first, I need to figure out why he won't.

After chatting about business for a while more, Aidan, Brick and Slade leave the living room and head off in separate directions.

As usual, Aidan has work to do and retreats to his study, Slade heads to the kitchen, and Brick heads downstairs to his basement. From some unusual noises I heard when he and Slade returned from their job, I'm fairly certain they didn't come home alone and Brick is about to have a long night doing what he loves.

I linger behind, standing near the entrance to the living room while Roman absent-mindedly flicks through channels on the TV.

I need to speak with him about what happened earlier. About everything.

He raises an eyebrow at me when he sees me just standing there, looking at him.

"You left the door open on purpose, didn't you?" I say, meeting his gaze. "You wanted me to watch you fuck her."

"Maybe." He smirks at me and shrugs.

"Why? Were you trying to make me jealous?"

He peers at me through his eyelashes, a small smile on his lips. "Did it work?"

"No. Saved me the time of fucking you after I saw your technique. You're like a fucking woodpecker with your cock. The least sexy fuck boy I've ever seen in the sack."

He smirks because I'm being ridiculous and he's a cocky asshole. He knows he's amazing in bed and his cock is nothing to be ashamed of.

That's why he carries himself so confidently, like the way he just strolled into my salon the other day acting like he owned the place.

"I think you're lying. I saw the way you watched, you couldn't get enough. If I really looked like a woodpecker while I fucked, that would mean you had some weird woodpecker fetish, the way you were rubbing your fingers all over your clit, matching the pace of my thrusts. The way you came all over Aidan's hand while you watched me burying my cock inside my date. You don't fool me with your insults, Angel. You wanted to be her."

My pussy clenches again. "I was just horny, I guess." I shrug. "It was just like watching porn. It did the job but I've seen much better. It would be a mistake if you thought it was anything more than that."

He smirks at me again, as if he sees right through me.

"Oh really?" He raises an eyebrow. "Do go on. Is there any other commentary you'd like to provide regarding my sexual prowess?"

"Yeah, actually, there is. Next time you fuck someone, you should really make eye contact with them. Instead of staring at another person standing in your doorway. It seems like maybe you wished you were fucking someone else, not the person you had your cock buried in."

In reality, watching him fuck his date was an intense experience and one I don't care to repeat again.

I saw the way he used his hips to rhythmically thrust into her, and the way her body responded to his touch. I saw the way he used his forearms and strong legs to dominate her, to position her body how he saw fit, to get at all the angles that brought him the most pleasure and delivered him exactly what he needed.

I saw the way he used her body while his gaze was locked with mine.

He was rough but intentional, controlling but sensual. Doing enough to make her think he was into her, but reserving his eye contact for me. Being sent over the edge only when he saw me come apart.

I want to see him do all those things again, but only if he's doing them to me.

Just thinking about it makes my pussy throb. I want him so badly.

As skilled as Aidan was with his fingers, I'm craving what Roman gave to his date tonight.

I need him inside me, and I won't give up until I get it.

As for any more bitches coming around, as far as I'm concerned, there will be no more dates.

I'm staking a claim to Roman.

He's mine now. They all are.

They just don't know it yet.

Chapter Twenty-Six

Angel

"We've come to a decision," says Aidan.

I've been summoned to the living room once again.

His tone is serious, and I can't quite pinpoint the expression in his eyes. He always looks a little serious and tense, even when he's being playful. And definitely when he's whipping my ass with a leather belt to teach me a lesson. Right now's no different... there's no amusement, but he doesn't look angry or sad. I'm usually good at reading people, but he makes it difficult, like he's in advanced mode when it comes to accurately interpreting his emotions.

The guys are once again perched on the couch and armchair. I'm sitting on the very end of the couch facing them. All eight eyes are on me.

After the whole Roman date debacle, I spent last night tossing and turning. Every time I'd fall asleep, I'd bolt back upright as nightmares and memories collided, full of stalkers and torture and evil. It was hard to parse apart real memories from my imagination, but all of it was terrifying.

So I'm feeling pretty groggy and disoriented, my brain fuzzy from lack of sleep and the residual emotional overload that comes from a realistic, traumatic nightmare.

Roman just came to collect me from my room and said they had something to tell me. I have no idea what it's about, but if I had to guess it has something to do with my future with them. It's the only decision I can think they'd take the time to announce to me.

"I'm going to need a coffee for this," I say, as a headache starts to form at the base of my skull. I don't actually expect anyone to get up and get me a coffee, but Brick bolts from his seat and comes back a couple of minutes later with an espresso in hand.

"Coffee for the pretty lady," he says, smiling and handing it to me.

"Thanks, Brick," I say, taking the piping hot espresso cup from him and inhaling a deep sip, enjoying the warming sensation as the smooth brown liquid runs down my throat and gives me life.

I turn to Aidan. "So, you were saying?"

"Great, now that the princess is partially caffeinated, I'll continue," he smirks. "I was saying we've come to a decision."

"Oh good. You've decided to kill me? Please get it over with so I can be at peace." I put my hands up in a praying motion. I half mean it.

"Two of us suggested that, but we were overruled," scowls Slade.

"Oh you did, did you? You really hate me that much?" I glare at him. I genuinely don't know why he hates me so much that he wishes me dead.

"It's nothing personal," he shrugs. "I just see you as an obstacle to our success, and part of my job is to make sure those types of obstacles are removed. Do I feel bad you're in this situation through no fault of your own? Of course. Does that change how I feel about it, in terms of the best course of action? No."

"You're a fucking charmer, aren't you, Slade?" I narrow my eyes at him. "So you're saying two people overruled two people? Not sure how that math works, but okay," I roll my eyes. "You could have had me be the tiebreaker and got your wish. And who was the other person who thought killing me was a good idea?" I glance around the room as if I'm being hunted, trying to figure out the second predator.

My eyes settle on Aidan, but I doubt it would be him, although he might see disposing of me as a form of risk mitigation given I observed one of his brothers kill someone. That said, he tends to have the final say on nearly every decision here, so I'm assuming he has something to do with the whole killing me plan being overruled. I'll keep him on the 'maybe' list for now.

I glance at Roman next, and his eyes meet mine. They're pleading with me, trying to convey an invisible message. I know he's a charming ladies' man and can put on an act when he wants to, but I can't imagine him wanting to kill me. At least not until after he fucks me. But then he also doesn't want to fuck me. Jesus, these guys are confusing.

Then I look at Brick. He looks away. "Brick!" I cry out, my voice wavering and tears threatening to fill my eyes. "Brick, did you say you vote to kill me?" This one really stings. I was beginning to think he cared about me.

"I don't want you to die, Angel," he says, his voice low. "I just said that if you did have to die, that I would rather do it myself so that it was quick and you felt no pain."

"You'd kill me?" My eyes bore into his. I want to know exactly where I stand with this man, and whether I can trust him.

"In the sweetest way," he says, shrugging.

"That's... cute, I guess?" I've never been more conflicted about someone's desire to end my life, but because it's Brick, I decide to give him a pass for now.

I glance around at the rest of them. "So, given this vote was overruled, I'm assuming a decision was made not to kill me immediately. That's nice. Was there anything else to this decision?"

"There was more," says Roman. "We want you to stay with us."

"You what? Stay with you?" I look around at all four of them in an effort to better understand what Roman just said. "What do you mean?"

"We want to protect you. You stay here and we'll take care of you," says Brick, smiling at me. "We'll make sure that nobody ever hurts you again."

"Oh really, how ironic," I glance at Aidan and he smirks. He glances at my ass. He knows exactly what I'm talking about.

"Except for us, to clarify," he says, and Brick nods in agreement. "We get to hurt you. But only if you want us to, only the good pain."

Brick nods some more. "Lots of good pain."

"Even if it attracts a homicidal lunatic to your doorstep?" I raise an eyebrow.

I don't think they realize the lengths my stalker will go to in order to get to me. These guys are strong and can take care of themselves, but I also doubt they've come across anyone like him before.

He's not a simple drug dealer or a thief or a human trafficker that has his eye on something logical like money or power.

He's a stone-cold killer, and he is fixated on destroying everything and everyone I care about before ending my life in a torturous grand finale. He can't be reasoned with, because there's nothing else he wants. There's no logic with him, just a deadly obsession.

If... when... he finds out that I'm here, all four of these men are going to be added to the list of people he'll use to get to me.

Brick grins and his eyes glimmer with cruel excitement. "Even better. I have a feeling he's going to be spending some time in my basement soon. I can't wait!"

"Are you planning on making me stay in my room again while I'm here? I know I was only meant to be out for a while, but I also didn't anticipate this being an ongoing situation." I raise an eyebrow. I have no desire to be locked in there all day, every day.

"No, you're one of us now," says Aidan. "You'll be free for the most part."

Slade chokes and starts to cough. It seems this part of the decision has taken him by surprise. "She's not one of us," he mutters under his breath, "and she never will be."

Aidan glares at him but doesn't speak further.

This is a lot of information to process. A moment ago these guys were my kidnappers, and I was their captive. Technically still I am. But now they're wanting to keep me here on a longer-term basis, with more freedom.

I don't have many options, really, when I think about it. No family or friends here. Nobody I really know.

Except for a psycho who's trying to hunt me down and kill me and doing one hell of a good job of the first part.

I'm clearly not going to show up on his doorstep, wherever that is, asking for a place to stay.

"Why are you being so kind to me?" I glance around the room, making eye contact with each of them one by one.

Slade looks away.

"Most of you, at least," I add.

"Listen, it's my fault you're here in the first place," says Roman. He looks at the ground as if he's ashamed to have put me in the worst situation of my life.

A weird thought occurs to me, and I snort involuntarily.

My snort is followed by a laugh that starts small but quickly builds into an uncontrollable belly laugh.

My entire body shakes as I cackle, my abs shrieking at me as my stomach clenches into itself with my unabashed laughter. This probably makes me seem like an absolute lunatic, but I just can't stop.

The guys all peer at me as if I've lost my mind.

"What?" asks Roman, squinting at me. "What's going on with you? Did we do some damage when we hit you in the head?"

That only serves to make me laugh even more.

"Jesus, we've permanently damaged her," Slade shakes his head.

I take giant gulps of air and put my hand on my chest in an effort to calm myself. Finally, my hysterics peter out to a giggle and I regain my composure.

"It's just that..." I resist the urge to start laughing again, pressing my lips together firmly to keep it all in, "ironically, I think you might have just saved my life, all four of you. Especially you, Roman. Fuck me, what a twist!"

"How so?" Roman arches an eyebrow.

"Well where do you think I would have been when... *he*... came after me if you hadn't brought me here?" I put my hands up in an exaggerated shrug.

The guys glance at each other, realization dawning in their eyes.

"Exactly. Either at work or at home. Two of the only places you'll ever find me. And there would have been a near one hundred percent chance I'd have been by myself."

I pause and nod at them.

"Yep, that's right. I can see you're getting it. He went to the only places I really go. In which case, I would almost certainly not be alive anymore. By committing a murder in front of my face, causing you to kidnap me... Roman, you saved my life!"

Roman's eyes grow large, and then he narrows them and smirks. "So... what you're saying, Angel... is that you owe me, big time?" He winks at me and grins. "Sounds like it might be time to pay up."

Without thinking, I jump up and race over to him, and plant a giant kiss straight on his lips.

He pulls me closer to him and kisses me back, hard, and I know my lips are going to bruise. But I don't care and in fact I kind of like it.

I close my eyes and tilt my head back and run one of my hands through his hair as our lips stay connected. He grabs me with one hand by the back of my neck, controlling the angle of my head, tilting it up to meet his.

The kiss turns passionate, and I moan softly as his tongue swipes through my lips and entangles itself with my own. We wrestle, each of our tongues trying to gain control.

I feel a throb beginning in my core as he deepens the kiss, pushing his tongue further inside my mouth. I respond by sucking on his tongue with mine.

He groans, cupping my ass with the hand that's not holding my neck, and grinds his body against me, his erection poking me in the stomach.

My pussy is throbbing intensely now, wet heat forming inside me.

I really wouldn't be alive right now if it wasn't for him. For these guys. The thought is exhilarating, my body electric at the realization.

"Get a fucking room, guys," snarls Slade, wrenching me out of my little mental bubble that only contains kisses with Roman. Out of the corner of my eye I can see he's glaring at us, but he doesn't look away.

I keep kissing Roman and close my eyes again to block Slade out. To block everything else out except for Roman's lips and his tongue and his hands. My mind flashes back to watching him and his date fucking, but, in my imagination, it's me he's sinking his cock into. I much prefer it this way.

"You know what?" asks Roman, not expecting nor wanting an answer. "Maybe we will get a room."

He grabs my hand and intertwines my fingers with his. "We'll see you later, folks," he grins. "I have a damsel in distress to take care of. She owes me big time!"

I giggle as he pulls me towards the stairs and we bound up them together, racing toward his room as the others look on. I glance behind me and Slade is still scowling as he watches us leave.

Brick has a funny grin on his face, and although I'm far away now, I swear I see a bulge in his pants.

And Aidan looks conflicted, but doesn't say anything. He just watches us leave.

Oh well, not my problem. Roman just saved my life. It might be in one of the weirdest ways I could possibly think of, but it still counts.

And I intend to show him just how grateful I am.

Chapter Twenty-Seven

Roman

Well, that's one way of thinking about what transpired over the past few days. I'm a murderer and a kidnapper, and now I can add a goddamn superhero to my list.

I saved Angel's life.

Sure, it was unintended and entirely coincidental, but she seems keen on thanking me for my efforts, so who am I to stand in her way?

I knew this day would come when I could be with her, and that it wouldn't be far off. It's just a little sooner than I expected.

She's an amazing kisser. The way she ran her fingers through my hair, her tongue wrestling with mine, was so fucking sexy. I could feel the heat emanating from her body.

And when she sucked on my tongue with her own... Jesus. She clearly knows what to do with that thing. I can't wait to feel it wrapped around my cock.

By the time Slade yelled at us to get a room, I was rock hard, and I didn't need any encouragement to grab her hand and bound up the stairs towards my bedroom.

She seems giddy, laughing and smiling at me, but I also recognize the lust in her eyes. I guess it's that 'saved by a superhero' afterglow that you see in action movies, where the hero saves the damsel in distress and she wants to give her body over to him immediately. Again, unexpected, but I'll take it.

This gorgeous woman is about to be mine, and I know all the guys are jealous, even Slade.

I open my bedroom door and tug her inside, not bothering to close it. I pull her to the bed and have her sit down next to me, and I turn to face her.

Our lips meet again, our kiss is more frantic this time.

I pull away, grabbing her ponytail and using it to yank her neck to the side so I can trail little butterfly kisses down her neck and over her throat.

I nip playfully at the side of her neck and she moans huskily, which only serves to make me even harder.

Using my other hand to cup her breast, I can feel through her thin top that her nipple is rock hard. Through the fabric, I roll it between my thumb and finger and she groans.

"Oh my god, Roman," she gasps, her breath struggling to keep up with the intensity of our kiss and my hands on her body.

I urgently need her breasts in my mouth, so I roughly yank her tank top down so it cups her tits from below. They're gorgeous, full orbs with rock-hard rosy nipples pointing at me, urging me to do bad things to them.

"Fuck, you have beautiful tits," I rasp, my breath coming heavy and hard.

Her body language suddenly changes, and she stills, her eyes meeting mine. The dark lust in her eyes has been replaced by something else. Her mouth is tight and her body looks tense.

"Do you really want to be doing this? Are you sure you don't want to just go on another date and bring them back here?" Her chin trembles slightly as she juts it out, perhaps a combination of anger and hurt. She bites her lip, but not in a seductive way. It's like she's clamping down on it with her teeth so that her eyes stop watering.

I dip my head and twirl my tongue around her nipple and she shudders, her jealous eyes clouding with lust. "Why? Are you jealous, Angel?"

"No, I've seen you fuck," she snaps. "I'm the opposite of jealous. I'm relieved." She frowns, but her voice is soft.

"Come on, now. You could see that I know what I'm doing." I try to tease her, gently.

"It seems like that performance was more for my benefit than yours."

"Maybe it was," I say, tugging her nipple gently with my teeth, causing her mouth to open in a quiet moan. "Maybe it was entirely for you. Did you enjoy it?"

Her face flushes, and she looks away.

Chapter Twenty-Eight

Angel

"You did. You enjoyed watching my cock slamming in and out of her, making her moan, didn't you? You enjoyed watching me make her come apart while you touched yourself, while Aidan worked you over with his fingers. While my eyes were on you."

My flush intensifies. My pussy is throbbing intensely from what his tongue has been doing to my nipple.

"It was only ever about you, Angel," he says softly.

He stands up, takes my hand and kisses it, and then guides me over to the full-length mirror at the end of the bed.

He stands behind me and I look down at the ground, but he grabs my chin and tilts my head so that I'm forced to look at myself.

I normally hate looking at myself in the mirror and try to avoid it for the most part, but seeing he's forcing me to look, I check out my reflection. My skin is a little flushed and I'm glowing.

"Look at you," he says, holding my chin in place. "You're beautiful," he whispers.

I cast my eyes down, avoiding my reflection again, looking anywhere but at the face that follows me everywhere I go.

"No, I'm serious. Don't look away. Look at yourself." He tilts my jaw up further. I sigh, shift uncomfortably, and then finally look in the mirror again. Properly this time.

My reflection stares back at me. I look okay, I guess. Maybe a little tired after waiting up for hours to monitor Roman and his date.

"You're fucking gorgeous. None of us can keep our hands off you. That woman I brought home was hot, but so what, big deal. There are lots of hot women around here. They're a dime a dozen, especially when the other guys and I look the way we do. Not to mention how women cream themselves when they realize we have power on this island, that we own bars and clubs and have a place in Tane's ranks. Their panties basically fall off when we walk past," he shrugs. He's a cocky asshole, but I have a feeling he's not exaggerating. "But you, Angel, are out of this fucking world. Off the planet. Exquisite. Nobody can hold a torch to you."

I don't know how to take his words. He's definitely a smooth talker, but as he holds my head in place, forcing me to see myself the way he sees me, his eyes remain locked on mine.

This doesn't seem like a line to get into my pants. I think he's pretty clear that I want him there, and he's the one playing hard-to-get for whatever reason. He could have just fucked me the moment we got into this room, but instead, he's taking the time to really make me look at myself, to make me understand how he and the others see me.

My body quivers as he keeps his eyes trained on mine, and, standing behind me, he lowers his hand inside my shorts until they rest on top of my thin sliver of underwear.

"I don't know why you bother wearing these around here, Angel," he growls in my ear. "There's really no point. You should just walk around naked all the time. None of us would complain."

My pussy clenches at the thought of never wearing any clothing in this house. Of wandering around stark naked, so that the guys have easy access to my breasts and everywhere else to touch and caress and pleasure at any moment.

"We'd need to put towels down everywhere. The four of you turn me into a perpetual puddle," I rasp, my voice husky at the visions of debauchery that play out in my mind.

He growls and sucks my earlobe into his mouth and drags his teeth over it, his cool breath making little goosebumps form on my neck.

He moves his hand up slightly and then slips it beneath my panties, touching my bare mound with his strong fingers and letting it rest there as we both watch in the reflection of the mirror.

"You're right, your pussy is soaking because you're so turned on. Do you like the way my fingers feel on your pussy, Angel? Are you craving more?"

I nod. It's as if he reads my mind. My pussy throbs at how close he is to touching me in my most sensitive places. I yearn for him, but he momentarily keeps his hand still.

"I enjoy having you around, Angel," he says, his voice husky.

I moan as he trails his fingers down over my clit and down over my slit, watching his fingers in the reflection as if he's touching someone else. But it's me this time. It's where he's meant to be.

"I can't stop thinking about how good you must taste. I'm constantly hard thinking about it. I dream about tasting your sweet cunt and letting it drip all over my face."

I grind back against him, feeling his hardness pressing into me. "Why don't you do something about that, then?" I ask, my eyes not leaving his. "Or why don't you let me take care of this?" I ask, reaching back and rubbing his rock-hard shaft.

"In good time, Angel," he rasps in my ear. "I'm going to dictate our pace. Be patient."

My breath grows ragged as he begins to stroke me, his fingers languidly caressing my slit and occasionally causing shock waves as they feather across my clit.

He removes his other hand from my jaw and moves it to the back of my head, where he pulls my hair back in a ponytail and wraps it around his fist, exposing one side of my neck.

He kisses and nips at the curve of my neck and my shoulder, and I cry out as his teeth drag along my skin.

"Why don't you want to fuck me, Roman? I can't stop thinking about what your cock will feel like buried deep in my pussy."

I've never had to beg a man before, but Roman seems to be playing hard to get with his cock, despite being generous with his mouth and his hand.

His eyes remain locked on mine, and I tilt my head back, gasping for air as he continues to massage my clit with his fingers.

He looks at my exposed throat in the mirror again, then dips his head. I moan as I feel his mouth suctioning onto the skin on my neck. He's marking me, showing the world I belong to him.

"Roman," I moan as he collects more arousal from my entrance with his finger and swirls it around my clit.

Without a word, he pulls me away from the mirror and leads me to the bed.

Chapter Twenty-Nine

Roman

I continue my trail of kisses down her chest and onto one of her breasts, where I circle her nipple with my tongue, resuming where we left off before I guided her over to the mirror.

It was worth the pause. She needs to know how I see her, how we all see her. How much she means to us, and how she's so different from any other woman we've ever met.

It was a struggle to get her to look at herself, really see herself, but she seemed to enjoy watching my fingers working her over in the reflection.

She moans hungrily as I suck her nipple into my mouth, dragging my teeth gently along her delicate skin. Her nipple is rock hard and pebbled, and I let my tongue swirl around its perimeter, savoring the textured feeling on my tongue.

She digs her fingers into my back and arches her own so that her breasts press up toward me, showing me she wants more.

I suck harder and then apply more force with my teeth and she cries out, her nails digging harder into my back.

I groan, my cock throbbing with desire.

The effect this woman has on my body is electric. There are so many things I want to do to her it's making me crazy.

This is only the beginning.

I think about paying equal attention to her other nipple, but I'm hungry for her pussy and I'm ready to feast.

I look up at her for a moment and almost come in my pants at the look on her face. Her mouth is open slightly, her breath fast and audible. She's flushed with a light sheen on her skin as she gazes at me. I can tell she's wondering if I'm going to bury my cock in her today.

She's fucking phenomenal, and this is just the surface.

I pull her down the bed so her hips are right at the edge. I unbutton her shorts and slide them off as she watches me. Removing her panties, I spread her thighs apart and kneel in front of her pussy.

"Fuck, you're gorgeous," I say, marveling at her slick, pink folds. "And you're so fucking wet. Does it get you off when I save your life, baby?"

"Mmm, yes. Saving my life is hot," she says back, dreamily. "You're my superhero."

I kiss her on her pussy. "Good, me too. Protecting you makes me hungry as well."

She smiles, her eyes dark with desire, and I dip my head, licking and sucking and gliding my tongue up and down her slit like I haven't eaten in days.

"Fuck!" I gasp. "How do you taste so good?" I definitely haven't had anything nearly this sweet.

She gasps as I gently lap at her clit and then lick my way down to her entrance. I plunge my tongue inside, savoring her sweetness. She's sopping with arousal and I want to taste every last drop.

I feel her body shiver with pleasure as I drag my tongue back up her slit and circle her clit. I merge my own saliva with her wet heat, flattening my tongue against her clit and making a sticky mess that smears all over my mouth and between her thighs.

She's fucking delicious, and the messier the better. I'll never wash my face again. She tastes so fucking good.

I want her all over me. I could eat her out every day, and I'd still never be satisfied. It would never be enough.

"Mmm," she moans. "I thought *I* was supposed to be thanking *you*."

"Oh, believe me, you are. I was hungry, and this is just what I was craving. Tasting your dripping cunt is exactly what I want right now."

She moans, and I make eye contact with her as I continue to feast on her pussy, tilting her hips so that she can see my tongue lapping at her like a starved man.

I increase the pace of my licks, and she gasps, her hips bucking forcefully.

I can tell that she's getting close as she wraps her legs around my head, grabbing my hair in her fists and pulling my face closer into her cunt. I groan, enjoying the feeling of my face being mashed against her wetness as I continue to suck on her swollen bud.

Her thighs tremble, and then I feel her whole body tense. Her back arches and she cries out, her hips wildly thrashing against my face. Her fingers grab fistfuls of my hair, almost ripping out handfuls, and I couldn't care less. I would go bald voluntarily. I'd lose all my hair to worship this pussy every day for the rest of my life.

Jesus, one taste of this woman and my priorities have flipped on their head. Slade was right. She's dangerous.

I groan as she cries out, her voice husky with pleasure, and I continue to lick and suck at her clit. She's not getting away from my mouth just because she came apart once under my tongue. I have more I want to give her.

She squirms underneath me and pulls my hair tighter as I continue to lash her with my tongue. I feel a few hairs come loose as she wrenches them from the root while she bucks and writhes against my face, but I don't let her go.

The air in the room hangs thick with her arousal, and I can't get enough.

I continue to feast on her, to devour her core. Her body tenses back up as I bite down on her clit and she comes again, arousal dripping and smearing all over my face as she arches her back and writhes against me once more.

"Oh my fucking god, Roman!" she screams, panting, gasping for air. Her cries are loud, and I am enjoying every moment of this.

It only adds to it that the other guys probably can't avoid hearing it if they tried. They might even be watching through the door that I intentionally left ajar, but I don't look up to check. I'm too focused on her, on bringing her pleasure.

If I hadn't technically saved her, she wouldn't be here for me to treat like this. I don't want to think about what could have happened if I hadn't taken her from the salon. But I force the dark thoughts out of my mind for now. She's here right now, and that's what matters.

I continue licking and sucking on her engorged clit, and she cries out as I make her come again, shuddering against my face.

As her orgasm subsides, she collapses across the bed. Her legs stay spread apart as she lays there panting, spent. I look up at her and lick my lips as I regain my own breath, well aware the lower half of my face is completely covered in her arousal. Her own thighs are slick with my saliva and her own wetness, and they glisten in the near-darkness of my room, illuminated only by my alarm clock and the dim light from further down the hallway.

My cock is rock hard, and I'd love nothing more than to bury it deep inside her sweet, soaking cunt. I imagine that's what she's expecting, the way she's lying there, looking at me, begging me with her eyes to fill her up.

But I just can't right now. It doesn't feel like the right time.

So instead, I stand up and walk out of the room without bothering to wipe my face, leaving her lying on my bed, probably wondering what the fuck just happened. I don't look back as I leave and head downstairs, my cock growing soft as I descend into the kitchen area.

Aidan and Slade are sitting at the dining table with their laptops out. They both stop what they're doing and glance at me, Slade glaring as usual and Aidan with that same conflicted expression on his face.

Brick is nowhere to be seen, which leads me to believe he might have been watching from the hallway and headed off in the other direction when we were done. Just a feeling. The dirty perv is probably jerking off in his shower right now. Not that I can blame him. Not that I won't be doing the same thing later when I replay the film reel in my head.

"Wash your fucking face," growls Slade, eyeing the mess smeared across my mouth and chin. "You're a fucking disgrace."

I grin back at him. "You're just jealous. Want me to wipe some on you?"

He narrows his eyes at me. "She shouldn't be here. She's a distraction."

Aidan furrows his brow and runs his hand through his hair. "Yeah, Roman. You're reinforcing Slade's concerns right now. Don't make me regret my decision. Go clean yourself up, you dirty fuck."

"Jesus, I just had a bit of fun with her." I put my hands up in mock defense. "You heard her. I saved her life, and she wanted to thank me. That's all it was. You know that's how I operate. I love fucking women, and pussy means nothing to me. That's all she is, and I'd never let pussy get in the way of our business."

Everything I just said is usually factual. I don't attach feelings to women. They're just a means to an end, a way to achieve the pleasure that I'm constantly craving. It should be no different with Angel, and I didn't intend for it to be.

But as the words come out of my mouth, I realize I'm not so sure that's the case this time.

Chapter Thirty

Angel

My body is feeling pleasantly relaxed from multiple orgasms delivered by Roman's mouth and tongue, but my mind is a little confused by our encounter.

I was sure he was going to be selfish, to just stick his cock in me and make me reward him for saving my life by letting him fuck me, but it was quite the opposite.

He was all about pleasing me, worshipping me. I've never had my pussy eaten the way he feasted upon it, as if he was starving and the only thing he wanted to devour was me.

And then he didn't even try to fuck me. In some ways, I want to say I'm disappointed, because my body was and is still craving him inside me, definitely his cock or at least his fingers. But his tongue was so talented that it would be rude to say. I was most definitely satisfied without needing those things. He didn't even need to add anything beyond his tongue to make me orgasm multiple times.

While I still want to feel his cock buried deep inside me, I feel good, sated.

But my feelings of satiety are being overridden by invading thoughts. Less pleasurable ones. There's too much on my mind. I'm worried about the guys inviting me to stay. It's a complex invitation and there's a lot to process.

They just murdered someone, and then someone tried to murder me and would have if the guys hadn't kidnapped me.

There are a lot of layers in this situation. A lot of volatility and uncontrollable variables.

If my crazy stalker hadn't gone and ransacked my salon and my apartment while attempting to find and slaughter me, what would these guys have done to me?

Because I strongly doubt they'd have said 'hey, just stay here and be our roommate because we've decided you're handy to have around.'

And what might they still do? I really don't know them all that well. It's only been a few days and the circumstances have hardly been normal.

I wonder if what happened between Roman and me, and before that Aidan and me, will change the dynamics in the house. What if the other guys don't like it, and want me gone? I'm pretty sure Slade already does. He's even told me as much. He already sees me as a threat. He hates me.

It's not like I have any other options other than trying my luck on the street. I don't think I'd last long out there, though, especially with *him* looking for me.

The thing is, I don't want to get my hopes up by staying here, thinking they really want me to be here for me. Because they could be doing this out of guilt, and from my experience, guilt wears off quickly.

They might change their mind and put me out on the street without any notice and then I'll be back to square one. Below square one, because at least I had a business and a home before, as modest as they may have been.

I can't go back to the salon and I can't go back to the apartment, that much is clear.

If I had to guess how comfortable they all are with the decision to invite me to stay, I think it's variable. I know for sure that Slade doesn't want me to be here. He's made that abundantly clear.

And it feels like Aidan is maybe on the fence, but for whatever reason is okay with it for right now.

Roman seems to want me around for sex... kind of, not that he'll actually fuck me, but who knows how long that will last?

And Brick is probably fine either way. He's a wildcard, and he doesn't seem to view life and death in the same way as anyone else I know.

I guess, for now, I'll stay and see what happens. It's the greatest shot I have at remaining alive at the moment, even though it's not guaranteed to last.

God knows Slade would off me in a second given the chance, and Brick is crazy enough that he just might help him.

Aidan might decide I'm too much of a risk to keep around.

For now, at least two, let's say two-point-five of them want me to stay.

But that means I'm going to have to let them help me, and I don't like that one bit.

Regardless of the quality of my accommodations, there's a killer on the loose. And he won't back off just because the thread count on my sheets has improved.

He's relentless, and he will stop at nothing until he gets what he wants.

Until he destroys me.

Chapter Thirty-One

Angel

The guys want to help take my mind off things, so we get up early and head out to one of their favorite breaks for a sunrise surf.

Even though it involves leaving the house for a bit, it feels like a safe option, and it's refreshing to be able to go outside.

There were no clues left at the salon that would tie me back to these guys. Roman was a walk-in, and The Asshole's body was long gone by the time Psycho McGee raided the place. Just a puddle of blood, and even though he's resourceful, there's no way he could have analyzed the guy's blood and tracked it back to us.

I know that sounds wacky, but he's incredibly resourceful and it's something he might try. At this point, I wouldn't put anything past him.

He's capable of anything, no matter how insane it sounds. Because he is fucking insane, the way no textbook could do justice.

There's no trace of the guys at my apartment, either. Brick's the only one who spent any time there prior to it being ransacked, and according to him, all he did was gather my stuff and shove it in a duffel bag. I have no doubt he rifled through my underwear drawer and sniffed my panties—and I know he kept at least one pair—but I doubt he would have left anything behind to link me to him.

Thankfully, this puts the lunatic on the back foot. He's tracked me to this island, but my apartment and salon are relatively far away from here. There's no logical connection between me and these guys, and no chance meeting or interaction online that he could stumble across. I haven't even had access to my phone since I've known them.

He's going to find me, and from how he's behaving I think it will be soon, but today I get to take a moment for myself.

A moment to back off from the coiled rubber band that feels like it's wrapped around my throat and my body at all times.

A moment to breathe.

The waves are mild, even though I know the guys could handle something way more intense. Growing up on the coastal mainland, the guys are used to volatile water, but they've decided to take me somewhere much calmer. And I need calm right now.

I have a feeling they brought me here so that I can join in and surf while they keep watch over me. Although I surf a few times a week, it's generally in gentle waves like this. There's a peace that comes with it, sitting atop these gentle rolling waves and letting you take them into shore. It's part of the reason I chose this island as my refuge.

They made it clear they didn't want me sitting on the beach by myself while they were out on the water. They didn't want me to be 'easy pickings', as Brick had put it, which sent a shiver up my spine as he said the words.

The thought of sitting on the sand, enjoying watching them surf, and suddenly being abducted by the lunatic, is the stuff of nightmares. I'm sure it will encroach on my dreams tonight or another night.

But, for now, I get to have a precious instant, a moment where I can forget the fear and darkness that I have learned I'll never escape.

Being around the ocean is therapeutic for me. When I'm in the water or coasting in on a wave, in those moments, I truly feel free. Like *he* can't get me. Like it's just me and the forces of nature propelling me.

I'm at the ocean's mercy, and it respects me as long as I respect it. If the ocean decided to take me under, it could, and I would be okay with it because it wouldn't be somebody else's decision.

Plus, it's something I get to enjoy alone, which is my preference for just about everything. The fewer people around you, the fewer people you let into your life, the less chance anybody will let you down.

It's different being out here with the guys than when I'm around my loose group of acquaintances, generally just paddling around by myself. I feel odd being part of a group activity where we're engaged in what everyone is doing, where I'm a member of this gang.

Lone wolves get all awkward when they're suddenly brought into a pack.

The guys show off a little while I'm out in the water with them. I dangle my legs over the side of my board a lot of the time, just sitting there and watching them having fun.

But they also help to coach me and they clap and cheer loudly each time I catch a decent wave. Even when I wipe out spectacularly, they cheer me on to catch the next one.

The whole outing is fun and light. It frees my mind in the moments that demand my complete concentration, as well as the moments where I find my head empty, just floating on my board and hearing the water softly slap against it. It tests my body, my focus and my balance, and it also lets me relax in a way that I generally find very hard to do. It's just what I need.

When I get back to shore, I lift my board above me and rest it on top of my head, the way I prefer to carry it. My arms are too short to carry it underneath my armpit the way some people can.

As I walk inland, a voice calls out to me from the ocean and I turn around to look.

It's Aidan, also heading in, asking me to wait for them before I get too far away from the shoreline. I nod, the board bobbing above me, and turn back around toward the carpark area.

As I turn, the board making a wide rotation with me, I almost crash into someone heading in my direction. They're also carrying their board on top of their head, and the long slabs of fiberglass and epoxy almost smack into each other at above-head height. I reel back, dodging at the last moment, barely avoiding a collision. That wouldn't have been good.

"Watch it, bitch!" the other person hisses at me.

I take a closer look at them. It's another female, wearing bikini bottoms and a rash guard. She has cascading red hair with pink streaks, and she'd be very pretty if she wasn't narrowing her eyes and curling her lip at me in a snarl.

"Watch where the fuck you're going!" she growls, her eyes blazing.

I glare at her. "I turned around for one second because someone was calling out to me. You watch where the fuck you're going, *bitch*! Loving the female empowerment around here." I roll my eyes.

She glares at me and darts around my board and heads into the ocean, lowering her board into the water. My eyes follow her as she paddles, heading out to meet a group of guys waving at her from another nearby break.

I frown. Not because I can't handle a rude bitch, but because it's remotely unsettling when I feel like I do something wrong when it comes to surfing etiquette. It's intimidating, the surf culture, even though I'm also fascinated by it.

I don't know how I could have avoided that situation, and a flush creeps up my cheeks as I realize my guys, and maybe hers, all saw the interaction just now.

I probably look like an awkward idiot, almost crashing into someone more experienced than me with my board. They're probably all laughing at me out there. I feel frazzled, the buzz of my time in the water already starting to dissipate.

Again, I don't normally care what people think of me, but surfing gets me out of my comfort zone in the best and worst ways.

As I stand and worry about losing all credibility in the ocean, the four Brixtons emerge from the water. Aidan and Slade each carry their boards under an arm, and Brick and Roman carry theirs on top of their heads like me.

Both methods give me a nice view of their strong biceps and rippling abs, and the rising sun bathes each of them in a golden glow, as if they're gods and heaven is shining beams of light across their gorgeous bodies.

They're all magnificent. My pussy clenches as I think about the things I would do to all four of these men, and that I'd let them do to me. And the things that some of us have already done.

I'm kind of surprised that Roman would risk ruining his hair, resting the board on his head like that, but then I think back to how hard I pulled it on the bed while his tongue pierced my opening. Maybe he lets his hair standards slide when it comes to doing things he loves. Like surfing and feasting on pussy. Who knows?

"You okay?" asks Aidan, concern in his voice. "What happened back there?" He gestures towards the woman.

"Just a rude bitch," I shrug. "Nothing I can't handle."

"What did she say to you? It looked like you were arguing?"

"It's my fault, I guess. Turned around and almost smacked her board with mine. I'm mortified, honestly. But like I said, it's fine."

"Nah, I saw her coming straight for you at speed," says Slade. He rarely speaks, and he's never said a kind word toward me, so it's interesting he's decided to defend me now. "I wouldn't worry about anything she has to say, anyway."

"Wait, you know her? Who is she?" I'm suddenly curious. I know the island is small and everything, but this person has done enough for Slade to have an opinion that he's prepared to voice. Fascinating.

"She's with some guys we know," explains Aidan, running a hand through his hair. "Rivals, you might say. They're out there somewhere," he says, gesturing at the water behind him but not wasting effort to look in their direction.

"*With* them? Like in a gang?"

"Kind of," says Roman. "Although I believe she's also intimately acquainted with more than one of them, from what we've heard."

"They're like a bunch of Peter Pans," scoffs Slade. "They're all in their forties, but act like they just got out of high school, always joking around, even when things get serious. Calling each other bro this, bro that. Wearing tank tops and shorts like they're ten years old. There's something wacky about growing up on the island. All the sunshine and sea salt have got them thinking they're ageless. Peter fucking Pan losers."

I look out at the ocean and see her having what appears to be a fun time with the four guys she joined out at the break. They seem to be having a similar experience to us, the guys all showing off and having fun, her watching and joining in now and then.

One of them slowly surfs past her on a long, rolling wave, sits on his board and kisses her on his way by. She leans in, returning his kiss as he makes his way past.

"Well, what do you know? Good for her," I say. I can't help it. It just comes out.

She might be a rude bitch but she's doing something right if she's got four guys like that. I can't see them up close but I don't need to in order to know they're all hot and incredibly in shape. "I didn't think something like that was possible. Truly good for her."

All four Brixtons glance at each other.

Brick wiggles his eyebrows.

Roman grins.

Aidan's expression is hard to pin down, but again I get the sense he's conflicted.

Slade scowls at me, his defense of me clearly only a passing reprieve.

I can't read their expressions, but it's like they're doing the silent communication thing again. God, they're frustrating. Grown men with their own secret non-verbal language, like they're psycho quadruplets.

"What?" I peer at them. "What's going on? Did I miss something?"

"Nothing," says Aidan, running a hand through his hair. He sighs. "Let's get back to the house. We have stuff to do. And we have something waiting for you at home."

As soon as we walk in the front door, my senses are assaulted by the overpowering fragrance of flowers. Walking into the kitchen, I see four enormous bouquets, each standing in an ornate vase, all in a row. They're artfully displayed, as if an actual florist spent hours tweaking every petal, every leaf, to the perfect angle to showcase the blooms.

"Oh my god. What are these? Is someone getting married?"

Aidan smirks. "These are to make you feel more comfortable, to make sure you know we want you to be here."

"Even you?" I narrow my eyes at Slade. "You got me one of these?"

"Don't push me," he growls, but his eyes are more gentle than usual.

"This is a lot of flowers," I say, walking closer to them. I lean in and sniff the first bouquet, and it smells heavenly. I close my eyes as I inhale the heady scent.

"We tried to get you one large one, but we couldn't agree on what best represented you," shrugs Roman. "We all have something we wanted to convey."

"Ha! I've barely received flowers from anyone, and when I did, I'm pretty sure they just grabbed the most basic offering from a nearby gas station. The whole nearly-dead roses in a plastic wrapping type of situation. Definitely not trying to convey anything except a desire to get into my pants. But this is... wow."

"Can you guess who got you which one?" grins Brick.

I look at the first bouquet and step closer to inspect it in more detail. It's colorful and elegant, a very full bouquet composed of a variety of flowers, including some bright yellow blooms that I recognize as carnations.

"Tell me more about the yellow carnations."

"Well, they're happy flowers, representing positive thinking. I thought they might help you get through this situation with the piece of shit that's stalking you."

"They also represent rejection, Roman," says Brick, his encyclopedic knowledge evidently extending from blood to floral symbolism.

"That seems accurate if these are from Roman," I say, with a hollow laugh. I swear, if that man doesn't let me sit on his cock soon, I'm going to explode.

"You called it, but not because of that," he huffs. "I had no idea they had that meaning. They just looked cheerful, and I wanted to make you smile given what you're going through."

"Sometimes it's the hidden meaning that means the most," I shrug, "but I'll take them at face value, I suppose. They're very pretty."

There's some fluffy greenery surrounding the blooms, which I recognize as fennel. "Is that in case I get hungry?" I grin at Roman.

"It's meant to represent flattery. I had to weave in my charming personality," he grins back, and I laugh. "Plus, it's not hard to flatter you. There are so many nice things to say." He grins at me.

I move to the second bouquet. It's quirky with a bunch of unique flowers I've never seen before, so I automatically assume it's from Brick.

"These are from you, I take it?" I ask, pointing at the bouquet.

Brick feigns surprise. "How did you know?"

"Maybe the skulls all over the vase gave it away, as well as whatever this sharp thing is sticking out the top looking like a torture implement," I laugh, and the others join me.

"They're not just any flowers, though," he says, proudly. "Want to know more about why I chose them?"

"Sure," I say, grinning. "Hit me."

"Well, obviously I have some black roses in there because they represent death and darkness, but they're also beautiful, like you. So that seemed appropriate, especially seeing you're my little Valkyrie. And then we have some chrysanthemums. They're meant to bring bad luck and nightmares."

"Gee, thanks," I say, and I can't help but laugh.

"No, you don't understand," says Brick, shaking his head. "My theory is, if you have these on your own terms, you get to control things. I know you have nightmares. Even when you're awake, sometimes, you'll go somewhere. I don't think you hear yourself scream, but I have. I want to put the control back in your hands."

"That's... quite sweet and thoughtful of you, Brick," I say cautiously.

He beams. "But wait, there's more! These ones," he says, pointing at an unusual flower with gray leaves and yellow petals that are almost sickly in tone but in a beautiful way, "are asphodels. They also symbolize death."

"Jesus, Brick. Should I be worried? Is this a death bouquet?"

"Death's coming for all of us, Angel," he says. "You may as well embrace it, learn to soak it all in. I mainly got these because they look cool, but when you give them to someone, it's meant to mean your regrets will follow them into the grave. I figured they were fine because I don't have any regrets, so nothing will follow you in when you die."

"Jesus, Brick!" Slade can't hold his opinions in any longer.

"Fucking weirdo," Roman snorts at Brick, and I do the same.

"Then we have some bird's-foot trefoil," he says, pointing at some bright yellow blooms with flecks of orange. "These symbolize revenge and actually contain trace amounts of cyanide."

"Wow, you're really going for the death and revenge theme here," I laugh. "They're really pretty, though. I'll just make sure I don't accidentally steep them and turn them into tea."

"Would you expect anything less from me?" Brick grins and wiggles his eyebrows. I get the sense he had a lot of fun picking these out.

I move to the third bouquet. It's simple, with tiny and brilliant orange flowers that look like little clusters of flames. I've never seen these flowers before, but they're simple and captivating. Something about their depth and fury reminds me of Slade. "I'm guessing these are from you, but I don't know why I think that," I say, glancing at him.

I'm skeptical that he got me something so pretty, and that he didn't just wrap some garbage up in plastic and hand it to me instead.

He nods. "You got me."

"What are these flowers?" I ask, pointing to the flame-like clusters. "They're gorgeous."

"You might not think so when you know the meaning behind them," he says, smirking at me, his eyes developing a tinge of the cruel glimmer I've become accustomed to.

"Try me," I say, narrowing my eyes at him. Only Slade could buy me flowers to offend me. I'm ready for anything.

"They're butterfly weeds."

"Oh okay, got it. You got me weeds instead of flowers. That tracks," I say, rolling my eyes. "They're still gorgeous, so I don't care. Did you really think I'm that easily offended? Do you really think my sensibilities are so delicate?"

"Ha, you don't get it," Slade sneers. "They represent solitude and the rejection of others. When you give them to someone, you're essentially telling them you want them to *leave*. Get it? I want you to leave. To go away."

Even though it's coming from Slade, and therefore I should have expected it, his cruel words feel like a slap in the face. Everyone else has been so nice with this little exercise, but he's clearly determined to ruin it.

"Oh, and the other flowers in the bouquet?" he says. "They're orange lilies. They symbolize hatred and humiliation. I couldn't resist." He smirks at me, his eyes cold.

"Slade, knock it off, man," says Roman. "That was harsh."

My eyes flick to Roman. "You don't get to speak for me."

I turn back to Slade and narrow my eyes. "Fuck you, Slade," I say, my voice low and cold. I blink back tears and resist the urge to run from the room. Or at least to grab the vase and dump them in the kitchen's large trash can. He clearly got these to upset me and delighted in telling me why he chose them. I can't give him the satisfaction of knowing he won. "I'm disappointed, Slade. No black dahlias? I don't know much about flowers, but I know they represent evil and dishonesty and betrayal. I think they would have been much more appropriate coming from you. Maybe some tansies to visually represent your uncalled-for hostility against me."

Brick lets out a low whistle as if to diffuse the palpable tension in the kitchen.

Sticking my jaw out so it doesn't tremble, not waiting for a response from Slade, I move to the fourth bouquet. "Anyway," I say, sniffing. "This one must be from you, Aidan." He smiles as I glance in his direction.

It's a simple bouquet, neatly organized with only a few different flower varieties. If it wasn't the last bouquet, I still would have guessed it was from him by the way it's been methodically arranged without any extra fluff.

Like Brick, he also selected some black roses.

"To symbolize revenge, because we're going to help you exact yours on your stalker," he explains. "They're a reminder that we're here for you. We're going to protect you, Angel. We will never let anything bad happen to you as long as you're with us. And you can ignore Slade," he narrows his eyes at him, "because he doesn't represent our collective view."

We return our attention to the fourth bouquet.

"What are these?" I ask, pointing at some pretty purple flowers.

"They're clematis," nods Aidan. "They're the 'queen of the vines' and represent..." He pauses and a flush creeps across his cheeks as if he's embarrassed by what he's about to share. "They represent mental beauty. They reminded me of you."

"Oh my gosh, Aidan, that's really sweet," I say, a flush building on my face, and I can't resist getting on my tiptoes and kissing him on his cheek.

"And then there's some dill because it's meant to be powerful against evil. And some gardenia, because you're meant to give them to someone who you think is lovely."

I smile at him. Of course, he'd thought this bouquet through as carefully as he does everything else.

"Thanks so much, all of you. All of you except Slade." I narrow my eyes and glare at him. "When I met you, I never thought the five of us would be standing here while three of you share how thoughtfully you picked these out for me. I feel so spoiled," I say, smiling at them.

"Actually, I take that back. All four of you. Even you, Slade. I'm going to channel the hatred in your selections. Take it as a sign that you spend far too much time thinking about me. Even though your bouquet was very cruel, clearly you must have put a lot of thought into it."

He grimaces, eyes narrowed at me. I appear to have hit a nerve.

After dealing with my psycho stalker for years, there's one thing I'm clear on.

Whether thoughts are loving or dark, they're still thoughts, obsessions, and energy focused on someone. That energy, whether it starts from dark or light, can be transformed and channeled and used in the ways you want.

You can make of Slade's thoughts what you will, but his mind is definitely on me, whether he likes it or not. And I intend to use his energy for my benefit.

Chapter Thirty-Two

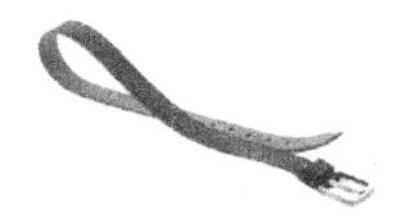

Aidan

"Hey," says Roman loudly, drawing all of our eyes to him. "Did you guys notice that a bunch of the options reminded you of those assholes that claim to protect the island?"

"Sounds like you have a crush," snorts Brick. "Did you want to get them a bouquet, too?"

Angel snorts.

"Actually, I did," Roman shrugs.

"What the fuck, man?" Slade winces at Roman. "Are you going to take them to a dinner and a movie next, and maybe buy them a box of chocolates so they'll suck your dick?"

"No, what I sent was just fine. If they know anything about flowers, the meaning will be loud and clear. It was too perfect to resist."

"What did you send them? Not poison ivy?" I ask, raising an eyebrow.

"That would be too literal," shrugs Roman. "I sent them a bouquet of aster."

"What the hell is that?" asks Slade.

"It's this purple flower, kind of matches Angel's hair," he says, glancing at Angel. "It's meant to ward off snakes, keep them away. I was sending them a message."

"Yeah, a message you want to jump their bones, you fucking idiot," sneers Slade. The rest of us laugh.

"Hey, it made sense at the time," says Roman, crossing his arms tightly over his chest. "I wanted to send them aconite because it represents hatred and would have made their skin itch and burn, but for some reason, the florist didn't carry it."

I can't tell for sure, but it looks like Roman might be flushing slightly under his tan.

This is what happens when I don't micromanage these guys. And why I always have my eye on the weird shit they come up with independently.

"What? I sent them a warning. The asters say exactly what I meant them to," says Roman defensively.

"I don't think it's the type of flower you sent them that's the issue, Roman," I say, exasperated. "It's the fact you sent our enemies a bouquet of pretty flowers and they're going to be wondering what the fuck your intentions are." I shake my head and the others laugh.

Angel seems to be particularly amused by this development, her neck tilting back to expose her throat as she cracks up at Roman's expense.

We haven't figured out what we're going to do with her yet. And we haven't dealt with the very real threat against her. But just for this moment, for this snapshot in time, she looks happy, lighter, as if her problems are far away and she's just in the moment.

I'm glad that Roman sent flowers to our enemies, even if they think he's trying to date them all. Because it made Angel laugh, and right now her happiness is the only thing I care about.

Chapter Thirty-Three

Angel

For a moment, for one precious and irreplaceable instant, I feel joy. These four guys went out of their way for me, to distract me and just give me a second to breathe.

They cared enough to plan out a surfing trip, to have bouquets deposited in the house while we were out. They'd each chosen them so carefully, even Slade, who channeled all his hatred for me into the tiny little blooms that look like flames.

It was a relief, a release to be able to laugh and howl at Roman's accidental romantic undertones toward the snakes. If only I could be a fly on the wall when the flowers arrive and they see his note. *'Standing in the flower shop, when I saw these, all I could think about was you guys.'* That's what he told us he sent them. I almost became deceased when he shared that part of the story, I was laughing so hard.

Now that the flower shenanigans are over, we've moved into the living room. Despite the tight squeeze, all four guys are on the couch with me like none of them could stand to be further away, even Slade. I'm sandwiched between Brick and Roman's large thighs and each has a hand protectively on my legs.

As Brick casually flicks through channels, finding something to watch, I stop him as an image I recognize appears on the screen.

"Wait, Brick, go back." I grab his arm. "Two channels back, I think it was."

He scrolls back twice and the screen lights up with what looks like an infomercial. Emblazoned in a banner across the bottom of the screen is 'Angel's Hair Salon'. My logo, just the way I designed it. But I've never taken out an ad, let alone a TV infomercial. I bet this cost a fortune. An uneasy feeling plants itself in the pit of my stomach and little goosebumps emerge on my arms.

"Turn it up," I direct Brick, and he adjusts the volume as a jingle begins.

"Get your sharpening on

At Angel's Salon
Do-do-do-do-do
You'll look your best
We'll peel your flesh
And stab you with a knife
We'll slit your throat from ear to ear
Your head will fall forward in the chair
You're living your best life!
I was a slutty whore back home
And nothing much has changed
But now I'm living on an island
Acting quite deranged
At Angel's... at Angel's.... Salooooooooooon."

The screen fades to black.

"What the hell did we just watch?" asks Slade. "Because, uh, that marketing is something..." His voice trails off.

"I take it that's not something you created," says Aidan.

"Jesus," says Brick, turning off the TV.

"He's a real sicko, isn't he?" says Roman. "Fucking hell. How did that get past the censors?"

"I know, right? I thought I was in a dream because it was so off the wall. My logo, a shot of my salon before it was destroyed. But you're all apparently experiencing it, too."

"Can multiple people hallucinate together?" asks Brick. "I've always wondered about group hallucinations."

"He has basically unlimited resources. I'm sure it will get yanked at some point when people complain, but for now... it's live."

"He paid money for that. It was really weird," says Slade. "Clearly sending you a message. Fucking with you. I just don't know how he knew for sure you'd be watching."

"I don't know that it would matter if she did or not," says Aidan, running his hand through his hair. "He could have narrowed down the algorithm, targeted her demographics for the primary audience, but our TV is linked to our preferences, not hers. In my view, it doesn't matter if she was one of the first to watch it or not. This ad is insane, and it's going to blow up on social media in no time. He's going to make sure her business dies and has no chance of ever being revived. This is a sick smear campaign."

"He's going to destroy the one thing I built before he kills me," I say softly. "This will never be over. Until the day he kills me."

I want to say more, but that's all I'm able to say before there's a large bang and the compound is plunged into darkness.

To be continued...

Chapter Thirty-Four

Angel

As the living room plunges into darkness, a shriek shatters the silence. The involuntary sound comes from me, and it reverberates in my ears as I glance around the darkened space to see what caused the blackout. My heart races so fast that it threatens to erupt from my sternum, and the intensity of my scream sends a shockwave through my entire body.

As all traces of light are vanquished from the sleek, modern living room, the myriad of electronic devices collectively turn off, resulting in a sudden silence. The power that typically crackles through the air ceases to exist and leaves a void of nothingness hanging thick in the atmosphere for just that moment.

Three of the guys leap to their feet. Brick is up first. His eyes flit around wildly, trying to identify the source of the blackout, his hands balled into fists as if ready to brawl with whoever is responsible.

Only Roman remains seated, and he reaches out instinctively to place his hand on my thigh in a comforting, protective gesture. He notices my leg trembling ever so slightly, and his concerned eyes flick to mine.

I glance out toward the dining room and kitchen area and the lights are all off there, too. Maybe it's the case for the entire compound. The guys are usually so in control of this space, everything managed with military precision, that it's disorienting seeing them being thrown off by this unexpected development.

Brick tilts his head as if he's looking for clues to the origin of the blackout, perhaps trying to identify any sounds that seem out of place. His eyes are intense, his ears pricked like he's a wolf poised to attack. I guess danger brings out his animalistic qualities, and I'm half-anticipating a primal snarl to erupt from his lips when he figures out the cause of the power cut.

I'm still highly agitated by the creepy advertisement that just played on the TV. It already has me jumping at the slightest movement or noise, so the instant descent into pitch-black almost did me in. Hypervigilance can be a real bitch.

I take a deep breath and repeat *relax, relax, relax*, in my head. Easier said than done when my deranged stalker might have just broken into this place after obsessing over me for decades. But I have four unapologetically powerful men on my side. Running around shrieking like a banshee while we're trying to figure out what's going on isn't going to help anyone. I'm definitely not going to be one of those ridiculous horror movie characters who runs up the stairs into a dark attic when the killer is chasing me. I'm here to fight.

The ad that we just saw was clearly targeted at me and my hair salon business. While TV marketing is meant to extend your reach and raise visibility for your brand, I for sure wouldn't have invested money into that creepy content. Clients are typically attracted to hair salons that will give them a solid cut and style, so they can be on their way looking their best. The promise of murder and gore during their bang trim isn't something that usually draws them in. Except if they're Brick, maybe.

The air hangs silently for just a moment, that brief period of inertia where power ceases to crackle across the hundreds of wires that span the living room, time seems to travel in slow motion. It makes me wonder about a simpler life without electricity, and what it feels like to live in the country without all the noise and radio waves and other stuff we're used to in cities, even on an island like this. After getting so used to the constant barrage of traffic and alarms and horn honking, the silence in the room has an eerie, deafening quality about it. None of us is used to operating in silence, with our mind as our sole narrator. It shows by the way everyone nervously fidgets while we try to work out what's going on. There's apparently a room somewhere that's so silent that it literally drives people insane in a manner of minutes. It has something to do with the horror of hearing your own heart beating and bones crunching as they grind together in everyday life, and I kind of get it.

Then, just as quickly as it disappeared, everything surges back to life, causing a brief flicker of lights and a buzzing sound as electrical components reactivate. It's like someone hit pause on the remote control and they just pressed play again. The regular crackling that tends to go unnoticed resumes, and it's almost comforting. We can once again see everything around us, and all is just the way we left it before the power went off. The living room looks normal. We look normal, except for Brick, who never does. We can all breathe again, at least for now.

"The backup generator must have kicked in already. Good to know it's working," says Aidan, running his hand through his hair, and his brow furrows as he contemplates our next move.

"But what the fuck just happened? There was a loud bang outside when the power went off. Is that lunatic trying to get into the compound?" Brick's nostrils flare and he grinds his teeth together forcefully as he storms back and forth across the width of the living room.

"I'm on it," says Roman, scrolling through his phone and frantically tapping at its screen. "I'll see if there have been any reports in the area that might be relevant."

A moment passes and Brick, impatiently hopping from one foot to another, paces all the way out of the room and down the hallway, no doubt checking every window to determine the source of the threat.

"Brick, man. Stand down!" Roman calls out after a couple of minutes as he continues to tap away at his phone. "I've found something."

Brick charges purposefully back into the living room, ready to take action on Roman's findings before he knows what they are. "What's up?" His fists clench and unclench as if he's preparing to make use of them on an unsuspecting victim.

Chapter Thirty-Five

Angel

"It looks like the power went down in the whole neighborhood," explains Roman, pointing at an update on his phone. "A truck crashed into a transformer just off the freeway. The system controls show that our alarm system is still on and secure. Our backup for that turned on immediately with the generator, and there was no downtime where the system wasn't tracking entry and exit points, so I'm confident nothing was breached."

"So it wasn't targeted at us?" Aidan asks, frowning, his gaze resting on Roman. "The timing of the creepy advert was just a coincidence?"

"Most likely," says Roman, and he shrugs. "It was a little too coincidental for my liking, but I don't think we need to get all paranoid about it."

"What about the ad, though?" Brick asks. "Even if timing really was a coincidence, that was a hell of a way to advertise Angel's salon."

He looks at me with concern and I return his gaze, pressing my lips together, not quite sure what to say. Yes, it was sure a hell of a way to advertise my salon. But we all know that garnering additional clients isn't what the ad was about. My own personal stalker just won't let up, and he'll do whatever he can to get to me, as outlandish as his efforts may seem.

"That's a whole other story," says Aidan, sighing as if he has the weight of the world on his shoulders. "Slade, why don't you try to get through to someone at the TV network? See if we can figure out who sponsored the ad."

"I think we know who paid for it, man." Slade gestures at me as if I'm the source of this entire problem, which I guess I am. "Her special friend, the mad stalker."

I glare at him from my spot on the couch, still snuggled up against Roman, who won't leave my side. I feel bad enough as it is that I've potentially put these guys on the lunatic's radar, and he doesn't need to rub it in further.

"Yeah, you know what I mean, though, man," says Aidan, running his hand through his hair again. "Any info you can find about the person who placed it. What name they're using, how they paid for the ad, their contact phone number or email address. Hell, if anyone can remember what their voice sounded like or if there was any background noise on the call, that would be helpful, too. Anything that might help us to track them down."

Slade nods and then disappears into the kitchen area, and I hear him muttering and huffing as he unsuccessfully tries to navigate some type of phone tree at the TV network. But eventually, I guess he gets through to someone because I hear him speaking in low murmurs. He returns to the living room a few minutes later, a strange look on his face that I can't quite put my finger on.

Everyone looks up at him expectantly.

"It looks like they used Angel's name." He glances at me and then looks at the floor. "The ad was paid for by an Angel Benson."

I feel the blood rush from my face as all four of them look at me, questions in their eyes.

"What? Why would I—?" They can't possibly think I would be responsible for the monstrosity of an ad we just watched. It would make no sense to come up with something that would literally stop people from wanting to set foot in my salon. Surely they saw that I was as surprised as they were when it popped up on the screen, the creepy jingle bearing my name.

"It's okay, we don't think you placed an ad like that," says Aidan, glaring at Slade. "Do we, guys?" Brick and Roman shake their heads in support of Aidan's words, but Slade just frowns. Noticing his lack of response, Aidan doubles down. "I'm sure that's not what Slade was implying, because that would be ridiculous, wouldn't it, Slade?"

"Don't we think she did it? Are we sure?" Slade raises an eyebrow and crosses his arms tightly over his chest. "They conveniently didn't remember the voice of the person who made the payment, and everything was done on the phone so nobody saw the face behind the name. It sounds fishy to me."

"Really, Slade?" I arch an eyebrow and I feel my lip curl involuntarily. He's got to be fucking kidding me. First of all, like I'd have money to spend on something as expensive as TV advertising. And second, if I did, as if I would insist on a murder jingle to promote my business. It's like he just wants to assume the worst in me, even when it makes no sense.

My body tenses up in frustration and discomfort at this type of attention being focused on me. The stalker's dark obsession is enough without Slade adding to it with his silly conspiracy theories.

"Hey, if it walks like a duck and quacks like a duck...," he shrugs. "You asked me to see what I could find, and I did."

"You're the duck here, Slade," I glare at him. "A big stupid duck hurling around serious and misplaced accusations. And you can duck right off. If you really think that I paid for that ad, there's a major problem with you." I want to say more—much more—but instead, I close my mouth. My voice is rising and if I keep going I know I'll lose it and start to yell, which won't help anyone. I want them focused on helping me to find out where this stalker is and put an end to things, not on the ever-increasing conflict between me and Slade.

"Leave it alone, Slade," sighs Aidan. "An ad like that is a sure way to put off potential clients, don't you think? Accusing Angel is kind of absurd. Clearly, the psycho knows her name because he is *stalking her* and has been for a long time."

Slade shrugs, and Aidan rolls his eyes.

"Ro, would you have gone to see Angel at her hair salon if you'd seen an ad like that?" Aidan turns to look at Roman, who still has his hand resting protectively on my thigh. He squeezes it gently in response to Aidan's question. "Fuck yeah, I would have! It would have intrigued me. I would've needed to find out more." He smirks. "That said, I might not have insisted on getting an actual haircut. It would have been more for the novelty, just to see what happens."

Aidan rolls his eyes. "Okay, fair point. I forgot you were a psychotic weirdo who's attracted to shit like that." He glances at Brick. "Speaking of psychotic weirdos, I'm assuming you would have signed up for VIP membership if the salon promised a torture show?"

Brick cackles, his teeth bared in a show of unabashed glee. "Yep, you bet! A bit of murder with a haircut sounds quite appealing. But only if I got to join in."

"Maybe you should visit a salon with Roman because apparently, that's exactly what happens when he goes for a haircut." I roll my eyes, and Brick and Roman smirk. "But Slade, for real, you really think I'd do that to my own business?" I can't get over it. My eyes lock with Slade's for a second, but then he drops his gaze. "Like, are you fucking serious?" I can hear my voice rising again, even though it's not intentional. My entire body feels like it's burning, and I know it's a combination of fear and rage and the uncertainty of not knowing what's going to happen next. "Your brothers here can see that me paying for this ad, or having anything to do with it, is a complete long shot. Like, there is absolutely no point in me spending money on something like that. Other than wanting to go bankrupt very quickly."

Slade reaches a hand to the back of his neck and rubs at it as if he's trying to work out a knot while thinking of the right way to respond. "I guess not." He takes a deep breath and then audibly exhales. "Look, I'm sorry. The information is flying thick and fast here, and I feel like I'm drinking from a fire hose. It's hard to know who to trust outside of these guys." He gestures at Aidan, Brick and Roman.

"And you don't entirely trust me..." I decide to address the elephant in the room head-on, my eyes locking on his while I speak. "Wait, I take that back. You don't trust me at all."

"Yeah," he glances at me and then at the floor, and rubs at his neck again. "I mean it's true. I'm working on it. It's not like I've known you for very long, and things have been a bit... volatile and unpredictable since you arrived here." He raises his gaze back to mine, his mouth pressed into a thin line. "If I take my feelings out of it, pragmatically, it feels a bit like this lunatic is trying to flush you out, or at least unsettle you."

I sigh. "Mission accomplished on the unsettling front." The net my stalker is weaving around me really feels like it's cinching more tightly, as if it started out loosely wrapped around me and all he has to do is tug on one strategic thread before it clenches about my entire body and renders me immobile.

He wants me to know he's nearby, that he knows roughly where I am, and that he won't stop until he finds me. The salon, the apartment, and now this ad. The island is only so big, and there are only so many places to hide. For now, he can't touch me directly, so he's finding all the indirect ways he can. He must be frustrated I wasn't at the first two spots he tried. He hates not having control over every little thing. Especially when it comes to me.

Despite his resourcefulness, however, he's had little realistic chance of finding me. His timing was off, thankfully. A day or two earlier and I would have been toast, completely oblivious that he'd come so close to tracking me down. But what a difference a day makes. What a difference a hot man looking for a short back and sides but ends up stabbing a man in his carotid makes. This compound wasn't even on my radar until I encountered Roman, and I wouldn't have known where to look for me, either. At least I have that, although, with my stalker's skillfulness at hunting me, it's only a matter of time until he finds this place.

"Maybe he figures you won't be able to resist trying to track him down yourself," says Brick, rubbing the beard on his chin between his thumb and forefinger. "Maybe he's set this up to lure you to wherever he is."

"That's how anybody could get to *you*, Brick," smirks Aidan. "Always champing at the bit to get the party started, to get the job done. Going after the person who's coming after you and killing them first."

Brick beams as if it's the nicest compliment anyone has ever paid him.

"Whatever it is, he's clearly making it known he's here," frowns Slade. "Drawing attention to your business, right after he destroyed the place and all. Surely he doesn't think you'd actually go back to work there any time soon, given he clearly knows that's where you'd ordinarily be."

As he lays the situation out like that, I feel a ball of something unpleasant growing in the pit of my stomach. The psycho has messed up my new life, destroying the two places that had become a sanctuary for me here. I just created this 'safe' new life and started getting used to it, even appreciating it, and now he's gone and taken it all away. Whatever happens, things aren't going to be able to go back to the way they were. A wave of realization and loss crashes over me. It's exhausting, always running and recreating and burning things down and building them back up. Each time it makes me stronger, but there's always a tingly feeling in the back of my brain that worries next time I might not be able to get back up. Maybe I've gone too far this time.

"Maybe he's letting you know he's about to strike," shrugs Brick, continuing to channel his energy into thinking like my stalker, his mind the only one anywhere near warped enough to almost get it. "Like a warning shot... like when you're playing hide and seek and the person is counting down until they start seeking you. Maybe this is that countdown."

An icy shiver runs down my neck and back. It feels so predatory, whatever my stalker's actual intentions are. I guess that's what stalkers are, predatory by nature. It's like a dark version of all the times I played hide and seek as a child and would conjure up imaginary 'bad guys' who were after me. I'd scare myself shitless while waiting for an invisible madman to come find me, even when the person actually looking for me was a friend or family member, and now, decades later, my imagination has managed to manifest itself into reality. Ugh.

"Why would he do that? Wouldn't he be better off to turn up unannounced?" Slade squints at Brick. "Leverage the element of surprise?"

"Tactically, yes. It would make it much easier to get to her if she didn't have any idea he was coming," Aidan nods in agreement. "But with this guy, I'm not so sure that's his priority. I don't think he's thinking in a logical, objective way. He wants to kill her in the end, of course...". He pauses, and my back clenches right in the middle. It feels like an icy invisible finger is trailing slowly from my lower back all the way up my spine. "But for him, from what Angel has shared, he seems to derive pleasure from the theatrical performance of it all. Of casting a wide circle around her and then gradually narrowing it down, letting her know that she's completely under his control and that his actions are all part of his grand, inevitable plan for her."

"Like a cat and a mouse, when the cat first loosely captures its prey, " says Brick, as if a lightbulb just went off for him. "The cat could easily kill the mouse straight away but instead, it toys with it, and starts off batting at it gently with its claws retracted. It's just enough to keep it within a broad perimeter and it gives the mouse an artificial sense that it could potentially free itself. That it has a chance at survival, even if it's small. It's about complete control and pacing for maximum enjoyment for the cat, and maximum terror for the mouse, which fuels the cat's ultimate enjoyment. The mouse knows the cat is toying with it and could take its life at any moment, but holds out a sliver of hope that during this 'play time,' it could find a way to escape. The cat knows the mouse knows it could end its life, but is holding out some futile hope the cat will become distracted or lose interest before it reels the mouse in one final time and strikes a fatal blow. So the cat teases the mouse, dragging things out until it can't take the anticipation any more and goes in for the kill." Brick glances over at me, where I remain sitting on the couch, trying not to vomit at the thought of being the mouse in this situation. "Oh, I'm sorry, Angel. You look pale. I apologize if I over-described that."

I wave him off. It's not his fault he's right, even though it hurts to hear it.

"I think you're right and it needs to be said to understand what we're working with here," says Slade. "It's like the thrill of a slow chase. He gets off on inflicting psychological terror, of getting his victims to the point where they're begging for death as a small mercy."

I shiver again. He doesn't know just how right he is. How I've been in that place with the lunatic in the past, more than once. When given the choice between having another chunk of my flesh removed, of having another vial of blood drained for his 'experiments'... or for him to straight-up drink it even, I've begged him several times before for the sweet slumber of death. To date, he's never given in, no matter how much he's been tempted. I guess he hasn't reached that quotient where he feels like he's extracted his maximum pleasure and broken my threshold for terror. The mouse is still free, but it's only a matter of time until the cat's claws come out.

They don't know how my pleading aroused him, and how he, in some ways, wanted nothing more than to lock eyes with me, absorbing my soul as the light faded from mine. He fantasized about that moment and would tell me about it in granular detail, as well as what he planned to do with my corporeal form in the days after he let my soul free. As he shared at the time, ultimately, he felt I had more to give while I was alive. That he could still absorb more of my terror and that ending my life early would be 'too easy' for me and a waste for him. That he could edge me toward the sweet precipice of nothingness and then cruelly jerk it back at the last moment, just another way to inflict physical pain and mental anguish.

But now he's circling me again, and the radius is starting to constrict in a tight, inevitable coil. I feel him getting closer to me, and this time, it's not just about me. There are more people I care about who are now involved. I promised myself I wouldn't let this happen, that I wouldn't put anyone else at risk from this madman, even if they are strong and powerful and self-sufficient. That he was a battle that I and I alone needed to face.

But I've broken the vow I made to myself, and the coil is wrapping its tendrils around me yet again. Around us.

And this time, I know he won't stop until he gets every last drop of me that he wants, regardless of how much or how little I actually have left to give. And no matter who else dies in the process.

***

As my mind races, a wave of fatigue washes over me, making it difficult to keep my heavy eyelids open. The guys are still chatting, but everything they're saying is a blur and feels like it's happening in slow motion. Seeing we've established we aren't in imminent danger of my stalker breaching the compound's perimeter, I feel comfortable enough to retire to my room to lie down for a while because, clearly, I need it. I say lie down because there's no hope in hell that I'll actually be able to nap with the stress of everything that's going on, and placing myself in a horizontal position is about the best I can do for the moment. My adrenalin is pumping, but I also know beneath that I'm exhausted, physically and mentally. The most I can hope for is laying on the bed with my eyes closed for a couple of minutes, hopefully thinking about anything but the demonic psycho who's on a rampage to end my life. If he does manage to find me, I need to be as sharp as possible, and right now I feel like I'm the pointy end of a pencil that's been crushed into a pad of paper until you can barely see the resulting nub, useless and bruised and broken.

The irony that one psychopath might be trying to get into the reinforced building containing four other psychopaths—five, if you count me—is not lost on me. It also speaks to the insanity of my stalker, and it probably gives him a thrill to know he'll be going up against more than just little old me.

As I ponder the critical levels of psychopathy housed under this roof as well as the complete lunatic hunting me from somewhere outside, I close my eyes and focus on relaxing my face, my shoulders, my chest and my back. As expected, having my eyes closed lasts all of three or four minutes and it's pretty obvious my body isn't going to respond to the sleep cues I'm trying to give it. Instead, my eyes feel dry and my body feels like it's been pummeled with the fists of fifty mad men, my mental stress manifesting itself physically.

I glance down at my denim cutoff shorts and black racerback tank and casually sniff an armpit. My armpits can get out of control sometimes when I'm stressed, and it's usually just one of them that goes rogue and decides the deodorant I'm using no longer works on it. Today is no exception. It's definitely time for a shower and a change of clothing. At least having a shower will be a momentary distraction from this madness, a normal act in the face of absurdity.

I sigh as I pull off my top, shorts and underwear and hop into the steamy water. Soaping myself up with body wash, I turn and face the shower head and let the water cascade over my body, cleansing me. For a moment, I allow the waterfall sensation to overtake me and temporarily clear my head, just feeling the calming drizzle of hot water streaming over my curves. For just this sliver of time, the only thing I focus on is the warmth and the way the steam wraps around me, comforting me and giving the illusion of safety. Because despite how good it feels, I know this is only temporary and death is tapping me on my shoulder. But I'll worry about that later.

Feeling physically refreshed at least, I step out of the shower and use one of the fluffy towels on the rack to dry myself, also using it to de-mist the mirror. As I rub moisturizer onto my face, I assess my appearance. I look okay, I guess, but there's a tightness in my features and it's not the plastic surgery version some people aspire to achieve. There's something about me that looks tense, drawn, like I'm waiting for the other shoe to drop.

And I guess that *is* what I'm doing. I'm staying here in this big house with four dangerous men I barely know, with a psycho stalker getting closer and closer to me, and

I have no way out, no plan. If he finds me, there's a good chance I'm dead. If I get to him first, the Brixtons might still decide I'm too much trouble to deal with. I know Slade already thinks I am.

It really does feel like a dangerous game of hide and seek where everyone is chasing me with chainsaws and throwing axes and giant stabby daggers that magnetize to my critical organs. I'm in the advanced mode of a video game, but I don't know who the ultimate boss will be that I'll have to face. Is it really the guy who has been taunting me for decades, or is that too obvious? There could be a bunch of them, each more terrifying than the next, some with whom I'm currently sharing a roof. All I know is I'll be finding out very soon, and there's nothing I can do about it in the meantime. I feel helpless, and frustrated, and I wish I could fast forward time just to get it over with, whatever *it* is.

This purgatory is crushing me, and it makes me feel like running far away from everyone and everything. I just don't know if I have the energy to start all over again, especially if he continues following me to the end of the earth. I can't keep running forever. I have to kill or be killed.

Controlling what I can, I add a swipe each of mascara and eyeliner and a dab of light pink lip gloss. I glance at myself one more time in the mirror as I loop my hair into a messy topknot. Not too shabby, and it will do for now. May as well look cute while I'm waiting to find out how I'll die. Not that it matters, but it's literally one of the few choices I get to make right now.

I head back down to the living room and the guys are all back in there, although Roman and Slade are wearing different clothing than before and seem to be deep in conversation, going back and forth in hushed tones. Aidan is tapping away on his laptop as usual, perhaps with a bit more intensity than normal, and Brick appears to be sharpening some kind of torture implement with a devious gleam in his eye.

They all peer at me as I enter the room and, apparently satisfied that I'm in a calm, post-shower state, they all go back to what they were doing. It's kind of sweet how they've already gotten somewhat used to me being in the house, even if for Slade it's just a favorite topic to complain about.

I need to get my mind off the creepy ad. My nerves are still on edge since the power went out, but at least he hasn't managed to mess with this building... yet. I'm jumpy, with my hypervigilance well and truly kicking in. They'd all better prepare themselves for the screams they'll hear if anyone gives me the slightest fright for the next few days, maybe more. I don't currently see an end to this situation… until he finds me and kills me, that is.

"So tell me the story about that girl at the beach earlier." I glance around at them and they all stop what they're doing to look back in my direction. "The rude bitch who you said was with those four guys who were out in the ocean. What's the deal with them, other than their living situation?"

It's a relief to be around these four protective, strong guys rather than by myself, innocently going about my day at the salon or apartment while a lunatic gets closer to me. It's a bit embarrassing to put it that way. I know that sounds like I'm depending on men to take care of me, like I'm some sort of frail damsel in distress, when in reality I'm quite capable of looking out for myself most of the time. But there has also been no luck stopping my stalker for the past two decades, and his obsession seems to have only grown worse while he was incarcerated.

Now, although they make me feel much safer than I would otherwise, I feel like I'm putting these guys at risk by staying in their compound. I may as well have spray-painted a giant target over their house that says *'Attack here'* and sent it to him. The guys are capable of attacking and defending what's theirs, but they're still human, and all humans have vulnerabilities. Even the toughest ones. None of us are immortal.

If something happens to any of them because of me, even Slade, I don't think I could ever forgive myself. Even though they kidnapped me, murdered someone in front of me, kept me hostage in their compound. None of those actions make them deserving of being brought face-to-face with my personal madman and all that entails. That's my baggage to bear, not theirs.

"They're kind of lame," Roman interrupts my train of thought, answering the question I'd forgotten about the moment the words left my mouth. "They have some type of legacy to do with 'protecting' the island, I guess they call it. We call them the snakes because they snake everyone out on the water, cutting in when it's not their turn. They say it's how they live their lives on the land, too." He rolls his eyes. "They do some of the same activities we do for Tane, but then they draw the line and tell him they won't do his real dirty work."

"And Tane's okay with that?" I raise an eyebrow. "It sounds like they're entitled little snowflakes, opting out of any work they believe is beneath them while everyone else has to suck it up." I'm surprised to learn they're allowed to act this way. Tane seems like someone who dictates the terms that others need to follow.

"It's some Robin Hood bullshit if you ask me," adds Brick, frowning. "You can't just pick and choose where and when you get your hands dirty. You're all in or you're out." He rotates his solid wrist, mesmerized by his tattooed knuckles.

"They'll never be anywhere near as powerful as we are," explains Aidan. "But it's good for us. They lose out on all the profitable activities around here. And our power is expanding whereas they've just about hit their ceiling if you think about it." He shrugs. "I think that's why Tane's allowing things to go on this way. They'll continue to be useful, he'll leverage their 'status' or whatever you want to call it, and they'll never get big enough to be any type of real threat to him or his closest connections."

"Why would they do that? It seems self-limiting." The way they're describing these guys, it's like they have some type of preferential access to a large pot of profits, but they've self-imposed a smaller cap within it as their maximum. Like they're at a casino with near-guaranteed winnings at the dollar slots, and they have buckets of dollar bills at their disposal, but they're insisting on sticking with nickel games and a lower probability of winning. It makes no sense, at least from where I'm sitting.

"I guess they have some morally ambiguous sense of right and wrong," shrugs Aidan. "They'll commit crimes, and participate in all sorts of illegal activities, but there are certain arbitrary lines they've drawn that they refuse to cross. Tane only puts up with them because of this legacy bullshit, which is tied to Skyler and his dad. Without that, they'd be in shallow graves up in the mountains." He glances absently out the window at the peaks that cascade down toward the city and ocean. I get the sense he knows for sure that the mountains are home for more than a scenic backdrop and a shiver runs through me as I wonder how many bodies these guys have left up there.

"Huh. And you guys don't have a morally ambiguous sense of right and wrong?" I glance at each of them, generally curious about how they view themselves in comparison to the other group.... these snakes or whatever they call themselves.

"We don't set artificial boundaries," says Aidan, and the others nod in agreement. "To use your words, we don't self-limit. There's nothing we won't do for money or power. Sometimes what we do is broadly considered to be right—like murdering someone who's abusing women and children on the island. And sometimes it's probably considered wrong by the broader population—like engaging in money laundering to help people like Tane, or moving certain illicit substances around. It doesn't matter to us which side of morality our work falls on. It's just business. A transaction. Our only loyalty is to ourselves and to the legacy we're creating."

"Jesus, that'll help me sleep soundly at night," I frown. There's something almost secure and almost like a safety net when a group has a moral code of some sort. It helps to know where you stand and to understand where people's boundaries lie. With these guys, it seems to fluctuate depending on the associated risk and reward. A clinical business decision about what is best for them in the moment, driven by the promise of acquiring money and power.

I try to shove thoughts down of a day when my being alive might not fit with their financial or power goals. The way Aidan's describing it, he makes it sound like outside of their inner circle. That they'd pick someone off without a second thought the moment they appeared to get in their way.

"You're one of us now, so you don't need to worry," says Brick, meeting my gaze and smiling at me. The curve of his lips is friendly and warm, his molten eyes boring into me with a deep hunger. My god, for someone so vicious and ready to torture people, he's a giant fucking sweetheart when he wants to be. A psychotic cinnamon roll vegan surfer with massive BDE. I really want to see this guy naked, because other than being incredibly hot, he's also fascinating, and his unique combination and brand promise nothing but a great time.

"No she's not one of us," snaps Slade, his eyes narrowing at me as he pulls me out of my carnal thoughts about Brick and what I want to do with him, "and she never will be."

"Wow. You're so hospitable, Slade," I roll my eyes at him. "I wish everywhere I went, I could be greeted with such warmth, such kindness. Have you ever considered working in hospitality with those skills? Maybe you could be a department store greeter because the warmth you exude shouldn't go to waste."

He glares at me, and the others snort.

I don't know why Slade hates me so goddamn much, but his anger that I'm still here is palpable. I sleep with one eye open when we're home alone together. His dislike for me is so strong that I wouldn't put it past him to take matters into his own hands and deal with the consequences later. He's adept with a meat cleaver and various other sharp blades from what I've seen in the kitchen, and it wouldn't take much for one to 'slip' from his grasp and embed itself in my body somehow.

I always make sure one of the other guys eats first, and that I dish up my own meal in case he tries to slip something poisonous in there. That might sound like a lot, but you can't be too careful in a house full of loyalty-free criminals, one of whom would prefer that you didn't exist.

At the same time, I *have* potentially introduced a lunatic serial killer into his life, so I guess I might not be breaking out the welcome silverware either if I were in his shoes. Regardless, a shiver runs down my spine as his icy gaze bores into me. All the guys make me feel safe except for Slade.

"The funny thing is, that girl you almost crashed into wouldn't be alive without us," Brick says, a big smile spreading across his face as he artfully changes the subject back to the previous topic. "I guess you could say we saved her, too."

"Wait, what? I don't understand." I raise an eyebrow. This feels like something I should pay attention to. I had no idea the Brixtons had a history with whoever that rude bitch was, and with these snake guys they suddenly seem to know so much about.

"Angel doesn't need to know about that," says Slade in a warning tone, giving Brick the cautionary look of a parent whose toddler keeps edging towards a busy road or a hot stove. He looks like he's poised to grab Brick by the back of his collar and haul him back to safety at any moment.

"What? It's not a secret. We can tell her," Brick shrugs. "Who's she going to tattle to? The unhinged psycho who we're trying to save her from?"

They all look to Aidan for his deciding vote, and he shrugs. "I don't think that there's a problem with her knowing. You're right. Who would she tell, anyway?"

"Yay, story time!" Brick claps his hands together with childlike glee, another dissonant departure from his brutish appearance and love of torture. "Gather around the campfire, children, while I tell you about the debt that helps us rake in extra profits each month, all because of misplaced love for a beautiful girl."

"Jesus Christ, that'll be us next if we let *her*," Slade hisses the word 'her,' and glares at me, "stay here for much longer. She'll fucking ruin us."

"I'm sitting right here, Slade, in the room. Listening to your every word."

I narrow my eyes at him and he glares right back, a familiar scowl twisting his mouth.

He really is extra hot when he scowls. I have the urge to tug at his lower lip with my teeth but instead, I just sit there, the recipient of his disdain. I don't know how looking so miserable can make someone more physically attractive, but somehow it works on him. Resting Slade Face is sexy as fuck.

"Anyways, as I was saying before I was so *rudely* interrupted," continues Brick, rolling his eyes at Slade, "the little snakes originally met that girl that you hate so much, doing a job for Tane. I believe her name is Devon or something like that. I prefer to think of her as a devil woman. Ha! That's kind of funny now that I think about it. They have a devil and we have an Angel." He grins at me, his eyes twinkling mischievously.

"Get to the point, man," Slade glares at Brick, bored by his words and unaffected by his devilish energy.

"Anyway, they were meant to protect her for Tane, and basically hold her captive and make sure she didn't escape until her father paid off some debt that Tane had purchased from someone else."

"What the fuck is with the guys on this island and kidnapping women?" I huff at all of them. "This is insanity! There are more kidnappers than just you? Everyone just... *takes* people here? Against their will?"

"There are countless kidnappers on this island, that's for sure. I've eliminated some but then others inevitably pop up to take their place," Brick shrugs and then he grins again. "We like to think we're special, though. We give our captives the VIP service." He wiggles his eyebrows at me.

"I mean, the bedroom I'm staying in is a big trade-up from the shackles and the filthy mattress downstairs," I reply, my face screwing up as I think about the remnants of whatever the hell it was that I'd had to sit on down there.

"Should have kept you in the basement, out of sight and out of mind," growls Slade.

I instigate the mutual glaring this time, which Slade seems happy to reciprocate, and then return my attention to the others, who are being far more hospitable.

"What would happen if her father didn't repay the debt? Would they have killed her?" I'm so invested in this story. I need all the details.

"Now the answer to that is kind of fucked up, actually, even for Tane," says Roman. He lowers his voice into a near-whisper. "Some might think death would have been an easier option than what was planned for her."

"Really?" I raise an eyebrow. "I don't get it."

"What could you do to someone that's worse than killing them, Devon?" quizzes Brick, as if he's my schoolteacher and I'm his student.

"Make them sit in a room with Slade all day while he pretends he's on Top Chef and gives me murderous looks from across the kitchen counter?"

Aidan snorts, and Slade shifts his scowl to him.

"That sounds really awful! But keep going... even worse than that!" Brick exclaims, amusement twinkling in his eyes.

"Fuck, I don't know. Torture?" I throw my hands up in the air. Brick's Socratic questioning style is taking too long, and I need to know more right now. "Just say the thing, Brick!" I huff, secretly enjoying the way he's dragging it out. He's such a tease.

Brick just smiles at me and sits there for a moment, unspeaking. He clearly has no problem stretching this out at his own pace, and my attempt at hurrying him is getting nowhere. I sigh and sink back into the couch. We're on Brick time now. I kind of love it.

"That could have been part of it," he shrugs, "but not at Tane's hands or those of his men."

"Wait," I raise an eyebrow. "You mean he was going to get someone else to hurt her? Why not just take care of it himself?"

"He wanted money for her, and that was his only concern. He was going to have her auctioned to the highest bidder. And they would have gotten to do with her as they chose. Snuff her, put her into sex work or other forms of slavery, rape her, torture her, whatever their sadistic hearts desired," explains Roman. "And god knows who those people would be. The only thing I know is that, whoever they were, they must have been insanely wealthy because that debt was *expensive*."

"So what happened? She's free now, clearly." I'm transfixed by this story. Who knew this bitch had more to her than being incredibly rude and confrontational on the beach? She's in a relationship with the snakes—all four of them—and now she has this whole Tane Brown connection. My questions are flying free and fast, because I simply must know everything. "Did her father pay off the debt?"

"No, apparently he's a weasel and he couldn't stump up the cash," Roman shrugs.

"A wealthy poor man. The skinny fat of gangsters," adds Brick.

I can't help but snort at the image, and so does Aidan.

Aidan picks up where Roman left off. "It sounds like he had some assets frozen somewhere and even when he was able to access them, they either weren't enough to cover the debt or he just decided it was better to flee than stump up the cash."

My jaw drops at the thought of someone treating their daughter like that, of thinking that her life had a price that he wasn't willing to pay. Of ultimately not caring enough, or at least just being so self-absorbed that he'd put himself first, instead of finding any possible way for his daughter not to be sold to another human being. Jesus.

I can't really relate, which I guess makes me lucky. Despite our various differences, my parents would have done anything for me. I *was* lucky, I guess you could say. Until my stalker brutally murdered my parents and brother because of their relationship to me, that is. And then went after my closest friends and ripped the lives of their families apart as well, excising them from my life in an attempt to reimagine it, so I had only him.

"So what happened to her father, then? Surely you can't just refuse to pay up on a debt to someone like Tane Brown?" I ask. Because they can't have just let the guy off the hook for not paying a very public debt. "I imagine he's the type that would come after you and use that kind of mistake to send a message."

Brick nods. "Yeah, her father is still out there somewhere, with a bounty on his back. I heard the little snake boys might even be tasked with offing him one day."

"Jesus," my jaw drops. "They'd be offing their father-in-law, basically? Do they even do murders, given their fancy 'moral code'?"

"I don't know that Devon would care if her father died, from my understanding," shrugs Slade, speaking up for once to say something that wasn't specifically critical of me. It must be his quota for the day, one or two poignant comments max, and then he's tapped out, emotionally drained, needing to retreat into the kitchen or something. "She'd probably spit on his grave, maybe piss on it, given what he did to her."

"I love family dynamics," I reply, and to my surprise, Slade snorts at my comment.

Did we just have some type of positive banter together? Weird.

"And to your question about whether the snakes do murders... it's definitely not within their 'moral code'," he says, his lip curling with derision at their 'standards', "but rumor has it they have killed for her. Some guys that tried to fuck with her have mysteriously gone missing and they were supposedly the last to be seen asking around about them."

"Wait, this happened here on the island?" I arch an eyebrow.

"Yeah, it sounds like she's a feisty one. Reminds me of someone we know," says Roman, his eyes locking onto mine and his mouth curving in a lopsided smirk. "She ran away at one point and made it as far as a local dive bar—."

"Wait, what?! She managed to get away from her captors and her first destination of choice was a... dive bar?" I interrupt because this is not where I saw this story going. And I like it.

"Yeah, I don't know what to tell you. But that's where she went, and some wannabe rapists put something in her drink. The snakes ended up finding her before anything happened to her, though."

There's a brief silence. "Wow," I exhale sharply.

"Yeah. Intense, I know," says Roman.

"And then they killed whoever tried to do that to her?"

"That's what the rumors say," he shrugs. "The guys who tried to hurt her were never seen or heard of again, and the snakes have never been quite the same ever since. A little more flexible in some ways, a lot less in others. Being around her has shaped their boundaries, I guess."

I release a breath I didn't know I'd been holding. If they're this protective of her, this willing to erase people who would hurt her, even though it goes against everything they stand for and isn't something they'd normally do... that's powerful. No wonder she has a loyalty to them, and no wonder she's decided to stay around. Especially if she's not used to loyalty and support from elsewhere in her life.

"And they were never charged or looked into for it?"

Slade smirks. "Like we don't all have the cops in our back pockets around here," he says. "They have much bigger fish to fry than snakes taking out some would-be rapists. Helps them with their jobs if you think about it, one more group of scum they don't need to worry about."

Jesus. It's a good thing I lost all faith in the criminal justice system a long time ago. It sounds like the corruption and back-pocket dealings I've heard about in big cities is also alive and well on the island. That said, by the sounds of it I can make an exception in this case. Devon's men's actions may not have been legal, but it sounds like they were just. I'm supportive of vigilantism when it's for the right reasons.

"Anyway," says Brick, ripping my attention from Slade and back to the conversation, "don't forget that she's still being held captive at this point, and it's for a reason, right? So once they have her back under their control, the guys protect her as instructed by Tane, for days, and then the day of the handover comes around. The father still hasn't stumped up the cash, and she's so sought-after by these wealthy sadistic pricks that there's been a bidding war and the price has gone up well past the value of the original debt."

"Jesus, does she have a golden vagina or something?" I cock my head at Brick. "I mean, she's hot and everything, but how does that even happen? It's not like she's in her 'prime' to be sold, I would think, either."

I truly don't get it, in terms of what determines the value of one human being over another. I would have assumed that bad men could be willing to pay high prices for women in their early twenties, and of course, teenagers would come at a premium, but someone in what appears to be their mid-thirties and hardly virginal? It's fascinating, but in a way that makes my skin crawl. Nobody is safe.

"People are just worth money, especially women. Especially attractive and feisty women that are likely to put up a struggle and defend themselves," Roman shrugs. "And she is really gorgeous."

"Oh, you think she's attractive do you?" I place a hand on my hip. There's a squeezing sensation in my gut, but I immediately realize how ridiculous I sound. She is pretty, I've seen her myself. But I don't like hearing Roman talk about it, it just reminds me that he's a player. I let my hand drop to my side and let out a breath. "Nevermind, forget I asked that question. You would fuck anything with a pussy." I smirk at Roman.

"Not just anything," says Roman, indignant. "I'm a reformed man with impeccable taste."

"Reformed? Since when?" I arch my eyebrow.

"Since yesterday," Roman winks at me, and I recognize hunger in his eyes. His gaze drops to my thighs and I feel heat generating in my core as I remember him feasting on me, his tongue exploring every part of me.

Slade rolls his eyes at Roman and me. "Whatever, guys. Stop eye-fucking each other, it's rude." He turns his gaze to Brick. "Anyway, continue your little story, Brick. I'm getting bored, there's no need to drag it out for so long. You could have just given her the TL;DR, and if you don't wrap it up soon I'm going to."

"How could you get bored? I tell *captivating* stories," says Brick in a singsong voice. "No need to be such a Debbie Downer, Slade. A Slade Sourpuss. A Brixton Bringdown."

Slade glares at him and looks like he's about to throw fists.

I smirk at the perfection of these names for Slade. These guys are fucking bizarre. I can't figure them out.

"So anyway," says Brick, "long story long, if the haters will pipe down over there... and I will take the time necessary to convey the true, beautiful aspects of this story whether you like it or not, *Slade*... the debt is really high, and the little snake boys liquidate all their assets and collect their savings and they still can't cover it in its entirety. Devon seems screwed, the sadistic would-be purchasers rubbing their hands together with glee as the countdown continues, preparing for all the sick things they want to do to her. It seems like there's no way out for their little captive, that she has no hope of ever being free. Her world is about to become a cage, her body a playground for the most evil men imaginable. But wait, there's more... guess who can cover the debt, even the inflated amount?"

"Hmmm.... you guys?" I raise an eyebrow.

"Yes, exactly!" he grins. "A+, little student! You have been paying attention!"

I snort and roll my eyes. Brick needs a backup career as a comedian or something. Torture by day, make people laugh by night. Although it's a dark and twisted sense of humor, an acquired taste that is far from mainstream. Yeah, on second thought it's probably better to keep him locked down in this compound where his audience is just us and the people he uses his scalpel on.

"And in return for bailing them out so they can keep her, or free her, depending on how you look at it, we now take a healthy share of their profits," says Aidan, ever the businessman. "They're racking up losses all over the place. We're shrinking their business while we grow ours. Our competition is literally paying us to eliminate them."

"Genius," I exhale. They really are very smart. I'm under no illusion that they helped Devon out of the kindness of their hearts. Saving her has helped to strengthen their power and bring in more money, the two things they actually do care about. The fact they saved her life is almost incidental, and something that needed to occur for them to get more of what they wanted.

"And they've stopped making it difficult to do our business on this island. We're exempt from some of their protection rules," adds Roman, "which means we can run an even more profitable enterprise. They were a pain in the ass when it came to our clubs and bars, making sure we were doing everything by the book, or at least according to their 'code'." He does quotation marks with his fingers as he says the last word. The fact the snakes turn down certain jobs clearly really bothers these guys.

"So what you're saying is your rivals owe you big time, and the reason that rude bitch is alive is because of you? Should I be happy about this?" I raise an eyebrow.

"It's good for business, so yes," says Aidan. "We make more money, we have passive income, and our operations are more efficient. So you can thank her, technically, even though she was rude to you."

I nod. "And so the snake... serpent... whatever the fuck they are, guys... do they technically own this Devon bitch now? You helped them buy her from Tane and his men, so now she belongs to them, right?"

She didn't seem like a captive when I almost ran into her at the beach that day. A real bitch, yes, but not someone being held against her will. She definitely could have run the time I saw her, with the guys all already out in the ocean.

"From what we understand, they let her go free, but she ultimately chose to stay here on the island with them. And they get to live happily ever after, all five of them," Aidan shrugs, simply explaining their curious relationship.

"That is, if happily ever after includes having to give us over a huge chunk of profits for their work," Roman grins, "which is definitely a happily ever after for us."

"And there you have it," says Brick, taking a flourishing bow. "The story has come to a close and now you know everything about... what are we calling her... 'that Devon bitch'."

I laugh. "You're some storyteller, Brick. Thank you for the comprehensive overview. It'll be etched into my memory forever."

This is all a lot of information to process, but I'm glad I asked. Definitely a story with many layers, some of which I haven't even begun to unpack. Jesus, this Devon girl might be rude but she's gone through the wringer, just like I have. Imagine your dad trying to sell you to wriggle out of a debt to one of the evilest men around. I'm surprised she doesn't have a bitter hatred for all men.

But she seems to have pulled herself up, risen from the ashes like a true phoenix, and crafted a life and lifestyle for herself here that sounds pretty fucking intoxicating. Four hot men who are incredibly loyal to her and would cross their own boundaries, who would kill to protect her.

And as for her behavior toward me? I'd probably be a bitch too if I were in her shoes.

Most people would probably say I kind of am one already.

Maybe we're not so different, her and I.

But I guess that remains to be seen. And she'd better not get in my way.

Chapter Thirty-Six

Slade

"Yep," I answer the phone on the second ring. The etiquette around answering the phone is one of those things that has never made much sense to me. It's a necessity, of course, but people do it in such a polite way. There's no way I'm ever saying something like, 'good afternoon, this is Slade speaking. Who am I speaking with?' because fuck that shit. A simple 'yep' does the trick just fine. Don't get me started on those goofs who call you on your cell phone, the ones you *know* are aware they're in your contacts, and they introduce themselves when they call. As in, you see an incoming call on your phone from let's say, Becky, and then you answer the phone and Becky says, 'hello, this is Becky calling.' I know who you fucking are, Becky. Jesus.

"Hey man, it's Chalky." The voice is a little gritty and raspy.

"I know it's you from your caller ID, man," I sigh. We have found another one. Chalky is in the gang of unnecessary introducers. "What's up, Chalky?"

Chalky is one of our longer-serving associates. He's been with us from the start, even before we relocated to the island. He takes care of a variety of jobs for us and has proven himself to be fairly reliable and conscientious about his efforts. It's uncharacteristic of him to be calling on the day of a job, and I know he has all the information he needs to get it done properly because he's done this type of pickup many times before.

"I've had an emergency and I can't collect the haul from the drop site today." I detect a slight tremor in his voice, like he's anxious to share he can't complete the job.

"Oh, really? What kind of emergency?" Chalky never calls out. Something must be seriously wrong.

"My wife's mother fell and broke her hip," he says, and I can detect the concern in his voice. "She took her to the hospital, but that means I'm stuck with the kids, at least for the next few hours, maybe for the rest of the day."

"And you don't have a babysitter or someone else who can take care of them?"

"Not at this short notice. I'm really sorry man, I tried to make other arrangements, but I've run out of options. I can't find nobody to come around." His voice wavers a little again, as if he's scared of how I'm going to react. It always makes me feel weird when people act like this around me. I'm not a complete monster, just a partial one.

"Well, I'm sorry about your mother-in-law, man. Is she going to be okay?" See? Not a total monster.

"Yeah, they said she'll probably need a hip replacement at some point, so we'll be saving up for that, I'm sure. But in the meantime, they have her resting and on pain meds. It sounds like she's comfortable. My wife is going to stay by her side until she's released."

"Alright man, well, take it easy."

"I'm really sorry again, boss." He still sounds anxious, but perhaps a little calmer.

"Yep." I click off the call.

I quickly google hip replacement surgery. It's expensive for someone without insurance, and I know for a fact Chalky and his family don't have it. Logging into our banking website, I wire funds to him anonymously that will cover the cost of the surgery and a little more.

Chalky is loyal, and while he's not part of our core family, he's an adjacent extension. Plus, we need him to be able to focus without worrying about financial trouble. It's when our guys owe other people money that they're most vulnerable to being compromised. It's better all around if I just help him out.

But this still leaves a haul to pick up.

Illegal alcohol distribution means we get booze for our bars and clubs that we can buy at a good price without all the taxes, helping us to turn an even nicer profit in an already lucrative business.

It can occasionally get a bit violent, picking up these orders. The logistics of being on an island mean that there's only so much stuff that comes in or goes out, and everyone wants the best deal. The taxes placed on items associated with people's vices—alcohol, cannabis, hotels where people come to deplete the island's resources while they lounge around and engage in all manner of hedonistic pleasures—are heavily taxed here, so the savings from this type of operation are substantial and enticing to a wide range of people.

The group who on-sells the alcohol to us has a tendency to invite more people than there are orders to fulfill, playing a little game of demand exceeding supply to further ratchet up their prices. It erodes the savings potential in our venues but still leaves the buyer with compelling savings. They couldn't care less if blood is spilled as a result of their little arbitrage game, as long as it results in more profits for them. I guess they're not so different from us in that regard.

"Hey, Brick," I call out from the living room to the adjacent dining area where he's pacing around for some reason. Or maybe the reason is simply because he's Brick and that's what he does. Psycho. "We're on liquor pickup. Chalky had a family obligation."

"Fuck yeah! I'm feeling up for a booze cruise." He enters the living room, grinning like a clown and holding a shiny scalpel in his hand. It's small, and he's at the other end of the room, but I can see some red marks on it. He has been having fun doing something down in his basement.

"What are you doing with that?" I arch an eyebrow.

"Practicing," he shrugs. "I have a little slug down in the basement that's been beating and groping old ladies on their way back from picking up their pension checks and groceries. I've been trialing exactly how deep I can go surrounding the vein without actually cutting through it." He mimics slicing through flesh with surgical precision.

"And?" I ask, mainly to humor him. He loves talking about torture stuff and I know I won't be able to get him to focus on the liquor pickup until he gets it all out.

"I've found a way I can almost cut around the vein without going all the way through it. So you can see the full thread of it, full of blood and everything. It's giving me flashbacks to dissection in biology class, but way more fun." He screws up his nose. "We've had a couple of mishaps though, where I've gone in too aggressively and severed the vein. But I've just glued everything back together as well as possible, and then we've moved on to another spot. Simple, really." He shrugs.

"Fantastic," I reply, not actually giving a shit. In fact, seeing someone's veins not attached to anything is fucking creepy. I don't mind cracking someone in the face or shooting them if need be, but I leave the full-on jerk-off torture fetish shit to Brick. "Alright, well, let's go get this liquor."

After a brief drive into a neighboring commercial area, we arrive at the drop point and there are some familiar faces standing and waiting for the supplies to be delivered. We're in a large space next to a dilapidated warehouse. The pebbled ground crunches under our footsteps as we approach. Palm trees and some other lush vegetation frame the large lot, and a couple of cars are parked at the edges, leaving a wide open space in the middle peppered with others also waiting for the drop.

We disembark from our vehicle and walk over to the waiting group. Nobody is talking, everyone standing there defensively with arms crossed and feet wide apart, trying to hold their own space. There's no orderly, single-file line. It's a cluster of randomly spaced people who are all ready to exert their dominance, eyeing each other up to see if they can guess who might make the first move.

It reminds me of how my grandmother's cats acted when I was growing up, stalking her to the cabinet where she kept their food and shoving in front of each other with increasingly loud cries and growls as the food got brought out. Hissing and clawing at each other when the food bowls made it to the ground, and they all realized there wasn't enough to go around. They were feral, just like these guys. Everyone's eyes flitting about for the first signs of the liquor being dropped, or of other groups trying to stage some type of ambush.

It's not just the picking up of the liquor that's where it ends, after all. You have to drive away from this place with a full vehicle and a bunch of people who missed out and want what you have. Shots have been fired before as vehicles have pulled out of the lot. Booze is a lucrative business.

I lead Brick over to two of the familiar faces. "Well, well, well. Look who we have here. Rake and Skyler. Two of the four little snake boys." I roll my eyes at the two men and take a closer look at them. Both are muscular, one significantly taller than the other. They're wearing their usual tank tops, shorts and flip-flops, like they couldn't decide whether to go to the beach or try to protect an island. "Why are you here? Trying to grab our stash? Or did you get lost on the way to T-ball practice?"

Brick snorts. "T-ball, haha good one."

"It's not your stash, last I checked," says Rake, the tall one, frowning. "It's whoever shows up first to get it." His voice sounds like he's trying to sound tough, making it a little lower than it naturally would be.

"Oh, so you're not too good for this type of job, then? Bootleg liquor doesn't go against your made-up moral code?"

"Fuck you, man," sneers Skyler. "We have standards, which is nothing to apologize for."

Rake nods in support, crossing his gangly arms over his chest.

I don't know Skyler well, but he's always seemed to have a big chip on his shoulder. Apparently, his dad was some fancy pants enforcer for the island back in the day, basically royalty around here. His son must be a real letdown, a major disappointment. Look at him, carrying on like this, defending their choice to turn down the real jobs and piss about with all the low-hanging fruit like liquor pickups. At least we normally have Chalky to take care of this type of task for us.

"Your standard has to be set really low," I scoff. "Must be a shit life, not having the ambition to ever accumulate any real power or money. To stay weak and poor. You'll never be anything like us."

"Nor would we want to be anything like you," Skyler spits on the ground, his saliva narrowly missing my shoe, and then narrows his eyes at me. He's lucky it didn't connect. Nobody fucks with my footwear. "It doesn't help that you're skimming a massive chunk of our profits. Makes it really hard to stay afloat around here. So thanks for your commentary on our 'shit life'. Maybe it would help if you acknowledged you're making it that way."

"You owe us, fair and square. We helped you to save her," I shrug. "You could have saved yourself the trouble. I know I would have."

Skyler nods. "I know, but it doesn't make it easier to turn a profit." He glares at me. "And I wouldn't change anything given the opportunity to do it all over again. She's more than worth it." Gross, he's like a walking human heart-eye emoji, weakened by some woman just because she's pretty or whatever. His eyes narrow at me. "But it doesn't mean I enjoy paying you your stupid cut every month," he sneers, "giving you a slice of absolutely everything we do."

"Aw, do we take all the profits away from the big bad snakes?" Brick asks, and Skyler's eyes flash with rage.

I turn my attention to Brick. "How much is this job worth, do you reckon?"

"Maybe five, ten grand?" He shrugs.

"You know what?" I glance over at the snakes. "Skyler and Rake, my little snake friends... which, by the way, is ridiculous. Can you come up with something better to describe yourselves? Anyway, I'm making an executive decision. This job is basically the scraps of this island." I gesture at the larger group standing around, hoping for a deal. "Here, you take the scraps. They're what you deserve."

"*What* did you just say to us?" Skyler steps forward, his eyes blazing. They're all so easy to trigger. You just need to insult their manhood and tell them they're less than. They get irrational very quickly. Especially Skyler.

I move toward him and get up in his face. Our eyes are inches apart and I can almost feel his breath on me. His nostrils flare and his eyes continue to blaze, but he doesn't say a word. He doesn't scare me. He's a skilled fighter, but so am I.

"I said," I say, enunciating each syllable, "that you can take the scraps. Because they're what you and your little friends deserve."

Without warning, Skyler smacks me in the face with a half-open hand and I don't even try to dodge it. He hits hard enough to knock my head sideways. I slowly move my head back to center, and then calmly crack my shoulders and then my knuckles.

And then it's on.

I rear my arm back, smashing it forward into Skyler's face. He reaches up to deflect it with his forearm, but he's too slow and it catches him on the jaw, his face flying backward and to the side.

Brick jumps in and punches Rake in the abdomen. It's a sucker punch because Rake is far too busy watching the interaction between me and Skyler. He doesn't see it coming at all and has no time to brace. Rake doubles over, gasping for air, but quickly regroups. Without fully standing back up, he swivels and spin-kicks Brick in a move he must have seen in an action movie or something, tripping him. They both end up on the floor, where they start pummeling each other. Brick jumps on Rake and pins him in an awkward pose that results in Rake's ass being inches from Brick's face. Rake tries to move but Brick keeps him firmly in place.

"Kiss my ass, Rake!" he yells, knowing Rake quite literally could in this position.

I'm so distracted by their almost-comical wrestling moves that I don't see Skyler's fist until it's too late. He delivers an uppercut to my chin and my head flies backward, little stars appearing in my peripheral vision.

I grimace as I feel my upper teeth sink into my lower lip and taste the distinctive metallic flavor of blood oozing into my mouth. That's going to hurt in the morning.

I spin around and deliver a high kick that catches Skyler on his side and knocks him toward the ground. Instead of crumpling, he dives on the diagonal and rolls, returning to standing at the end. He laughs, a little unhinged, and starts bouncing on the balls of his feet, fists up, while Rake and Brick continue to pummel and pin each other in the background.

By now, the entire parking lot has turned to watch what's going on between us. I suddenly feel a bit self-conscious and hear Aidan's voice in my head telling me enough is enough and that it's time to wrap things up.

"Okay, calm down Muhammad Ali," I smirk at Skyler as he continues to bounce from foot to foot.

"I was going more for Rocky Balboa today," he grins, his fists still up in a boxer's stance.

Neither of us makes a further move, and we stand there, a polite distance apart, even though our feelings for each other are far from courteous.

It's like we've momentarily got whatever it was out of our system, and the energy has shifted. We're almost amiable.

"Fucking hell. Where did I find you guys?" I shake my head and let out a deep breath.

"Here on the island. Where, unlike you, we grew up," Skyler says, his eyes glimmering.

"True. Would you like a prize? I grew up in a shithole on the mainland. Do I get a sticker for that, too?" I roll my eyes but decide not to take the conversation any further in that direction because I know if I do, we'll just start brawling again. "What the fuck are these two doing?"

We both look over at Rake and Brick, and they're still rolling around and pummeling each other. There are grunts and a lot of swearing, but nobody seems to be delivering any damage to the other. The bearded vegan and the ultra-tall, lanky guy, sliding around on the ground, grunting and trying to pin each other like they're TV wrestling.

I glance back at Skyler, and we both stifle a laugh and shake our heads.

"You know what? Fuck this." I walk over to the wrestling guys and pull Brick off Rake. "Come on, man, we've got bigger, more important shit to do. Let's leave them for now. We'll get most of their profits from this little gig, anyway. The venues are fairly well-stocked according to Roman, and we can just get the next drop when Chalky is back up and running."

Brick disentangles himself from Rake, and then stands up and takes a flamboyant bow. "Until next time," he says.

Rake waves back like he's the queen of England or something.

I don't know what just happened, but I want to block it all out. Fucking weirdos.

We're going home without the haul we were supposed to pick up.

But we're going to profit off the transaction anyway, so that's a win. Maybe should have just approached the situation this way in the first place.

Nevertheless, the snakes have me feeling a little ruffled, a little frazzled. The lengths they'd go to in order to protect the woman they love. It's stupid and naïve to put everything on the line for a woman, especially when she could just end up betraying them in the end. That's what women do, after all.

They're going to regret it. But they seem so steadfast in their decision.

They're choosing love over strength. Love over profits. Love over power.

What a bunch of fucking idiots.

Chapter Thirty-Seven

Angel

Brick and Slade arrive back at the house, and they're more quiet than usual. No snarky banter between them, and their posture is a little deflated, their shoulders slightly slumped. They've returned from a job empty-handed, and Aidan has words with them. I'm not sure of the details, but I guess they were meant to pick something up for one of their businesses, and there's a lot of head-shaking and hands held up in defensive postures.

Slade ends up getting pissed and storming off up the stairs. I hear his door slam halfway down the hallway.

I wonder what happened. They're usually such a tight unit and seem willing to jump in and help each other when things aren't going as they should be. But I get the sense that Brick and Slade screwed something up in Aidan's eyes.

As for Slade, his little tantrum just now got me thinking. Maybe he's just angry all the time and there's no specific target, just whoever is in his line of fire at that moment. Maybe his scowling is just the way he is, and has nothing to do with me or anything I've done. I'm not an idiot, and can tell he clearly doesn't want me here, but it's suddenly not feeling as personal as it was before.

I steer clear of them all, plucking some kind of thriller fiction book off the shelf in the living room and flicking through the pages absentmindedly while a reality show plays on the TV in the background.

Someone has made notes and highlighted sections in the book in what looks like careful color-coding, which I find more interesting than the contents of the book itself. I seriously doubt it was Brick because if he wanted to note something in a book he'd probably stab the page with a knife, or excise the quote with a scalpel and then glue it to his basement wall. Aidan seems like he would read things online, he's always attached to his computer screen. I'm guessing either Roman or Slade might have done it, but which one of them I'm not sure.

Eventually, Slade re-emerges from his room. He seems much calmer now, and after a brief discussion in hushed tones, he and Aidan leave the house together to go do another job.

Roman's already out taking care of something at one of the clubs.

It seems to be a busy day on the island.

Within a minute of everyone else leaving, Brick gets up from his stool at the breakfast bar and walks over to me in the living room.

"They've left us alone together." He winks at me. "This is the first time, I think!"

He plonks himself down next to me on the couch, dips his head and nips me on the neck, and I yelp and squeeze my shoulder to my ear.

He laughs, nuzzles his head back into the same nook and kisses it better. His lips make my neck tingle, and it spreads down my shoulder and back.

"What are you looking at?" he peers over my shoulder at the book I'm flicking through.

"It's some random book from the shelf," I gesture toward the floor-to-ceiling shelving jam-packed with literature on all sorts of topics. "Someone's made all these notes and highlights throughout it."

"Ah yeah, that's probably Roman," nods Brick. "He probably thinks it makes the book look pretty, doing that. Or maybe he thinks it will impress the ladies if they ever see it."

I glance at him sideways. This seems like something more personal to whoever did it than something intended to be shown off. Like it was meaningful to them regardless of whether anyone might eventually see it or not.

"Does it impress you, Angel? His color-coding?" He nips me on the neck again, playfully. "Does it make you want to ride his cock, seeing how he's used the color blue for dialogue he likes, and pink for the spicy scenes?"

I laugh and grin at him. "You know more about his book markings than you're letting on, by the sounds of it. Maybe they're *your* markings. I think *you* did this!"

"I don't mark books, I mark people," he replies, shrugging, and I can tell he means it. "And I'm going to mark you as mine, Angel. By the time we're done, everybody will know who you belong to." His eyes light up as he speaks, and it seems like he's been thinking about this for a while.

"I don't belong to anybody, Brick." I narrow my eyes at him. "I don't know why you think I do."

"That's where you're wrong." His tone is calm and confident, like he doesn't have a shadow of a doubt about what he's saying. His eyes bore into mine and the intensity of molten lava makes me melt a little. "You became ours ever since we laid eyes on you."

"What? You looked at me so now I'm your property? That sounds a little misogynistic, no?" I arch an eyebrow.

"Yep, that's pretty much how it works. You're mine, and yeah it probably is a bit misogynistic. But I take what I want, and I want you, Angel. I'll never apologize for wanting you."

"So do you think I belong to all four of you, or just you?" I raise an eyebrow.

"Yeah, basically. All four of us. We share everything, you know. But I'm the only one home, so you're all mine for now." His gaze trails down my body and he bites his lower lip.

I gasp as he leans over and licks the shell of my ear, an enjoyable shiver running along my neck and down my spine.

"How do you feel about us, Angel? Do you find us attractive? I think you do. I've seen the way you look at us. I saw how wet you got with Roman. I know what Aidan did to you, and how much you enjoyed your punishment."

My pussy clenches at the thought of Roman and me together, as well as my interaction with Aidan and his leather belt. I can almost smell the leather and feel the air whipping by as he cracked it down on me. Both memories get me hot just thinking about them.

So Brick was watching Roman and me, probably from the door, the same way I did when Roman fucked his date. But this time would have been better, because this time Roman was with me and not some stupid bitch he met at a bar.

"You watched me with Roman?" I raise an eyebrow.

"Of course I watched you with him," he shrugs and his eyes cloud with desire. "I couldn't look away. I've listened to your wetness and learned your scent. The gorgeous lines of your body as you arch your back, and the way your voice gets husky when you moan with pleasure. You're beautiful when you come, you know, Angel."

A deep flush creeps up my cheeks. Nobody's ever spoken to me quite this way. It's like he's studied me and likes what he sees, and is vowing to become an expert. A connoisseur of my body, the same way he is with his bevy of torture implements in his basement.

It's a little unusual to think he was looking at me while Roman's tongue explored my most sensitive spots. But it also turns me on, thinking about him watching, touching himself, while Roman lapped at my clit and ordered me to come all over his face.

There seems to be something about this house and watching people engage in intimate activities. My mind goes back to touching myself when Roman brought home his date, except there seems to be no jealousy involved in this case whereas I still want to kill that dumb bitch.

"Afterward, I jerked off at least three times thinking about you," he growls. "The way you arched your back and writhed on his face and moaned his name when you came. I couldn't help but think about what it was going to be like having my tongue swirling over your clit, and slipping my tongue inside you and tasting you and slurping down every last drop of your juices until you cry out my name. The things I want to do between your thighs." His eyes grow dark with lust.

My pussy clenches and throbs deeply as I remember the way Roman skillfully unraveled me with his tongue until I couldn't bear it anymore, my thighs trembling as he undid me over and over again. The thought of Brick doing the same but with his own spin on it is compelling. I want his fingers in me. I want his cock buried deep inside me. I want his own brand of crazy.

I bet he fucks rough, and I need someone who'll challenge my body right now. I need him to hurt me. I need him to make me forget, even just for a moment.

"And now I'm going to make you come apart for me," he rasps, as if reading my mind, licking his lips and tracing his finger from my clavicle down to my belly button. "What do you think about that, my Angel?"

My pussy clenches at the thought of me being alone with Brick, who has been thinking about how much he wants me for the past few days, planning all the ways he wants to dominate my body and consume me. It's quite a delicious situation to be in.

"You can try," I say, "but just so you know, my expectations are high."

"How so?" His gaze drops to my mouth and he bites his lip again.

"I want you to break me apart and put me back together again. I want you to make me scream your name until my voice cracks, until there's nothing left."

"Fucking hell," he groans, reaching down inside my shorts and panties and sliding two of his long fingers through my slick folds. With his free hand, he grabs a fistful of my hair and pulls it so my head tilts back, exposing my throat.

I moan at the feeling of his touch against my soaking slit and he pulls his fingers out, trailing the wetness up my stomach.

"Jesus, you're fucking dripping, Angel," he growls. "You're making me so fucking hard. You feel so good and I can't wait to bury myself in you."

My pussy is clenching in anticipation of what comes next. I tilt my hips toward his hand, grinding my clit against his palm. My body is screaming for his fingers to be inside me again, his tongue on me, and his cock to fill me up.

He hooks his hands over my shorts and pulls them down along with my panties. He slides his fingers through my folds again and finds my entrance, soaked with my arousal. His fingers are big and strong, their slightly rough texture dragging pleasingly against my walls.

"Watch me fuck you with my fingers, Angel," he says, my hair still tightly wrapped around one of his fists, and I gasp as two of the fingers of his other hand glide easily into my pussy. The only noises in the room are our breathing and the sound of his fingers plunging in and out of my wetness, the scent of my arousal thick in the air.

"Fucking hell," he growls. "You're so fucking tight. I can't wait until your pussy is clenched around my cock."

I moan as he slides his fingers out of me and then starts stroking my swollen clit. I grind against his hand, trying to create more pressure from his touch, trying to move faster.

"Look at me, Angel," he growls. "I want to see you come. I want to see your pussy convulsing while you come apart for me, begging to be filled by my big hard cock."

I stare back at him, this fucking hot man manipulating my pussy with his strong fingers. He definitely knows what he's doing.

He adds another finger, plunging all three deep inside me, and my pussy shudders, seizing around him and releasing more of my wet heat over his fingers.

The noise increases as my arousal begins to slide down my thighs. I can't remember the last time I've been this wet.

He increases his speed and the pressure on my clit, giving me everything I was trying to grind against him for. My body tenses as I buck against his hand, and I cry out his name as a powerful orgasm rips through me. I see stars in the corners of my eyes, and bold colors flash through my vision, pleasure radiating throughout every part of my body. He groans as I maintain eye contact with him, my body riding the wave.

He pulls his hand away and I moan, my eyes pleading with him to put his fingers back and slide them into me and all over my clit.

"Don't stop," I whisper, even though I just came. I want more of him, here and now.

He holds his hand up, his fingers still slick with my arousal and cum, and he locks eyes with me as he licks them off one by one. "Fuck, you're delicious," he says, savoring the taste of me.

He lowers himself from the couch to the floor, on his knees in front of me. My body trembles as he grabs my knees with his hands and spreads my thighs apart, opening my pussy to him, and baring me at his eye level.

"I can see your cum dripping out of your cunt," he rasps. "You're craving my tongue and my cock, aren't you, Angel? You want to come all over my face and then feel me buried deep inside you."

"Yes, baby," I moan. "Please, give it to me." My pussy is throbbing uncontrollably now. I want him inside me so badly I can barely breathe.

"What a greedy girl, wanting more after you just came all over my fingers."

"I need more," I rasp, my pussy tingling with anticipation. I mean it. He can't stop. I need more of him, all over me.

He dips his head and I moan as he licks me slowly from my ass up to my clit. He flattens his tongue and does it again, and then plunges his tongue deep inside my entrance. He groans, and I gasp at the way it makes my pussy seize as he swirls his tongue to explore my walls.

"I need your cock, Brick. Please," I beg. "Raincheck on your tongue because you're really good at that, but I need you inside me. I need you to fuck me right now, and I need it to be rough."

He pulls his head away for a moment and looks at me. "Are you sure, Angel? Because my rough is next level."

"That's what I was hoping you say," I pant, my legs still spread wide apart by his strong hands.

"Your wish is my command," he says, dipping his head and plunging his tongue into my pussy again like he wants one more taste before he destroys me with his cock.

"Fuck, you taste amazing. I could eat you out all day," he says, his voice husky. "And another day I will. But you've asked so nicely for me to pound you with my big hard cock, and that's what I'm going to give you. That's what you get for being a good girl."

His words make my pussy clench tighter than ever, and little tingles of anticipation spider out throughout my body.

He stands up and grabs me by my wrists, then pushes me down and stretches them above my head as he leans over me. He transfers one of my wrists so that he's holding them both in one hand, and closes the other around my throat. Bringing his lips to mine, he tugs on my lower lip with his teeth and sucks it into his mouth.

I moan as his lower body presses into mine, his hard cock digging into my throbbing pussy through his pants. I wrap my thighs around his waist, making his cock press into me even harder and he groans.

"Spread yourself for me while I take these off," he says, gesturing to his pants as he lets go of my wrist and throat and stands up.

I do as he says, placing my feet on either side of me on the couch so that I'm as open as I can be, ready for him to be inside me. He groans as he looks down at my wet, bare pussy, as if he can't wait to plunge himself deep inside me.

His pants off, exposing his thick cock, he lines it up with my pussy and slams it into me, knocking me backwards onto my forearms. My legs fly into the air and I instinctively throw them over his shoulders and wrap them around his shoulders, pulling him further inside me.

"I have an idea," he says, and while he's still very much inside me, he stands up with my legs still wrapped around him. I cling my arms around his neck and he carries me, my breasts bouncing, through the kitchen and dining area and down the hallway, down the stairs and into his basement.

Standing in the middle of the room, he mashes his lips to mine. Our teeth clash and our tongues wrestle. He carries me a little further into the basement, my thighs still wrapped tightly around him. He lowers me so my pussy once again impales on his hard cock, and presses my back against the concrete wall, just beside where the shackles are suspended.

For a moment, I think he intends on restraining me like he does his torture victims, but instead, he presses me more firmly into the wall, his hands cupping my ass, and he begins to fuck me hard. My back grazes against the cold, hard concrete as he pierces me with his cock, over and over. I cry out and wrap my legs around him even more tightly, angling myself so he can get further inside me.

"Harder," I gasp. "More!"

I wrap my arms around his neck, burying my hands in his hair, and I bite down hard on his shoulder which momentarily distracts me from the pain of the friction of the concrete wall on my back.

He growls at my touch. "Break my skin, baby. Make me bleed."

I do as he says, biting him harder, and he growls again. The sounds coming from him are primal, animalistic, and his hands squeeze my ass so firmly that I cry out.

"I like making you scream," he rasps out as he continues to thrust into me. "I'm going to make you bleed one day and I'm going to drink it. I have a feeling you'll taste like a fine red wine."

The veins in his neck throb from the exertion as he holds me up and slams into me, and I can tell he's close by the pace of his thrusts, the talk of blood play carrying him almost over the edge. His hips continue to grind as his cock presses into me, and I match his rhythm using the wall behind me as leverage. I savor the delicious feeling as his piercing drags against my walls.

"You like that, baby? A little pain while you're getting fucked?"

"Mmhmm," I moan.

"Make yourself come all over my cock, baby," he grinds out as he impales me over and over again.

I angle my hips so that my clit rubs on his pubic bone as he continues to thrust in and out. My pussy spasms and he groans as I feel my orgasm releasing throughout my body, stars in the back of my eyes. His thrusts are even harder now and he groans as I milk his cock, and he grunts as he throws his head back and releases into my body.

With his cock still inside me, he gently carries me to the basement counter and sets me down. He pulls my legs apart again, but this time it's so that they can dangle either side as he moves his body in close and wraps his arms around me. He's tender, gentle, and he kisses me softly on my forehead. "You're so incredible, my Angel. My Valkyrie," he says softly. "You're my dream girl."

He takes my hand and gently helps me off the counter. "We just added some new body fluids to the basement," he grins. "It's official, there's semen down here now, too."

"More fun than the usual kind of fluids down here," I smile back.

"Well, there's always a place for blood," he says, a devilish glint in his eye. "I'll use the scalpel next time."

"Do you promise?" I look at him through my eyelashes and I swear he starts to get hard again.

But instead of going for another round, he squeezes my hand gently and we head upstairs side by side.

He insists on walking with me to my room where he takes me into the bathroom and gently wipes me down with a warm wet cloth. His touches are gentle and attentive, a far cry from the brutality with which he slices and dices people who generally deserve it for their terrible acts.

My tender, gentle psycho. To everyone else, he's an unhinged, terrifying weirdo. And to me, he's quirky and really super sweet like a cinnamon roll.

Except when he's railing me, burying his cock deep inside me. Because in those moments he's animalistic, primal, consumed by carnal bloodlust. In those moments, he's everything I need.

Chapter Thirty-Eight

Aidan

Despite Angel distracting everyone's cocks, including mine, my mind is still in the game. We've received a report that someone is trying to rip off our underground casino, and we need to put a stop to it quickly. Word spreads quickly around this island, and if one person telegraphs that you're soft, that you can be fucked over, everyone comes out of the woodwork to try the same. So it's important that any time someone tries to compromise a weakness or vulnerability, you set them straight and send a very clear message to anyone else who's thinking about trying to undermine you.

"You drive. I'll ride shotgun while I review the transactions," I say to Roman after I pick him up from the club where he was supervising inventory.

Roman shrugs. He doesn't mind driving, but usually, he's the one riding shotgun, admiring himself in his phone camera and taking selfies while any of the rest of us drive. But we don't have time to indulge his vanity today.

Scrolling through the casino's reports, I can see that there have been roughly eight transactions to a single individual. On their own, each wouldn't raise an eyebrow, but I know the odds at our casino and this person's combined winnings are statistically impossible. That tells me one thing—there's someone helping this individual on the inside. One of our employees.

If there's one thing I can't handle, it's a betrayal by someone who we've let into our world. We take care of our people, and when they betray us, there's no coming back.

I get that people are often living paycheck to paycheck, but we pay our people well. It's an insurance policy to make sure they stay loyal. Unfortunately, being around stacks of money at the casino can make people greedy. And usually, when someone dares to try to rip us off, it's because they're desperate, battling their own demons which they can no longer afford. That's not our problem though, we're not a fucking charity. They might have bills to pay or a debt they owe, but that's no excuse for compromising our business.

Roman and I roll up to the front entrance of the restaurant that houses the casino.

"Those fuckers have been siphoning money from us? Jesus, Roman. I thought you did background checks on all of them."

"I did. They were clean when they started with us, but it looks like they've been compromised. Zero and his men started the job, and Swarenski took over from him more recently. They go after their families, threatening them and their livelihoods, so they have no choice but to try to steal from people like us."

"Fuck. How bad is it?" I rake my hand through my hair and let out an exhale.

"I'd estimate they've been stealing around ten grand a day for the last week or so. They're very methodical. They know when shifts start and finish, they've memorized the security protocols and the sentry detail. Somehow they've gotten hold of the codes for the safes where we keep the money."

"Well, that's not fucking good enough, is it?" My blood is boiling. How did we let this happen?

"Aidan, you've got to calm down. We'll fix it. It's different here than on the mainland. You knew that when we moved here. We all knew that."

I sigh and run my hand through my hair again. He's right. I did know it was going to be like this, the connections running so deep. We will always be outsiders here to some degree. No matter how powerful we become, there really is a home-court advantage. And it's not ever going to be our home court to the same degree as someone who grew up here.

That means we have to be sharper, hungrier, and stronger.

As we move through the restaurant, I feel the gaze of patrons as they raise forks to their mouths. They look up from their tufted booths and their giant plates of steak and lobster. The food is solid, if a bit pretentious for my liking, and the chef is a rising local celebrity, so the spot has been doing a roaring trade.

Most people in this city know who we are, and the regulars that frequent this restaurant know it's ours. The chef is becoming too high profile for our liking, her recent accolades drawing the attention of several prominent media outlets. Given we're running this place as a front for a gambling den in the back, we might have to swap her out soon for someone a bit more low-key.

Roman pushes open the door to the casino and we step through, closing it carefully behind us and nodding discreetly to the suited security guard who stands off to the side. Jazz music plays in the background, and a bar making classic cocktails lines the back of the room. Throughout the main space are a series of tables, poker and blackjack, mainly. There's a roulette table off to the side, as well as a couple of slot machines, but most people are here for the cards. Cigarette and vape smoke intertwines and wafts through the area, and the scent of whiskey and rum pervades the space.

Roman whispers in the door guy's ear and he nods and tips his head in the direction of a couple of the croupiers as well as a cashier. Roman nods and gestures for him and me to go upstairs.

We enter the security booth, and the guard on shift nods at us and slips out the door to do his rounds, leaving us to it. We cast our eyes over the complicated bank of screens that play security camera footage 24/7.

"When did we first notice something was off?" I ask Roman. "You said like a week ago?"

"Yeah. It was on a Tuesday." He types a password into the desktop computer in front of him and then starts to tap away in a browser.

"We should cross-reference the casino schedule with the dates the money went missing."

"Already on it. Okay, it looks like the three suspects the door guy has his eye on are Don Wong, Sophie Cutler and Bill Townsend. Those were the only three employees working all days the money went missing."

"I know Don from way back. I'd be really surprised if it was him. He's our top bartender, and people come here from miles away just to see him. He's our highest-earning bartender, and while I know having access to so much cash could be tempting, it would hardly be worth the risk for him. At least, I'd have to think so. He usually works out front, too. Doesn't spend much time back here in the casino."

"People change," shrugs Roman.

"That's true. We don't know what's going on in his family life. He might have developed his own gambling addiction, being around this all the time." I gesture at the bustling casino in front of us. "Someone could have a health issue and he needs to pay for surgery. It could be a number of things."

"You're becoming too soft and empathy-filled in your old age," laughs Slade.

"Oh, when we figure out who it is they're going to pay. I'll show no mercy. I don't care why they did it. They still fucked with the Brixtons. We can't let that slide. But it doesn't hurt to think about why sometimes."

"Really?" Roman seems surprised. "The more I have to hurt someone, the less I want to know about them. I like it to be clinical, objective."

"I like to know exactly how dark my actions are, in order to understand the full story. Feel the whole thing, understand it all."

"Doesn't that make it hard to sleep at night?"

"No," I shrug. "If anything, it makes it easier. Sometimes I have to lean into something before I can fully pull away. It gives me closure in some way, the ability to intentionally experience the full fucked-up nature of it all. It also helps me to understand how others are likely to respond, knowing what drives them. It keeps us safe in a way."

Roman shrugs and nods.

"Alright, Sophie was the second one." Roman pulls up her file. "Thirty-six-year-old mother of three. Has been working with us for two-and-a-half years. Runs the cashier station and has access to money. Record is clean, has never had any disciplinary issues."

"Seems unlikely, but we should still vet her," I say, and Roman nods.

"Alright, then," he says. "Third suspect is Bill Townsend. He's rotated around a few of the tables, has some kind of certification in blackjack and poker. Has had a couple of write-ups for coming in late with no excuse, and one for a verbal altercation with a supervisor a few weeks ago."

"My money's on this guy," I point at the photo on Roman's screen. "There's just something about him, and he's the only one with any disciplinary issues. It would just seem completely out of character for the other two."

"Yeah, he's apparently into some... pursuits that cost money that might be outside his means. They're a relatively new development and this is only based on gossip among the team. Nothing on his record that we could have caught when we brought him on board."

"Let's go have a little conversation with him, then," I say, and Roman nods.

We locate Bill and take him into one of our special rooms just off to the side of the main gambling hall. He's a man of average height and build, with close-cropped dark hair and brown eyes that flit about nervously. An Average Bill.

"We know you've been stealing from us, Bill," I growl. There are two ways interrogations can kick off. The first is where you pretend to be on the person's side and gradually lure them into a trap where they can't cover their own lies. I don't have time for that today. I'm going with option two, which involves just putting the accusation out there from the very start. It tends to result in immediate defensiveness, but the person on the receiving end knows you mean business from the outset.

"I don't know what you're talking about!" he protests, his voice squeaking at the end, his eyes looking everywhere except at me. They finally meet mine and he winces almost imperceptibly, but I see it.

"No, no, no, we're not going to do it this way," I say, shaking my head. "We're not going to go around in circles for hours while you deny everything, and make up stories about various other people it could have been. We're going to do this quick and dirty."

Roman points a gun at Bill, and Bill gasps. "Please, please don't shoot me. I'm not the guy you're looking for."

"Who is it then, Bill? You have five seconds to tell us who it is that's been ripping us off."

He looks down and I notice his hands are shaking.

"Five seconds, Bill. Five.... Four... Three-."

"Randall! It was Randall!" His voice cracks and his eyes glance left and right as if he's figuring out an escape route.

"Randall was on PTO visiting family in another country, you ass. Don't you think we checked the schedules to narrow things down to you?" Roman uses his gun to hit Bill in the side of the head. Bill cries out as the pistol whips him in the temple, raising a hand to staunch the pain.

"Tell us the truth, Bill, and we'll make this go quicker for you," I say.

"It wasn't me." His voice is low and unconvincing, perhaps the result of defeat and resignation settling in.

Roman hits him again, harder and to the front of his face this time. Bill's lip splits and he spits a blood-covered tooth into his hand.

"Fuck! Okay, okay! Please stop!" he cries out. "I've been taking the money. I didn't think anyone would notice. There's so much of it."

"Are you stupid? You don't think we know exactly how much money flows through this place, down to the dollar?" I arch an eyebrow at the moron.

"I—I needed cash." His eyes are glued to the floor, his voice still low.

"Yeah, we've heard about your habits and predilections. You're fucking disgusting, man."

Bill hangs his head and blood trickles from his nose.

"We could have dealt with basically anything else you could have shared, Bill." I speak slowly and clearly, so he absorbs every word. Let him be a warning to others. "But the one thing we just can't tolerate is lying. You see, we have to be able to trust everyone that works with us implicitly. You've made us a bit of a laughing stock over the last week or so, siphoning money from us and thinking you'd gotten away with it. That's how it even came to our attention in the first place. You may as well have been big-noting around town, telling people you got one over on us. Unfortunately for you, Bill, we can't just let that slide. We need to treat you as a message to anyone else who would try to do anything like what you did. It didn't need to end this way, but you only have yourself to blame. Do you understand?"

The whites of Bill's eyes grow large and he whimpers as Roman pulls his gun from his holster and screws in the silencer. His whimpers grow louder as Roman raises the gun to Bill's head height and shoots him between the eyes. He crumples to the floor, and the room is silent.

Chapter Thirty-Nine

Angel

"You look like a Slade, you know," I say as I take a seat at the breakfast bar and peer over the counter to see what he's doing. It would probably have been easier to steer clear, but with everyone else out of the house and nothing new on TV I can't help poking the bear.

"What the fuck does that mean?" he growls and rolls his eyes.

"Seriously, you do. If I had a dictionary, right next to the word 'Slade' there'd be a picture of you, glaring back at me from the page. There are more Slides out there than you, but you're the iconic one. The face of all Slides."

"What do you want? You can see I'm trying to cook." Slade brings my words to life by doing exactly what I just described, glaring at me as he aggressively chops some peppers and garlic on a chopping board.

"Wow, you sound like that grumpy TV chef," I smirk at him. "You even have the mean chef glare down. Don't you like company when you cook? It can be like one of those chef's tables at a fancy restaurant, where the chefs interact with the guests and explain what they're doing."

"That sounds like an actual nightmare," he scoffs. "Not to be dismissive of your night terrors, but I might have one tonight at the thought of it." Great. He's heard my screams.

"What's so bad about human interaction, Slade? Afraid someone will find you out? That they'll deem you to be less worthy than them? Realize you desperately need a personality transplant?"

"No, I just prefer to be left alone. I like the isolation and solitude of concentrating on the food I'm preparing. Without interruptions or small talk or having to explain myself. I get lost in measuring out the ingredients, in tasting the food. Of figuring out which combinations go together the best."

For the first time, I see Slade in a different light. Instead of the brooding, scowling man who barely speaks, he's animated and gesturing as he talks, and there's an energy about him that I haven't seen before. I've heard him say more words in the last minute than I think I have since we met. His voice actually broke out of monotone, and I saw or at least imagined the hint of a smile.

"You're making cooking sound kinda sexy," I grin at him. I cock my head to one side as I examine him in more detail, and I like what I see. "I believe cooking brings you joy, Slade."

"I suppose it does," he shrugs. "When I'm not being distracted." He narrows his eyes at me, and I'm worried he's just going to go back to the way he was before. Maybe I pushed him too far, pointing out that he seemed a bit lighter, and that he was actually enjoying something for once.

But instead, he beckons to me, inviting me into the kitchen with him. "Come around here and make yourself useful."

"*You* want *my* help? After your song and dance routine about how you only like to cook by yourself?" I maintain eye contact and smirk at him as I walk around the kitchen island and stand between him and the counter.

"Don't push it, Angel," he growls, grabbing me by my wrists and pushing me back against the edge of the counter until I have to tilt back slightly. He presses against me, his body melding into mine, and he leans forward so that his stubble grazes my jaw. "There are sharp objects and fire in here, you know. I wouldn't test me," he growls, his voice growing husky. I feel him getting hard as his cock presses into my lower abdomen, and my pussy clenches. He really is a very attractive man and now I'm squarely within his domain, within the area of the house that he fully dominates and controls.

"Or what?" I ask, breathless as his girth continues to harden against me. "What will you do to me if I push it?"

"You don't want to know," he says, pulling away to hand me a chopping board and a knife, as well as an onion. "Here, chop this."

"You trust me with a big sharp knife?" I arch an eyebrow.

"Trust is a strong word, Angel," he grins. "But I'm risking it just this once. Don't make me regret it."

"I'm not great at this. I exist on takeout and ramen noodles."

"Why doesn't that surprise me?" He rolls his eyes. "But I'm sure you can chop a fucking onion."

I do my best to neatly chop the onion while he prepares some other ingredients, and he leans over my shoulder at one point to inspect, his stubble once again brushing against my face and sending little goosebumps up my neck. "Nice job, Angel," he says, "for someone who doesn't cook, you can chop an onion okay." His deep voice is doing things to me, and my pussy begins a low throb.

"What can I do to help you now, Chef? How can I be of service?" I look at him through my eyelashes and bite my lower lip.

He glances over at me from the saucepan where he's flicking some ingredients with his wrist. I've never been able to do that. I've tried before, but the contents flew across the counter and the floor, my wrist clearly not made for such efforts. Never again. But Slade makes it look easy, flicking this giant heavy saute pan like it's nothing. It's mesmerizing to watch.

"Nothing else needed from you," he says. "You've reached your peak with those onions, I think. So you're dismissed." He smirks at me and I pout.

Suddenly all I can think about is distracting him. I grab the chopping board covered in onions and carry it halfway across the kitchen.

"What are you doing?" he asks, confused. "I need those. Bring them back."

I look over my shoulder and smirk at him, and then turn back around so my back is to him, and drop the chopping board on the ground. "Oops!" I say, as the board clatters to the floor and diced onions fly all over the tiled surface. "I guess I'll just have to pick them up."

Without bending my knees, I lean straight over, my short shorts riding up as I lean down, giving him a good look. I'm not wearing panties, and I'm sure he knows that now, too. I can almost feel his eyes boring into me. I kneel down and proceed to sweep the onion into a pile with my hands, my butt still stretched into the air.

He groans behind me, almost imperceptibly. "Jesus fuck, Angel."

"What? It was an accident." I look over my shoulder at him, through my eyelashes, feigning innocence.

"Get up," he growls, my ass still in the air, taunting him. His eyes are hungry. He wants me, there's no question. Fuck, he's so hot, and I can feel myself getting wet.

I stand up and face him and he grabs me by my upper arms and pulls me to him, mashing his mouth against mine. I kiss him back, urgently, and he reaches down and cups my ass with both his hands. He growls as I graze my teeth against his lower lip. His husky voice does things to me and my pussy's throb intensifies. My lips are going to be bruised and I don't mind one bit.

I reach down to touch his cock and it's rock hard. I start to rub it through his pants but then he pulls my hand away.

"What's wrong?" I ask, and a shadow passes over his eyes. I press my chest into him and his eyes dart to my breasts. He's still hungry for me, and I'm not sure why he pulled away. He stands there for a moment, still, but I'm not convinced this is over yet.

He suddenly grabs me under both arms and hoists me onto the kitchen counter so that I'm sitting on it. He yanks up my shirt and pulls down my sports bra underneath my breasts, exposing both nipples. They immediately harden in the cool air, and he leans down and sucks one of them into his mouth, twirling his tongue around it and tugging at it with his teeth. I moan as pleasure shoots from my nipple to my core like a lightning bolt straight to my center. While he sucks on my nipple, he reaches down and undoes my shorts, and then growls, "Hold on to my neck, Angel." I do as he says, and he lifts me up just enough to slide off my shorts and my panties.

Chapter Forty

Slade

I pin her to the kitchen counter, one hand clamping down on her shoulder while I crush my mouth to hers. She's fucking intoxicating, and it infuriates me. She wouldn't take no for an answer, distracting me while I tried to cook. I tried to put her to use, but she was even distracting while chopping onions. I couldn't stop looking at her exposed neck while she narrowed her eyes in concentration, trying to impress me with her geometric onion cuts that were clearly a struggle. I don't want to like her, but she's making it fucking hard. She's adorable. Ugh.

Speaking of which, then the manipulative little bitch went and dropped the entire chopping board of onions on the floor, making a giant mess. Then has the audacity to torment me with her gorgeous ass. She knows she's not wearing underwear, and her shorts are a tiny piece of material that barely covers anything. When she bent over, she made sure I got a good look. This is all part of her act and I don't know if I can trust her, but I couldn't tear my eyes away.

So now, she's going to get it. She wants to distract me? I'll let her distract me just this once. But she tried to touch my cock, and although part of me wanted nothing more than to slam it into her tight cunt, that's a no-go zone.

Instead, now that she's bare in front of me, I roughly spread her thighs apart so she's exposed to me, her pussy glistening for me. Her arousal begins to make a small puddle on the counter. Not entirely sanitary, but that's what cleaning products are for.

I slide a finger through her slick folds, and she's soaking wet. It gives me an idea, something fitting for the kitchen. I pull her tank top over her head along with her bra, throwing them to the side and leaving her completely naked.

"I don't think I can wait until dinner is ready," I growl, looking down at her gorgeous tits, her rock-hard nipples pebbling under my gaze. "I'm hungry now."

I get some olive oil from the counter.

"I always make sure I get the best kind they have," I say, showing her the bottle. "Good quality makes such a difference... to the texture, and to the way it makes things taste."

It's in a pourer that's meant for drizzling, so that's what I do. I drizzle the oil so that it runs down her chest, moving it from side to side so that little rivulets of oil slip over each nipple and then cascade down her breasts and over her abdomen, down to her pussy. I pour a little directly on her clit and she moans as the cool, thick liquid makes contact and begins to slide over her. I place the oil bottle back on the counter and she moans as I massage her breasts, paying special attention to her nipples, which I roll between my thumbs and forefingers.

"Your nipples are rock hard," I say as I tweak and twist them. She's so slippery now, and she moans at my touch."It's hard to get a grip on you with all this oil."

I get her to prop her forearms up on the counter, and I lift her hips up to my chin height. She gasps as I blow cold air so that it fans across her slick folds. I dip my head and slide my tongue between her folds, devouring her with my tongue. "Fucking hell, you taste so sweet," I groan, as I move my tongue upward to her swollen bud. She gasps as I suck her clit into my mouth and begin to massage it with the flat of my tongue.

"Fucking hell, Slade!" she screams.

"Call me chef," I grin at her.

"Yes Chef!" she pants.

"Good girl," I growl, and her eyes cloud with lust.

I lock eyes with hers as I continue to feast on her pussy, tasting her arousal and moving my mouth and tongue over every inch of her that I can get to.

"Do you want to come for me here in the kitchen, Angel? Will you come all over my face for me?"

"Yes. Yes Chef," she pants again. She's a quick learner, calling me by the name I ask her to. She seems less stubborn when she's on the verge of an orgasm, her feistiness replaced by pure lust.

"Are you sure?" I ask, pulling away just for a moment.

"Yes! Fucking hell, Slade. *Yes*!" She wraps her legs tightly around my neck and attempts to pull me back onto her, but I resist just for a moment. To remind her that I'm the one in control here.

"Okay, just checking." I bury my head in between her thighs and suck and lick at her delicious juices until she arches her back and screams my name as an orgasm rips through her.

Lowering her hips, I let her sit back down on the counter. I slide my fingers through her soaking folds, slicked with a mixture of her wet heat and the olive oil. "Jesus, Angel. You're like a human Slip 'N Slide."

She giggles, but it comes out more like a moan as I slide three fingers into her as far as they will go, with no warning.

"Just don't tell the guys we did this on the kitchen counter. Brick wouldn't care, but Aidan gets funny about stuff like that."

She laughs. "Even when Aidan's not here, he's got you all trying to be on your best behavior. Although that's a relative term when it comes to you psychos." She gasps as I slam my fingers back into her soaking cunt. I have no intention of being gentle. This little bitch has been causing me nothing but concern and I'm going to take it out on her the only way I can think of that will end well for her.

I plunge my fingers into her repeatedly and she gasps, lifting her hips up to give me better leverage and access to her hole. I fuck her with my fingers as she grinds against my hand, the kitchen amplifying the sound of my fingers ramming into her wetness. "You dirty little slut, begging me to finger fuck you on the kitchen counter," I growl, our eye contact unwavering.

She doesn't say anything and I slow down my pace, dipping my head to twirl her nipple in my mouth.

"More!" she cries out.

The oil and her arousal make loud slippery noises, and I can smell her sweet scent above all the ingredients in the kitchen. It's making me even harder, but I can't go there, so instead, I focus on annihilating her pussy with my fingers. I slam them in and out and she bucks and cries out as my pressure and pace increase.

She's flushed and covered in a thin sheen of sweat, and her breath is beginning to grow ragged as she writhes against my hand. I bury my fingers inside her over and over again and curl them up towards me, my palm flattening against her clit.

I feel her body start to reach a crescendo and she starts thrashing wildly against my hand, trying to get more pressure on her clit.

Suddenly, a screeching beeping noise starts blaring from the ceiling in the hallway. *Fuck!* It's the smoke alarm. But I can't do anything about it. My fingers are still buried deep inside her. She doesn't stop either, and instead grinds against me harder. I can tell she's imminently close, and she gasps my name as her whole body visibly tenses. The smoke alarm continues to blare and I notice dark smoke billowing from the saute pan. My fingers still deep inside of her, I use my spare hand to grab the pan and dump it in the sink. The scorching hot cast iron connects with the cold water on the bottom of the sink and it sizzles and hisses, sending smoke billowing into the air.

Her pussy starts spasming violently against my fingers, her hips still bucking wildly as she crests her peak. She screams my name and I can hardly hear it over the beeping.

Aidan and Brick suddenly run into the kitchen.

"What in the actual fuck?" Aidan yells as he sees my fingers embedded in Angel's cunt. He grabs a wooden spoon and uses it to tap the button on the smoke alarm, which is just out of reach on the tall ceiling. The beeping stops. "On the kitchen counter? Really? An entire house to yourselves and you pick the one place we prepare food?"

She looks slightly dazed, gasping, as I slide my fingers out of her. "We knew you were going to say that," she smirks. Brick cracks up laughing as I walk to the sink to wash my hands, and she hops down from the counter to retrieve her clothing.

I grab the all-purpose cleaner and some paper towels. "Clean up after yourself. You made a giant mess." I hand them to her and she narrows her eyes at me but then shrugs and cleans it up, still completely naked, her arousal and the olive oil sliding down her thighs.

"You have all lost your fucking minds," Aidan shakes his head and runs a hand through his hair. "I think you were right, Slade. Having her here was a terrible idea. Now she's gotten to you, too."

Chapter Forty-One

Angel

"So you're really going to let me go shopping... by myself?" I still can't quite wrap my head around it. After what feels like months, I'm being allowed out of the house unsupervised. It sounds kind of crazy, but there hasn't been a need to leave ever since I've technically been able to. I've had everything I need right there and plenty of disincentives to have my face seen around the island.

"Yeah. Just for an hour or so," says Aidan. "You are free, you know. But it wouldn't be sensible to come and go as you please with a lunatic stalking you."

"What makes you think this is going to be safe? I mean, I want to go, it's just... I'm a bit scared if I'm honest. He's clearly good at tracking me down."

"It's a public place and we'll make it difficult for anyone to track you. Even if he knew you were staying here, we're going to have multiple vehicles and you won't be visible. We'll have you duck down until we arrive at the shopping mall, and we'll park close to the door."

This is so exciting. The thought of just being a normal human being for a moment, of walking past artfully designed displays and window shopping. Of running my hand along a row of clothes neatly placed on hangers. It sounds so... normal. And there hasn't been much of that in my life for what seems like forever. It's sweet that they have thought this through so carefully, knowing that the items Brick grabbed from my apartment are running low and I could do with replenishing some skincare and cosmetics as well as some additional clothing.

The guys do as promised. We hop into three different cars in the garage. I'm with Aidan and Roman, and then Brick and Slade each take separate vehicles. They have me sit in the back and lie down across the back seat. With the heavily tinted windows and the added precaution of me lying down, there's no way anybody would be able to track me. And it's not like I have my own phone anymore. That's long gone, so we don't need to worry about my stalker finding me that way either.

"Here you go," says Aidan, handing me a small rectangular package through the gap in the seats.

"What's this?"

"A burner phone so you can reach us if there's an emergency, or just to let us know when you want to be picked up if you get bored before the hour is up."

"I doubt I'll get bored. There are hundreds of stores in there! Not that I can afford any of it," I sigh.

"Keep looking in the bag," says Aidan.

I gasp as I remove the cell phone box and see a stack of hundred-dollar bills underneath. "What the hell?"

"It's a gift from us. Buy yourself something pretty," he smiles.

Roman glances back at me and grins. "It would be difficult to find something you don't look gorgeous in. But we hope you find something you really like that brings you joy when you wear it. Me, personally, I'd love it if you got some sexy lingerie that I can peel off with my teeth, but it's your gift, so do what you want with it." He wiggles his eyebrows and I laugh, my pussy clenching at the thought of him doing just that. There will be some lingerie shopping today, that's for sure.

We pull up at the shopping center and, as promised, they drop me right beside the door to one of the department stores.

As I get out of the vehicle, I reflect that this is one of my first outings on the island in a very long time. It seems ironic, being in this gorgeous tropical environment with its warm, sunny weather, sandy beaches, crystal-clear water and lush greenery, yet here I've been stuck inside a sleek, shiny, mega-secure compound that could just as easily be located in any city on the mainland.

It's not what I expected when I moved here, and where I'm staying is very nice, but it's definitely not the relaxed, laid-back atmosphere I was hoping for. Instead of natural beauty and stunning sunsets, I've been encapsulated in a high-tech wonderland. To be fair, the compound is full of hot men, so that's a plus.

I glance around before heading into the building, inhaling the slightly sweet, salty air that wraps its humid arms around me and holds me close as I walk through it. It's like an invisible gravity blanket, making me feel comforted and secure. This is more reflective of the island lifestyle I'd been hoping for and that I'd gotten to live for a brief moment before these guys and my stalker turned everything upside down.

Even the carefully curated landscaping of the mall reflects this gorgeous island paradise. The sidewalks ringing the building are lined with palm trees, providing natural shade and a picturesque backdrop. Tropical flowers and a variety of other plants and trees are clustered in planter boxes attached to the exterior cladding. The air is filled with the sweet scent of blooming hibiscus and plumeria, and even in this bustling commercial area, you can often hear the sounds of birds and other wildlife in the distance. It's gorgeous. For a moment, I take in a deep breath to soak in these surroundings. This is how life is meant to be.

Pulling the heavy front door ajar by its large golden handle, I inhale deeply as I enter the department store. The familiar scent of cosmetics mixed with a variety of perfumes invades my senses. There's something magical about upscale department stores, the promise of something exciting and new blended with a comforting familiarity, even when you can't afford to do more than window shop.

I walk all the way through the department store and exit on the other side into the main part of the mall. People walk past, mainly in pairs and small groups, chatting and laughing and sipping on fancy coffee and enjoying snacks from the adjacent food court.

Walking past the escalator, I take a peek at the store directory and find one of my favorite stores on the same floor on the other side of the mall. I turn around and make a beeline for it. Walking fast, I almost smack into someone hurtling in the opposite direction. I stop just in time and she whips around to face me as I essentially slam on my leg brakes.

"What the—?" she locks eyes with me, and recognition dawns.

Oh my god, it's *her*. I know nearly nobody on this island, and this is the person I almost crash into in the middle of a shopping mall? Come on.

"You're that bitch that almost ran into me at the beach a while back." I narrow my eyes at her.

"As I recall, it's *you* who almost ran into *me*." She narrows her eyes right back at me. "Staying in your own space and walking in a straight line both seem to be real issues for you."

"I've been wanting to ask you about something," I say. I may as well take the opportunity to ask her what I want to know. "Is it true that you're in a relationship with all four of those guys you were surfing with?"

"You're really going to almost crash into me a second time and then open up a conversation with a nosy ass question like that?" She arches her perfectly manicured eyebrow at me.

"I'm just curious. If you'd like to talk about the weather and other 'safe' topics, that's fine. I'm also down to debate religion and politics. Look, it seemed to be a straightforward question, unless it's something you're ashamed or embarrassed about."

"Why would I be either of those things, if that is, in fact, what was happening?"

"Oh, I don't think you should be, if that's what was happening. I just don't know why you wouldn't be more open about it. Why you'd shut me down for asking."

"What's it to you?" she snarls, narrowing her eyes at me. "Did your little Brixton gang ask you to ask me that?"

"No, I was just curious. If so, good for you." I shrug.

She observes me curiously. "Why do you hang out with them, anyway, the Brixtons? They seem like terrible people."

"Why do you say that? Because they don't put up with other people's shit? Because they don't come up with some lame moral code like your guys?"

"My guys can sleep well at night. I imagine yours find that difficult."

"Actually, they all sleep quite soundly, from what I've seen."

"They sound like soulless monsters, honestly."

Hearing her say that really pisses me off. What an ungrateful bitch. "You're just mad because they're taking a cut of your guys' profits," I snarl. "When they totally deserve it, bailing you out like that. It's a debt." My voice rises. "In fact, you're lucky you're alive. You actually owe them when you think about it! Maybe you shouldn't be so rude. Maybe you should be thanking them."

"Wait, they did what?" Her eyes grow large, but only for a moment, and she quickly regroups and tries to act casual. I'm not buying it, though.

"Oh, they didn't tell you?" She must be messing with me. She has to know how she got out of her catastrophic situation.

"Oh, um... yeah, I guess I misunderstood for a moment," she says quickly. "I heard you loud and clear. Yeah, I know all about that whole debt situation and bailing me out. Yep."

She's lying. Her eyes flit up and to the side as she speaks, and she twists her fingers against her thumbs.

"You didn't know, did you?" I observe her, and her mouth trembles slightly, but she stays quiet. "I'm sorry if I spilled the beans. I wasn't meant to say anything to anyone, and I guess the guys thought you'd be the last person I'd be having a polite conversation with."

"This is a pretty fucked up polite conversation," she says, her voice low.

"So you didn't know...?"

"No... I didn't." She wraps her arms tightly across her chest.

"Sorry, I didn't mean to—."

She cuts me off. "It's not your fucking fault, Angel. And yes, I know that's your name," she glares at me. "I'm just fucked off that they lied to me. They made it seem like... I don't know... that they took care of it themselves, without... outside help. Especially help from... them."

"They didn't act like your father paid it off, did they?"

Her eyes narrow. "Jesus, you know about him as well? Fuck, your guys have their noses all up in everyone's business."

"Well, it's kind of common knowledge around here," I smirk.

She rolls her eyes and glares at me. "Well, no, I didn't for once think my dad paid it off. I know he's slunk off back to the mainland and he'll be on the run until someone finally catches up with him on Tane's orders. Tane is twisted enough that he might even get my guys to take out the hit, knowing full well they're with me."

"That is fucked up."

"The thing is, I wouldn't hold it against them for a minute if they did it. Hell, I might demand they let me do it myself. Because trying to sell me to get rid of a debt is way more fucked up than anything I've done to him. Death seems like an easy way out, considering all the shit he's pulled."

"Wow... but I kind of get it."

"You do?" she squints at me, her brow furrowing. "I highly doubt that. How?"

"Let's just say my family is fucked up as well."

She nods, and we stand there quietly for a moment, both deep in thought.

"So you thought your guys stumped up the cash somehow and didn't realize they had help and now have a debt?"

"Yep." She smacks her lips together loudly. "It sounds like all four guys have some explaining to do." She walks away.

"See you around!" I call out as she heads in the opposite direction.

She doesn't look back. If only to be a fly on the wall when she gets back to wherever she lives. Because there's one thing that's for sure. Shit's about to go down.

Chapter Forty-Two

Slade

"Brixton," Aidan answers the phone curtly, and an inaudible voice murmurs something into his ear. "Wait, who's this?" his voice rises.

I look up. It's rare for Aidan to sound confused about anything. He's usually the master of control, everything meticulously planned out and all potential scenarios accounted for. We're similar in that way, but it's for different reasons and it manifests itself differently. As in, he's a hero and a leader, and I'm a surly asshole.

A shadow passes across Aidan's face. "She *what*? Oh, Jesus fucking Christ. Are you sure?"

There's a loud garbled voice on the other end of the line that I can hear from across the table, although I can't make out their actual words. Someone isn't happy. And I'm pretty sure there's only one 'she' that whoever it is could be referring to.

"Look, sorry to hear that, dude. Seriously. I know we have our differences but.. Jesus. Look, I'll deal with it. I'll be back in touch. Okay, bye."

His face is stony as he hangs up.

"What did she do? It was her, wasn't it? The fucking she-devil has fucked something up just by being alive." I knew it wouldn't take long for her to do something to compromise us. I don't know what she's done, but she's clearly done something. I'm going to enjoy being right about this.

Aidan sighs and runs a hand through his hair. "Yep, you were right. I should have listened to you instead of Roman's dick. Jesus."

"Well, what did she do? It would be helpful to know the details so I can help you think through what to do next."

"She fucking told that Devon girl about us helping her guys pay off her father's debt. That we're responsible for saving her. She didn't know."

"Wait what? She hates Devon, and from what I could tell, it's mutual. And they don't even really know each other. How the fuck did that even happen? Did she track her down on purpose to upset her?"

"I don't know. But either way, I guess those guys had told her a different story, and she's on a rampage, possibly murderous. If I were them, I'd be protecting my dick from sharp objects right now."

"When did they even have an opportunity to communicate? She was only out of the house for a couple of hours this entire time."

"I guess they were both at the mall at the same time."

I let out a low whistle. "What are the fucking chances? But then again, I knew we shouldn't have taken the risk, and should have just sent Brick to get more stuff."

Aidan sighs. "Look, can we focus on how to fix this rather than pointing fingers and talking about how you were right over and over again? It's not helpful."

"Yeah, fine," I sigh. "But Jesus. I knew she was trouble the moment I saw her."

"It is kind of on them, though, when you think about it." Aidan shrugs.

"Why are you protecting her? She did a cruel thing for whatever reason. Maybe she's fucked in the head like that. Jealous of Devon or something."

"Why would she be jealous of her?" He arches an eyebrow.

"I don't know. Devon's pretty and lives with four guys who are, by conventional standards, pretty decent-looking."

Aidan looks around the kitchen and puts his hands out in an exaggerated shrug. "Um, Angel is fucking stunning and look where she's living and who she's with."

I roll my eyes.

"Look, she seems like a conniving, manipulative bitch who uses her pussy to get what she wants. And now it turns out she's a cruel bitch, too. This could put our business deal with those snake guys at risk, too. A condition of our arrangement was not to fuck with Devon."

"And we haven't," Aidan says, but he's frowning. He sighs. "They might just not see it that way."

"Well, if she hadn't said anything, it wouldn't even be in question."

"Yes, but they also could have told their girlfriend or whatever she is the truth."

"I knew Brick shouldn't have said anything." I sigh. What a fucking mess.

"Listen, let's get her side of the story and try to understand what actually happened. There's no point in jumping to conclusions just because they suit your narrative that she's some fucking devil spawn out to ruin us."

"It might not be intentional, but it might be the result. She might have really fucked us on this one, Aidan."

He sighs and runs his hand through his hair again. I see his Adam's apple bob.

I can read Aidan like a book, and I can tell he knows I'm right.

Whether we are completely fucked remains to be seen, but we're going to find out very soon.

Chapter Forty-Three

Angel

"Angel! What the fuck happened today?" Aidan's eyes flash at me in a way I haven't seen before. With a scowl that big, he reminds me a bit of Slade.

"What do you mean?" I genuinely don't know what he's talking about.

"What happened at the store today?"

It's a weird question. What the heck? "I went to get some clothing and other stuff. You know this Why?"

"Did you try to reach out to that girl that you had the run-in with at the beach? Devon?"

That's strange. I wonder how he knows I spoke with her.

"I didn't reach out to her," I shrug. "We walked past each other and struck up a conversation."

"It sounds like it was quite the conversation. What did you talk about?"

"Girl stuff, mostly. You know, Scandoval, nail polish, dick sizes. That type of thing." I shrug and smile sweetly.

He glares at me. "Angel, don't lie to me. I know you talked about more than that."

Oh shit. A little pit grows in my stomach. I know I shared some information with her that maybe I shouldn't have, but I didn't expect it to get back to these guys, at least not so quickly.

I sigh. "Okay, listen. We were talking about why you guys hate her guys so much and vice versa, and I mentioned that I was surprised given you'd helped her guys to bail her out of the whole debt extravaganza."

Aidan places his head in his hands and shakes his head.

"What?" I shrug. "I didn't have a clue that she didn't know! I assumed she did, seeing they're in a relationship and all! I had no idea they didn't tell her. I felt so bad for her when

I realized this was the first she'd heard of it. It was all a bit embarrassing and cringe, really, so I didn't say anything. I didn't want you to think I'm a complete idiot. Why? How did you know?"

He raises an eyebrow at me. "You really think she didn't run straight back there and tell her guys about your little conversation? That they're not on the lookout for any little thing to say we did wrong?"

"Well, I don't know the dynamics of their relationship pentagon or whatever the fuck it is, do I? I would assume a relationship like that requires extra trust, not less. Seems like a pretty big thing that they should have told her about. Saving her from being auctioned off to a creep. Seems like something they should take credit for, not hide."

"They were likely trying to protect her. You know, because guys like to protect their women. Like we protect you."

"I'm your woman? Aww!" I grin, and my chest flutters a little.

"Watch it," Aidan growls, and the grin disappears from my face immediately. He's not in the mood to play around. "You might have fucked us on our deal with her guys, Angel," he explains.

Fuck. "How? I don't have anything to do with your business dealings."

"The main condition was that we wouldn't do anything to fuck with her. And whether intentional or not, and Slade is particularly skeptical of your intentions, as you may imagine, your actions could be perceived as fucking with her. With all of them."

Shit. "Oh my god. Please believe me, I had no idea. And that wasn't my intention. I can be a real bitch when I feel like it, but that's not what happened today."

Slade rolls his eyes.

"What can I do about it? How can I fix this? I really am sorry." Fuck, they're going to toss me out on the streets and I'm going to be shredded to pieces by my stalker.

Aidan runs his hand through his hair, which I notice is something he does when he's thinking, when he's worried, when he's conflicted. I guess it's just something Aidan does a lot.

"You can get the fuck out of this house, for one," says Slade. "That would help the guys know we had nothing to do with your little stunt."

"Oh, so you'd prefer me to die than to figure out an adult solution to this? That's lovely of you, Slade. You can fuck right off."

He glares at me, but then his face softens. "I forget about that piece with the crazy slasher dude. I just want you to go away so you don't destroy us like you seem hellbent on doing. I don't want you to actually die."

"That's a change of pace."

"Sometimes I'm not good at saying what I mean."

Jesus. Slade is perhaps the most confusing man I've ever met. Is he getting a soft spot for me? Part of me wants to tease him, but I don't think I should push it right now, although I fully intend to put him to the test later. For now, I just need to figure out this mess.

Chapter Forty-Four

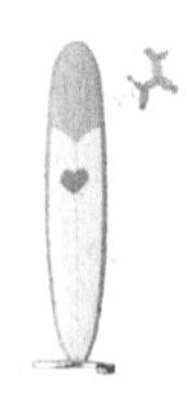

Brick

My dad leads me into an industrial building clad in corrugated metal. Several large trucks are parked out front, ready to collect their haul first thing the next morning.

Smoke stacks pump out filthy gray smoke.

A sign with a logo of a pig says Floyd Brothers Meat Works.

Inside, the walls are covered in safety signs. '5 days since last accident' is emblazoned proudly under a health and safety banner, along with a memorial for a team member who was crushed in a piece of factory equipment. I shiver. What a place to die.

The building is noisy, even though it's late and most people have completed their shifts for the day. Metal clinks against metal, and it sounds like heavy chains are being dragged across the floor. A conveyor belt takes slabs of carcasses into the adjoining room, metal whirring as cogs turn and flywheels spin.

In the distance, I hear backup warning beeps indicating someone is stacking crates with a forklift. Now and then, there's the clank of heavy boots on metal stairs.

There's an odd smell, a thickness lingering in the air. Over time, I will come to recognize it as the scent of death. It permeates every surface of the building, wending its way onto any porous surfaces and remaining there forever.

He has me wait for him in this strange room while he retrieves the guy from the car. The guy that he'd found in his bed with my mother. The guy who has a reputation around town for harming women and children, and who she brought into our home and allowed around me and my sister. He's not a good man, but my father has many reasons to be angry.

A pile of coals sits in a pit on one side of the room. Steam emanates from them, and my father moves them around with a poker until they glow red hot. Once satisfied they're hot enough, he uses them to heat a pair of large, industrial pliers with a fine point.

The man screams as my father yanks out one of his fingernails with the pliers, begging for him to stop.

"This is for you," my father says, handing me the fingernail. "It's a reminder of what happens when you don't play by my rules." I look at the fingernail, turning it over in my hand. It's brittle and yellowed, the ragged end of it covered in blood and some fragments of the nail's roots. I didn't know nails had roots. "What happens to his finger? Will the nail grow back?"

"Sometimes. It can take six months for a fingernail and 18 months for a toenail."

The man groans.

My father is always teaching me new things.

"You know how they used to do it, back in medieval times? They'd take the finger and insert a sharp wedge of wood between the flesh and the nail. They'd hammer the wedge underneath the nail until it was torn free."

The man whimpers.

"Another option was to dip it in boiling oil, which would give you more surface to work with under the nail bed."

"Please, no!" the man cries out.

"Oh, shut the fuck up. We're not savages. We're just using pliers, the modern way."

He slices the man's clothes from his body, leaving him hanging naked from the hook that holds his shackles. The man writhes, trying to get out of the metal clamps, but he has no chance.

"So you thought you'd fuck my whore of a wife, did you? Thought you'd encroach on another man's slut. Take her for yourself?"

"I—please, I didn't know she was married. She didn't tell me!" He gulps in air, inhaling big rasping breaths. His eyes bulge, unblinking, as he attempts to convince my father he didn't know the truth.

"Liar!" My father balls his hand into a fist and smashes it into the guy's face. He cries out as a loud crunching sound rings out, the man's nose taking on an unusual angle.

"Oops, got your nose," says my dad. He turns and grins at me, a sadistic look in his eyes. I can tell he's enjoying this.

"Want to tear a fingernail out for yourself?"

"I'm not sure," I say, feeling a little uncertain about removing body parts from a person, even if it's only a fingernail that will eventually grow back.

"What did you say, boy? Don't you fucking disappoint me now. Get over here before I pull one of yours out as punishment for being such a pussy."

I shrug and walk over to my dad. He hands me the industrial pliers. "Get his thumb," he says.

I walk over to the man and he laughs in my face. "What are you going to do to me, little boy?" he asks. "Trying to act all tough? Well, you're just a loser, like the rest of us." He spits at me, blood and saliva landing on my shirt.

I feel a twist in my gut, like something is coiling within me. I haven't really felt this way before. It's a combination of discomfort and excitement. Maybe this man deserves what I'm about to do. Maybe I'll even enjoy it.

I take his free hand. He tries to wrench it away but I'm quick, clamping the plier down against either side of his exposed nail, and I yank on it as hard as I can. Initially, there's resistance, but then there's a funny sensation, like something's moving that isn't meant to, and his nail slides out. I rush back and crash into my dad, holding the tweezers outstretched in my hand with a bloody nail attached to it.

The man howls.

"Who's the loser now, asshole?!" I yell at him.

He's crying now, blubbering, snot running out of his nose and mixing with his tears and saliva that's making its way out of the corner of his mouth.

"Bravo, son," my dad claps at me and beams, his face full of pride for me for the first time in as long as I can remember. "Bravo."

He places a cordless drill, a rusty serrated saw and a scalpel on the table behind us, lined up neatly in a row.

"It pays to be organized," he says. "You want to maximize your time inflicting pain. You don't want to be hunting around, trying to decide what you want to use, and then needing to figure out where you left it. Just like a chef does mise en place in the kitchen, we do the same here. Everything in its place. Would you like to start with the drill, the saw, or the scalpel?"

I assess the options, first squeezing the drill handle so the drill bit whirrs as it rotates. I turn the saw over in my hand. Its blade is serrated, sure to drag along the skin and inflict maximum damage. And the scalpel, so minimalistic and precise. My hand lingers over it, and my father notices immediately.

"You want the scalpel?"

I nod, worried I've disappointed him. The sliver of pride he just showed in me has left me craving more.

"That's my boy. I'll teach you where to cut depending on whether you want to maximize blood loss or damage. Myself, I'm going to start with the drill." He picks up the drill and whirrs the drill bit in his hand.

Our captive begins to rouse, groaning as he opens his eyes and groggily assesses his surroundings.

Seeing the tools in our hands, he squeezes his eyes back shut as if trying to will us away, as if he's hoping that when he reopens them, we were just a mirage.

"Perfect timing," says my father, smiling at the man with an evil glimmer in his eyes. "We're going to use you as a guinea pig for our little lesson today. Isn't that right, boy?"

I nod. We both advance on the man, and then we get to work.

It's been two hours, and we're finally done.

Our captive's soul has well and truly left his body. He's in pieces now, chopped up and ready to be discarded at the bottom of the dumpster where animal meat scraps and organs go.

For once, my father is proud of me. It was easy, maiming the man who made him so angry. Watching my father hack up his lifeless form was interesting. He was so precise with his incisions, choosing every tool so carefully. Breaking him down like an expert butcher, which I guess he is.

I'm covered in blood, the metallic scent lingering in the air and on my skin and clothing. I feel brave, like a warrior who has just shown the world his power.

He leads me into the next room, each of us carrying plastic bags containing pieces of the man's chopped-up body. We walk past meat saws and meat grinders and sausage machines. There are coolers and freezers lined up along the wall. There are meat mixing areas where giant mixers churn spice blends with ground meat. And there is a lot of floor drainage, with various trails of blood making their way into the gaps in the floor.

He leads me into another room, still carrying pieces of our chopped-up buddy.

I look around and a gasp bursts from my mouth. There are rows and rows of animal carcasses in here, dangling from the ceiling on heavy metal hooks. Sheep and cows and others that are so mangled I can't recognize them.

Shrieks suddenly ring out in the background. It sounds human, like a large group of women are being stabbed in a frenzied attack.

"What's that noise?" I ask my father.

"Those are the calves and the lambs bleating. They're being slaughtered out there, just like this guy."

"Did they do a bad thing, too? Like this guy?"

"No, they're just food. They're less than us. They serve a purpose."

This doesn't seem fair. I get why the guy had to die. He tried to break up a family, and before that he'd done some very bad things to women and children. That makes sense to me. He behaved badly and had to face the consequences. I glance down at the bags that hold various pieces of his body.

But chopping up a defenseless animal to use as food just because it's a protein source, when there are so many other options available? It feels like the slaughter of innocent beings is literally overkill. I think back to spending time on my uncle's farm when I was younger, and how I befriended the cows and sheep and goats, naming each of them and feeding them long blades of grass and food pellets out of the palm of my hand. I blink back tears as I imagine them being brought to a place like this, if they were the animals strung from the ceiling, if they were the animals screaming because they knew they were about to be killed.

It's here and now that I make a pact with myself. I will torture, I will maim, and I will kill. I will even enjoy it. But my activities will be strictly confined to humans. Because humans deserve pain and suffering. Animals deserve to roam free.

I am both human and animal. And I don't know which side of me will ultimately take control.

Chapter Forty-Five

Roman

"Want to come and take care of something with me?" I raise an eyebrow at Angel.

She looks so cute and sexy, sitting there on the couch with her legs curled up underneath her and her vibrant purple hair cascading over her shoulder. It's too hard to rip myself away from her, even though I have work to do. Bringing her with me will be the best of both worlds. I might even get to show off a little in the process.

"You mean, like, a work thing?" She glances at me, confused. I guess we have kept her trapped inside the compound since we originally brought her here, except for the one outing to the mall... and look at how that turned out. Taking her back out into the wild has some risks associated with it, but she could also come in useful for what I have planned. And getting her out of this captive environment surely has to earn me some points.

"Yeah, I have some business to do down at one of our clubs."

"What kind of business?"

"You'll see." I tap her on her leg as I stand up. "No more questions. Now go get ready, unless you want to stay here for the rest of the day."

After quickly changing and grabbing my keys, I pull the car up to the front of the compound. Angel hops into the car and we drive to the largest of our clubs, an upscale venue in a trendy part of town. Running a high-volume venue with a sizeable area for private events and live shows is lucrative when you operate it as efficiently as we do, especially given we attract the high society types that live in the area. And it's even more profitable when you're also using it as a way to distribute high-end substances.

There's been some trouble, though, recently. We pride ourselves on our reputation for distributing top-quality product. But some lowlifes have been cutting in on our business, selling drugs that are low-quality, cut-down versions, and passing them off as ours in our own venue.

It's resulted in more than a few accusations that we're compromising our quality on purpose, and that we're intentionally trying to rip people off. That the people hocking these subpar goods are somehow affiliated with us and doing it under our authority. It's eroding trust with the local community, and if it goes on much longer it could tank our reputation within the industry. We need to shut this down and fast.

I explain this to Angel as we fly down the freeway, high-rise condominiums and apartment buildings towering on either side, giving the occasional glimpse of ocean out to the west. Traffic isn't too bad at this time of day, thankfully. It can be a beast at typical peak hour times, slowing to a crawl that can make it take a long time to get even the shortest distance. One of the drawbacks of island life, I suppose. The price of paradise.

"Do you think it's an employee or a guest doing it?" she asks.

"It's almost certainly an employee," I sigh. "I can't see any of the regulars doing that. We have a fairly good handle on who comes in and out, and there's a general rule that you don't shit on other people's turf. People know this is our club. And it needs to be someone who's meant to be around a lot of the time, someone who doesn't look out of place."

"That makes sense," she nods and meets my gaze in the rear-view mirror. "But don't you check employees out when you hire them? Some kind of intensive background screen?"

"Yeah, we vet people very carefully when we employ them," I shrug. "We end up knowing more about them than they know about themselves, most of the time."

"So do you think it's possible someone just slipped through the cracks, then?"

"I guess that's what had to have happened. The background screening isn't foolproof. People can get backstops to verify their fake history easily enough. There are online services that'll do it for really cheap. We don't know who we're actually talking to half the time, what with free online numbers and voice-changing software." I sigh. "But we do the best we can. Sometimes it means we make a mistake and end up having to pick up the pieces."

She chews on her lip, deep in thought. "I guess circumstances change for people over time, too. Someone who might have taken a job with you to earn an honest living might have hit hard times and... loosened their boundaries a bit."

"Yeah, it can be a slippery slope when it comes to ethics. Everyone has vulnerabilities, and some make it easier for others to exploit them. It might not be immediately apparent, and like you say it might not even exist when they start with us. A dire financial situation, or a sick family member, for example. They can come up at any time, and it's not like they send an updated resume through when it happens. We've seen these types of situations threaten the loyalty of some of our best employees over the years."

"Hmm," she twists a strand of her hair in her fingers, deep in thought. "So how can I help with this?"

"Just keep an eye out for anything that seems off. I might get you to do some recon for me depending on the suspects and where they go in the building. As a female, you're going to have access to a couple of places I don't usually go. But remember, everyone who works here knows who I am and so they're going to be on high alert."

"Oh, your employees suddenly stand to attention when you walk past? Just about salute you?" She smirks.

I laugh. "Something like that. You'll see."

Chapter Forty-Six

Angel

We hop out of the car and approach the club's front door. A large bouncer stands at the entrance wearing a charcoal suit, an earpiece, and sunglasses. I feel a little out of place. The last time I was in a club like this was what feels like several lifetimes ago. I half expect a song about apple-bottom jeans or poker faces to suddenly start blasting from the sound system, but for now, the club is apparently sticking to heady bass-forward remixes by chart-topping musicians.

A line of clubgoers waits patiently to go inside. They stand in pairs and small groups, chatting away. Occasionally raucous laughter permeates a huddle, punctuating a joke or funny passing comment. For the most part, the females wear short, tight-fitting dresses and heels and clouds of makeup and perfume, and the men wear collared shirts, designer T-shirts and jeans. I don't know where they find people that dress like this on this island. Everyone's normally so casual and laid-back, and these tight-fitting sequined outfits are a huge departure from comfy board shorts, tank tops and swimsuits. I guess you can find whatever you want in the evenings in most places. No matter where you go, there's always a club. There's always someone looking for trouble. There's always someone just as lonely or messed up as you.

I glance down at my outfit and take a deep breath in. This skin-tight black minidress is a departure from the shorts and tank tops I've been wearing most of the time lately. But it shows off my curves in all the right places. Even though I had to get ready in a hurry, I managed to swipe on some makeup and put my hair down so that it flows around my shoulders. I know I look decent, but glancing around at how put-together the people standing in line look would make anyone feel a little self-conscious.

Roman approaches the man at the door, and they nod at each other.

"Hey Lenny, how's it going tonight?" They shake hands. "This is Angel, by the way," he says, gesturing at me.

The large, suited man nods at me, the same way he just did at Roman. I guess that makes me officially welcome in this fancy establishment.

A couple of cabs and rideshare vehicles pull up and couples get out and make their way to the line. He glances at them before returning his gaze to me. "Hi miss," he says, and then gestures toward the club. "Welcome in."

"It's starting to get busy in there," he goes back to speaking with Roman. "The DJ just had one of his songs enter the charts, so it's got some buzz going with the locals."

"Nice to hear. Thanks for the heads up, man," Roman says as the door guy opens the heavy door, letting out some of the thudding club music the DJ is spinning inside.

Strobe lights flicker and pulsate in time to the music against a dark backdrop. It takes a moment for my eyes to adjust to the visual cacophony of darkness interspersed with blinding bursts of light.

The club has several rows of VIP tables that cascade down to the stage where the DJ nods his head to the music while standing behind his equipment. Each table has a booth wrapping around it. There are two long bars flanking the space. They mirror each other, each with premium alcohol displayed in front of strategically backlit and mirrored walls.

The club smells like a combination of pungent air freshener and the plastic-like burning scent of overheated speakers and sound systems, masking what I'm sure is some intense body odor and sticky spilled drinks. It doesn't matter how much people pay for a VIP booth, rich drunk people are still sloppy.

The bartenders expertly churn out high-volume drinks. Under the bass-heavy music, I hear the sound of metal scoops digging for ice, and the noises of multiple drinks being stirred and shaken simultaneously. The bartenders operate like an orchestra, fluidly placing their prepared libations on server trays and handing them to guests who stand and lean against the bar. One bartender in particular spins and flips his shakers, pouring ingredients from high in the air and flicking the jigger behind his back and catching it.

"That's Donny, he's some type of flair bartending competition winner," Aidan explains, and I nod. "I'd be smashing liquor bottles and shattering glasses if I tried that."

I laugh. "Me too."

"Wait until you see Brick try to do it," Aidan grins and I snort, imagining Brick balancing a bottle of liquor on his nose like a trained seal, or trying to slash it halfway through the air with one of his deadly scalpels.

The bar surface itself is kept clear except for the drinks and bins filled to the brim and replenished frequently by the venue's efficient barbacks, containing lemon and lime wedges, cherries and other garnishes. One bartender fills a row of shot glasses with an amber liquid, Fireball I think by the looks of it.

Skimpily dressed cocktail waitresses hustle by with glowing trays of drinks. One walks past with a line of people following her, holding up a bottle of champagne with crackling sparklers exploding from the top. People clap and sing behind her, and cheer when they get to the table that ordered it. The group is celebrating a birthday or an anniversary party, maybe.

As the DJ continues to spin tracks full of bass and auto-tuned voices, women gather in clusters to gossip and check out all the attractive men in the club and take selfies. Groups of guys hang out doing the same. Small groups dance on and around the large speakers that flank the stage. A few people make out in the darkness of their booths, their hungry hands and mouths grabbing and touching each other in intoxicated abandon, not caring who sees them exploring each other's bodies.

Roman cranes his neck over my shoulder and I turn to see what he's looking at. I notice an attractive brunette in the venue's uniform heading inside the women's restroom.

"Friend of yours?" I ask, automatically assuming she's on Roman's roster of pretty women.

"No, employee," he says, not picking up what I was putting down. "I'm pretty sure if there's something going on, she's involved somehow. She hasn't done anything overt, but she just seems to be well-connected around here and if she's not directly involved, she knows who is."

"Want me to follow her, seeing you can't go in?"

He nods. "Yes, exactly. See what you can find out. Befriend her if you can. Just try not to be too obvious about it. Everyone knows you're with me, ever since we walked in here together."

I take a deep breath and straighten my dress. No pressure at all. But at least I look good.

"You've got this, Benson," he smirks at me. "And you look good. Real good." His eyes trail over my body. "You're absolutely stunning, in fact."

"I know," I wink at him as I grab my purse, and head in the direction of the door the brunette just slipped through. Undercover-ish with the Brixtons. Whoever would have thought? I don't let him see the blush creeping onto my cheeks. It's weird feeling this comfortable in my own skin, and I'm still getting used to it.

I follow the employee into the restroom as Roman instructed. Some venues like this have employee-only restrooms, but I guess this isn't one of them. She glances back as I pretend to be doing something on my phone, and doesn't seem to think anything out of the ordinary of a girl in a skintight dress scrolling through her text messages.

The air is full of gossip and bickering over things that happened years ago, emotions heightened by too many vodka sodas and the general buzziness of the club atmosphere.

I can hear someone sobbing in a stall, her friends leaning against the door to try to comfort her and figure out what's going on. They don't seem to be having much luck, and one of them rolls their eyes as their friend's incoherent words are punctuated by hysterical sobs. Judging by their body language, I get the impression this isn't the first time they've had to take care of their messy friend in a venue like this.

Another group of women monopolizes the mirror in the bathroom, each of them checking their hair and makeup and adjusting their cleavage. Satisfied, they all turn and pose and take a group selfie.

Two girls stand off to the side, leveraging a counter to snort lines of white powder. They glance furtively around as if they're trying to be secretive while also doing drugs in plain sight. Apparently, they don't realize that's what bathroom stalls are for at a place like this, no doubt a convenient ledge bolted to the side of each one for just this purpose.

The employee I'm following goes into one of the empty stalls and I see her taking her phone out right before she closes the door. I walk along to the row of basins and wash my hands as I try to listen, and I feel like a bit of a creep for trying to hear what's going on in the stall. After a few uneventful moments, I hear her voice, muffled by the thudding music.

"Yeah, Manny. I've got the stuff." She pauses. "Yeah, I've sold some. Look, I told you I don't feel comfortable with this, okay? We have our own stuff here. This is making things complicated."

There's another pause.

I can no longer hear her conversation as the door to the restroom is thrust open, letting in the thumping beat of the music and the voices of the small group of women that trickle in, four of them. They're talking loudly and laughing and squealing. There's no way I can hear the employee's phone conversation over all of this.

I stand patiently until they each find their way into stalls and the restroom is relatively quiet again.

"Why are you holding that over my head?" I can hear the employee's voice again. "It was just the one time." Her voice is pleading. "I've paid it off. Just don't make me keep doing this. Please."

Satisfied with what I've learned, I put my phone in my purse, wash my hands and leave the bathroom as I hear the employee unlatch the stall door. I avoid the urge to glance over my shoulder as I move back into the main club, the music still thumping and sweaty bodies gyrating on the dance floor.

I find Roman standing where he was when I left, a glass of amber liquid in one hand while he scrolls through his phone with the other, occasionally glancing up to observe his patrons and employees.

He glances up and sees me approaching. A small smile plays over his lips, his eyes hungry as they roam my body. He clearly appreciates this new look, and I wink at him, finding it hard to keep a big smile from bursting from my own lips. I feel a little giddy, having found something useful for Roman, and I can't wait to tell him. I'm like an eager kid in school, excited to show off a good grade or a well-drawn picture.

"What did you find out? Anything helpful?" He looks over my shoulder as if expecting to see the employee following along behind me.

"I think so," I say, letting out a deep breath. "It was hard to hear, but it sounds like she has been selling something on behalf of someone. I couldn't hear exactly what it was, although my guess would be drugs. But she was definitely trying to get out of it, to go back to how things were before, whatever that means."

"Hmm," he presses his lips together in a thin line, his eyes thoughtful. "Anything else?"

I remember a crucial detail. "She called the person on the other end of the phone, Manny."

A strange cloud passes over Roman's eyes and his mouth turns up in a snarl. "That little fucking weasel."

"You know a Manny?" I arch an eyebrow.

"Yeah, he works here," he nods. "I took him in, under my wing, when nobody else would. Gave him a chance when he got out of prison. He worked his way up from barback to bartender and he's one of our best high-volume guys now." He sighs, his smile replaced by an anguished frown. "I trusted that shithead and look how he repays me. This is why we don't have a moral code, Angel. This is why we put our own interests first. Because other people sure as hell aren't going to."

Still frowning, Roman strides over to a manager who is standing at the end of the bar, observing patrons and making sure the staff has everything they need.

He looks up and startles as he sees Roman approaching with a dark frown on his face, and glances around furtively as if to ensure everything is in its place and that he's not the target of Roman's obvious wrath.

I follow along behind, partially out of curiosity but also because I don't know quite what else to do in this situation. There's nothing I'm less interested in than standing alone at a club where people assume I'm single and approach me, and Roman only took two steps away from me before I felt the curious gaze of other clubgoers trailing my form. No thank you, not today.

The manager sees me approaching over Roman's shoulder and his own eyes rove over my body. He's dark-haired with an average height and build, one of those nondescript bar manager types who blends into the background but also doesn't seem to miss a thing. Always watching, observing, listening in. The type of person I typically try to avoid. I don't like being observed like that.

"Is Manny working tonight, Silvio?"

Silvio nods. "He sure is. He's out back on break."

"Wait here," he says to me. "I'll be right back."

"I want to come with you," I say. Standing around watching Silvio work seems only marginally better than standing alone in the middle of a club in the early hours of the morning.

"Fine." Roman shrugs and gestures for me to follow him.

He leads me behind the bar and through a door out to the back. We walk past the kitchen where the aroma of fried foods pervades the entire space. Staff in aprons and white hats assemble all manner of wings and fried chicken, burgers, chicken tenders, and overflowing cardboard boxes of fries. I haven't been feeling particularly hungry, but this carb heaven is enough to make my stomach growl.

We walk down a short hallway and into a spacious breakroom with tables and chairs, a microwave and a few vending machines. It's one of the nicer staff break rooms I've seen in an establishment like this. I'm not sure whether the space came this way and Roman and his guys just decided to use it as is, or if he intentionally wanted to do something right by his people, giving them a space where they can escape from the madness for a few precious moments during their shift. In either case, it's very nice.

Sitting at one of the tables, a tall, slender guy wearing a collared shirt and a name tag is drinking what looks like cola out of a plastic container and scrolling through his phone. His nose is hooked, and his eyes are a flat shade of brown, like filter coffee that's been sitting in the jug for a little too long and mixed with some shitty creamer. He has a half-eaten burger on a plate in front of him, and as we walk in, he picks it up and takes a large bite.

"Manny!" Roman confidently walks over to the man and slaps him on the back, a little hard from the way the guy jerks upright. "How have you been, man?"

The guy glances up at Roman. For a moment, his eyes get a little wider and his mouth grimaces almost imperceptibly, his eyes flitting to the exit behind me. But he quickly regroups himself, meets Roman's gaze and plasters a big smile across his face.

"Hey Roman, man! It's been a while. How are things going? And who's this beautiful lady?" he asks, turning his smile to me. His words tumble from his mouth a little too fast, his chest rising and falling a little too rapidly for someone with nothing to hide.

"Cut the shit, Manny," Roman growls. "You don't need to know who she is. It's none of your business and not at all relevant to you. But I do need to know why you thought it was okay for you to come into my club and betray me and my brothers."

The color drains from his face and he places the burger down, pushing his plate toward the center of the table. "I don't know what—."

"Don't lie to me, Manny," Roman leans in closer to the man, his eyes boring into him. "Or it will only get worse for you. I can promise you that."

Manny glances at the table and his eyes flick back up. He starts to speak, a little too quickly. "I—."

Roman puts a hand out to silence him.

"Before you say another word, I want to remind you about that little chat we had when I first took a chance on you, way back when you first started. Do you remember that chat, Manny?"

"Yeah," he replies, his eyes turning down. He pushes his plate even further away and sighs. "I remember." His gaze meets Roman's again and his expression is hard to pin down. Frustration, resignation, and maybe even a hint of sadness.

"What did I tell you during that chat, Manny?"

"That honesty is the most important thing. That you can get over many things, but deceit is where you draw the line. That it's the one thing you can't come back from."

"So, what do you have to say for yourself?" Roman arches an eyebrow.

"Look, I'm sorry, okay? I'll stop doing it." Manny nervously bites his lip.

"I'm afraid it's not that easy, Manny," says Roman, eerily calm and clearly in control. "When you do the type of thing you've been doing, other people hear about it. They think, 'oh, well if this chump can do it, I can take what I want from the Brixtons as well. No problem. They won't do anything about it because look at Manny over here, taking a cut of their potential profits by selling his subpar product at their club.' Next thing you know, we've got all sorts of assholes up in the club hawking drugs and god knows what else. We start to be associated with the shit you're selling, rather than the top-quality experience we're committed to providing to our clients." He pauses, and Manny squirms uncomfortably in his seat. "So we've got a problem here, Manny. And it's about to be your problem. We need to send a signal that this type of behavior is unacceptable and comes with severe consequences. We need you to be a deterrent now."

"Wha—so I'm fired? I can grab my things right now. Again, I'm really sorry, man."

I smirk at the man's feeble attempt to just finish out the situation in this way. He's delusional.

"Firing you would just be an easy way out for you, Manny," scoffs Roman, shaking his head, a small smile forming on his face. "It wouldn't send the right message to people who aspire to behave the way you have been. So no, Manny, we aren't going to fire you. We're going to invite you back to our compound to continue the conversation. My associate, Brick, is looking forward to welcoming you to his special part of our house."

The remaining color drains from his face. "Please, man. Just let me go. You'll never hear from me again. I promise, I'll never do it again."

Roman just smiles at the terrified man. "Oh, I'm confident you won't. And I absolutely insist that you come and experience the hospitality that we reserve for a select few."

Chapter Forty-Seven

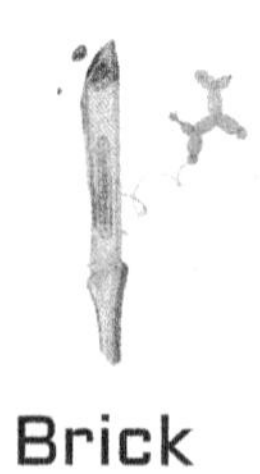

Brick

The tall guy trembles as he looks around at the basement.

"Stop being so fucking nosy, looking around like you're trying to figure out my secrets," I smirk at the man. When they tremble it just adds to my excitement, the fear that I've created within their mind leaching to their body and causing a physical response.

I smash my fist into his face and he cries out, his lip splitting on impact and oozing blood onto his chin. I punch him in the face again, and this time there's a satisfying crack as his nose breaks under the force of my knuckles. Blood flows from his nose and lip, some of it dripping from his chin onto the cold concrete floor. I love the sound of my knuckles connecting with flesh and bone.

I glance over at Angel and see her eyes flicking between me and the shackled man. She looks fascinated, maybe even a little excited, by what is taking place.

There's something primal about the crunching sounds that fists create when they connect with the human body. Sometimes the sound alone is enough to whip me up into a frenzy, and there have been times I've come out of my haze to find dead men, their faces and bodies pulverized into oblivion at my hands. Only time will tell whether that will be Manny's fate. It all depends on how excited I get during our time together.

"Making a mess of my basement, Manny," I growl. "I'll use you to mop it up later."

"Please," he begs, his voice squeaking as he pleads. "I didn't even sell that much."

I smack him in his broken nose, and he whimpers as more blood splatters across his cheeks.

"Go easy on him, would you?" says Roman, wiping off some blood that splattered on top of his hand. "We want to teach him a lesson, not kill him... for now at least."

Manny whimpers in the background.

"Shut the fuck up, loser," Roman snarls.

Manny clamps his mouth shut, his eyes watery and bloodshot and pleading.

"What's the point then? He fucked us over," I snarl. "Don't give me a toy and tell me I can't play with it."

"Yeah, he did fuck us over. That's why he's here," says Roman, calmly. "And so we need to send a message. So do your thing. Have fun. But make sure he's going to be employable again some day. To someone else, anyway."

"Why do you care if he's employable?" Roman confuses me sometimes. He doesn't care about anyone but himself, but then he suggests not killing this shithead because he feels some kind of pity for him.

Roman shrugs. "Just humor me, okay?"

I shrug and walk over to one of my cabinets. I place a hand on my hip as I glance inside, checking out my treasured collection of torture implements. It's taken me years to acquire this variety of tools, and I brought many items across from the mainland when we moved. They go where I do. Non-negotiable.

I tap my foot and nod as I map out a plan of attack to give Manny the fright of his life. Clearly, his lesson needs to involve pain that he'll never forget. And Roman says I can't kill him and he has to remain employable, but that leaves a lot of options. Disfigurement isn't out of the question, and I have a lot of leeway as long as I leave his hands and face relatively unscathed.

Satisfied with my plan, I nod to myself and return my gaze to the man. "I've figured out just the plan, brother."

Manny whimpers as I grin at him, pulling a scalpel out from one cupboard and a rusty serrated blade from the other.

"Oh god, please, no!" he whimpers. "I'm so sorry. I promise I'll never try to cut into your business again. I'll do whatever you want, just please don't do this! I'm really sorry!"

"Actions speak louder than words, Manny," I growl. "And your actions have shown us that you're a disloyal, opportunistic piece of shit who needs to be taught a lesson."

"I—I didn't even do it for very long! I barely sold a thing!"

"Only because we figured out what you were doing straight away, or you would have kept going," growls Roman. "And don't pull that 'didn't sell that much' bullshit on me."

Manny has officially hit a nerve, and I stroll over to him with my tools in hand. "Yeah, quit with that line of argument, *Manny*." I spit his name and take a pause as he tries to avert his eyes from what I have in my hands. "That's like telling me the meal you're giving me just has a little bit of meat, a little bit of dairy." I narrow my eyes at the terrified man. "It's still the same. It still involves animal byproducts which are bad for your health and the environment, not to mention cruel to the animals involved," I hiss, my mouth close to Manny's ear. "And what you were doing, back at the club? There's no such thing as just a little bit of dishonesty, or just a tiny lack of integrity. It's a slippery slope, Manny, and today I'm going to help to ensure you get right back up that slope and never think about going down it again. Do you understand me?"

He nods, feebly, and a single tear falls from one of his eyes and splashes onto the floor below, mixing with the puddle of blood that's already starting to settle there.

"Is—is there anything I can do to stop this? Please?" he begs again. "Pay you back the money? I'll find a way. I'll do anything you ask!"

"Oh, you will pay us back the money, Manny," says Roman, fully confident that Manny will. "And then some. But that's not what it's about, and it surely won't be enough to teach you a lesson. Or to send a message to anybody else. You've made your bed, Manny, and now you're going to take a nice, long nap. Doesn't a nap sound nice right about now?"

"Yeah," I smirk at the scared man, "It is going to be a little like a nap. Except it's going to be a very painful one. And you're going to be awake the whole time."

Manny's head slumps as he realizes there's no way out, there's no reasoning that would stop what's about to happen.

Our torture session begins, and Roman leaves us to it.

Angel decides to stay with me and Manny, and her eyes sparkle as she watches me try out a selection of tools to extract maximum pain without doing any major damage. She's been quiet this entire time, but her eyes have been fixated on everything that's taken place. She's soaking it all in, and doesn't look at all upset by the damage I've done to Manny's slimy body. In fact, her eyes are sparkling with an intensity I recognize because I've seen it in myself. She's enjoying the show.

If I had it my way, I would have gone harder, but Roman has specifically requested I take it easy so I'll behave this time. After slapping Manny back into consciousness for the third time, I glance at Angel and hold out my scalpel, offering it to her.

"Do you want to try?"

She smiles at me as if I've offered her a nice gift, which I guess I have. Her eyes zero in on Manny's face as she takes the scalpel from me and advances on the tied-up man.

"You made a big mistake," she says, clinically. "And you're lucky you're still alive. I want you to know that I don't take kindly to people ripping off my men." She pauses for a moment, and Manny's eyes grow large as he sees the intent in her eyes. My chest flutters a little and my cock jerks at how possessively she just described me and the other guys. 'My men' has a nice ring to it.

She continues. "Roman may have told Brick to go easy on you, but I didn't receive the same instructions. I can do whatever I want with you, with no repercussions. And unlike your friend Roman, I'm not feeling very nice today."

I feel another little flutter in my heart, hearing her talk dirty like this. My cock twitches in my pants.

"You should be more scared of her than you are me or anyone else," I growl, and I mean it. "I wouldn't fuck around if I were you. Do exactly as she says or you'll regret it."

We have a little more fun with Manny, nicking and slicing and making little incisions wherever we please, until he passes out for a fourth time while his blood drips into a growing puddle on the floor. Angel asks me questions along the way as she picks out all the perfect spots to inflict excruciating pain while also keeping the man as conscious as possible. She particularly seems to get off on nicking both of his Achilles heels, actually laughing as she takes a satisfying slice across the back of each foot while the man yelps and screams, his feet jerking involuntarily. His passing out once again gives us some alone time. I'm incredibly turned on after watching this queen work her magic with the scalpel. My beautiful Valkyrie has some secret skills and I am very much into it.

She turns to face me, and her eyes are dark with desire. This is turning her on, too.

I groan and bite my lower lip as I see the hunger in her eyes. There aren't many women who would be as aroused watching me break bones and yank fingernails. Who would get enjoyment by actually joining in and being willing to learn and put her own spin on things. She's very special, our Angel. My angel of death, my Valkyrie.

All of a sudden her body is pressed against me. She stands on her tiptoes and brings her face to mine. "You're so confident when you work," she moans breathlessly, her tongue sliding into my mouth to wrestle with my own.

I'm not used to having an audience in my basement. It's usually my solo time... well, me and whoever is on the receiving end of what I have to dish out. Her being here makes me want to turn it into more of a show. To pick out the perfect implement to use each and every time. I want to be the best version of myself for her, to make her proud, to make her wet when she watches me exact retribution on anyone who crosses our path.

I would die for this woman. I would torture and kill anyway because I find it fun, but I'd do it even more for this woman. I would follow the souls I destroy into whatever purgatory or hell they're headed to and destroy them over and over again, if doing that would make her happy.

Her eyes darken with lust as she wraps her arms around my neck. I hoist her up on the counter and yank her dress over her hips. In the background, Manny hangs unconscious by his shackled wrists, bruised and bloody from the beating and torture he just took. The heady thickness of violence hangs in the air, and I can smell Angel's arousal intermingled with the comforting scents of blood and sweat. My cock is like an iron bar, primed by the exhilaration of what we just did together and anticipation for what we're about to do.

I grab her by her hair and yank her mouth to mine again, our lips and teeth clashing and our tongues tangling around each other.

She moans as I cup her breasts, lowering the top of her dress on one side so I can caress her exposed nipple. It immediately hardens under my touch and she groans as I suck it into my mouth, twirling it under my tongue.

I hook my fingers inside her panties and stroke her pussy. She is soaking, excited from watching me show off for her in the basement and from having her own turn at inflicting pain and injury. She's turned on by violence and darkness, and I have plenty to give her. Maybe even more than she can handle.

"You're fucking soaking, you dirty little slut," I grit out as I trail my fingers over her slick folds. "You're getting off on being down in this basement, and joining in while I work, aren't you, Angel?"

"It's not my fault you're so sexy when you're deep in torture mode." She reaches down and rubs my hard shaft through my pants. "Or that it's fun giving it a go myself."

I groan as she caresses her hand against my cock.

"You seem to be turned on yourself," she says. "I want you to bury your cock inside me to celebrate." She grinds her pussy against my hand and I groan as she strokes my hardness.

She undoes my pants and pulls them down to my hips and I yank them down the rest of the way. She moans and bites her lip as she gets a good look at my pierced cock as it unfurls in front of her. I slide her ass to the very edge of the counter, and it lines up with me very nicely. "Look, your pussy is the perfect height for me and this basement," I growl, as my erection pokes her entrance. "We're meant to be together, just like this."

"Oh yeah?" she asks, her voice husky with desire. "You want to fuck me here in your torture basement, baby?"

"Yes, you're home here with me. I've never wanted you more," I grit out as she grinds her entrance against me, enticing me to enter her.

"Mmhmm," she murmurs as she grabs my cock and lines my tip up against her folds. "Don't be gentle. Fuck me like you like to torture people."

I groan and grab her hips, slamming myself deep into her pussy with one firm thrust.

She cries out as I fill her up. "Fuck, Brick! You're so fucking big. And the piercing, oh my god!"

"I'm going to destroy your cunt," I growl in her ear as I begin to slide my hard cock in and out of her. "You're going to be feeling me for days."

She moans, her mouth gently parted, and I dip my head down and suck her gorgeous, plush bottom lip into my mouth and tug on it with my teeth. She cups my ass with her hands, clawing at it with her nails as I repeatedly ram into her pussy.

I reach down and strum my fingers against her clit as I continue to impale her on my cock, and she moans, arching her body to increase the pressure on her clit. She lifts her hips to meet each of my thrusts, joining me in mid-air, our bodies releasing and then reaching back for each other, slamming into each other as hard as they can.

Manny groans from off to the side but we both ignore him. Who cares if he regains consciousness? I couldn't care less if there's an audience. All I care about in this moment is fucking this woman, our Angel, our queen.

I lift her hips up to get more leverage and rail her pussy, the echoes of my cock slamming into her wetness bouncing off the walls, the scent of sex thick in the air. My chest pounds as she gazes at me, taking my cock like a good girl, clamping her cunt tightly around me. I can tell she's going to come soon, her body coated in a thin sheen of sweat. She glows as I fuck her.

"Fucking hell, Angel," I rasp. "Why is your cunt so perfect? I want to be buried balls deep in you at all times."

She cries out as I continue slamming into her. "Me too. Fuck, baby. Harder. I want more!"

I don't know if I can fuck her any harder than I am now, but I'm up for the challenge. I lift her hips a slight bit more and then slide my cock out almost all the way, so that just my tip is inside her.

She screams as I slam myself back into her repeatedly, her body tensing as I impale her with my full length.

"Brick!" she cries out as I flick her clit with my fingers and then pinch it. She grinds against my hand and screams, her fingernails digging into my ass as she bucks her hips to get my cock as far inside her as possible.

Her eyes roll to the ceiling and she arches her back, her tits curving up toward me. I lean down and suck one into my mouth, biting and sucking as her body writhes beneath me. Her pussy clenches on my cock, shoving me over the edge to my own release which spills inside of her with force. She continues to grind on me until I'm done.

Wrapping her legs around my waist, she pulls me to her, my cock still buried inside her, and I wrap my arms around her.

I kiss her on the top of her head. "My Angel, you're so fucking perfect. I'm falling in love with you, you know," I whisper.

I tilt her chin up with my finger and her mouth meets mine. We kiss, gently.

"I'm falling in love with you as well," she whispers back.

"And my brothers?"

Her gaze meets mine. "All four of you."

"But my cock's your favorite, right?" I grin, still holding her to me, my finger tracing a path along her delicate jaw.

She smiles. "It's one of my four favorites. They're all amazing. Each has their own perks. And it helps that I also think the guys they're attached to are hot as hell."

I can't help beaming at her.

Glancing over at Manny, I sigh. "I need to excuse my cock from your pussy right now because I have this loser to take care of. But I want more of you later, okay, my sexy queen?"

She nods and laughs. "I don't care how sore I'm going to be after this. I want more of you as well."

"You're feeling raw?" I ask, and she nods. "I'll kiss it better later."

"I was hoping you'd say that," she smiles at me, her eyes hungry. I wish we had more time right now, but business is calling.

She jumps off the counter and pulls her dress back down. She's just as stunning as before, but now her hair is tousled and her dress is slightly crinkled. I groan, because somehow she just managed to get even sexier, as if that was possible.

"I'll leave you to it," she says, standing on her tiptoes and planting a kiss on my cheek. "Have fun."

I watch her leave, her gorgeous ass and hips swinging as she walks up the stairs, giving me a peek at the curve of her cheeks from below.

The moment she closes the basement door I turn to Manny. "You interrupted my fun with my Angel," I growl. "And I don't care that I was instructed to go easy. Nobody's here to police me any longer, so I'm just going to go with the flow. Wherever the wind takes me."

Manny groans, resignation filling his features as I advance on him again, scalpel in hand.

A smile plays across my lips as I look at the man and the torture we've inflicted so far today. Adrenalin flows through my veins. It's time to make my Angel proud.

Now I'm really going to make him pay.

Chapter Forty-Eight

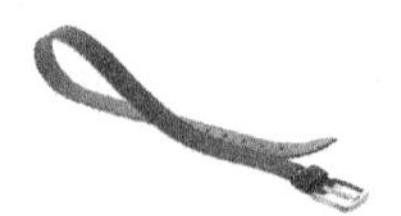

Aidan

The next day

"Don't you care that the drugs end up in the hands of children?" Angel raises an eyebrow at me, but she's not frowning, and I don't hear a hint of judgement in her voice. She looks more curious than anything.

We're sitting in the living room, relaxing. Angel is leaning up against the side of the couch with her legs dangling over mine. I let my fingers trail languidly up and down her smooth shins. It feels comfortable, just relaxing like this with her, as if she's meant to be here. As if she belongs here with us.

"No. It's not our problem," I shrug. "We're just doing a transaction at the end of the day. We're not selling drugs to children, and if someone else chooses to do that, it's on them."

"But aren't you providing the means to do it?" She arches an eyebrow.

"Listen, if someone wants to do something that badly, they'll find a way. If we weren't the ones distributing, someone else would be. And they'd be the ones making the money," he shrugs. "So instead, we're going to leverage our networks and continue to grow our business. If you have a problem with it, then maybe spending time with us isn't the place for you, sweetheart."

I didn't mean to be condescending, and I don't think she's necessarily judging us, but her questions are a little unsettling. I'm confident about our business, and her getting all philosophical about why we do what we do only serves to make me question things. If this line of questioning continues, Slade could be right... Angel could prove to be a distraction, and that's the last thing we need.

"Don't fucking call me sweetheart," she glares at me. It seems like an overreaction, but I think she can sense she hit a nerve with her questions. "That sounds so condescending, like something Slade might say. And I didn't say I had a problem with it. I'm just trying to get a sense of your moral code. What you are and aren't prepared to do, and how you think about it. How you sleep at night."

"It's easy," I shrug again. I've thought about this a lot so the words come easily. "We don't have a moral code. And I sleep very soundly."

"Makes sense to me," she shrugs. "Viewing anything as a transaction helps to make things more objective. I like to think that nobody is entirely good or bad. They just are the way they are. Everyone does what they need to in order to get by. And some people have bigger aspirations. I admire that about you." She places a hand on my arm, her gaze locked on mine.

"Oh really? You're not disgusted or terrified by our business dealings?" I'm impressed by how objectively she's able to think about our business. Not clutching her pearls, not glorifying us as some gang of benevolent Robin Hoods. Just seeing it for what it is, no more and no less. It's like she gets us.

"I actually find them fascinating. I'm enjoying learning about it. It's like a fast-tracked MBA for people who have what it takes to take over this place."

She grins at me, her sexy lips distracting me with their plumpness. My cock twitches as I think about them being wrapped around it. Suddenly, all thoughts of business go out the window. She is distracting me now, and I couldn't care less.

"By the way, Slade missed a massive opportunity when he finger fucked you in the kitchen," I growl. I've also been thinking about *this* a lot.

Angel smirks at me. "Are you still mad that he did that on a cooking surface?"

I smirk. "I'm over that. In fact, if I was in his position, I would have done something more fitting for the location." I graze my top teeth over my bottom lip, and my eyes rove down her body, stopping at her core. "Anyway, stop talking about him," I growl. "You're mine now."

"Oh, really? And what exactly does being yours now entail?" Her eyes caress my body and then move upward to meet my gaze. Her chest rises and falls and I can see her nipples protruding through the thin fabric of her tank top. I know she wants me just as badly as I want her, and my cock twinges at the thought of being buried deep inside her.

"First, I'm going to make you come for me." I pause and kiss her on her jaw as I reach down with a hand and cup her heat.

She moans and arches her back.

"Fuck, your pussy is generating so much heat. I bet you're soaking wet for me," I growl in her ear, and she grinds against my hand. I pull it away so she can't anymore. She's going to go at my pace today. "I'm going to take you to the edge over and over again, and make you come when you can't take it anymore. And then I'm going to fuck you so intensely you'll feel me for days. You'll be screaming my name. The way my cock feels buried deep inside you will be all you can think about, and you'll spend your whole life wanting it again."

She gasps, short of breath from my words and my touch, her hips grinding onto my hand to generate more friction for her clit.

"Is that what you want, Angel?" I rasp in her ear and she tilts her neck, exposing it so that my breath fans across it. "Tell me how much you want it."

She smirks at me, challenge in her eyes. "Brick has a bigger cock, but you know how to use your hips. Your pussy eating is average at best. I'm going to need you to practice some more if you want to be anywhere near as good as the others."

Okay, I wasn't expecting that. I thought I'd broken her down, that she was so thirsty for me she'd just go along with what I was saying.

"His cock is what?" I narrow my eyes at her. "And fuck you, Angel. That's not nice."

She shrugs. "I never said I was nice."

She smirks at me. The fucking bitch. Using my words against me, and now of all times.

Chapter Forty-Nine

Angel

He pushes me back onto the couch and yanks off my shorts and panties.

I've made him mad, and his visible anger is turning me on. It's making him animalistic, primal. I may have taken things too far with my dick size and pussy eating comments, but I have no regrets. Even though none of it was true and we both know it. His cock is ample, and he knows how to use it, and as for his tongue... my words were full of lies. He knows exactly what he's doing with it and is extremely talented in that department. Still, it was fun to assault his ego a little, and now maybe he'll try to prove himself. At least, that's how I'm hoping he responds to the challenge.

He drags my butt to the very edge of the couch, so it's almost hanging over the edge. He gets down on his knees and peels my knees apart, baring me to him completely.

"You're so fucking wet. I can't wait to taste you again," he says, burying his face between my thighs.

His hot tongue swipes its way from my clit down to my asshole and back. He trails it languidly over my slit a couple of times, purposely not letting it touch my clit, holding back from giving me everything he knows my body is craving. I moan as he finally trails his tongue up to my clit, and he starts lapping at it hungrily. I moan as he sucks it into his mouth and lets his teeth graze against it. He pushes my knees back toward me more, further exposing me to him and granting him better access to my hole as he eats me out. He uses his tongue to pierce into me, feasting upon me, collecting my wet heat as he fucks me with it. He maintains eye contact and my eyes roll back as he moves his tongue back up to focus on my swollen bud, and slides two fingers into my pussy as a replacement. He begins to slam his fingers in and out while he eats me out and feasts on my clit, the noise of my arousal being manipulated by his fingers the only sound in the living room in addition to our rapid breathing.

"Flip over for a moment. I need to taste all of you," he growls.

I turn over and get on my knees, my clit already craving his tongue again, my ass in his face. He slides his fingers back inside of me from this angle, finger fucking me from behind as he explores my asshole with his tongue. I back up against him, grinding my ass into his face as he plays with my back entrance. I moan as he spears my asshole with his tongue and eases it in while he continues to finger fuck my pussy. I gasp as, using his other hand, he slowly eases a finger into my ass while he works my cunt over with his other hand, double penetrating me with his fingers. I cry out as he gets a finger the entire way in, and slowly slides it in and out of my ass.

I reach down and begin to rub my clit as I grind back against him.

"There we go," he growls. "You're all mine now, baby. I own every part of you. Do you like having me inside both of your tight little holes?"

"Mmhmm," I cry out and push against both of his hands as they dominate my pussy and my ass, fucking me in two places. I can't help but wonder what it would be like if he had his cock stuffed into me while one of the other guys did the same.

"Do you want to feel my cock buried in your ass as well, Angel?" he grits out, and then dips his head back down, his tongue continuing to explore me.

"Yes, Aidan!" I cry out as his tongue rams into my back entrance while his fingers manipulate my pussy. "Oh my fucking god!"

"That's right, Angel. I am your god," he growls before resuming his hungry lapping of my ass.

The thought of two of the Brixtons' cocks being inside me, and of him fucking me in the ass right now, is enough to send me over the edge. I scream as he makes me come apart, slamming both hands into me at the same time, white stars flashing behind my eyes. I lean against both of his hands as hard as I can, and then my entire body shudders as my orgasm crashes through me. I feel my pussy and ass clenching tightly around his hands, my ass so tightly that he can't move his finger for a moment. "Jesus, you're so fucking tight!" he groans. "I can't wait until my cock is buried deep inside you."

He pulls his fingers out of me and I flip back around.

"So about my ass..." I look at him through my eyelashes.

"You're going to have to wait," he growls. "Show us you're a good girl. That you deserve it. And then we might let you have it."

Fuck.

Chapter Fifty

Angel

I'm a little surprised Aidan, Brick and Slade invited me to go on another job with them, but I'm not complaining. I finally get to leave the house another time. They've let me out for some surfing, which has been fun, but it's been my only reprieve from the compound, other than that one time at the mall. I think I did a good job gathering intelligence at the club for Roman, but obviously Slade doesn't trust me, and my being out in 'the wild' of the island presents an inherent risk. I get the sense they've been trying to avoid any further run-ins between me and Devon, and of course, there's that small matter of a stalker that's trying to hunt me down so he can kill me. Lots of reasons to keep me locked inside like a precious glass bird.

We ride in the car in silence. Aidan drives, and the rest of the guys strap themselves with guns and knives. Of course, Brick has a couple of extra tricks up his sleeves just in case, judging by the bulky backpack that sits on the floor at his feet. Palm trees and homes whiz past as we transition out of the commercial development and onto the freeway, taking us in the direction of another entertainment district. But this time, I'm not dressed for the club.

My outfit is practical. Shorts and a tank top with combat boots. There's no way I'm going to slow the guys down because I've twisted my ankle in heels. I'm wearing two holsters, with one gun at my waist and the other attached to my thigh. As far as I'm concerned, it's important to be prepared for anything.

After taking an exit ramp, we descend into a trendy industrial area dotted with warehouses. Large murals are painted on the side of large concrete structures, lending an artistic, quirky feel to the otherwise nondescript area. If you drove by during the day, you would likely assume this area was truly just for manufacturing and a wayward artist might have happened upon the blank concrete walls and decided to decorate them. But in the evening, it's very clear that this neighborhood has been carefully curated as an entertainment destination.

We drive past the main strip, and a few blocks later we pull up outside an industrial building that looks a little more dilapidated than the popular venues we cruised past earlier. The building is coated in corrugated iron and is relatively un-noteworthy, and unlike the other places this has no flashy entrance announcing it's a club. In fact, there isn't any signage at all, and the parking lot is empty except for a poor attempt at landscaping, and unkempt weeds sprouting from a couple of planter boxes that sit neglected by the sidewalk.

"This looks super sketchy," Slade mutters. I agree with him, but Slade also seems to think everything looks super sketchy. Including me. I bet he's an enneagram six with this bullshit.

"I don't like it either," says Aidan, running a hand through his hair as he inspects the building from the security of the vehicle, his brow furrowed in concentration.

"Where's the entrance? I don't see it," says Brick.

Slade sighs. "Yeah, and if we get out of the car and try to find it on foot we'll be sitting ducks if Zero's men are here to ambush us."

"Are you sure this is the right place?" Brick asks nobody in particular. We're all as lost as he is.

"I think we should circle around and see if there's an entrance on one of the other sides of the building," says Slade.

Aidan nods and reverses the car back out onto the street. We crawl forward, headlights on dim, trying to find any sign of a way to get into the building.

After making three turns we finally spy an entrance at the very corner, near where we started. Aidan pulls the car to a stop and we all hop out, not seeing anybody nearby.

Suddenly, three men burst from the building and bullets start flying.

We throw ourselves to the ground behind the vehicle. Shards of glass spray over us as bullets continue to fly in our direction, the vehicle shielding us from most of them.

Brick and Slade move stealthily to either end of the vehicle and return fire. I hear a grunt and assume that's one of the three men. They continue to fire back, bullets and glass scattering everywhere.

Finally, the bullets stop and everything is silent. Brick is pressed flat against the ground peering under the vehicle. He turns to us and gives the thumbs-up signal. Slade puts up three fingers and looks at him as if asking a question, and Brick nods to confirm all three men are dead or severely injured.

We all slowly get up. I'm half expecting more goons to come running out of the club, but it remains still.

Aidan pulls out his phone and calls Roman. "Ro, what the actual fuck? He sent three goons out to shoot us. Are you sure this is the right place?"

"The call sounded a little off when it came in, but they knew enough about our shipment to appear credible."

"Do you think it was Zero fucking with us again? He really seems to be trying to... um... zero in on our turf."

"Maybe. They've been doing a lot of hacking into phones and computers and shit, lately. I wouldn't put it past them. They've been obsessed with taking over this area since we got here."

"Then we probably shouldn't go into that building. If he's sending three out as a welcome party, there have to be more inside, protecting him."

"That could be it. And this also could be our only shot to get to him for a while."

"Well in any case, if this is a trap and he just tried to have us killed, we can't just leave with our tails between our legs," says Aidan, running his hand through his hair. "We'll lose all credibility around here. We have to fight back, to show them that their traps don't mean shit and that we'll smack down anybody who disrespects us."

Aidan turns to me. "Are you ready for this, Angel? I have a feeling shit's about to get messy."

I grin and nod. "Alright, just how I like it."

"Yeah girl," grins Brick, high giving me. "Me too!"

He gestures for us to follow him into the building and we all do.

Chapter Fifty-One

Aidan

As expected, there are more henchman-looking guys inside the building.

Methodically, we execute each one as they pop out from around corners.

Brick gleefully sets off a series of flash-bang grenades as we enter new areas within the space, giving us smoky cover as we pick off each goon one by one.

This goes on for some time and we operate like a well-oiled machine. It's easier when you've done it as many times as we have.

"Uh, guys—?" I glance around, panic building from deep within my core. "Where the fuck is Angel?"

We run to each of the corners of the room. The air hangs heavy with smoke and gunfire, and the industrial building creaks from its foundations up. Pipes clank somewhere off in the distance.

"Angel?" I call out, trying to project just far enough to get the attention of someone in an adjacent room. No-one replies. "Angel!" I call out, slightly louder now, but there's no response.

"Was she hurt back there?" We rush back, and my heart sinks as I steel myself, preparing to see Angel in any condition from unconscious to severely injured or worse. But despite retracing our steps from the front door—and we know she definitely entered the building with us—and peering around every obstacle that could obscure her frame, there's no sign of Angel.

I feel sick. If anything has happened to her, I really don't know what I'll do.

"Do you think she ran away from us while she had the opportunity?" Slade asks.

"As much as you'd like that, man, no I don't think that's what happened." I run my hand through my hair and exhale hard. "We need to find out who took her and fast. I have a feeling that these guys won't keep her around for long."

"They sound smarter than us, then." Slade rolls his eyes, but I can tell he's worried too.

Chapter Fifty-Two

Brick

After retracing our steps and not seeing a sign of Angel, we move further into the building and find a room with several people inside. Unlike every other person we've encountered during this visit, none of these individuals appear to be goons. Instead, they're dressed like normal people, still employees but without the directive to kill us on sight. They're wearing suits and seem more corporate, and they're bustling around like they have important business to attend to. God, I'm so glad I managed to escape that humdrum corporate existence, toiling through work every day to build wealth for already wealthy people. Torturing evil people is way more fun.

But I'm not here to think about how I escaped a boring existence. I'm here to find Angel.

If people took her, and I think that's what happened, I will kill them. Every single one of them will be looking right at me as the light goes out of their eyes. I'll absorb their darkness as I drain each one of their life energy, and use it to fuel my revenge for my Angel, my Valkyrie.

I let off a warning shot, which might be overkill in a small space like this. Everyone in the room stops in their tracks and a couple of people shriek and gasp, dropping to the floor as their eyes take in our group of heavily armed men. We get them all to kneel down in a row, hands behind their heads.

I'm ready to shoot. They'd better start talking.

Aidan senses my readiness to get started, and he puts a hand out to stop me. "I've got this," he says, and then turns to face the row of terrified people. "You have our girl. We will keep coming for you until you give her back to us. If you know anything, anything at all, speak now. Even if it seems like an irrelevant detail, you *will* tell us where she is."

A few people turn to speak to the person next to them, while others adjust themselves awkwardly in their kneeling position. People know more than they're letting on, but Zero seems to have them under some kind of spell, locked down by a visceral fear that keeps them from talking.

"It really is in your best interests to tell me. You're staying loyal to a dead man. Mark my words. By the end of the day, Zero will be dead and you're going to end up much better off being affiliated with the Brixtons."

"I—I know something," one of the women says, her voice breaking out of the murmurs of the group. Everybody turns to look at her.

"I heard one of Zero's men saying they were taking her to their main compound."

"Thank you," says Aidan.

I'm tempted to shoot them all between the eyes just for being affiliated with the people that took her, but I behave myself for now.

Chapter Fifty-Three

Angel

I don't know how we get separated, but suddenly the guys are nowhere to be seen and I'm running down an empty hallway by myself. The walls are metal, blank canvases that give off no clue as to where I am. I think I'm running in the right direction to escape, but I'm not sure. For all I know I'm actually just going around in circles, making no progress. There has to be an exit around here, but this place is like a maze and I don't really know if I'm getting closer to the perimeter of the building or further toward the center. There are no windows or signs to guide me, and time stands still as I try to figure out the best direction to go to get the fuck out of here.

I turn a corner and pause for a moment, deciding whether to continue straight or go left. A hand closes around my shoulder as I stand there trying to figure out which direction to turn, and it grips me tightly. I try to shrug it off but I can't. I move to turn my head and the hand shoves me forward, and I almost lose my balance on the grated floor.

Looking down, I see a foot behind me. I stomp and try to kick at my captor's shin but I miss. I try stomping on his foot again and this time I connect, crunching the top of it under my combat boot. He yelps and I wrestle myself out of his grip and start to run. Grabbing my gun from my holster, I turn around and fire it in his direction, two shots that both hit him in the abdomen. He groans and grabs at his stomach as he falls to the ground. One down. Not sure how many to go.

Two more men appear and glance at their friend, and then notice me. They run toward me and right before I turn to race away from them I see one pulling his gun out of his holster. I take off toward what I now realize is the exit, hoping I'll have more of an advantage on neutral ground. It seems to be some kind of break room with various pieces of old furniture. There's a door in front of me and I slam it shut from the other side and pull a heavy couch across it. A shot rings out as it smashes through the door, sending splinters flying. It was a couple of feet away from me but still too close for comfort, so I race out a side door. This area looks more familiar, and after making a couple of turns down the winding hallways I make out the familiar entrance that we came through when we arrived. It's just what I've been looking for.

Right before I get to the entrance a large figure steps in front of it, blocking my way.

I raise my gun and aim it while I'm running, and fire straight in front of me. It hits the man in the head and his body stays upright for a moment before it topples to the ground. I yank at the door, willing it to open, but it won't budge. The guy's dead weight is pinning it closed. I have to put my gun on the ground as I try to lift him. He must be at least two hundred and fifty pounds of solid muscle. I reach under his armpits, looping my hands underneath his arms. I bend my knees, heave his upper body off the ground, and manage to get him away from the door just enough so that he's no longer in the way. I pick the gun back up, holstering it and then pull hard on the door.

Footsteps ring out loudly and they're headed in my direction. The other guys have almost caught up to me after taking a detour. I try one more time to yank the door open and it groans and then springs outward.

I leap through the door frame and thrust myself outside, squinting as my eyes adjust to the bright sunlight. I look left and right and see the car. Running toward it, I hear the footsteps drawing closer and while I'm sprinting as fast as I can I can tell this person is faster. A large hand once again curls around my shoulder. Fuck.

The two men that chased me are followed by five other men who all rush outside and circle me. This isn't good. I could probably inflict pain on one or two of them, but there are just too many of them for me to make a real dent. I pull my knife out of my holster, waving it toward them in an attempt to warn them off.

One of the goons standing toward my back moves forward when I'm not looking and seizes my arm, clenching my hand and causing the knife to clatter to the ground. Fuck.

I try to punch and kick as the other men descend on me, but they're too much. I'm overpowered. They're all so big and muscular and I'm exhausted from the chase.

I tense my body, steeling for the pain. They're going to knock me out again, for what will be the fourth time this week, I know it. But instead, an arm wraps around my neck and a finger presses firmly against my carotid.

I see stars, and then everything turns red and then black.

***

I wake up with a splitting headache. It reminds me of the feeling I used to get after a few too many vodka sodas out at the club with the girls. But instead of the usual feeling of amnesia and regret and the compulsion to text my buddies to try and figure out what the hell happened last night, I'm just concussed.

Fucking hell. This is the third time I've been knocked out in a week by some random guy. This needs to stop. I'm beginning to feel like I'm a professional football player or something, but without the shoulder pads and the celebrity girlfriend. Brains aren't meant to experience this much trauma.

But this time I don't think it was one of the Brixtons that knocked me out. Who was it? Fuck. My memory is like a black hole. There was something about a club. Roman wasn't there but was giving directions from a phone if I recall correctly.

Slivers of memory filter hazily through the cracks in my mind, like I'm deep underwater and somehow the tiniest streaks of sunlight are managing to permeate the darkness. Ah. Now I recall more. Zero's men and the ambush. We came here to do some deal, there was lots of gunfire and Brick let off some flash-bangs. But then I lost them and everything went downhill.

I need to get the fuck out of here and find my guys. But first, I need to figure out where the hell I am.

The room is dark and my arms are tied behind me with something scratchy that I assume is rope. I'm sitting on a chair in the middle of the room, and there's a piece of some type of cloth wrapped tightly around my mouth. I try to move my mouth and tongue and lips to push it away but it's been tied firmly and won't budge.

Tipping my head to the side, I hear a noise in the corner. There's a burly guy sitting on a chair in the dark, scrolling through his phone. I'm not sure what he's doing on his phone, whether it's a dating app or Candy crush or an engrossing exposition on the state of international affairs, but he's extremely absorbed in whatever it is and he hasn't noticed that I've regained consciousness yet.

I wriggle my wrists to get a sense of how tightly they're bound. There's a tiny bit of wiggle room and I begin to test how much I can rub them together, seeing if I can bend and flex them in a way that loosens the rope. This material is far more flexible than the metal shackles that bound me last time, back in Brick's torture basement where I was last restrained and held captive. I'm not sure that I can get myself completely free, but I at least stand a better chance with this rope.

After a few minutes of subtly adjusting my wrists and seeing what I'm working with, the strange man glances over at me. His eyes land on mine and, realizing I'm awake he places his phone down, and presses his hands to his thighs as he pushes himself to his feet.

He approaches the chair and peers at me. He's a large guy, with a shaved head and stubbled chin. His nose stretches across his face prominently, flat and slightly bent, like he's been in a few too many bar brawls, and his eyes are a dull, dead green. A scar runs down one side of his face, cutting an angry dent into his chin that mars his profile view.

"You're awake," he growls, reaching behind my head to undo the gag wrapped around my mouth. As he pulls it off, I cough at the sudden rush of fresh air hitting my face. My mouth is bone dry. "Where the fuck am I?" I manage to croak.

"Never you mind," he snarls.

"Do you have any water?" I ask, my voice still very hoarse.

"What the fuck you think this is? The Ritz?" He looks at me like he thinks I'm a complete idiot. Nevertheless, he walks over to a shelf at the side of the room and pours a not-quite-clear substance from a jug into a dirty plastic cup. He carries it over to me and I eye it with suspicion. Suddenly, I'm not so thirsty anymore.

"I'm good, thanks," I say, jamming my mouth closed as he moves to tip the cup to my lips.

"Make up your mind, princess," he hisses. But he shrugs and puts the cup back down on the shelf and I get the feeling he's not surprised I didn't want to take a sip.

I glance around and see a variety of knives and other sharp items. "Is this your place? Your special room where you like to inflict unspeakable pain on people?"

He smirks at me. "Something like that."

"This is a pretty lame torture chamber. I've seen much better," I scoff, and I mean it. I think about Brick's basement with its extensive library of torture implements, catalogued by type and size.

The strange man glares at me. "What don't you like about it?"

He's defensive, like I'm in his living room criticizing his wallpaper.

"Oh, you know. It's just not very organized. I've seen an arrangement where all the implements are catalogued by the type of pain they are used to inflict. And then by size within those categories. It was just so logical." I feel like Brick's hype man, telling other torture artists all about his pimped out basement.

"And here I am with my clutter all over the counter? Are you really judging me for the organization of my torture chamber? Do you really think that's fucking wise seeing you are tied up in here? You're crazy," he sneers at me.

"At this point, what do I have to lose? Maybe if I piss you off enough, I'll go swiftly."

He narrows his eyes at me and then turns to face his tools, digging around in a pile on a nearby counter to figure out what he wants. Brick would be so disappointed in this sorry excuse for a torturer.

While his back is turned, I work my wrists extra hard. I manage to get traction with one of them, feeling the rope give a little. It doesn't move much, but it's enough to give me hope. There's no doubt both of my wrists are bleeding now, and it's acting as a lubricant that's helping me to slide one of them free. That's all I need, just one little wrist freed from captivity.

The discount version of Brick hums to himself as he continues to rifle through his implements. "Where are you, Mr. Scalpel Man? And where's your friend Mr. Serrated Knifey?"

Jesus, these torturers are all batshit crazy.

He continues to potter about, looking for just the right tool. There are only so many implements on the counter and he's bound to find what he's looking for soon. I squeeze my wrist into the tiniest shape that I humanly can and clench my jaw so that I don't scream as it feels like my thumb is bending into my palm so hard it might snap at any moment. Right before I tap out, something gives and my hand slips through the fastening.

He glances over briefly, continuing to hum his tune, and I still myself and pretend to be looking around. Anywhere that won't draw attention to my wrists or otherwise make him come back over to me.

As soon as he turns back to the counter, I free my second wrist from the now-loosened rope. He doesn't hear as I slide my hand down my lower back and pull out the knife I hid there earlier when I was getting dressed. As I lift it out of my clothes I see my wrists are bleeding pretty badly.

I ignore the pain and leap onto the man's back, yanking his neck back as I wrap my legs around him from behind. I let out a primal scream as I raise the knife and thrust it down, stabbing him forcefully in the neck in a move I learned from Roman back at my salon. He tries to move his arms upward but I stab him in the shoulder, yank the blade back out and pierce him in the neck again.

He wobbles under my weight and I continue to embed the knife in him.

"Fuck you!" I yell. "I'm so sick of fucking assholes like you, kidnapping and torturing me and trying to control me. I'm done!" I probably should keep my voice down so I don't attract any other henchmen, but at this point I don't care. I'm livid. This is the last straw.

I leap from his back and jump away from him. He swivels around, clutching his neck as blood gushes from it. He locks eyes with me and growls. It's a feral sound, but my rage at least matches his. I lunge forward, slashing at his face. He shrieks as one of his cheeks is sliced in two, blood spurting like a fountain from just below his cheekbone.

I rebalance and lunge at him again, this time impaling the knife deep in his gut. He groans, his hands flying around like he doesn't know what wound to press them against to still the flow.

I use his distraction and agitation to my advantage and I move forward, this time stabbing him in the eyeball. He belts out a bloodcurdling scream as I yank the knife back out of his eye and a suction sound rings out in the room as his eyeball comes with my blade.

"Oops!" I say, giggling at him through my eyelashes. "Bet you didn't see that coming!"

He crumples to the ground, grasping his abdomen while blood gushes from his face and neck, the sleeve of his shirt also coated in scarlet from his shoulder wound.

I stand over his face and kneel down slowly as his eyes bulge. "Remember to smile!" I cackle and he shrieks as I use the knife to extend his mouth from ear to ear. "Smile, bitch," I whisper in his ear as his face begins to peel apart, blood gushing from the fresh wound, and then push myself to standing. I wipe my bloody hands off on my shorts as his remaining eye grows large and his hands fly to his helpless face.

I run out of the room and down a hallway. There's a noise off to my side and I spin around as another man launches at me. He's holding a gun, and he starts to raise it at me. I lurch forward and slice his wrist that's holding the gun and it clatters to the floor.

Distracted by the gun and deciding whether or not to try to pick it up, he doesn't notice as I raise the knife up to his neck height and slice him across the throat.

He howls in pain and puts his hand up to slow the bleeding. I stab him in the stomach as well, lodging the blade deep in his gut as he howls in agony.

As he drops to his knees, clinging to his abdomen, I step behind him and grab him by his hair. I tip his head back and slice his mouth from ear to ear as well, and then do the same with his throat for good measure. I'm not taking any more chances. I am just so sick and tired of all of these guys trying to hurt me. No more. I am done. He screams so loud it rings in my ears and then the noise recedes into a soft gurgle.

Stepping over his body I see the exit at the end of the hallway. I run and let out a sigh of relief as the door pushes open when I press against it. I burst out into the sunshine, a wave of humidity cloaking me as I sprint toward the parking lot, my bloody knife still tightly grasped in my hand.

I glance left and right and suddenly Aidan and Slade and Roman and Brick are all sprinting up to me.

"Angel!" a couple of them call out my name at the same time.

Aidan reaches me first. "Angel, are you okay?"

He glances at my knife, coated thick with blood, and his eyes flick up to mine.

"Yeah, I'll be okay. You should see the other guys."

He smirks, but the concern in his eyes remains.

The other guys have caught up and are standing with us. Brick grins proudly as he notices my knife. "Did you try out anything I taught you?"

"I did, actually," I say. "It's refreshing to be a woman telling a man to smile for once."

"Jesus," says Roman, shaking his head, knowing exactly what I mean.

"You look like a psycho running around with that blade in your hand, covered in blood. Very sexy. I like it," grins Brick. I glance down and he clearly has a bulge forming in his pants at the sight of me immediately after a murderous rampage. Of course he does.

"Do you know where Zero's number two guy is located?" I ask. This place is like a maze with all sorts of building configurations. All are very industrial, unnamed. No big flashing lights that say 'Big boss is here'.

"Yeah, we've tracked him to the main building," says Aidan. This was the second most secure of the facilities, and now we're going to the max. We should expect more guys, more weapons, and for them to be on high alert given what's just happened. We might let things settle for a bit before we take our shot."

"Your torture basement is way nicer, by the way," I say to Brick. "You're much more organized and have a better variety of tools than they did here."

He beams.

"We're getting closer but we can't be complacent," says Aidan. "Once we get to Zero, which will be soon, the next person on the list is four down from Tane Brown on the list of the island's most powerful men. There aren't many to go until Tane is the next big fish on the list. But as simple as the math looks, things are much more complicated in reality. There's not a gentle ramp-up to get to the next boss. The power of each man remaining, including Tane, is exponentially more significant each time you go up one position on the list. It's like going from a teacup to an ocean."

"Yeah," Slade frowns and glances at each of us. "We need a warship. Instead, it feels like we're on a sturdy rowboat, one step higher than a dinghy, or maybe a very small yacht. We're making progress, but we still need reinforcements. We're nearly ready for Tane, but not quite. And when we do go after him, I hope we beat him rather than die trying."

Chapter Fifty-Four

Aidan

"So, I don't mean to sound insensitive, and I know it's hard for you to talk about. But can you tell us a little bit more about this guy that likes stabbing sharp implements into walls and leaving you little love notes all over the place?"

We're back at the compound in the living room. It's been a few hours since we got back, and everyone's coming down from the adrenalin high created by our earlier adventure. I'm not sure how many men we killed today, but the body count is definitely in the double digits. More impressive is Angel's role in this, including her ability to get away from being held captive by a torturer, and killing both him and at least one other of Zero's men.

Angel visibly shivers. I feel bad for asking, but we need to know what we're working with here. We might have just taken down one of our strategic business rivals, but she still has a stalker hunting her down and presumably he's getting closer. It's important that we arm ourselves with as much knowledge as possible—how he likes to operate, the speed at which he's likely to track her down again and so on. Because one thing's for sure, we're going to be prepared for him. Ideally, we'll get on the front foot ourselves and hunt him, and I know that's what the other guys will instinctively want to do. But we need to be intentional and understand the risks involved, rather than going in with guns blazing. I need to protect her from him, and I need to protect the other guys from themselves, too.

Angel takes a deep breath as she steels herself for this conversation. I know she's been avoiding going into too much detail, and I want to protect her from the bad memories, but the risk of not sharing this information is too great. Her life is at stake. Everything we've worked for is at stake.

"We met when I was younger. I was a teenager and he was this mature guy, you know? He'd traveled a lot, and was knowledgeable about all sorts of stuff that I'd never even heard of before," she says, biting her lip and looking upward as she tries to channel memories.

"Like eighteen or nineteen year old teenager, or younger?" Slade asks. I was wondering the same.

She flicks her head to him and narrows her eyes.

"No judgement, just curious," Slade puts his hands up defensively.

"Sixteen," she replies. "I was sixteen when it began. And the age difference didn't seem strange at the time." Her gaze drops to her hands which she has clasped neatly on her lap. "Everything started off so well. It was perfect or at least I thought it was. I didn't know any better," she says, her voice quiet, a sad smile playing out over her plump lips. "He'd take me places, like restaurants. Not fancy, stuffy places, but places that were interesting. With cuisines from destinations he'd traveled to. He knew all the origins and would tell me about when he first tried each item, and how he wanted to take me to get the real thing as well. It was exciting planning trips with him, and it really did feel like the world was out there waiting for the two of us to go and conquer it. We'd go to museums and he'd talk about all the paintings and artwork. He did take me on a couple of vacations, and they were amazing. The hotels and the food and the hospitality, it was like nothing I'd ever been exposed to before. It's like he opened so many doors for me that I didn't even know existed." She sighs. "I know it sounds cliche, a young woman with an older, worldly man. He just knew so much about things that I was clueless about. But he also seemed cool, like not pretentious."

I want to ask questions, but I hold back from interrupting.

She cocks her head to one side as if trying to recall more.

"One day, everything just changed," she says. She closes her eyes for a moment and winces, as if she's trying to recreate the memory in her mind. "I can't quite put my finger on it. Maybe there were signs before, but I was young, and I guess I ignored the red flags. Sure, he'd been possessive, now that I look back. He'd order for me at the restaurants we went to, and would get angry if I wanted to pick something for myself. He'd isolate me from my family and friends, although at the time I just thought he really liked me and wanted to spend all of his spare time with me. Pretty soon, they stopped calling and reaching out and I guess in a way, I can't blame them. I used to, but I've come to realize what he was doing was isolation. At first it felt warm and fuzzy, like we were in our own little love bubble together. It was comforting and fun. Like having a sleepover every night with your best friend. But that phase of our... relationship or whatever it was... didn't last long."

She pauses, taking a deep breath as if she's steeling herself for what's to come out of her own mouth.

"It turns out he's a really bad guy. A hardened criminal."

I clear my throat. It's not like my brothers and I are upstanding citizens in the eyes of the world.

She glances at me, and I can tell she knows what I'm thinking.

"Not like you guys. At least I hope not," she says. "Things turned violent really quickly. It turned out he'd been grooming me all along. The wining and dining, the sophisticated teachings. He was a sex trafficker, and he was 'loosening me up' in his words. He would..." her voice trails off and she rubs at her forehead.

"Angel," I say, placing a hand on her shoulder. "If you can't finish telling us right now, it's okay."

"No...no," she says quickly. "If I don't say it now, I might never get it out."

She takes a deep breath, steeling herself to continue.

"That's when the rape and torture began. He started passing me around to his friends, and they weren't gentle. He'd keep me locked in a room, and only let me out when he wanted me to 'perform', I guess you could call it, for him and the other men he brought around." Her voice cracks as she speaks, and her lips tighten into a snarl.

"And then the beatings began," she says, her voice continuing to get lower. "He'd always been a little bit violent, but it started off with him making sure he only hit me in places that didn't bruise, or where people were unlikely to see his marks. But at some point, he stopped caring. He was beating me every day, telling me what an ugly waste of space I was. He even encouraged me to kill myself on a few occasions. It was incredibly cruel. I really think he wanted to see if he had broken me down so far that I would do that just because he told me to. To see if that's the level of power he wielded over me."

Her eyes fill with tears, but she holds them back and clenches her jaw, tilting her chin up slightly. "But I refused, and it only made him madder and the beatings more savage. He started using tools on me, which is how I got all of these scars." She gestures at her torso and her limbs through her clothes, and I know that the marks cover her body. Some are raised and prominent, and others are tiny silver lines. I still think she's beautiful, but it's clear that they bother her, that they bring her back to that time. And from the look of them, they must have caused a hell of a lot of pain.

Her eyes cloud and she bites her lip. "Then one day, he... brought me a kitten. He said he was sorry that he hadn't been treating me right lately, and that he promised to do better. Of course, I didn't believe him, but I wanted to so badly. I needed one tiny sliver of hope. Sometimes when you're in deep darkness, when you're truly desperate, you'll cling to anything that makes life seem less awful. Even when it makes no sense, your mind will search for survival. It'll ignore all the warning signs just to chase that sliver of light, of hope. So that's what I did."

She presses her palm over her mouth and squeezes her eyes tightly shut. "He let me bond with the kitten for several days, and for the most part, he left me alone. Didn't lay a finger on me for once. He was kind and attentive, and brought me nice food and made conversation. He asked me questions about my life rather than just regaling me with his experiences. I was allowed to walk around the house more freely. The kitten was so cute, she would rub her little face against me and purr, and snuggle up against me as I slept. I named her Ziggy." Her eyes fill with tears and this time she doesn't blink them back.

I feel a pit of sickness swirling in my stomach. Pretty sure I know what's coming.

"But then a couple of days later, he came into my room with the kitten held up by its neck and he sliced its little throat right in front of my face. I don't want to remember her like that, blood spurting out everywhere. I swear she gave me this helpless look as it was happening. As if she was begging me to save her."

Tears start flowing freely from her eyes now. She clutches her chest as if she's trying to staunch the pain of this horrible memory. "And that's when he threw the kitten's little body to the side, and turned to me coldly and smiled, this icy, evil smile. And do you know what he said?" she asks, and I know she doesn't want an answer. She rocks slightly and holds her elbows tightly against her side as if she's soothing herself, preparing herself for what she's going to say next. "He calmly says, 'You're next, Angel. You think I've taken away everything you've ever had. You think you know darkness? You're about to. And let me just forewarn you, there is no dawn."

I glance at Brick and can see a vein twitching in his neck. Slade's mouth is curled, and he's breathing heavily. Roman's face is tight and stretched in a snarl. They're all expressing exactly how I feel but in their own way. The terror she must have felt at the hands of this psycho. Not only inflicting unimaginable physical pain, but psychologically manipulating her and breaking her down piece by piece. I try to remain calm and neutral so that she keeps talking, but inside my heart is pounding and my body has never felt this tense. I don't want to scare her off. The rest of her story needs to be told, and we need to know what we're dealing with to be able to help her. And hopefully, so that all of us are alive after this.

"It turns out he'd gone to the homes of my parents and my brother, and he'd killed them. He also murdered the two friends I'd ever talked about with him."

Jesus. I didn't think he could do anything more to hurt her than what she'd already shared, but clearly I was wrong. He annihilated everyone she cared about and made himself her everything.

"I managed to escape one night," she says. "I'd been a 'good girl' as he called it, and he decided to give me privileges. He was acting a little careless after murdering everyone I'd ever cared about, like it's all he could think about. It's like it emboldened him, and the thrill of killing people somehow made me seem like less of a threat to him." She pauses and her eyes flick up and to the side as she recalls what happened next. "So I was able to help him around the house, cooking and cleaning. He even let me out in the garden a few times. He supervised me, of course, and was always heavily armed. But everyone needs to sleep, even him. And one night he got complacent. As I cleaned up, he watched TV and at some point he dozed off. I could maybe have killed him then and there, and we wouldn't be having this problem, but I was more concerned with getting away. He's so much bigger than me, and so cunning, that risking waking him and angering him without being able to escape just wasn't worth it. So as soon as I saw the opportunity to get away, I slipped out the front door and I ran and I never looked back."

My god. She's literally been through hell, and she's so brave.

He woke up not too long after I fled and I hid in the bushes while I heard him looking for me. He drove up and down the street and searched on foot and I thought he was going to find me. He wouldn't let up for hours, going back and forth along the street calling my name and trying to flush me out. He got close a couple of times and I thought for sure he'd find me, but somehow I managed to stay quiet and hidden enough that he kept just missing me. Eventually, he took a break and I ran until I got to a nearby house. The people who lived there immediately took me to the police station and I told them everything that happened."

I want to ask so many questions, but I can sense she wants to keep going and I don't want to throttle her flow of consciousness. These details, while disturbing, might just help us take this freak down, so instead, I just continue to listen.

"He ended up being arrested after police hunted him for about a week," she explains. "They found him hiding out at a campground not too far from where he'd held me captive. They found all of his notes about me in a shed at the back of his house. He was completely obsessed with me. He wanted to disfigure me, throw acid on my face so that he would be the only living person who knew what I looked like beforehand, so that he would be the only person who wanted me. He wanted to continue to mutilate my body even further, and he'd mapped out the scars he wanted to add and the tools he wanted to use to wound me. He'd obsessed so much that he'd started to think about me as some kind of science experiment. He wanted to perform surgeries on me. He wanted to remove pieces of my flesh. He wanted to cook and eat parts of me."

I resist the urge to retch or recoil in front of her, but it's nearly impossible. There's nothing I want more than to reach out and comfort her, but in this moment I can tell that she doesn't want to be touched.

She spins the bracelet on her wrist and continues to rock gently. "They found the acid and the tools that he was going to use to do it with." She's biting her lip so hard now that it's starting to bleed. Her face has grown pale.

Brick's nostrils are flaring, and Slade is tapping his foot. Roman is staring at her with deep concern. I place my hand on hers.

I'm not sure that she's going to continue, but she takes a deep breath as if to steel herself again.

"And he's been in prison for the past seventeen years. But I guess he's gotten out and he hasn't forgotten what he promised to do." Her voice cracks as she continues. "He's here on the island, stalking me, and he's not going to stop until he finds me and carries out his plan."

She leaps up from the couch and runs to the bathroom, and soon there are sounds of loud vomiting. I don't blame her for a moment. Her story made me want to throw up, too. But more than anything, it filled me with a deep rage, and I know that the other guys feel similarly without even looking at them.

Roman goes after her, while Brick looks around for something to punch. Luckily, he comes up empty. Slade remains on the couch seething and likely forming a revenge plot in his mind.

"For fuck's sake," Slade growls. "We need to kill this fucker. By the time I'm done with him, he's going to be unrecognizable."

Brick and Roman nod in agreement.

I'm just as full of rage and hatred, and my need for vengeance is just as strong. But I need to make sure that none of them does anything stupid. We are going to kill him, and we're going to take every sliver of pain he caused her and magnify it so that he feels it exponentially. But we need to play it carefully. I can't lose Angel or my brothers in this fight.

There's one good thing about this situation, though.

This guy sounds fucking psycho, and very dangerous.

But so are we.

Chapter Fifty-Five

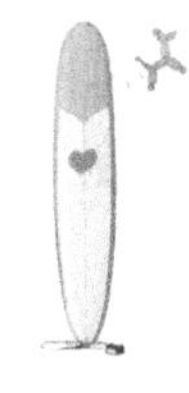

Brick

Blood rushes in my ears as Angel tells her story of pain and darkness.

My hands won't control themselves, balling into fists and then flexing repeatedly, my tattooed knuckles cracking loudly.

I've met some very bad people, but this guy sounds like pure evil. I want to go after him and make him suffer. I can feel it in my bones that I will kill him.

I want to do all the things to him that he threatened to do to Angel. I want to make him pay for each scar that he gave her, even though I think they're part of what makes her so beautiful, so unique.

Sure, I get joy out of torturing people and killing them. But they've all inevitably done something to deserve it. They've crossed someone, not lived up to their end of the bargain, or hurt people more vulnerable than them.

Angel has never done any of those things. Angel is perfect. The things this lunatic did to her and the people she cared about are unspeakable, and he has to pay.

She doesn't deserve to have gone through so much pain and suffering because of him.

And now I'm going to delight in making sure he experiences just as much pain as he's ever put her through and more.

He will be begging for forgiveness, but just like the dawn he tried to withhold from her, it will not come.

Chapter Fifty-Six

Slade

I really want to hate her, because things would be much simpler that way. But it's becoming increasingly difficult.

Angel is a distraction. There's no question. But I think my visceral reaction to her isn't because of anything she did or didn't do.

I'm reacting to the darkness and pain within her that I see in myself.

I resent that seeing her is like holding up a mirror. I don't want to see my reflection, and I want to smash the glass into tiny little shards.

She comes across as so feisty and outspoken, whereas I shut down and create a world within my head. Her fiercely independent nature is out there for the world to see, and she gives no fucks, and mine is trapped inside my mind.

I distance myself from others because that's how I cope. It doesn't mean I don't want to be around them. It's just easier not to be.

I clench my jaw and grind my teeth. Maybe I've really fucked this all up.

When I peppered her with scowls and unkind smiles. When I cursed at her loudly or under my breath, and when I argued with her for no reason. When I shunned the source, even when she was just trying to help by providing information or an opinion. When I belittled her, snapped at her, and repeatedly told her I thought it would be easier for everyone if she was just dead. I wanted to throw her out of the house to fend for herself. She deserved none of it. That was all about me. By Angel being her authentic self, it made me reflect on myself, and that's a highly uncomfortable area for me to be in. It was never about her. She's perfect the way she is.

What she just shared, the unspeakable things that this evil psychopath did to her, I can't even imagine how she's still standing. And she's not just standing, she's strong and fierce and brave. And yet here she was, so vulnerable, opening up in a way that I've never known how to.

I'm beginning to realize how much I underestimated her, and how my hatred was misplaced. I don't like this feeling at all.

Chapter Fifty-Seven

Angel

I can't believe I just shared what I did. I've never uttered those words out loud, ever, even though the flashbacks to those times haunt my dreams until I wake, screaming, heart racing, covered in sweat and full of dread. After he was locked away, I was enrolled in therapy and I went along for a few sessions, but I couldn't bring myself to describe what took place. The words were too ugly, too real. The thought of bringing them to life by uttering them in front of another human being—even a trained therapist—much too terrifying. But somehow, with these guys, I managed to get the words out.

They sounded like a stranger was saying them as they came out of my mouth. My dark nightmare brought back to life with words. I feel dizzy, and it's difficult to swallow, like my throat is deciding to stop me from sharing any more. My heart is pumping, and the vomit has left a sour taste in my mouth.

"Come on, Angel," says Roman, rubbing my back. "Come and sit back down with us. We'll get you anything you need. We will take care of you, no question."

I don't try to fight it, and I let him lead me back to the couch where he sits down slowly next to me as if he doesn't want to startle me.

He pulls me to him, and I melt into his side, my energy spent just from getting those horrific words out. My nightmare shared with these men.

It was cathartic, but now I'm almost more worried. They don't seem to be judging me, and I know it's not my fault. But it's terrifying having this out in the open.

And a little part of me, buried deep down, wonders if by sharing this I've cracked open some door that my stalker can now walk through to inflict even more pain.

Chapter Fifty-Eight

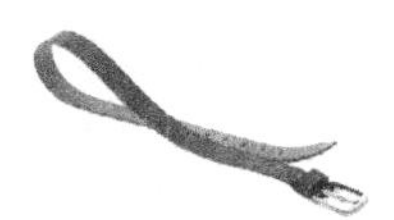

Aidan

After Angel shared her story, I could tell she was extremely drained, which is more than understandable. She left the living room to go and lie down, leaving the rest of us in the room.

"We have to do something. I'm going to kill the guy very slowly," Brick snarls.

"Not if I get to him first," growls Slade.

"Get in line." Roman's face is stony.

"I agree," I say, "but we need to be careful. He's clearly dangerous, and we can't unintentionally put her at risk by exposing her to him in some way."

"Okay, Mr. Practical. How do you think we should go about it?" asks Brick.

"We have some more digging to do. We'll figure out where he is and we'll go after him. But first and foremost is making sure she's safe."

They all nod. Thank goodness they appear to be listening and nobody seems about to go off on a vigilante mission. For now, at least.

"I can't believe all she's been through," says Slade. "I feel like I really misread the situation. I feel pretty bad."

"Stop judging books by their covers, man," says Brick. "You can be cute and still damaged, too. Look at me, for example." He wiggles his eyebrows, and Slade throws a cushion at his head.

"Alright, enough of the bullshit. Get to work, guys."

We all head off in separate directions. We're going to find this psycho stalker before he finds Angel. That's the only option.

Chapter Fifty-Nine

Angel

After napping for a few hours, I wake feeling exponentially lighter. I'm surprised I could fall asleep at all, a heady mix of adrenalin and fatigue warring over my consciousness. I guess the fatigue ultimately won out. Sharing my story with the guys was draining, each spoken word feeling like my brain was being scraped raw against a box grater as I relived my experience.

It frayed my nerves as I recounted my story, like wires spliced open with their fibers spilling everywhere, and I'm doubtful that they'll ever be able to find their way to their original places again. But, at the same time, it was also invigorating and empowering to finally get it all out. In sharing with the guys, I wanted to make sure every detail was accurate, too, and not gloss over anything.

They needed to hear it all if they're going to understand me, if they're going to truly know me. And there's also something about letting the words out that seems to have released some of the power they've been holding inside me for far too long.

I've done a little energy healing work before, and learned that when you cut a cord with something that doesn't serve you, that you should throw it back into the light... the opposite of burying it deep down inside, which I've been doing for more than half my life. For far too long. That by releasing the dark energy that holds you down even when the dark deeds themselves have long been done, the same energy that has been doing you harm can completely transform into something else. Someone can repurpose it into something positive, something beautiful. It made sense as a concept, but I'd never thought it applied to me.

Isn't it funny how you can hear about a concept and it makes complete sense... when it comes to everyone else, that is. And this isn't coming from a narcissistic place... quite the opposite, really. It's almost like *they* are deserving, *they* get to have the thing, *they* get the benefits of whatever that thing is, but you don't. I don't. This line of thinking is something I'm working on but haven't quite managed to overcome yet.

Today, I told the guys things that I'd told nobody before, and it felt good once they were out, even though each syllable was a struggle. They're no longer a secret, and no longer only mine to bear. I feel validated by the concern each man displayed based on what I shared. I'm almost giddy. Not that I want to go around telling everybody all of my traumatic experiences, but I took a risk and now I feel like part of a team instead of being so alone. It's a new feeling for me, but it's one that I'm not opposed to.

I've done therapy a few times over the years, but it never felt like this. I didn't feel nearly this comfortable opening up to a professional in a clinical environment, with their buzzwords and the way I could tell they were analyzing my every word, my every facial expression and my body language.

Sitting on a therapist's couch, it felt like I was being judged or dissected as a subject rather than a human being. It didn't matter who the therapist was, and I cycled through a few trying to find the right fit, but was ultimately unsuccessful. I was there for the hour, or forty-five minutes, or whatever it was, each of us furtively glancing at the clock as time counted down. Them, ready to collect their payment and send me away with some homework that always seemed too simple. Me, waiting to be dismissed, wondering what they'd actually have to say without their professional filter, their impenetrable clinical facade devoid of true human emotion. Some days, I assumed they were silently judging me, thinking I was some kind of lunatic that they couldn't wait to leave their office. Other days, our conversations seemed so normal, so benign, that I thought they might wonder why I was even there. Someone indulging in sharing their minor day-to-day frustrations for a while. So instead, I'd shut down and tell them as little as possible. It was just easier that way.

That's all to say my time in therapy didn't last long, and the many sessions I went to cumulatively couldn't hold a candle to the impact of my sharing my story with the guys today.

There was something else that set this sharing session apart as well. I could tell that any of my four men would have insisted on taking the pain I endured on my behalf if they could have, no questions asked. Their facial expressions and body language were so raw, so authentic. There's no doubt in my mind they're all in for helping me put a stop to my stalker.

And Roman's reaction struck me in particular. He was so compassionate and tender with me.

I feel safe with all of them now, strangely even Slade, which is a bit of a shock.

But I have unfinished business with Roman, and I could use a pleasant distraction.

CHAPTER SIXTY

Roman

I'm sitting on my bed thinking things through. I press my back up against some pillows stacked against the headboard, and my legs are straight out in front of me. My body is comfortable, but pain torments my mind.

My room feels both large and small, and I think it's because my mind is actively trying to put things into perspective. Angel shared so many stories today that transcend both time and geography, all raw and real and horrific.

I don't get upset about a lot of things, and neither do the other guys, but today all four of us were. And one thing I know about us is that when we do get upset, it's for a reason, and this type of emotion tends to transform itself into rage and a thirst for vengeance. Nobody gets to make us feel like this without consequences. And this isn't at all on Angel, this is on *him*.

The horrors Angel has endured at her psycho stalker's hands are unthinkable, and each of us hung onto every word, every syllable, as she recounted the sick acts he perpetrated on her over an extended period. Knowing that he's here, on this island, continuing to pursue and torment her has us clear on one thing. We will end him. And it will be on *her* terms.

At this moment, though, I just want to make Angel feel better. To distract her. The only way that I can think of is with my cock, but that might not be quite what she needs right now. After all, she just shared some of her deepest, darkest secrets and fears, and some might think it's too soon to flick from those dark topics to something more primal.

Or maybe it's exactly what she needs.

It's abundantly clear that she's been wanting it, even though she's had three others available under this roof for various activities. Despite that, she's been clear that she's still craving me, but I couldn't give it to her until this point.

Not because I didn't want to. That's certainly not the case, and I've lost count of the number of times I've jerked off thinking about burying myself deep inside her. But she's different from all the other women because she actually means something to me, and it's been giving me some kind of anxiety that I'm just going to fuck it up.

It has to be special with her, because she's special. She's taken up an important space in my life.

Actually, that's an understatement.

Angel is not just special. She's not just important to me.

She's everything.

As I ponder whether to make a move, and as if she's reading my mind, Angel appears at my door, wrapped only in a towel.

She looks like a weight has been lifted off her shoulders from earlier. Her shoulders look visibly more relaxed, her upper body far less tense. She even has a cheeky little grin on her face, like she's up to mischief.

God, she's so fucking cute.

She's an impressive human, too.

Some people would have shriveled and wilted after what she's been through, but here she is, standing in my doorway with an energetic strength radiating from her. Dressed only in a fluffy pink towel.

That's it. It's done. I'm in love.

"Can I come in?" she asks, peering up at me through her eyelashes with the gorgeous little smile continuing to build on her face. As if she needs permission, and as if there's a chance in hell that I'd say no.

"Sure," I smile back at her.

She walks into the room and then stops when she's about halfway to the bed.

"Oops," she says, dropping the towel so that it cascades to the floor behind her, revealing her gorgeous body. Jesus. My cock is instantly rock hard. She's got my attention on so many levels. I could just sit here and look at her all day, although of course I want to do more.

Fast or slow, everything or nothing. I'm okay with whatever she wants as long as I get to be around her. If the other guys could hear my thought process right now, they'd wonder what happened to the 'real' Roman, or at least the Roman they thought they knew.

When it comes to women, the Roman they're used to has always been about getting what he wants, when he wants it, and it generally has taken little effort to get that. But clearly, Angel has happened to me. I'm still the real me, but I've evolved, and I'll never be the same. I know I'm not alone in this. She's had a significant effect on all of us. Even Slade, although he tries to hide it.

Her hips sway as she walks toward the bed, highlighting her ample, shapely thighs and the curve of her waist, her breasts bouncing gently with each step she takes. My cock jerks in response to her body simply walking toward me. She's just so fucking perfect.

"Are you sure you want to do this?" I ask as she approaches me.

She's the one initiating this interaction, but I want to be sure. Especially now, especially after all she shared with me and the others. It's been a massive day for her, and I want to make sure we take things at her pace, that she doesn't feel pressured to do anything she might regret later. She's had enough bad things happen to her to last many lifetimes, and the last thing I would ever want to do is add to that list.

Without responding verbally, she climbs onto the bed and straddles me between her gorgeous thighs, and I cup her breasts with both hands. I take this as a yes, that she wants to do this. Her nipples are rock hard, and I lean up and kiss each one gently. She lets out soft moans, almost inaudible, both times, but I hear them.

Although she's displaying confidence in her actions, I see a flicker in her eyes. It only lasts a fraction of a second, but I know what it is. She's worried that I might reject her because we haven't gone here yet. She's not entirely sure why I haven't crossed this line with her yet, and deep down inside, she's concerned that it's because I don't want her. That's the last thing I want her to think. I need to fix this, so she never worries about that again.

"I've wanted this ever since I saw you in the salon, Angel," I growl. "I need you to know that the reason I didn't try had nothing to do with you. It was all about what was going on in my mind, and what I thought was the right thing to do."

Her gaze locks onto mine. "If you wanted it, then why didn't you take it?" she asks as she undoes my pants. "And since when have you been concerned about the right thing to do?"

I slide my pants off, leaving me naked from the waist down.

"Too many clothes," she says as she glances down my body, pulling off my shirt as well so that we're both completely naked.

"Because you're way more special to me than anyone else, Angel." I pull her face to mine, gently kissing her. "I don't want to fuck everything up. You deserve the world, and for people to treat you with respect."

"So you withhold your cock? Unfair," she pouts, her plump lower lip jutting out. I can tell she's half joking. "I like that you respect me and all, but respect shouldn't mean I don't get to have this type of fun with you when we both want it."

"Okay, okay, you can have it now," I laugh, putting my hands up in mock defense and then returning them to her hips. "But only if you really want it."

"Oh, I *really* want it," she grins, reaching down behind her and sliding her hand along my shaft. I groan at her touch. "I want you on top of me, to show me you mean what you just said," she says.

Together, we flip over so that I'm now on top, my forearms propped on either side of her head. She's soaking wet, and as much as I enjoy an extended foreplay session, I can tell she wants to get down to business just as much as I do. I dip my head and we kiss. It's passionate from the outset, our tongues interlocking and exploring each other with a mutual hunger. She moans and wraps her arms around my neck. "I need you, Roman, now. Please."

I line myself up with her entrance, and in one thrust, I slide myself all the way inside her to the base of my cock. She gasps as I fill her up. "Fuck, Roman!" she cries out.

I groan as she clenches so tightly around me I can barely move.

"That's what you're doing. We're fucking and I'm Roman." I grin at her.

She rolls her eyes and grins back, her gaze full of desire. "I knew your cock was going to feel amazing."

"Well, that's funny, because I've been wanting to bury it inside your gorgeous pussy for days. I was confident you were going to feel amazing, especially based on what I'd heard."

"From what you'd heard?" She arches an eyebrow at me as if demanding an explanation.

"Well, I'd heard rumors. To be fair." I smirk. "No complaints from the other guys, only effusive compliments. A+. Five out of five."

"You discussed that with them? With Brick?" A flicker of concern crosses her face. I guess that must feel a bit weird, hearing that a houseful of guys are talking about you in that way. But it really wasn't like that. Everyone is just so mesmerized by her, she's become one of our principal topics. We can't get enough.

And most of it isn't about what she's like naked. It's about her interests and her hopes and fears, how funny and smart she is, how she's changed our worlds in such a short time just by being around us. By being herself. We're so lucky she's part of our chosen family. At least for now.

There's a giant 'what if' shadow hanging over our heads in terms of how long this will last for, and what will happen next, but as much as possible, we're all living in the moment, just enjoying having her here. We're committed to helping her take her psycho stalker down. After that, nobody really knows. We'll figure out the rest later. In the meantime, she's part of us and we can't get enough.

"Not in detail," I say, not wanting to get into all the things I've just been thinking about right now, but hopefully just enough to put her at ease. I caress the curve of her waist with both hands. "Nothing disrespectful. I just know enough to be aware they had a great time and no regrets."

She laughs, and it makes her clench around me tighter. Jesus, this woman. "Seems like a shame you waited then. We could have been doing this the whole time."

"Nah, it was worth building up the anticipation." I shrug, grabbing hold of her by her hips. "It's not like we didn't have other fun. And besides, it would be rude to keep you all to myself. You're quite popular around here, you know." I wink at her and she moans as I thrust slowly in and out of her, teasing her, not wanting to rush this.

"You don't mind the... sharing?" she asks, her voice coming out in a soft gasp as she looks down to watch as I plunge my cock deep inside her.

"If you're asking if I mind my brothers railing you, then the answer is no. I don't mind. There's enough of you to go around." I shrug. "Besides, jealousy isn't my thing. Any of our things, really. But if you don't mind, I'd prefer to stop talking about their dicks being inside you and focus on mine. Be in the moment and all that."

She wraps her legs around my waist and her arms around my neck, and part of me melts inside. This one gesture makes me feel strong and powerful, and part of me regrets not having done this sooner because we could have been doing it a lot this whole time. Then again, it feels like everything has led up to this moment for a reason.

"That's totally fine with me," she moans, arching her hips up toward me. "From now on, I'm one hundred percent focused on your cock."

I thrust my cock in and out of her, faster now, rolling my hips to give her a variety of sensations deep in her core. She moans at the change in pace, and a shiver runs through me as she rakes her nails down my back while I pump myself deep into her and extract myself again, over and over.

"Fuck, Angel," I rasp, my breath ragged from the effort. "I feel like your pussy was custom-made for my cock. You're so fucking tight and wet."

She digs her nails more firmly into my back and I feel them catch against my flesh, drawing blood, almost sending me over the edge.

I flip her over so that she straddles me, her hair cascading wildly around her shoulders as she smiles mischievously down at me. "Ride me, Angel. Show me how you can ride my cock."

She slowly raises herself up and I guide her by the hips to slam back down on me, her wetness and our heavy breathing the only sounds in the room, the scent of her arousal pleasantly thick in the air. I use my grip to impale her repeatedly on my shaft, and she gasps each time I bury myself inside her from below.

She angles her hips ever so slightly so I can get a little deeper.

"Good girl," I growl. "Angle yourself so that your clit rubs against me, just the way I know you like it. Use me."

I'm guessing, but I seem to be on the right track as she grinds herself on me, and I loosen my grip on her hips, letting her take control and work herself into a frenzy. She moans and I know that she's close, her speed increasing and the pressure of her grinding continuing to build.

"Fuck, you feel amazing, Angel," I groan. "I'm so close."

"So do you, Roman," she cries out. "And so am I."

She tilts her head back and cries out again as her pussy seizes around me, and I feel her spasm wildly, shuddering as she comes, releasing her juices all over my cock. Her eyes roll back and her mouth opens as she reaches her peak and she continues to clench around me.

As her orgasm subsides, I grab her once again firmly by the hips. She gasps as I hold her still while I fuck her from below, driving my cock into her over and over again until I release deep inside her.

I kiss her gently on her gorgeous lips once more, and then gently pull her off me and bring her to lie in the nook of my arm as we both regain control of our breathing. She nestles in, fitting perfectly into the curve of my armpit, and smiles up at me. Another little piece of my heart feels like it's melting. She's global warming and I'm an iceberg. I'm completely screwed, but I'm okay with that.

"You felt even better than I thought you would, baby," I say, smiling back at her.

"Oh, you're saying you like my pussy?" She curves it in toward me so that it gently touches against my hip, as if to make sure I know exactly what she's talking about.

I bite my lower lip. "I fucking love your pussy, Angel." Reaching up with both hands, I play with her nipples. "I'm going to spend the rest of my life thinking about how much I want to be buried deep inside you twenty-four seven."

"That's high praise from someone with your... experience," she grins up at me, her eyes sparkling through her gorgeous dark lashes.

I pick up a pillow and smack her gently with it. She laughs, hopping off me and laying down beside me, and snuggles into the nook of my arm. It feels so good, just laying here like this, basking in the afterglow of fantastic sex with this beautiful creature.

I pull her closer and close my eyes.

I don't tell her it's not just her pussy that I love.

I'm pretty infatuated, some might even say obsessed, with everything else about her, too.

Chapter Sixty-One

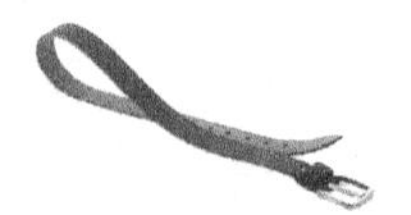

Aidan

"Where are they?" I glance into the living room and the kitchen, but both rooms are empty. I haven't seen or heard from Angel or Roman for a while, and it's making me nervous. She's at huge risk right now, with her psycho stalker on the loose and all, and the last thing we need is for Roman to take her somewhere that makes her vulnerable to an attack. I also like to know where the guys are, and if Roman has gone on some job without at least mentioning it, let alone a vigilante mission, I'm going to be pissed.

"I have no idea. It's weirdly quiet in here," Brick shrugs and randomly opens the pantry as if they might be hiding in there. He picks up a container of Lucky Charms and shakes it.

"What are you doing, Brick? You think they're hiding in there with the marshmallows?" I arch an eyebrow.

"You never know," he says, shrugging and continuing to shake the container and peer inside. "Worth a check. Weirder things have been known to happen around here. Imagine if they found a way to make themselves tiny, though, the size of the cereal. Like with a miniaturization machine or something. It would make for a good hiding place, a box of Lucky Charms. Unless somebody didn't know and they poured you into a cereal bowl, poured milk over you and ate you, I guess. That wouldn't be a good ending."

I smirk and shake my head. This guy. I have no idea where he comes up with this shit.

"Do you think they went out somewhere?" Slade asks, glancing toward the front door. "Roman had said something about needing to do inventory at the club sometime soon. And I know Angel likes to get out of the house more than she's been able to lately."

"I fucking hope not," I huff. "It looked like all the cars were here, and I'd like to think they're not that stupid. Besides, I strictly told them to stay put. That lunatic seems to be getting closer. We need to be on the lookout for any potential traps. They'd be putting us all at risk if they decided to get up and go just because they felt like it, especially without telling us."

I walk up the stairs to the hallway, and Brick and Slade follow along behind. It's silent up here as well, except for the sounds of our footsteps and the rustle of our clothing as we walk.

As I pass Roman's door, I notice it's slightly ajar and there are faint sounds coming from inside. I peek in.

He and Angel are both in there laying on Roman's bed. I turn and gesture to the guys to be quiet, but show I've found them by pointing into the room so they can also see.

They peek in and see Angel, fast asleep with Roman's arm wrapped around underneath her, snuggling into him, her leg wrapped comfortably over his, both breathing softly. Slade and Brick turn around and raise their eyebrows at me, and I nod.

"Jesus, he's got it bad," says Slade in a low, deep voice.

"I know, her knee is like snuggled up into his balls," says Brick, staring at their human origami. "And that's his cardinal rule. Always send them home after fucking. Never let them sleep over in case they catch feelings."

"I think you were right to be worried, Slade," I sigh, observing how peaceful they look snuggled in each other's arms. "Because Roman, playboy extraordinaire, appears to have been the one who's broken his own rule and caught feelings."

What I don't say out loud, and what I try to keep to myself as I wrestle with it internally, is that so have I.

Maybe we all have at this point.

In other words, maybe we're all completely fucked.

Chapter Sixty-Two

Slade

The next day

I walk into the main dining room where the other guys are sitting, preparing for the day ahead. We have actual business to do today, more than just being distracted by a girl.

They look up and see my facial expression, their backs all straightening. They can tell something is up.

"What's going on, man?" Aidan asks, his brow furrowed.

I clear my throat.

"Zero's men have intercepted one of our hauls from the mainland. Somehow they found out where the drop was taking place, yet again." I sigh as I say it, not enjoying being the bearer of bad news. "We have to make them pay. And then, at some point, we need to figure out how they're getting this intel."

"Jesus, didn't we just shut down another major supplier?" Brick growls. "Do they just keep creeping out of the woodwork and taking each other's places? It seems like a never-ending cycle."

"Yeah, that's how this works, man." He knows how this works, but I can understand his questioning it. It's like whack-a-mole all up in here with these mafia guys. New versions just keep coming and coming and coming, no matter how many you knock down. They're relatively indiscernible from each other, but some just wear better suits.

"It's fucking annoying, if you ask me." Brick has a tendency to pout, a bit kid-like, and today is no exception. "I mean, send them all my way and I'll have some fun, but I like to feel like we're making some kind of progress."

I tap him on the shoulder for reassurance. "You can say that again, bud. We are making progress, though. Today, for instance, and what we're about to do. Let's go."

We don vests and grab our weapons and head out into the car. Guns are the appropriate choice for this mission, and fortunately, we have plenty. Normally Aidan would already be inside, waiting for us in the driver's seat, but he's not today, so I hop in and take the wheel.

After a brief drive to an adjacent neighborhood, we reach Zero's location. It's not a secret where he lives. It's a big place, and he's proud of what he does and who he is to the island. He's just powerful enough to be annoying and just a little dangerous.

Their compound is lit up with perimeter lights. It's a large residential building, originally historic architecture but with a variety of contemporary-looking wings have been added over time. Tall hedges that partially obscure even taller fences line the property, and the fences are topped with razor wire. Several security cameras are perched high on poles. I know they have a giant security detail keeping tabs on the property 24/7.

Of course, they see us coming. Zero's guards pour out of the building as soon as we pull up, all heavily armed as expected.

Brick and I pick them off one by one. Normally, we'd have Aidan here to call out positions, but he was busy, and we actually feel comfortable going in just the two of us this time. Generally, we're like a well-oiled machine, Aidan's leadership and knack for understanding how humans move, and Brick's and my precision shooting. It feels a bit like a video game, but with more grunting noises and a little less blood. Today, it's just Brick and me and our instincts. The fact Aidan didn't insist on coming to chaperone us was actually a compliment to us, a testament of his confidence in our skills.

When the guards out front are on the ground and have all mostly stopped moving, Brick keys in a code and the gate opens. He might be crazy, but he can get into just about any building regardless of the security system, and that's an extremely useful skill to have in so many situations. Even if it means you end up subjected to the odd lecture on veganism and animal rights.

A couple of guys are groaning on the ground and we put them out of their misery. For a moment, things are silent except for our breathing and our footsteps.

We step over the bodies and enter the house.

We sweep the bottom floor and it's clear, and the two of us slowly climb the stairs.

At the top of the stairs, we find ourselves in a long hallway with three doors on either side. The house is silent, but we know Zero is in here, no doubt with some of his toughest goons. These guys are highly predictable, leaving their weakest out front and having their most powerful men glued to their hip at all times.

We kick open the first door on the left, and it's a fairly empty room. It looks like a guest bedroom largely devoid of personality, furnished only with a bed and some side tables. It's immaculately made up and as if nobody has ever stayed in it. Some cookie-cutter-looking artwork hangs on the walls, and some generic books sit on the nightstand. We check under the bed and in the closet, but both are clear.

We kick open the second door. It's another bedroom, but it looks like someone has been sleeping in it recently judging by the tangled sheets strewn across the bed and clothing crumpled on the floor. We hear rustling from somewhere inside the space. Brick yanks the closet door open to reveal a man hiding in it. He whimpers when he sees Brick and the unhinged grin stretched across his face.

Without wasting a moment, Brick shoots at him, exploding the guy's head, and his body instantly crumples to the floor. Brick turns around to face me and he's splattered with blood. He grins at me, and his teeth are red. He looks like an absolute lunatic. Like himself, in other words. In his happy place.

The third door squeaks open and disappointingly, it's only a linen closet, items neatly folded in tidy rows, the potent scent of laundry detergent permeating the small space. I move a couple of items around just to make sure there's nothing hidden behind them, but it's just full of sheets and towels and regular household items.

Behind the fourth door is a bathroom. The room is clean and impersonal, only a couple of toothbrushes in a holder and a towel on a rack that looks like it's been hastily folded, showing it's ever been used. The room is obviously empty. This is disappointing. I want to hurt someone.

We creep along the dimly hit hallway to the fifth door. If there's someone behind it, they've got to know this is the next door we'll be opening. We've been coming down the hallway in sequence, left to right. Whoever is in there will almost definitely be armed, so we need to be careful.

I nod at Brick. He reaches out a hand and flicks the door handle, sending the door open, and leaps back. Gunshots ring out, bullets spraying the wall opposite the door. We're on either side of the door as a line of goons comes running out, at least six of them, and we pick them off one by one, taking care not to accidentally shoot right through one of them and hurt each other. Their defenses are terrible, and they're like lemmings running out in a row, easy pickings. Once they're all on the floor, we step over their bodies and collect a couple of their guns as backup.

That leaves one more door. Door number six. Zero has to be in here.

Brick carefully leans in and flicks this door open as well, but this time there's no hail of gunfire. I carefully peer inside, and Zero is calmly sitting in an executive chair, flanked by three more goons. These guys look more sinister than the last group, and they're heavily armed. Unlike the others, they're in full defense mode, and there's no chance of them making the first move. They're here to protect their leader, but on his terms. It feels like maybe he has something to say before this goes down, or they would have started shooting already.

Zero is behind a large, ornate desk that dominates the space, and he leans forward and crosses his arms on top of it. He's a muscular man of medium height, wearing a dark blue suit. His attire is obviously custom made, clinging to his well-developed torso and biceps just the right amount. I can picture an older lady stretching a measuring tape across him to make sure everything is exactly to measure, making sure everything is just right. Okay, that's weird, Slade. Get a grip. You're here to kill this guy, not visualize him with random seamstresses.

"I thought you'd never arrive," he says, calmly, even though we just tore up his house and killed nearly all of his men. "Men?"

I guess that's his cue. There's suddenly a massive flash and an explosion, and both Brick and I jump back as smoke fills the hallway. Coughing, I shield my eyes and then a bullet flies right past me. Fuck! It must have been a flash-bang grenade, and the goons are shooting at us. Clearly, they're copying Brick's chaotic style. I dodge and weave as I try to get my bearings. We need to be careful or Brick and I might end up shooting each other because of all the smoke.

"Ca-caw!" Brick shrieks, and I fly to the ground. I know his code. Two silenced shots take down two of the goons. As I get to my feet, the smoke clears and I see the third goon standing behind him, aiming his gun at Brick.

"Duck!" Brick immediately dives to the ground and I shoot. The third goon groans and lets out a gurgling sound as the bullet nicks his neck, blood spurting from the wound. He crumples to the floor.

This just leaves Zero.

He's still sitting at his desk, but he's looking very pale and fidgeting with his hands. I think he was expecting his guys to take us down pretty easily, judging by how he's looking right now. His confidence is gone, and he no longer seems so poised. I'm still not sure why he had his goons pause before opening fire. He said nothing profound before the flash-bang grenade went off.

"You know why we're here, Zero?" I growl.

He gestures around. "You enjoy interior decorating?" It's a feeble attempt at a joke, and I can see the fear radiating from his eyes. "You like what I've done with the place?" His voice squeaks, betraying him and his attempt to show confidence.

"Stop with the attempt at small talk or humor or whatever the fuck that is," I growl, my voice low. "You stole from us, Zero. We really don't like it when people steal from us."

"I—I—." His eyes fall to the ground and then flicker up to meet mine, but he can't find the words.

I put up a hand to silence him.

"We caught your guys on tape, Zero. But that's not what we're really mad about," I shrug. "See, you really fucked up. You sent one of your guys to murder our brother, Roman, while he was working. But you weren't successful, so then your men kidnapped and attempted to torture our woman. You weren't successful with that either, so then you targeted one of our drop sites. Nobody fucks with our brotherhood, nobody fucks with our business, and nobody fucks with our woman."

"I'm sorry, I—." He knows he's done, and it's not worth trying to articulate a feeble excuse.

"Repent in hell, you stupid fuck." Brick shoots Zero square between the eyes, blood and brain matter splattering on the family portrait behind his desk. "Bye, bitch," Brick grins and waves at the man's body. "Good riddance to a colossal waste of a carbon footprint."

We pick up the stolen haul that sits egregiously in the corner of Zero's office in a large cargo bag, and then walk out of the house the way we came, smoke still billowing in the hallway. The smoke reminds me of a technique I learned at culinary school. I might need to make barbecue sometime soon.

We head back down the hallway and down the stairs, out to the front of the compound. After stepping over countless bodies, we hop into our vehicle and drive home in silence.

Chapter Sixty-Three

Aidan

Slade and Brick arrived back at the house a little earlier, both covered in blood and dust and grime. They tried to sit on the couch and tell me all about it, but I made them go take showers and change. Filthy fucks. I don't know what state this place would be in if I wasn't around.

It would probably look like a homicide scene in here, the amount of times we've all come back drenched in the blood of our enemies, streaked with dirt and mud and god knows what else. But that's par for the course when you're in the line of business that we are.

It's a relief to have Zero out of our lives. I knew that the two of them could take him down without my help. This wasn't one of those situations where three or four of us needed to go in guns blazing. He wasn't the strongest man on the island, but he had a decent-sized team and they were always trying to mess with our drops. Like a hundred noisy mosquitoes buzzing around your ears when you're trying to focus and be productive, always having to swat them away.

When Zero's guys tried to mess with Angel, I knew we needed to take care of him for good. When they messed with our drop, it seemed like the perfect time to address things all at once and put an end to him.

Now that he's out of our hair, we can focus on people with more power than us, and how we can take it from them, rather than stopping Zero and his men from trying to mess with ours. We need to focus on the bigger fish, not the annoying little minnows nipping at our ankles.

After they cleaned themselves up, Brick and Slade went out to run a few errands, and I'm waiting for them to come back and tell me more about what went down. I'm sitting in the living room absentmindedly flicking through TV channels. My mind drifts to what we observed earlier in Roman's room. I wasn't jealous when I saw Angel snuggled up against Roman, but it made me realize how much I want that for myself. She seems to trust me, at least more than she did at the start, but I feel like I need to show her how much I care about her.

If I can be the one who finds her stalker and helps to end her pain, I think it will show her how much I want her around.

My phone beeps and I look to see who's reaching out.

Anonymous: I know about the girl.

Aidan: Who is this?

I don't normally have time for anonymous texts, but anything that might be about Angel is, of course, going to pique my interest. Assuming that's the 'girl' the message is referencing.

Anonymous: That's not your concern. I believe she goes by Angel now, but that's not her real name.

Aidan: Wtf, who is this?

Okay, this *is* definitely about Angel. And this person seems to know about her past. She's been pretty up front, but we've only heard things from her perspective. I think she was telling the truth about everything, but what if there's more to it?

Anonymous: I have much to share. Meet me at the park beside 14 Palm Street. Don't tell your friends and definitely don't tell the girl.

Aidan: You've got to give me more info than that, man. It sounds like I'd be walking into a trap. What would I need to learn about her from you?

Anonymous: Do you want information on the girl or not?

Aidan: What kind of information?

Anonymous: Trust me, it'll change your mind about her.

Aidan: Trust an anonymous tester? Good one, bro. Go fuck yourself.

What kind of information could this person possibly have? Hearing it will change my mind about her is concerning, though. I'm certain this person is playing with me, but why is there a little voice in the back of my head saying I should find out more?

Anonymous: She'll destroy everything you ever worked for. You need to hear this.

Aidan: How do I know you're for real?

What if she's done this before? What if she's capable of ruining everything we've worked so hard for? Ugh, why am I letting an anonymous texter needle me like this? I'm losing my mind. But this might be important information, and I need to protect the guys.

Anonymous: Let me put it this way. If you don't meet me, I'm going to call the cops and let them know that you're harboring a captive. I'll also let them know about the not-so-little blood puddle I found on the floor of the salon.

Shit. I'm pretty sure we can figure the part out about the captive, assuming Angel would have our back and deny that's what was going on. And I think we did a reasonable job of cleaning up the evidence in the salon.

And what if we really can't trust Angel? What if she said we really were holding her captive against her will and corroborated witnessing Roman murder someone at the salon? The last thing we need is Roman in prison for homicide. It would be such a waste and would definitely tank our plans. I feel sick. We've worked way too hard to be taken down by something like this.

Aidan: I don't know who you are, and I don't know what you're talking about.

Anonymous: Meet me as instructed, and all will become clear.

There are clearly many things that are off about this exchange. I don't trust whoever this is for a minute.

It might be our only opportunity to get some background on Angel from someone other than her, and we need as much info as possible to track down her stalker, and also to figure out what to do with her after we catch him. But this sounds like a trap, and not one that I'm willing to fall for.

Yes, there's a chance she made up her entire story, and she's not the innocent woman she claims to be. She could be the one tormenting other people, but that seems unlikely. She seems really authentic and vulnerable, but you can't be too careful around people. There's always someone trying to fuck you over. Maybe she's not the exception I thought she was.

God, I'm sounding like Slade, all cynical and mistrusting. But that's what's kept us alive and able to build our empire so far. If we took everyone at their word, we'd all be under the dirt by now.

But who was she before she created her life on this island, before she created this new Angel identity? I need to know, and soon. This might be our only chance, and it's going to have a big impact on her fate.

This still feels like a trap, though.

And I guess this could be her stalker taunting me if everything she said was actually true. In which case, maybe he's volunteering himself to me. Part of me thinks I need to take whoever this is up on their offer so I can at least find out.

If it is him, we already know he's going to pay for everything he did to her, and everything he put her through. And this might just bring us one step closer to finding him and doing what we need to do before he has any hope of touching her again.

No, that's silly. This is clearly a trap. I don't fall for traps that easily.

I'm so conflicted. I should just leave it alone.

We're going to find him without needing to engage in whatever this is.

A couple of minutes later, my phone beeps again. This time it's from Brick's number. Which is a bit weird, because Brick isn't much of a texter. Prefers 'old fashioned voice conversations', he says. Enjoys hearing the sound of his own voice, more like it. Likes to talk on the phone and tell stories while he gets to the point. But I guess he does text from time to time, so it's not completely unheard of.

Brick's phone: *Hey man, I got a text from an anonymous number and they have information on Angel.*

Aidan: *So did I. I'm pretty sure it's a trap.*

This anonymous texter must be doing the rounds. Makes them seem desperate, trying to find the weakest link. Or maybe they're just thorough. I'm not sure which, but either way I don't like it.

Brick's phone: *I need to follow the clues. I'm going to meet the person.*

Aidan: *The fuck you are. Stay away. Come back to the house.*

Brick's phone: *Sorry, man. I can't pass up this opportunity to learn more.*

Aidan: *Listen, what have I told you about being impulsive? And how it puts us all at risk?*

He's always like this. Never vets things out properly. Acts and reacts without thinking through any of the consequences. It's going to bite us in the ass one day... it already has a few times, but luckily, the impact has been fairly minimal. But the stakes are getting higher, and it could only take one wrong move to lose all we've worked so hard for.

Brick's phone: *Well, then talk to Slade. He's already gone to meet her.*

Aidan: *Excuse me, what did you just say?*

Brick's phone: *Yeah, I told him to wait for me, but he was anxious to find out more about Angel.*

Aidan: *Of course he was. He's been trying to find out anything bad about her from the start. When did he leave? Where did he go?*

I am fuming. Slade… the most risk-averse human I know, always seeing the worst in anything. But when he has a bone to pick with someone, when something might validate one of his conspiracy theories, he's suddenly almost as reckless and impulsive as Brick.

In this case, of course Slade would have been the first to respond. He's been aching to find out something bad about Angel. Searching for it, needing it, to prove she's some kind of terrible person. If this really is a trap, which I'm realizing it almost certainly is, he is their prime target. Putty in their hands. If whoever this is doesn't get to him first, I'm going to teach him a lesson after this.

Brick's phone: He said something about Palm Street. Which is the same address the number texted me about.

Aidan: For fuck's sake. Why did he go alone? That's stupid.

Brick's phone: I don't know what to tell you. But I'm going to go meet him now. You should come, too.

Aidan: Don't tell me Roman went as well.

Brick's phone: No, but bring him with you. It can be a party.

Aidan: Brick, just wait for me, please. I'll come meet you somewhere and we can go together.

Brick's phone: There's no time, man. I need to know more now. If you want to join me, come meet me over there.

Aidan: Brick, just wait, please.

Brick's phone: No time, sorry Aidan.

I try calling Brick's phone, thinking maybe hearing my voice will get through to him, but it goes straight to voicemail. Fuck, these guys just don't listen sometimes. Their habit of wanting to rush in and fix things without thinking them through has put us in countless dangerous situations. Generally, I'm able to talk some sense into them, but now and then they can't be stopped.

Then again, I also almost went racing to this address to meet this anonymous texter and find out information about Angel. If I was about to be that impulsive, Slade and Brick didn't stand a chance.

I feel a little tingle at the base of my neck. It usually happens when my subconscious senses that something seems a bit off. Brick's texts sounded like him or the most part, I guess, but his writing was maybe a little more precise than normal. Or maybe I'm reading too much into it. I'm on high alert with everything going on, and I'm infuriated that Slade would go off without either of us, and that Brick would follow behind. I'm looking for something, anything, that can explain the insanity of what's happening right now.

Against my better judgement, I'm going to go and meet them. I hope they're both okay. I'm pretty certain this is a trap. Who it's a trap for, and who built the trap, remains to be seen.

After a twenty-or-so-minute drive in my SUV, I roll up to Palm Street, which, like the name suggests, is lined with tall palm trees as well as carefully curated hibiscus and plumeria trees and other landscaped greenery. A few cars are parked on the sidewalk, and remnants of kids' activities are strewn about in the form of forgotten toys and basketballs lying in gutters and on the curb.

It's a quiet suburban area, almost like a cul-de-sac in terms of nothing interesting happening except for Tupperware parties and kids running around playing ball on the street. But instead of it being a dead end, there are quiet intersections at either end, and the odd vehicle will rumble by at sporadic intervals. Seems like a strange choice to meet someone with intel on Angel, but it's the only option I feel I have right now. Plus, I need to find these idiots and make sure they don't do anything stupid.

I glance around for signs of life. The homes are fairly quiet, with just the gentle sounds of people rousing from their slumber and making breakfast. Through open windows, I hear dulled notes of conversation and the occasional clanging of cooking utensils. In a few of the houses, I see people gathered around kitchen counters and dining tables. Do people actually make pancakes and bacon and eggs for their kids like on TV? Must be nice. Not the childhood I experienced. Growing up, I was lucky to get a knuckle sandwich for breakfast from most of my stepdads.

Where the fuck are these assholes? They're probably wandering around together laughing at how they got here before me. How they'll get credit for finding out info about Angel first. Or maybe I'll find them tied up somewhere and I'll have to rescue them. Ugh. Brick is so fucking heavy, I've had to drag him across the room before and it sucked all the energy out of me. I'm not looking forward to that, if that's the case.

"Aidan." A deep voice emerges from near me. I turn to my right to look, expecting to see Brick, and all of a sudden my brain reverberates in my skull. I put my fists up defensively, but it's too late. What the fuck. I'm a good fighter, but I just got sucker punched. This is so embarrassing. Everything is fading to black and I fucking deserve it.

Chapter Sixty-Four

Angel

I'm pottering around my room, straightening things up. The guys all seem to be out doing something or other. When they get back, I'm looking forward to just relaxing with them. It's been so hectic around here and I just want some quiet time, to get to just enjoy their company. Of course, if that leads to other things, I will not complain. There are perks to living with four hot men, after all, and I intend to enjoy every one of them while it lasts.

My phone beeps. Oh, that sound is so refreshing. It's nice to have a phone again, to be trusted. I'm following Aidan's rules and I haven't reached out to anyone I know. I know that this is a dangerous time, and the last thing I need is to be tracked down by my stalker because I texted a friend here on the island. Besides, I don't want to put any of them in danger. And this phone is new, with only the guys' numbers in it, and I'm staying off social media. Everything should be fine.

Grabbing the phone off my nightstand, I glance down and it's from Aidan. A little smile forms on my face. I love it when the guys text me to let me know they're thinking of me.

I check the message.

Aidan's phone: Angel, I need you to come look at this.

Angel: What is it?

This sounds interesting. He's never texted me to go meet him somewhere before.

Aidan's phone: I found some info on the guy that's looking for you. But don't tell the other guys.

Angel: But you tell them everything. I don't understand.

Aidan's phone: There's no time. I think we have what we need to stop him. And you're the only one I can trust with this info.

Angel: Really?

Aidan's phone: Yes. Can't wait to show you. Hurry!

Angel: Okay.

He follows up his latest message with an address not too far from here. I know the general area, partially residential and part commercial. He's so risk-averse, there must be a reason he doesn't want the other guys to know about whatever he's found. They seem to tell each other everything, but these are unusual circumstances and there's always a method to his madness, and I've grown to trust him, mostly.

I pull on my black bomber jacket and tuck my bright purple hair into a wool hat. Despite the heat, I also pull on some black jeans. I'm not in a disguise per se, but I don't need to stick out like a sore thumb. I won the bomber jacket by doing a ton of Pilates classes one month as part of a challenge, and I feel good when I wear it because it reminds me I can kick ass when I want to. I guess I feel cute and strong, and that's a pleasant feeling.

It's exciting, going to meet Aidan like this without the other guys being aware. I've been feeling like they have the inside scoop on everything, and I'm the last to know, the outsider. So having Aidan reach out and confide in me like this, our own special time together, makes me feel a little giddy. Maybe the tables really are turning. Maybe I'm in the inner circle now, and more than just a captive, they don't know quite what to do with.

Okay, I'm probably delusional. It was just a text. Calm down, Angel, for fuck's sake. Sometimes someone says one thing with a hint of possibility and my mind spins it into a whole narrative where I'm at the center. The queen. Ridiculous.

As I walk toward the address Aidan sent through, I realize there's a lot to think about in terms of my future. I don't want to get ahead of myself. The guys are only keeping me around out of some sense of obligation, some feeling that they need to protect me, to defend me, from the evil psycho who has tormented me for more than half of my life. With their help, I think we have a chance to take him down and end his reign of torment once and for all. But once the threat is over, and it sounds like it will be soon, the guys may not see any reason for me to stay around. I'll just be back to what they saw me as in the first place. The witness to a murder that one of them committed. That doesn't bode well for me. I'll be a loose end again, and we know Aidan prefers dead ends to loose ends.

Even if they showed me some mercy and let me back out into the world, I don't know where I'd go. I'm assuming that they wouldn't want me staying around here, knowing what I know and having seen what I've seen. I created this island life to escape from the psycho. There's nothing left for me back on the mainland. He destroyed any remnant of that. If I went back, I'd have to reinvent myself again, in another town, under another name where my past couldn't follow me around. The thought of it is exhausting. Cultivating new ties, making excuses why I haven't established a solid work history or credit, inventing a solid back story, knowing nobody and then meeting people who I can't tell shit.

On the very slim chance that they didn't banish me from here, I guess I could stay on the island and continue the life I've been building since I got here.

I enjoy running the salon, and the island is gorgeous.

The surfing is amazing, and the lifestyle is relaxed, except for the whole murder aspect.

One step at a time, though.

We have a psycho to destroy before I can start thinking of the possibilities, whatever they may be.

Chapter Sixty-Five

Angel

Following my phone's map directions, it takes me about half an hour to get to the neighborhood of the address Aidan sent through. On my way there, I spend the time thinking about how much has gone on since I met the guys, and wondering why Aidan wants me to meet him here. It's exciting to get out of the house, but I can't shrug off a sense of unease. I attribute it to wondering what happens after we take my psycho down, after I finally get to stop running from him.

As I head down the street lined with rows of tall palm trees, I hear a rustling behind me. I glance over my shoulder, but see nothing out of place. Shrugging, I turn back around. I need to get to Aidan, and he's probably impatient that I've already taken so long to get to him. But I walked fast and was trying to be sensible, not taking an Uber from the compound or anything like that which would leave a trail.

I hear another rustling noise behind me and turn again. This time, a shadowy figure steps out from a nearby tree and darts toward me. I try to run, but the figure moves too quickly, and suddenly they're right next to me. I cry out as I feel a sharp prick in my arm. And then everything goes black.

I wake to a bright light shining directly in my eyes. I squint and try to shade them with one of my hands, but my arms are not cooperating. I can't lift them at all, and I realize I'm tied down to the surface I'm laying on. It feels cold and smooth underneath me, my shoulder blades digging into what feels like metal. I try to move my legs, but they won't budge either. I look down, still squinting, and see they're bound at the ankles, too. I writhe around, trying to free myself, but the bonds are tightly secured. Where am I? How did I get here?

The room is clinical, with white walls, and some generic paintings hung on them. Stainless steel counters sit flush against each wall, the perfect place to set out sterilized tools and medications. I don't know where I am or exactly what type of facility this is. It could be a hospital of some sort, or maybe even a laboratory or scientific research facility.

Then I hear the cruel laugh, and it instantly sends an icy shiver down my spine. The unmistakable sound of Brett Wolf, my very own psycho stalker. I've blocked his name out of my mind, but with him in the same room as me, I'm finally letting myself think it. Not just Brett, never Mr. Wolf, always both names at the same time.

Brett Wolf, the man who tormented me for years, bringing out my darkness, leaving his horrific marks all over my body and my mind. Brett Wolf, the man who has never let me go, over the almost multiple decades he's festered in prison, thinking about me, obsessing, waiting to hunt me again. Brett Wolf, finding a way to get out of prison much earlier than expected and tracking me down on this island despite my efforts to bury my old self and start anew. His name, long blocked from my mind, now perforates every synapse in my brain, flooding all my senses. *Brett Wolf. Brett Wolf. Brett Wolf.* And now he's found me.

"Oh hello, there! You're awake. That's just... *perfect*," he whispers, almost theatrically. Even his whispers are full of excitement when he's doing something evil. I remember them well. "I've been waiting for you for seventeen whole years, but these few hours, while you were passed out, were the hardest by far." He paces around me, his gaze never breaking from being locked on me.

I shiver uncomfortably under his stare, trying to avoid direct eye contact, but it doesn't make a difference. I can still feel his eyes on me.

"I was so tempted to get started early, but I reminded myself that I needed to be patient. I enjoyed knowing I could do things to you while you were unconscious, like I used to, but the greatest pleasure has always been in making sure you're fully aware of what's about to take place. I had to hold myself back earlier, knowing that waiting for you to wake up will bring me the most enjoyment with what's about to happen."

His thin lips twist in what I can only imagine he thinks is a smile, even though it's the stuff of nightmares, revealing his chiclet-like teeth and the tip of his creepy pointy tongue.

He's really let himself go over the years he withered in prison. His skin is mottled and drab, likely no access to the expensive skincare products he was accustomed to on the outside. I can't believe I ever found him attractive. But I guess seventeen years of prison and being an evil maniac will do that to you.

I guess sometimes people are ugly on the inside and it eventually soaks through to the outside. It doesn't happen to everyone, but it has happened to him. He was always so proud of his appearance, and he's probably still better-looking than a lot of men his age. But I know he must hate looking in the mirror, and he must despise what he's aesthetically become. A minor victory, I suppose.

His body is still muscular, and he's much bigger than me. I'm sure he continued to work out throughout his time on the inside, determined to maintain his physical strength so he can continue to exert dominance over people weaker than him. He probably sees his physical upkeep as a testament to his mental vigor, something that he could still control from the inside when he had little control over anything else.

I shiver as his gaze runs over my body. "You still look like an angel when you sleep, you know," he says, his mouth hinting at another warped smile.

"I found it curious that you chose the name Angel when you attempted to hide from me, to start a new life. Like you were almost teasing me by pretending you wanted to start anew. Naming yourself something that I used to call you. It's almost like a special signal to me, a gift to let me know you were thinking of me. That you didn't really want me to stay away."

I want to vomit in my mouth. Gross. That is not at all why I chose the name. But now it makes me sick I didn't connect the dots at the time I picked something. I must have blocked out that he used to call me that as he inflicted wounds all over my body, typically while I was in and out of consciousness. Fuck, maybe I really do need more therapy.

"You've really been thinking about me this whole time? You couldn't find someone else to obsess over?" I narrow my eyes at him because that's all I can physically do right now. I wish my eyes could throw poison darts into his stupid body. I hope he feels my hatred as viscerally as I do.

"There's nobody else worth this level of focus, this dedication," he says softly. "You are my masterpiece. The work I am most proud of." His voice is surgical and precise, like everything he does. "Everyone before you was just practice."

I shiver. I knew I wasn't the first, and I'm not sure how many there were before me.

My Stockholm Syndrome was so bad for a while that I felt almost flattered that he saw me as being at the peak of his horrific acts. I was almost proud, almost felt special. I hated myself for those feelings, and they still make me feel very uncomfortable.

I shiver as he caresses my jaw with his hand. His fingers are long, but they're no longer nicely manicured, like they used to be. They're rugged, a little rough, no carefully buffed fingernails or neatly trimmed cuticles. He must have come straight to the island after being released, no time to refresh himself. He'd normally take the time to make sure everything was perfect and controlled. Maybe he's changed a little over the years, and he's not as prepared as usual. Maybe that's something I can use to my advantage.

My skin is crawling even after he removes his hand from my face, just like it always has since he started hurting me. To think at one time I was okay with, and even enjoyed, his touch. That didn't last long, but it still feels really creepy to know that at one point he made me tingle in a good way.

"And now I get to follow through on what I promised almost two decades ago. But now it's even better, because I've had so much solitary time to plan." He rubs his hands together and bounces from one foot to the other, jubilant. "Do you know what it's like to be completely solitary, *Angel*?" He laughs, more than a little unhinged. "It still sounds so funny to me, calling you that. Do you mind if I call you by your real name?"

He peers at me with one eyebrow arched, as if genuinely asking my permission. It makes one of his eyes look almost comically bigger than the other. His eyebrows are no longer neatly manicured like they used to be, but it's almost an improvement because he used to overdo it.

God, I'm tied down by my arms and legs, about to be tortured, and I'm critiquing this asshole's appearance. But he looks so different and yet the same, and it's the small things sometimes that keep us on the brink of sanity.

"Angel *is* my real name." There's no way I'm letting him call me by the other name. It's taken me a long time to get used to the new one, and hearing him call me by the other one might take me back *there*. I can't let him. I'm glad he didn't just automatically start, that he's almost deferring to me on this one thing.

"No, it's not, and we both know it. It might slip out. Sorry in advance." He winks at me, badly. He never could wink properly, something that probably really got to him. A weakness, the inability to wink, even if not useful. "Anyway, it's just a name, and I've always enjoyed calling you Angel while I worked on you. So I'll humor you for now, but apologies in advance if I accidentally slip back into old habits." He shrugs like someone might shrug to a friend if they did something annoying but still kind of cute. I shiver again. He lost his mind a long time ago, and it's clear he still hasn't come close to finding it.

"I'm not that person anymore. You have no right to call me by that name anymore." I jut my chin out defiantly. This is a test. I'm telling him not to do something, and I want him to know I've changed. Will this be enough to send him even further over the edge? If so, I'm fucked. It would mean he's completely lost control and I don't know him anymore.

"That's where you're wrong, though," his voice takes on a huskier tone, but it's still measured and precise. Thank goodness. I might be able to unravel him on my time and take advantage when he finally snaps. I think that's the only way I have a chance of getting out of here. "You'll always be that person, *Angel*. You can't run from yourself. You know I'll always have a hold over you, that I know you better than you do. Don't kid yourself."

I shudder as I remember him thrusting himself into me against my will, screaming my old name as if he truly believed I wanted it. The name that I can't bear to write or speak out loud anymore. That's what that name means to me now. Him, violating me against my will. Allowing other people to violate me. Hearing them say it out loud when they were ravaging my body, while I was trying to block out their grunts and groans and think of something else, anything else. Hoping they didn't snuff me out in the course of their perverted excitement.

I still can't quite believe I made it out alive back then. Sometimes I wonder if this is all just some kind of purgatory, that I really died and the universe doesn't know what to do with me.

His voice rips me from my thoughts. "You can run, you can change your name. You can call yourself Angel or Barbie or the Easter Bunny. You can pretend to be whoever you want. But it's all a facade." He grins at me again, his sharp incisors sticking out like fangs against the smaller nubs that line his evil mouth. "You're still a weak little girl who will succumb to my control and will. It's not your choice. You're just so damaged and unfixable. You always have been. Who cares what name you go by? It's your essence to be frail and vulnerable. Pitiful, really. I probably should have chosen somebody stronger to manipulate. More of a challenge than you."

He stares at me intently, his eyes overly bright. To me, he'd always had an intense gaze, but now I can see that it's fanatic, his emotions all tied to me. He lives to hurt me. His only goal is to destroy me in the most depraved way he can conjure in his sick, twisted mind.

But something has shifted within me, and this feels different from all the times he's tried to cut me down before. I'm so used to him telling me how weak and shitty of a person I am, that instead of decimating my self-esteem, instead of shredding me down to a husk of myself, his words now don't even scratch me. Instead, they make me feel sorry for him in a way.

It's been a while, but I've developed calluses in my soul, and I've become immune to those types of comments from him. I suppose the internal scars will never go away now. They're just there for all time, like my physical marks. But in this case, it's useful. My stomach isn't churning at his vitriol. I'm just enduring him and this moment. I can see through him, can finally see him for what he is.

How can I be his ultimate masterpiece if he really desires someone more challenging to manipulate? That makes no sense. He's gaslighting me, trying to diminish me with cheap shots. He hates me because he hates how obsessed with me he is. He hates that I make him lose control just by existing. That gives me power, and he doesn't know that I know it. But I do.

He peers at me more closely now, his eyes scrutinizing every inch of my face. "You have changed little, you know, Angel. You look just the same as when I last laid eyes on you in person seventeen years ago."

He circles around the table where I'm tied down.

"Must be the moisturizer I've been using. Keeps me looking young, just how you like us." I can't resist, even though I know he can't handle me being a smartass and it's going to cause me pain.

"Shut the fuck up! Don't you give me lip, you stupid little girl." He slaps me open-handed across my face.

It stings, but it was worth it. If I'm going to die, I'm going to piss him off in the process. Trust me, I'm not just going to lie here and take whatever he's trying to dish out on his terms.

"I've memorized every single detail, every single *pore* on your face, *Angel*. Every night, in my cell, I would dream of you. Of this day." A dreamy look spreads across his face, his mouth and eyes almost melting into his broader features. "And now it's here. I just want to savor it." The corner of one of his eyes tics a little, and he bites his lower lip as he continues to gaze at me. Jesus, if he keeps this up, he's going to come in his pants. I guess that's better than him trying to touch me, though. What a disgusting, evil monster.

"Haven't you tortured me enough?" I meet his gaze, and am pleased my face remains set in a scowl, no tremble giving away the residual fear I feel inside. "Don't you see that my body is already covered in scars because of you?"

His eyes trail down my body, as if he's admiring his own artwork through my clothing. "Oh yes, I remember how I inflicted every single one of them. To be honest, sometimes I jerk off to the memories of the ones I especially enjoyed creating." A grin spreads across his face and I swallow hard to keep the bile down that's threatening to exit my throat. "But that's just cosmetic. I know I've done far more to you than that."

"Yes, you fucking did!" I'm exasperated and I can't help my voice from rising. "You killed my soul! You made me dark inside!"

"Oh Angel darling, that's simply not true," he says, his voice dripping with condescension. "You give me far too much credit." He smiles a wicked little smile. "You had plenty of darkness within you already." He shrugs. "It's actually what drew me to you. I could see your... potential. And wasn't I right? Look at you now, trying to come across as so headstrong, but in reality very much still under my control."

"Fuck. You." I want to call him a psychopath, but I know he would just enjoy that. He's a lunatic. Unhinged, deranged, insane, obsessed with me. And he loves it. I do not.

"I wanted to haunt you in your dreams, you know," he says, nodding as he continues to study me. "I studied astral projection and lucid dreaming while I was in prison. My goal was to visit you every night, just to remind you I was there, waiting, biding my time until we could be together again."

Of course he would try to attack my dreams and my reality. Nothing is off limits for him, as if I'm not even allowed to nap without him trying to invade my inner thoughts. My brain conjured him up regardless, allowing my own sick version of him to haunt my dreams, my nightmares, and my every waking minute. So I guess he wins, even though he wasn't able to transcend dimensions and literally manipulate my dreams. And now here we are.

He pulls out a scalpel and twirls it gently so it sparkles under the light. He smiles as he admires the shimmering blade, and then turns his deranged grin to me. "Isn't this a beautiful tool? Worthy of being used on you, my dear Angel?"

I eye the scalpel as it glimmers. "Haven't you sliced me with one of those enough already?" I don't shrink away from the scalpel because he's used so many on me it may as well be a run-of-the-mill dinner fork or a butter knife. This fool has me desensitized to things that would have many people passing out from the fear.

"Oh, *Angel*, it's not the amount of times you do it. It's how much joy you get each time you do!" His voice booms with excitement, reverberating off the walls of the clinical room. "And I derive a lot of joy from slicing into your creamy flesh and leaving my mark on you. Mmm."

I shiver, my skin crawling as he describes marking me as his property. As I remember the slicing and singeing and the crispy burning odor as he branded my flesh. My blood, pouring from me, that he would scoop up in his hands and smear across his face and chest like some kind of war paint. That he would even drink it at times. The sick fuck.

"I suppose you're hoping those four men of yours will protect you, aren't you, Angel?" He peers at me as if he's trying to pick the best spot to slice me with the scalpel. "Not to be the moral police, but it seems slutty of you to be going around fucking four guys at once. Especially when they all live under the one roof."

I narrow my eyes at him again. It's about the worst I can do to him in my current predicament. "Oh, please stand there and continue to slut-shame me. Ironic, given you used to rape me and allow your rapey acquaintances to do the same. That's what you were doing, you know. That's what it called when you perform sexual acts on someone against their will."

His face darkens for a moment, and I think he's going to deny it, to insist that I wanted all those things to happen. But just as quickly, it returns to normal and goes back to his current version of 'normal'.

"Oh, I think I hit a nerve," he grins. "I'll be hitting more of those later when I bring out some of my other tools. This is going to be such a fun evening, for me at least." He rubs his hands together again with anticipatory glee. "I hope you get some enjoyment out of it too, *Angel*. This should be enjoyable for you as well."

I glare at him, adjusting my shoulders against the metal surface below me to try and get more comfortable. "You don't need to keep saying my name like that. And you never cared much for ensuring anything was enjoyable for me, so please don't feel the need to start now."

"I don't *need* to do a lot of things, *Angel*, but I choose to." He shrugs. "As I was saying, your friends won't be able to save you because I sent them on a wild goose chase. Similar to how I lured you here." He smirks, clearly proud of himself.

"Wait, the guys? What have you done to them?" A lump instantly forms in the pit of my stomach. This was my biggest fear. Forget what plans he has for me and what he ultimately ends up doing to my body. I'm concerned about the guys being brought into this. I know they're big and strong and can handle themselves against some terrifying people, but this is my psycho stalker and I don't need him interacting with the only good part of my life right now. This is my battle to face.

"Oh, I cloned their phones," he grins, looking very proud of himself. "Your little Aidan was so worried about you. He didn't come to me at first, but I told him little Bricky-dicky and Sladey-wadey were on their way to me, and he fell for it hook, line and sinker. And as for them, well, I led them to believe you were somewhere else on the island. They should be just about as far from here as they possibly could be without leaving the shore."

My heart sinks. "What did you do to Aidan?"

"Oh, you're worried that I hurt your boy? How... sweet of you. I must say, I'm a little jealous that you care about someone other than me. I'm going to take it out on him as soon as I'm done with you."

He's said too much. His little slip just now means Aidan is alive. A wave of relief washes over me as I realize he's prioritizing destroying me over ending the lives of the men I care about so much.

"Anyway, I'm sick of talking about them," he says, his eyes narrowing. "I want to talk about you, Angel, and how I'm going to separate your body into tiny little pieces while you're still alive. How I'm going to savor every moment as I destroy you after all these years. Mmm, this is going to be my best work yet."

"Whatever." I roll my eyes at him. "It's not like there's anything you haven't done to me before already. Do your worst."

He glares at me, and I see him ball one of his hands up in frustration. But this time, he resists the urge to hit me.

"Come on, Angel, please," he says, his eyes pleading with me. "This isn't how I imagined it. It's not how it's meant to go." His voice is almost whiney, like a little rich kid having a tantrum because he didn't get his full allowance or because not all of his friends showed up at his party. Pathetic. "It's not as much fun torturing someone when they don't care whether they live or die. I prefer it when they struggle. I like to see the fear in their eyes. The situations where they start off trying to be heroic, to save their own life. Where they summon their strength and give it their all, and then I get to see the light extinguish from their eyes. The moment they figure out they're not good enough, that they're not powerful at all, and that they're going to die and there's nothing they can do about it."

"So, you get off on human suffering? That's hardly a shocker. I mean, look what you did to me." I gesture at my body. "Haven't you done enough already? You've hurt me so much that you've made me numb. I'm like a drug addict that can't get high anymore.

You've made my resistance super strong. I'm completely desensitized at this point. If you don't like my lack of reaction, you only have yourself to blame."

"Oh, I still have plenty of ways to hurt you," he growls. "And I'm going to do something I haven't done before. I'm going to destroy your face. I can't wait to take away your beauty. It's the one thing I've preserved this whole time, the one line I didn't cross. I've never touched your face."

He moves to the side of the room and picks up a vial of something that's bubbling despite no apparent heat source. Is that acid? Jesus. He twirls it in his hands. "I'm going to wait to use this, although I've fantasized about it for a very long time. Watching your flesh disintegrate, making you into a grotesque creature that only I could love. Your men will think you're hideous once you're all melted. It's going to be wonderful when I'm the only one who'll even be able to bear looking at you."

"That's it? You want to make me ugly? That's your major goal? Good one." I roll my eyes, even though I'm terrified of acid chewing at my flesh. That really would be a new form of torture, and one that I won't be able to hide with long sleeves or pants.

"Beauty is pain, *Angel*," he shrugs. "And you're my most beautiful masterpiece." He smiles at me again, his hideous teeth bared. I shiver, and I'm feeling actual fear at this point. He's reaching new lows, extra levels of crazy. He's threatening me with actions that can't be undone, and ones that I might not survive.

Fuck.

"So, while they're off hunting you down on the other side of the city, we're going to have our own little fun and pick up right where we left off all those years ago." He puts the vial down for now, thank goodness, and returns to my side.

He caresses my jaw again and I try to move my face away, but he holds it in place, controlling me like always. God, I desperately want to vomit all over him, but I need to remain calm and pretend to be doing what he says while I figure out how to escape. He continues muttering about our time together before he killed my family and all my friends. How much I mean to him, how much he enjoyed causing me unbelievable pain. He's so repetitive that I tune him out, even though his words are completely insane.

One thing is clear. He's even more deranged than the last time I saw him. Seventeen years on the inside have not treated him well in terms of his mental health.

He's so busy taking a trip down memory lane that he doesn't notice me squeezing my right wrist ever so slightly, trying to slip it through my restraint, or at least loosen it. I'm determined to get out of here, even if I get injured in the process. Better off injured than dead. I don't even care if he disfigures me at this point, as long as I leave here alive.

"Your family couldn't protect you," he sneers. "Honestly, I don't think they cared about you enough or they would have figured out a way. It's a bit sad, really, having a family that doesn't care enough to save you." There he goes again with his hurtful comments. "And now neither can these men." He shrugs. "It's a bit of a pattern you've got going for you, isn't it, *Angel*? Everybody close to you seems to let you down. To leave you here on this plane to fend for yourself. It must make you wonder to yourself, is it something about you? Are you not somebody worth sticking around for? Are you not capable of being protected because you're just so... broken and irreparable on the inside? It must make you feel sick, realizing that you're not somebody that's worth saving."

His words used to break me down, but now I just listen as he rattles off his psychobabble, trying to manipulate me into my old sorry state. This time, I see how he tries to slice me deeply with every word choice. He's physically holding an extremely sharp scalpel in his hand, but nothing could cut as deftly as his words. Using his knowledge of my family life against me. Preying on my vulnerabilities.

But instead of cowering and crying and thinking dark thoughts about my self-worth, I just let it all go. I forgive myself for falling for this bullshit in the past. I see him for all his manipulation, and how he's actually very skilled at it. Younger, more inexperienced me didn't stand a chance.

But he doesn't know who he's up against now.

What he doesn't realize is that I'm out here in this world now just trying to get by. Like we all are. But I don't have an anchor to guide me home. I'm rudderless. I'm my own anchor. And that's scary sometimes, not having a backstop. I look at all my friends and their family relationships. They might seem like a pain sometimes, like more trouble than they're worth—the obligations and feelings and baggage that come with them. But at the same time, they provide a foundation and roots and a place to go when the world is crumbling all around you. But in my case, I only have myself. And I do have my chosen family, but as I've learned, those relationships can come and go. There's not the same permanence that you find with a 'real' family. I am my own rock, and that's a big role to fill sometimes. I've been told I'm brave many times, but really, I'm out here just trying to exist. What he doesn't realize is that I'm done with his suffering. No matter what he does, he can't hurt me anymore. Not like he used to. And I don't have anybody centering me, making me weak. I thought my being anchorless was a weakness, but I've come to realize it's my ultimate strength. I have nothing and everything to live for.

His words have lost their power over me. But instead of letting on that he's not affecting me, I indulge him, playing along as if he's getting to me. Tears spring forth from my eyes and he looks pleased, because he thinks he's the cause, when really, it's the pain of squeezing out of one of the wrist restraints. I inch my hand along, folding it in on itself as much as I can, and I can feel that it's slick with blood, lubricating the restraint and assisting my hand along. I grimace, and he assumes it's in response to another of his stinging verbal attacks, but it's because my thumb feels like it's going to buckle in on itself as I squeeze it out of the restraint, leaving my hand loosely inside the fastening.

He's so enthralled by watching my reactions to his words, so consumed by my every micro-expression, that he fails to notice what's going on so close to him. He's so obsessed with me, with thinking that his words have such an emotional impact on me, that he misses what's right in front of his face.

"I love hurting you," he growls. "I love watching the way you are so weak against my words." He's clearly aroused, and I'm sure he's on the verge again of coming in his pants.

"Yes, stop hurting me, daddy." It slips out, and I want to vomit, but his eyes light up and I know I said the right thing to keep him distracted. He always loved it when I called him that. Let him think that's what this is about. Pleasing him, fulfilling his every desire, including ultimately destroying me. This sick fuck is going down, and he has absolutely no clue. I love it, and I'll be gross and say exactly what he wants to make it happen.

My fingers inch along above me until I feel them tap against a long, thin object. Ha! The fucking idiot placed a scalpel on the bed for later use, too busy luxuriating in his nostalgia. Too busy staring at the pores on my face to notice me escaping right under his eyes.

"Anyway," his eyes grow dark and a scowl forms on his face. It's the first negative emotion I've seen from him in a while. "I can't stop thinking about you and your four men. You stupid slut."

"Oh, for fuck's sake, Brett Wolf."

His eyes light up as he hears me say his name out loud.

"How is that any different from the men you forced on me for your entertainment?" I arch an eyebrow at him. " Or was it different because you were in control of that situation?"

His eyes grow darker. He's distracted, wild. I've hit a nerve. "What is it about these four guys, though?" His voice is whiney again. "They seem like vile human beings to me, *Angel*. If I had anything to do with it, they'd be dead. And that's exactly what I'm planning on as soon as I've finished with you. Ideally, I'd force you to watch as I slowly kill them one by one. But it's taken me seventeen years to get to you again, and I can't take any risks. Believe me, each one of them is going to die a slow and grisly death."

The scalpel is now firmly in my grasp, my wrist free. My heart is racing, and blood is pounding in my head. I can't stand to hear him talking about my men like this. Any fear that existed within my body has fled the scene. I'm breathing fast, adrenalin coursing through my veins. He's threatening my guys. I might not know what they will do to me after all this is said and done, but for now, they're all I have. And it's time to shut him up.

"Stop talking about my fucking family!" I scream and slash at him with my free hand. My use of the word 'family' to describe them isn't lost on me, but I'll process that later.

He jumps back and I use the scalpel to slash my other wrist to freedom, and quickly do the same for the ropes attached to my feet. I jump off the bench that I've been tied to throughout my time in this room, and wildly slash in his direction.

"You fucking bitch!" he screams, his voice hollow and raspy as he tries to stay just out of my reach. I'm out of control and so is he now, just like I know he hates. "This isn't meant to happen! You're meant to let me finish you, to let me take what you owe me."

"I owe you *nothing*!" I scream, blood slamming against my temples with force. I'm so worked up, so rageful, that I'm worried I might black out. "I have already given you *everything* and more! You took so much that didn't belong to you. There is nothing left to give you!"

Unfortunately, he regains his composure remarkably quickly as I scream at him, as if my 'acting out' makes him take on the condescending parental role once again.

"Now, *Angel*. I know this must be very difficult for you, taking a long, hard look at yourself. You're acting out of control. This is why you need my help." He shrugs, his voice once again oozing with condescension. "Why don't you just use the scalpel on yourself now? You could rid yourself of the darkness so easily. You know where to cut. I've shown you before. You have a few options... here, here and here." He gestures to the parts of the body that really shouldn't be sliced if you want to stay alive.

I ignore him, blood continuing to rush to my temples. A loud heavy metal song blares in my brain. I've learned to drown out his words with imaginary music, and it's kicking in as if I'm at a death metal concert. We circle the table where I was restrained just moments before. I hiss at him, chasing him, scalpel in hand. He jumps backwards, but again my wildness seems to calm him and he moves toward me.

Without warning, he leaps to the side and picks up another of his tools from one of the stainless steel counters. It's a longer, much sharper knife. There's no way that I can reach him with this much smaller scalpel when he's holding that thing. I try to circle around to the door to make an escape, figuring I can plot revenge later if only I can get out of here, but he realizes what I'm doing and he just laughs.

"Oh, *Angel*. How silly you must think I am. Falling for that? Do you think I would let you escape so easily after seventeen years of waiting to take what's mine?" He cackles, the same unhinged laughter that has haunted my nightmares for decades.

I feel my eyes narrow. An attempt to make him and his atrocities look smaller, maybe. "What the fuck is your problem? Why are you so obsessed with me? What is it about me?"

"Like I said, *Angel*. It's the darkness within you that attracted me to you in the first place. Seeing it pouring out of you energizes me. I dream of the times I used to cover myself in your blood. It was invigorating, energizing. And I'm so looking forward to drinking more of it tonight. The most I have ever consumed of you, my darling. There won't be a drop left by the time I'm done."

What a fucking nutter. I have to keep him talking while I figure out how to escape.

He leaps onto the restraint table. I don't even know how he gets up there, but it's an impressive athletic move. Maybe it's the adrenalin fueled by his obsession, but suddenly he's way too close to me with his sharp knife in hand. He hops down from the table on the side closest to me, no longer a barrier between us.

Now he's laughing, his eyes boring into me, as he corners me. There's nowhere to escape. For more than half my life, I've feared that I'd die at his hands. That I'd succumb to his psychopathic obsession, and he'd trap me in my darkness forever. And now that time has come.

I resign myself to my fate, but I'm determined to at least cut him a couple of times in the process. Inflict a bit of pain before he kills me. I'll fight until the last moment. That's a guarantee. I crouch into a staggered position the way I would on a surfboard, my center of gravity low, knowing that will afford me the most balance, and I lash out and slash one of his shins with the scalpel. The blade cuts through his flesh like butter and I feel it scrape against bone. He screams in agony, almost dropping the knife.

"You fucking bitch!" he cries out, his eyes narrowing and turning from dark brown to pitch black.

As he advances on me with the knife pointed toward my heart, I realize I'm probably going to die in the next minute. There's nowhere for me to run. He's bigger, his knife is bigger. I'll still fight, though. I won't give up. I can't give up.

He circles around me, still pinning me into the corner because of his hulking presence. He's blocking me from the door. Getting through that slab of wood is my only chance to stay alive, and he knows it. He advances on me, the blade only inches from my torso.

Suddenly, the door to the room flies open and a baseball bat smashes Brett Wolf in the head, sending him crumpling to the floor. I soon see that attached to the bat is Brick's large hand, and of course, the rest of Brick. He comes into full view, and so do Slade and Roman.

Slade runs to me on one side, Roman on the other, and they help me to my feet.

"Are you okay, Angel?" Slade asks, his eyes full of concern.

I can't form words. This is so much to process.

"Talk to us, Angel. Please," says Roman. "Are you alright?"

I try again to formulate words, but something's missing. Then it clicks. "Wait. Where's Aidan?"

"Brett Wolf smacked him on the back of the head and knocked him out," says Roman. "That's why you thought Aidan texted you. It was really this psychopathic piece of shit." He kicks at Brett Wolf with his foot. "I guess he cloned our phones and tricked Aidan, and then sent us messages saying you were somewhere completely different. We were able to track Aidan's phone and figure out where you were." He glances around. "It looks like we got here just in time."

I nod.

"Oh my god," I gasp. "Aidan...is he okay?"

"Yeah, the doctor was coming around to check him out. Should be there right now, actually. But based on our quick phone conversation, he seemed to think it was just a moderate concussion. Sounds like this asshole," he points his thumb toward Brett Wolf, "sucker punched him out of nowhere."

"As for this guy," Brick kicks Brick Wolf in the center of his back while he lies unconscious on the floor, "he's coming with us."

"What are we going to do with him?" My eyes are wide. I've been so resigned to him ending my life that I haven't even thought about what I might do if suddenly I gained control over him.

"It's pretty simple, really," says Slade, his eyes narrowing at the unconscious figure, finally scowling at someone who actually deserves it. "We're going to kill him, and we're going to make sure it hurts."

"We sure are," grins Brick, his eyes dreamy. "It's going to be a fitting performance. He's going to regret the day he ever met you, my Valkyrie. Nobody fucks with our queen and lives."

"What do you mean? How will you do it?"

"It's a bit of a case of choose your own adventure, really," says Brick, unusually cryptic. His gaze meets mine. "I need to ask you a very important question, Angel."

"Like what?" This is a weird time for Brick to be randomly quizzing me. But Brick is a kook, after all, so here we are.

"Like... what's his biggest fear?" His gaze is even more intense than usual. "Not just something he doesn't like. His actual biggest fear, the thing that he has nightmares about."

I think about it, and I've spent so many years fearing my stalker and what he's capable of that I've never really considered what he himself fears. Then again, I've spent a lot of time with him, and that's unfortunately lent itself to me getting to know him and his delusional mind well. After a moment of mulling it over, a lightbulb goes off in my mind, and I grin. It's so obvious.

"Not being in absolute control."

Brick nods, and then his face explodes into a broad grin. "Excellent. I have just the idea."

I feel a ripple of excitement. The thought of exacting revenge on the man who has made my life a living hell seems almost too good to be true. After hunting me, stalking me, abusing and torturing me, raping me, annihilating my entire family and everybody close to me, it felt like he was the unstoppable one.

Getting out of prison and coming straight after me was a bold move, but it only points to how unhinged he is, how he's been festering in his jail cell, thinking only of me. My skin crawls as I imagine him obsessing over what he wanted to do to me once he was out.

"You ready to go?" Slade asks, a rhetorical question clearly. Why would anyone want to stay around here after what just happened?

Without a word, Brick grabs Brett Wolf from underneath each of his arms and Slade grabs his legs. They carry him to the car and throw his bulky body into the trunk. As they toss him in, the impact causes him to rouse. His eyes slowly open, and he groans and gives Brick a questioning look. He attempts to prop himself up onto his forearms, but he can barely hold himself up.

"Oh haiiiii! I've heard you're quite the planner," Brick grins. "And that's such a lucky coincidence, because we have quite the plans for you! A win-win, if you will. A mutually satisfying exchange! I can't wait to show you what we've come up with! But now it's nap time, nighty night!"

In a familiar move that all the guys apparently know and love to use, Brick pulls a gun out of his holster, rears it up behind him and brings it down hard on the top of Brett Wolf's skull. He crumples back into the trunk, and Brick closes it with a satisfying click. "Baiiiii!"

Chapter Sixty-Six

Angel

I'm not sure what to expect when I get to the basement. The guys made me go upstairs to wait until they have everything ready, and now that I'm all set for whatever they have planned, every minute feels like hours. Standing around waiting to be called down has me on tenterhooks. I can't quite believe we've taken my captor captive, and not only do I get to live, I get to get revenge!

Brick told me to dress in my wildest outfit, to channel the most elaborate version of myself that feels most empowered and powerful. To wear what I believe will terrify Brett Wolf the most, and sear into his brain as the last thing he sees. *The last thing he sees.* It sounds so surreal, but it needs to happen. My brain is still processing. This is all so unbelievable, but it's actually happening. What a trip.

I've picked an all black outfit. Tightly fitted leggings, matte black, and a slightly sparkly corset that I've never had the courage to wear before. My tits look great in it, but that's for me, not for Brett Wolf.

My makeup is bold, and I extend the wings of my eyeliner far beyond where I normally would, dramatic and intense. My lashes are thick and dark, my lipstick a striking red. I did not come to play today.

For shits and giggles, I've adorned my back with fairy wings. It might be a bit extra, wearing wings, but Brick inspired me. If there's one thing he's taught me, it's not to be afraid to be my authentic self, no matter the cost. I've carried them around for years, always wondering if I'd get to the point I'd ever actually wear them. Today is that day. They stretch broadly behind me, making me look broader, bigger, more powerful. Ready for revenge.

Unusually, Brick also gives me a corsage to wear, promising me that today would be 'like the best prom you've never been to.' I shook my head and smirked at the time, but

I've put it on over my wrist as instructed. It's a beautiful black rose that would make a nice tattoo now that I see it on my hand. He's so hot yet so fucking weird, but in a way that makes me feel like a princess. No, not a princess, an absolute queen.

Finally, after what seems like forever but was probably only about an hour, the guys call me down to the basement. I'm so ready, but still not sure entirely what to expect. I just need to trust. They know everything I've been through now, and I'm confident they'll have put a lot of thought into whatever they've come up with, especially Brick given the venue is his precious torture basement. Every little detail will have been accounted for, and all I need to do is show up.

I walk down the wooden steps that normally descend into darkness, but it looks and sounds a lot different today. The basement has been completely transformed. Instead of a clinical concrete room built for torture, it's now an insane, noisy, and colorful carnival of horrors.

Garish masks with mouths snarling in horror and torment cover the walls and hang from the ceilings.

Loud, disorienting music blares from surround sound speakers. Strobe lights dance across the walls, and flashing lights surround vintage funhouse signs. The high-pitched beeps of carnival games reverberate off the concrete walls, creating a wild cacophony of chaos.

There's a touch of fairytale madness down here, too. Black and white rabbits and playing cards and black-light and neon artworks featuring torture scenes and wild sex acts also adorn the walls. I'm guessing that Brick chose these, and I'm not going to question how he got hold of them so quickly. It's cluttered and loud and a barrage of disparate sensations, which I can immediately tell is exactly what it's intended to be. This place is designed specifically to disorient, to mess with your senses, and it's working in the best way.

There are even containers of freshly made popcorn, the salt and butter scent pervading the room, and cotton candy sitting on a stand off to the side, covered in real worms that slither over the contents.

It's hard to feel anything like control in a place like this. Brick has received the memo and has executed on the assignment. This stage of it, anyway. I can't wait to see what happens next.

"It's time!" Brick calls out, grinning broadly.

As if he's completing a regular errand, Slade casually wheels my psychotic stalker into the room on a cart, and with the help of Aidan and Brick, he secures him to shackles suspended from the ceiling. A piece of material tied tightly around his head gags Brett Wolf's mouth. Which is wonderful and surreal for me—someone has finally got him to shut the fuck up.

It's refreshing to be in the same room with him without hearing his unhinged laughter, his condescension, his attempts to make my entire psyche crumble from the slices of his cruel words. Now he's just a gagged man shackled to a ceiling. I love it.

Brick moves back into position behind a podium near the center of the room, right in front of where Brett Wolf is suspended from his shackles. He picks up a microphone. "Testing, testing, 1-2-3!" The microphone screeches and the sound quality improves, Brick's voice booming out of surround sound speakers.

He's wearing a blazer that's completely covered in multicolored sequins. It's loud and garish and fits right into this chaotic environment. He's lined his eyes with thick black eyeliner and drawn lipstick on his face in a manner reminiscent of a deranged clown. It's definitely crazy, but it suits him. He is just perfect. At this moment, I realize I love him so much. I have the urge to make out with him here and now, but we have more pressing matters and that can wait.

"Well hello there, Brett Wolf!" booms Brick. "Welcome to the island's newest game show, *All Your Dreams Come True!* I'd say 'come on down!' but you're already here!"

Brett Wolf jerks awake at the sound of Brick's game show host voice blaring from the speakers in the basement. He squints at the bright spotlight shining directly in his eyes. Ironic, considering that was my reaction when I woke up in the clinical room where he planned to torture *me* to death. The metal shackles connected to his wrists rattle and clank against the pipe above as he attempts to move his arms.

"No point in trying to struggle, Brett Wolf - we've got you safely secured for the duration of this game show! But I appreciate the enthusiasm!" Brick winks at Brett Wolf. "Wriggling around is futile and will just spend your valuable energy, which you're almost certainly going to need to be a worthy contestant and make it all the way to the end!"

He tries to kick his legs and flail about, but he's tied up so tightly that his toes and the balls of his feet barely graze the floor. "Now, now, we haven't reached the dancing stage of the evening, Brett Wolf. You're jumping the gun. It's best if you just stay still and await further instructions. Be patient!"

Brett Wolf groans and blinks repeatedly. He tries to adjust his posture in his restraints but doesn't have much luck. His shoulders adjust in resignation. He stills and sighs deeply, waiting for what's next.

Slade approaches him and undoes his gag, removing the fabric and revealing a bitter scowl. Brett Wolf coughs and splutters as he inhales deep breaths through his mouth.

"Now, tell us a bit about yourself, Brett Wolf! We like to get to know our contestants at the start of each show!" booms Brick. "We want to know what makes you tick! What do you like to do for fun?"

"I—who the fuck are you?" he growls, but his eyes are wide. I'm not used to seeing him scared. It's kind of fun, I could get used to this.

Recognition dawns on his face as he scrutinizes Brick more closely. His sparkly outfit clearly threw Brett Wolf off, which is fair. "Oh, you're one of those *men* that Angel has been fooling around with, aren't you?"

"It doesn't matter who I am, but I suggest you play along, Brett Wolf," Brick grins. "Because if you don't, there are going to be bonus prizes, and I'm not so sure that you'll like them."

Brett Wolf snarls, but that's about all he can do from where he's shackled. Who's the captive now? A little grin spreads involuntarily across my face. I just can't help it. I feel giddy with anticipation.

Brick pulls a scalpel out of his pocket and holds it up so that it glints off the bright lights in the basement. With the brightly colored carnival lights, there are glimmers of blue and red and yellow and green and purple. It's beautiful. "I warned you, buddy. Slade, will you hold the microphone for me while I do the honors?" Slade nods and Brick tosses him the microphone.

"As you can see, Brett Wolf here has earned himself the first bonus prize of the evening! And Brick here is going to administer it to him directly." Slade has a surprisingly legit game show host's voice as well, deep and resonant. I might suggest it to him as a backup career if this whole mafia-type gig doesn't work out, and I suppose if he can't become a chef, which is clearly what he was born to do.

Brick walks over and holds the scalpel in front of the spotlight so that it glints directly in Brett Wolf's eyes. He squints and flinches as Brick descends on him. Brick deftly slices off one sleeve of Brett Wolf's shirt, leaving his arm bare from the shoulder down.

Because Brett Wolf's shackles are suspended above him, the smooth, sensitive skin of his inner arm is exposed. Brick runs the scalpel along Brett Wolf's arm, from his armpit to his wrist, breaking the skin and carving so deeply that it takes a moment for the incision to bleed. It'll no doubt hurt like hell, but Brick made sure not to cut so deeply that my tormentor isI at any risk of bleeding out. I don't know exactly what the guys have planned, but I know we need this psycho to be conscious for the game show to work.

Brett Wolf's eyes grow wide and his nostrils flare as he stares at his bleeding arm. He screams in agony as the pain hits him, writhing as if trying to free his hand to hold in the blood and gore that Brick has just split wide open in his grotesque act of butchery. I'm sure he's not feeling the full extent of the deep gash, his body protecting him by partially throwing him into shock.

"I'm sorry if you're right-handed, Brett Wolf. You might have trouble signing your name for a little while!" Brick shrugs as if he's explaining something quite trivial. "Lots of tendons and other important things for motor function just got a little messed up there, bud."

The blood is trickling out of his arm in a steady stream. Not torrential, but enough to know that significant damage has been done. Sometimes deep cuts hurt so much that they stop hurting. You're just numb. But you still know they're there. It's the case for both physical and mental injuries. I'm not sure which is true for him right now, whether he's in agony or not. Either way, I know he's terrified. His breathing is fast and ragged. I sense him trying to regain control of it, but he can't. He must really hate this. Almost as much as I love seeing him like this.

"Now, are you ready to go back to playing the game, or would you like another bonus prize?" Slade raises an eyebrow in his direction.

Brett Wolf shakes his head, his face pale and covered in a light sheen.

"What was that?" Slade booms into the microphone. "I need to have a verbal answer from you for it to count. It's game show regulations, you see. Nodding and shaking your head doesn't cut it. We need audible acknowledgement. Would you like to play the game now, or would you prefer to take another bonus prize? Keep in mind the bonus prizes get bigger and better the further you advance in the game! Brick just gave you a little... slice... of what's to come, if you'll excuse the pun. Things will only get crazier from here on out!"

"P-play the game!" Brett Wolf stutters, saliva flying from his mouth. "Play... the gam e..." His voice trails off. It probably feels surreal for him too, calling out to continue this insanity.

"You got it!" Slade says, and Brick returns to take the microphone from him.

"Excellent, thank you for standing in there for me, partner." Brick high fives Slade, who steps back off to the side where the rest of us are standing, watching.

"Alright, so back to where we were," booms Brick. "Tell us a bit about yourself, Brett Wolf. What do you do for fun?"

"I—I don't know," he says, his eyes wide with panic, the whites showing around the entire iris.

"You'd better come up with something, Brett Wolf," Brick insists, his voice echoing off the concrete walls and only dampened by the plethora of garish carnival decorations adorning the space. "The clock is ticking! We need to know *all* about you if you want to survive this game!"

Brick presses a button on the podium and a chaotic, high-pitched tune plays, accompanied by a loud *tick-tock! tick-tock!* sound.

Brett Wolf's eyes dart around wildly, and then finally settle on Brick. He clenches them tightly shut, and yells, "Photography!"

"Excellent! Brett Wolf has selected photography as his first category!"

We all turn to Brett Wolf and applaud enthusiastically, as if his 'choice' of category is truly exceptional. He doesn't look so sure, his eyes bugging as the sound of our synchronized claps reverberates off the walls just like Brick's voice.

"Now our co-host, who I believe you may know, is going to ask you some questions and put you to the test to see if you can make it through to the next stage. Come on down, co-host! My beautiful Valkyrie, or as you may know her, Angel!" Brick makes a flourishing gesture to welcome me onto our 'set'.

I step from the shadows into the spotlight so that I'm silhouetted in front of it, and I curtsy flamboyantly to my left and then to my right as the guys all clap loudly for me.

Brick reaches over and hands the microphone to me, as well as a stack of cue cards. Noticing my reflection in one of the basement's many shiny carnival games, I can see I really am wearing an outfit inspired by a Valkyrie. I knew Brick would like my choice, and it seems fitting for the occasion. An Angel of Death. That's what I am today. I added a few extra touches to my outfit right before I came down. My face is now painted with stripes that run from below my eyes, halfway down my cheeks. I added more black eyeliner so that it sweeps out and up even further, making my eyes look extra intense and dramatic and wild. The wings flare out broadly, and they twinkle under the wildly colorful lights that surround the basement space. The ensemble makes me feel powerful, confident, ready for the war we're waging today. Exactly how Brick intended for me to feel down here. I'm here to face my demons, and for once, I have the upper hand.

Brett Wolf squints, trying to figure out who I am, to make out my features. For a moment, it frustrates me he doesn't immediately guess it's me, but after all, he's always claimed to believe I'm weak, and right now I'm definitely in a position of power over him. He's not used to seeing me move confidently like this. He's not used to seeing me thrive in my element. I move closer to him to give his eyes a chance to adjust and take in the entire spectacle.

I want him to soak in every inch of me right now, to remember what he tried to create and to see instead how I've transformed into something far stronger than he ever imagined. Sometimes life is cyclical. Sometimes when you turn light into darkness, that darkness grows more powerful and ends up ultimately destroying you. I guess he took that risk and lost, and now is his day to pay the price.

"A-angel?" he snarls and narrows his eyes, his tone condescending despite his predicament. "Let me down or you'll regret it." I can't believe he's shackled to the ceiling with four men in the room who are determined to end his life, and he still has the audacity to threaten me. Actually, on second thought, I can believe it.

"Always so controlling. Always making me believe you're in the power position. Even when it's clearly a lie, like right now." My voice is firm and unwavering. I circle him, and on my way past his calf muscles, I kick one with the point of my shoe so that his wrists wiggle in the air above him. He jerks awkwardly, swaying in the air before coming to a complete stop.

When I'm satisfied he's not moving anymore, I finish my circling and stand in front of him again.

"So for your first round, the topic is photography, by your choosing," I say calmly. "Now tell us, Brett Wolf, what type of photography do you like to do?"

He lowers his brow and blinks rapidly, his eyes wide each time he opens them.

"The clock is ticking!" Brick says, leaning over so the microphone picks up his voice. "No time for dilly-dallying, contestant number one!" He plays the high-pitched carnival tune with the accompanying *tick-tock!* sound again. It echoes wildly off the walls, and Brett Wolf clamps his eyes closed as if trying to will a palatable answer into his mind. Or maybe he's trying to will himself away from this madness.

He blinks rapidly again. "Flowers!" he yells.

"Oh yeah? Flowers, you say? What kind of flowers?" I ask, arching an eyebrow and smirking at him. This man doesn't know shit about flowers, and he knows I know it. "I didn't pick you for a florist, Brett Wolf! Where did you develop your interest in flowers? And what types of flowers float your boat?"

"I don't know," he groans meekly, sweating under the harsh spotlight. "Any growing in the garden, I suppose. Wherever I see them. Colorful ones with leaves!"

I flip over the cue card in my hand. "I'm afraid that's the wrong answer, Brett Wolf! Honesty is a very important part of this game."

The guys standing behind me nod and murmur, "Very important."

"We're going to need you to fess up to your real preferred type of photography. Or otherwise Brick's going to give you another bonus prize. The more honest you are in this game, the more likely you are to live. Simple stuff, really."

Brick grins at Brett Wolf, probably hoping Brett Wolf is going to tell another lie so Brick can have some more fun with him.

"Okay—okay!" Brett Wolf pants, on the verge of hyperventilation. The balls of his feet each slip out from under him, one after the other, as he tries to gain balance, making him jerk awkwardly underneath his shackles.

He eventually regains his footing. His skin is flushed, and his eyes dart from me to the shadows where he knows the men are standing and watching, ready to jump in. But then, he seems to solely focus on me, and he gets the look in his eye that causes a shiver to jolt down my spine. The look he used to give me when I was under his spell. He's regaining control, figuring out how to fixate on his obsession despite all the noisy and colorful distractions around us.

"I like to take pictures of sluts like you," he growls, then spits in my direction. "Ugly loser whores who are so thirsty for a man. You're so gross. No man would ever want you."

"Oh okay," I nod. I hear Slade growl in the corner. "Thank you for the feedback. Anything else?"

"You weren't a virgin when I met you. You were spoiled. You are a disgusting mess that nobody would ever want. You're destroyed. Your parents don't even like you and wish you were never born."

"Okay then. Thanks again. Keep going." My voice is calm and steady, which just serves to agitate him more. Which is exactly what I want to happen.

"You're insecure and your tits are too small. Your ass is so fucking gross."

Slade growls again, and out of the corner of my eye, I see Aidan holding him back.

I nod. "Okay, thank you for all of your valuable input. I appreciate your transparency and candor." I resist the urge to roll my eyes.

I turn and walk toward Brick, but then change my mind, flip back around and walk back up to Brett Wolf.

"I have another question for you. Why are you so obsessed with me?" I peer at him and laugh, scrunching my shoulders up and grinning at him side-on, letting out a loud and crazy giggle that echoes off the basement walls like a creepy doll come to life in a horror film.

His eyes are enormous, his face red, and I can see he's about to yell.

"You don't deserve to be alive! You're worthless!" he screams. "You should have killed yourself when I told you to the first few times. You should still do it now. The world would be much better off without you in it. Do everyone a favor. End it now."

I hear shuffling in the background and I put a hand out to gesture for them to stop. I know they're all there, behind me, ready to destroy this psychopathic loser for saying the stuff he used to on the daily. But we need to let this play out rather than let him out of this the easy way, as tempting as it may be.

I review the cue cards in my hands and as I read, I can't help but flick forward a few. Holy shit, mind blown. So much thought has gone into this game show and I'm here for it. I'm fully on board with what's planned. But I try not to give Brett Wolf any idea about what's happening next. I want him to dream up wild scenarios in his head that won't actually be nearly as bad as what's about to happen to him. As he always taught me, anticipation of the unknown is half the mental torture.

Turning to Brett Wolf, I slow clap. "Wow, Brett Wolf. You must've been waiting a long time to get out all that controlling psycho rage. It must have been building up inside you the entire time you were rotting in prison. In fact, I'm very impressed by all the things you had to say today. So impressed, in fact, that you've earned yourself another bonus prize. Didn't he, guys?"

The four of them step out of the shadows, and each is holding a baseball bat. Slade slaps his bat against the palm of his outstretched hand, creating an ominous smacking sound that echoes off the walls.

"Congratulations! Here is your prize, Brett Wolf! See, these four guys think the opposite of all the things you said, and they have a problem with you lying about me. They protect me. I'm their queen. And I told them what you did to me. They're not very pleased about it. Are you guys?"

I look over at the guys, and they all shake their heads enthusiastically.

"The rule for this bonus prize is one crack each with a baseball bat," I explain to Brett Wolf. "No hitting in the head, because we want to be able to finish out the game. But anywhere else is up for grabs!"

I glance around at each of the guys and their bats, smiling at all four of them, then turn and look at Brett Wolf. "Oh, this is going to be so much fun! I can't wait to see where they pick on your body to make contact with!"

Slade goes first. He stretches the bat high above his head and bends side to side, before twirling the baseball bat over his shoulder and taking a few practice swings.

"First up is Slade!" I call into the microphone. "Slade weighs in at... who the fuck cares, but he's a large guy! His interests include cooking—remember that for later," I chuckle. "He also likes to hide his feelings and pretend he doesn't have any, when really he's constantly simmering just under the surface, ready to boil over at any moment!"

Slade lifts the bat over his left shoulder and brings it down in the center of Brett Wolf's back. It makes a loud cracking sound and sends the man flying by his wrists, his legs lifting in the air. He cries out and swings back and forth by his wrists, scrambling with his toes to find equilibrium.

"Great job, Slade! Come on down, Roman and Aidan! Next up, we have a double whammy! Roman, the house's resident playboy, who is the reason that I am here! Roman prides himself on his good looks and his ability to kill in cold blood, as long as it's profitable. Aidan is a born leader, always thinking five steps ahead, including the most impactful way to inflict pain and injury with one swing of a bat. With Aidan involved, you know this has been well thought through!"

Roman and Aidan stand on either side of Brett Wolf and look at each other, one a lefty, one a righty, and count down, "Three! Two! One! Go!" They nod and raise their bats behind them, and then at the same time, they swing at Brett Wolf, each connecting with a kneecap. He screams as his body flies up behind him, and again he scrambles to find equilibrium.

Brick moves in last. "And last but not least, and probably the one you should be most scared of. It's your new favorite, Brick! You're on his home turf here, in his very own torture basement. It doesn't normally look like this, but he's so excited to entertain you that he had the interior especially designed just for today, and especially for you! Come on down, Brick!"

Brick steps up behind Brett Wolf, who whimpers at the sight of him with the bat in his powerful hands. Brick's eyes are even more wild than usual.

"What are you gonna do?" I ask. "Give him a preview!"

"You never said anything about his balls," says Brick.

He swings his bat up behind him, and Brett Wolf whimpers as he smashes it in front of him, right into Brett Wolf's crotch. The psychopath shrieks in agony as the bat makes contact with a satisfying crack, his legs bending up in the air against his body for a moment before falling back down again. He squeezes his legs together, unsuccessfully trying to find a position where he's not in extreme pain.

"What a fun bonus game! Good job earning that by... how did you earn it again, Brett Wolf?"

"Lying!" He answers without a pause. Clearly he's learning how this game works!

"So you have one more chance, one more life left or you'll lose the game. So speak wisely now. What kind of photography do you like? Let me make it easier for you. We'll do multiple choice. Was it A) pictures of food, B) pictures of your cock, C) inappropriate pictures of humans who it's illegal to have them of?"

"B!" he shrieks.

"And?"

"And C!" he yells without hesitation.

"That's fucking disgusting," I boom into the microphone, starting to get the hang of this hosting gig. "And we just got your confession on tape. Not that you'll have a chance to go anywhere near a courthouse the way you're going. Your freedom is shriveling by the minute. That said, you did technically complete the task, so you're onto the next stage. And... would you believe it? We've got you a special guest to take part in this round! Bring him out, and I'll hand over the microphone to you again, Brick!"

"Slut!" Brett Wolf growls. Even as he bleeds and lays there with grievous bodily harm, he has to get in another sexist insult, trying to get his power back.

"I'm getting really sick of all he has to say right now," growls Slade.

Brick holds up the scalpel he used earlier. I glance at the cold metal tool while I think about the situation.

"I'd like to do it," I say, "but make it the serrated one. I want him to feel this." He grins and nods like it's the proudest I ever made him, and hands the serrated scalpel to me. I strut right up to Brett Wolf with a confidence he's never seen before.

Slade walks over, prying the man's mouth open so I can access his tongue. I extend it as far as I can from his mouth, and then I saw through its fibers, letting the little serrated edges drag across so that they pull on the muscle tissue, like slicing a steak that you need to saw back and forth a little just to get through. He tries to pull his tongue back but Slade helps to keep it sticking out enough for me to cut. Brett Wolf shrieks, hyperventilating, as I finally get to the other side of his tongue, severing it completely. He retches as I hold it up to him, blood pooling in his mouth.

"What's the matter, Brett Wolf?" I ask, batting my eyelashes at him. "Cat... no, what was it? Slut got your tongue?" I grin, and hear Brick cracking up in the background. Roman steps forward and hands me a rag that I use to wipe Brett Wolf's blood and spit off my hands.

Aidan walks over with a plate. He bows and hands it to me. "Ma'am, for later, correct?"

"Yes, we'll need that for later," I reply, unable to prevent my mouth from forming into a small smile as I think about the depravity that 'later' entails.

Slade wheels out an indoor portable stove and a cart with some ingredients all set up to cook. He wears a chef's hat and a fake mustache that makes him look like a hot version of one of the Super Mario Brothers. He places his cart in position in front of Brett Wolf so he'll have a prime position for the cooking session. Chef's counter, if you will.

"Excellent, thank you Angel! Isn't she wonderful?" He winks at me and waves as I leave the main game show 'set' and head back to the shadows to observe what happens next. "Now, Brett Wolf, meet your special guest!"

He looks over as Aidan wheels a man into the room on a dolly cart. He's also tied up and gagged, his eyes frantically trying to acclimate to the wild cacophony of lights and darkness of the basement.

"Here's your cousin Freddy!" booms Brick. "Now, you're already well-acquainted, aren't you? I'll spare the introductions! But don't speak to each other, or Brett Wolf here will receive another bonus prize. And as you know, they get bigger and better every time!"

Both of the men's eyes are like saucers, Freddy grunting but unable to get words through the fabric tied to his face, Brett Wolf too scared to talk. Brett Wolf stares intently at Freddy and zips his lips together as if to reinforce the importance of Freddy not trying to earn him another bonus prize.

"Alright, now we're onto round two. I understand that you and Freddy both sexually assaulted Angel and other women. Is that correct, Brett Wolf?"

I don't know where they found Freddy, but now that I get a good look at him, I remember his face. He was definitely one of the guys Brett Wolf would invite around. Being able to block things out isn't the healthiest defense mechanism, but I'm immensely grateful at times like this when I can't remember all the painful details.

Freddy goes to shake his head, but Brett Wolf is nodding vociferously. He really is a quick learner. I'd say I'm proud of him, but I'm not. He makes my stomach want to hurl out its contents, but it's also quite enjoyable making him squirm.

"This round of the game show is called *Eat a Dick*! We heard you were quite interested in the taste of human flesh, Brett Wolf. So we thought we'd get Freddy to help you out. Keeping it all in the family, some might say!"

Brick hands me the microphone and grabs a very sharp chef's knife from the tool table. He strolls over to Freddy as if he's on a Sunday walk, yanks the man's pants down, pulls his flaccid dick out of his underpants and lops it off with one slice. There's no fanfare this time, just straight-up castration. This man is the means to an end, and we have a lot more planned for the primary focus of this very special event. Freddy screams in agony and writhes in his wrist fastenings, but there's no way he can get free. Blood drips beneath him from the area formally home to his penis.

Brick throws the penis over to Slade, who catches it. He takes a closer look and cringes.

"Glad I'm wearing gloves! And damn, this is an especially ugly one," he laughs.

He clicks the stove on and it lights up with flames on two of the elements. He puts a sauté pan on each and adds a little olive oil and butter to both. "Gives it more flavor. Seasoning is key," he explains to Brett Wolf, winking and nodding at him as if he's his prize pupil in a beginner cooking session. Brett Wolf looks on in horror, coughing and spluttering blood from his de-tongued mouth, the pallor of his skin white as a sheet.

While the oil and butter get hot, he seasons both the penis and the tongue, doing the Salt Bae arm when he adds the salt, causing all of us except for Freddy and Brett Wolf to laugh.

The temperature is where Slade wants it to be, so he puts the penis in one pan and the tongue in the other and they sizzle. The smell isn't great, and I scrunch up my nose, but the reward of seeing him tortured this way is well worth it. I can't wait to see him ace this challenge!

Slade whistles as he skillfully flicks the sauté pans, one in each hand. Once they're done to his liking, he turns off the elements and places the cooked meats on a board to rest. "I find keeping things simple is better in these situations," he explains.

Once they're rested, he places them on a chopping board and slices both along the bias. "It makes it juicier when you cut it this way," he explains, nodding at Brett Wolf. He artfully places them on a plate with a micro green garnish. "To add a little pop of color," he says, gesturing to the dish. "And now we're all set. It's time for you to feast!"

As Brick and Slade approach Brett Wolf with a beautifully plated meal of his cousin's penis and his own tongue, he screams. His body violently flails about and as he gasps to control his breath, he seems like he might be about to pass out. His eyes dart around the room, failing to connect with a particular point. He's feral, out of control, but under our control.

Slade seems in charge of propping Brett Wolf's jaw open tonight, and this time Brick cackles with glee as he feeds spoonfuls of his cousin's dick and his own tongue into his mouth. He gags and tries to spit it out as Brick shovels it in, but Slade clamps his jaw together and growls, "Chew or it's time for another bonus game!" As Brett Wolf whimpers, I see his Adam's apple bobbing wildly as he swallows.

I half-snort, half-gag at what's happening before my eyes.

"Congratulations!" exclaims Brick. "You have passed the *Eat a Dick* challenge! No other contestant has ever got this far!" He beams at Brett Wolf as if he's truly in admiration of his getting to the next point in the game. "To be fair, you're our very first contestant on this game show," he adds. "Ooh, I have an idea! Let's celebrate with a bonus prize." I cackle at the unfairness of it all, Brick's rules changing by the minute. He skips around, clapping his free hand to the microphone and presses an absurd big red button in the center of the room that I didn't notice before. A loud siren goes off, the room lighting up in red and white, on and off, on and off.

Tears pour from Brett Wolf's eyes, his head down and his mouth frozen in a grimace. He makes a whimpering, choking sound. He's not so powerful anymore, now that he can't use his tongue to tear me to shreds.

Brick assesses him, his thumb and forefinger pressed to his chin, and then goes back to the big red button and presses it again.

"Ha! Change of plans, folks. I don't think he could endure what we had planned for this bonus round as well as the finale. And the finale is definitely the most important part of this exercise."

Brett Wolf whimpers again, and this time I sense a twinge of resignation, an understanding that he has no say in what happens next and an understanding that it will not be good for him.

"Alright, Brett Wolf! We picked this final challenge out specifically for you. You should be honored at the attention to detail that went into preparing this. We wouldn't give this challenge to anybody else. It's especially for you, VIP, just like you've always told people you are when you were abusing them. So we've made sure this challenge reflects your power! It's called *See How You Like It!*"

He whimpers and tries to swallow, but it comes out like a splutter. He's going to have to get used to that stump. Or actually, there's probably no point. He won't be around much longer.

Slade walks to the side and collects a sharpie and a piece of paper with a diagram on it.

"Do you know what Slade is holding in his hand, Brett Wolf?"

His eyes are now vacant, the wildness beaten out of him already. He instinctively tries to say 'no', but it turns out you generally need your tongue to say that word, so instead, his mouth just forms a pathetic 'o' shape, a monotone grunt coming out instead. To double down, he shakes his head.

"Slade has a Sharpie in one hand. In the other, he holds a diagram of each and every scar and mark you left on Angel's body. There are 128 of them in total, and there would have been more if you'd had an opportunity to inflict more injuries on her. We are going to draw each and every one on you in exactly the same place as Angel has hers. So we will be here for a while, but once it's done, you will have matching wounds. Isn't it only fitting that you get to experience your own creation for yourself? You're a fucking monster. And you've messed with our Angel. That was a big mistake."

One by one, one-hundred-and-twenty-eight times, Slade asks me which tool or method Brett Wolf used to carve or chisel each of my scars onto my body. With every lash, every slice of metal, every tear of barbed wire, every hot branding iron, scissors, peeler, grater... more blood runs from Brett Wolf. I watch as Brick painstakingly administers each one. After he makes each incision, he goes back to look at the diagram and then compares his handiwork like a proud artist. The entire exercise takes several hours, but it goes by in a flash for me. It's surreal seeing the injuries inflicted on me being inflicted on someone else, to the person who did them to me.

By the time Brick and Slade are done, Brett Wolf has passed out many times and been slapped back to consciousness, so he is forced to endure every sliver of pain.

Freddy, still restrained and dickless, is also passed out, probably from a combination of blood loss, the horror of having his penis chopped off, and what he just saw happen to his cousin.

Brett Wolf's posture sags against his wrist restraints, and like the rest of him, his wrists are bloody and raw. He is flayed, carved, stabbed, hooked, sliced, and butchered, just like me. It's the only thing we ever had in common, and now it's visible. I'd say we are both human, but he's not really human. So that just leaves this. My scars are because of him. And his wounds are because of him as well. The difference is that my conscience is clear.

His eyes are vacant and watery, and he's barely coherent. He slips into semi-consciousness once again. I know he's close to death. But he can't end just drift away quietly, because that would give him control over his final act. This has to end on my terms.

"Brick," I say, my voice firm and calm. "I would like to complete the game now."

Brick nods and hands me the machete. "As you wish, my Valkyrie."

I walk up to Brett Wolf and slap him twice, hard, so that he wakes from his subconscious stupor.

He blinks at me, his vision clearing enough so that recognition dawns in his eyes, snapping him back to where he is. I see pain flash in his gaze as his physical condition registers. All he can see below him is his own blood. And some pieces of dick and tongue meat that fell out of his mouth. His eyes grow wider and he gags.

"Brett Wolf, I'm really sorry, but you didn't pass that last test. What a fucking pussy. I didn't pass out once when you tortured me. Given, you didn't inflict every one of my injuries at one time, but you're still a weak man." I don't love being derogatory about a person's masculinity or lack thereof, but I know it will get to him, so I'm making an exception in the circumstances.

I carefully trim one of my fingernails with the machete and admire the results before turning back to face Brett Wolf.

"And now the time has come for my revenge. You thought you'd turned the tables, that you were going to end my life. But, the truth is, I'm smarter than you and I'm more powerful than you. Always have been, but I just didn't know it. You stripped away my innocence and my youth. You introduced me to evil. You encouraged me to find my darkness. Well, here it is, fucker."

His eyes, despite their fatigue and pain, flash with fear as I let out a guttural scream that echoes off the walls. I lift the machete high above my head and then spin around with it horizontal to the floor. As I pirouette in Brett Wolf's direction, it makes contact with his neck and slices through like butter, just like Brick promised it would.

Brett Wolf's skull bounces to the ground and rolls off to the side.

His body, now separated from his head, crumples to the ground with his wrists still dangling from the shackles.

I walk over and take a closer look at his skull. I need to nudge it with the point of my shoe because it landed face down. His face is like a horror film, his eyes wide and his lips curled in a fearful snarl. Looking down at him, I see how truly pathetic he's always been. He's dead, and he can't hurt me anymore.

It took me a long time to see it, to see that his power was just a construct. He was always as human and vulnerable as anybody else. He was just a complete sicko. Delusional, deranged, a master manipulator. And now he's gone for good.

Brick walks over and does cousin Freddy a favor by injecting him with a lethal concoction of goodness knows what, giving him a more peaceful passage to hell than his cousin.

With the two men who don't belong here dead, the remaining guys all turn to me. Their eyes convey a mixture of emotions—concern, pride, their own fatigue after this extended performance.

Part of me feels numb, but as I take one more peek at his scowling skull something snaps inside me. My body heaves and I gasp for breath as tears burst from my eyes. I'm not much of a crier normally, but my body racks and shudders at the release of having the burden of my psycho removed from me. For hours and hours we tortured this man, and it didn't scratch the surface of the cumulative time he spent inflicting countless horrors on me. Our physical wounds may have matched by the time he died, but he didn't endure the same level of psychological pain that he built up for me prior to and during his crimes. My soul feels crushed, my body heaving at the loss of someone who cared about me more than anyone else in the world, even though that care came in the form of a deadly obsession.

The guys are all looking at me. They're probably wondering if this is what a psychotic break looks like. Maybe that's what's happening to me. I can't stop crying, even though my eyes are swollen and my face is puffy and I'm gasping for breath. He's finally dead, unable to torment me any longer, but it's like a part of me died, too. I'm so glad it's over because this has all been too much. I can't stand any more torture today, no more death. My brain needs to process what just happened, because I feel raw and numb, happy and terrified, energized and exhausted.

As my body wretches and tears continue to cascade from my eyes, Roman steps toward me and wraps an arm around me, pulling my face into his chest, where I continue to sob. His touch is comforting, and finally, I regain my breath with my face buried in his shirt. He continues to hold me, not rushing me, and eventually I look up at him.

"Angel, we're going to clean up here, and get this taken care of," says Aidan, his voice gentle but very much in control, "and then we're going to come and check on you. You don't need to be here for this. Roman will take you upstairs and be with you, okay?"

I nod. Everything seems surreal. Brett Wolf is dead. I always thought he'd kill me. It might take a moment for me to process this.

Roman escorts me upstairs.

"What do you need, Angel? Right now, what do you need most?"

I think about it. "I need a shower," I decide. I can't think of a better thought than washing off the mental and physical residue of Brett Wolf.

"Same," says Roman.

We walk upstairs and Roman leaves me at my door, ready to walk down the hallway to his room.

"Wait." I reach out and grab his hand. He stops, turns and raises an eyebrow. "Stay with me. We can shower together."

"Are you sure?" He arches an eyebrow. "I thought you might want some time to yourself."

"I've never been more sure of anything in my life." I pull him through the bedroom and into the bathroom with me, and shut the door.

I turn the shower on as hot as it will go, and the room fills with steam as we both remove our clothing. I breathe it in deeply, letting the steamy air fill my lungs. Turning the temperature down just a bit, I hop into the shower and pull Roman in with me.

My face paint pours off me and swirls down the drain in a black spiral as Roman and I crowd together under the shower head, our now-wet bodies mashed together. I feel heat generating in my core as my breasts press against his muscular torso. He uses a finger to tilt my head up, and meets my lips in a deep kiss, the warm water splashing down on us. I kiss him back, my tongue pressing against his, hungry for him.

I moan as he dips his head and sucks one of my nipples into his mouth, and rolls the other between his thumb and forefinger. I run my fingers through his dark hair while the water splashes over me, hot and wet, as he teases me.

He stands up and I kiss him again, my arms wrapped tight around his neck.

I reach down and he groans into my mouth as I stroke his hard cock, running my wet hands along his smooth shaft. Fuck, I want him inside me so badly.

He slips his fingers through my folds and slides a single finger inside me, followed by a second. "You're so wet, baby," he rasps. "Did that turn you on back there? Destroying the evil that's haunted you for so long?"

"That, and being naked in a shower with an incredibly hot man who has his fingers in my pussy while I stroke his big, hard cock. That has something to do with it too, I'm pretty sure." I smile up at him and he grins back before kissing me again, this time his tongue exploring mine.

"I want you inside me, Roman," I whisper, my voice husky from the steam and my desire for this incredible man. "Fuck me until I forget everything. Get me dirty while you get me clean. Don't be gentle. I want it rough. I want to feel you for days."

He groans and picks me up, and I wrap my legs tightly around him as he presses my back into the tile behind the shower head, the water continuing to rain down on him as he slides into me in one go. He fucks me hard and fast, and I cry out with every thrust. My clit rubs against his body every time he slams into me.

The combination of the water and steam and the sensations he's generating inside of me create an almost sensory overload, stimulating every part of me. It distracts me from what just happened, my attention focused solely on Roman and the way our bodies meld perfectly together. It almost feels electric, the water creating the sensation of sparks between us.

I scream his name as I come, clenching around his cock while he continues to bury himself deep inside me. His pace increases and he mashes his lips to mine as he comes, releasing into me.

As our orgasms subside, I unwrap my legs from his waist, and he carefully places me on the ground, the water continuing to rain down over us.

"Is that what you had in mind, baby?" he asks, smiling down at me, his arms wrapped protectively around me, the shower continuing to stream warm rivulets between us, on us, around us.

I kiss him again and smile back. "It was absolutely perfect," I whisper. "Thank you for fucking my pain away."

Chapter Sixty-Seven

Angel

Slade and Brick have me sit between them on the couch. I happily squeeze into the gap, their strong thighs pressing against either side of me.

Each of them laces a hand in mine. They both look at me thoughtfully, as if they're trying to read my every expression, and I lean my head back against the back of the couch so it's easier to glance at both of them.

"How are you feeling?" asks Slade. For once, he's not scowling. He's not smiling, either, but Resting Slade Face is gone for now.

"Okay, I guess. I don't know." I've been asking myself the same question and haven't found the right words to describe it.

"Just okay?" Brick frowns, his disappointment palpable. "I thought today was going to be cathartic for you. That you might feel some excitement, some relief."

I'm not sure how I should frame it for these guys in a way that won't sound ungrateful. It's important that I'm honest and don't pretend that everything is suddenly perfectly okay, but I also want them to know how much I appreciate them making this happen for me. I take a deep breath.

"I'm just processing, I think. I always assumed he would find me and kill me one day. I'm glad that he didn't. I'm glad that we did what we did. That I was able to do what I did. But I don't feel... I don't know how to explain it. I'm glad he's gone. It was exhilarating at the time." I shrug. "There's just a lot to think about."

"Well, you were great," beams Brick. "Gave me a giant boner right in the middle of it, seeing the way you took control down there. I'm so incredibly proud of you... in fact, I'm in awe. And when you sliced off his head, and it rolled around on the floor, I just about came in my pants."

I laugh and Slade snorts. This time, instead of scowling at me, he leans over and kisses me on the cheek. I guess we really are allowed to find the same things funny now.

I feel like I should continue to explain how I'm feeling. They're not pushing me, but saying it aloud is as much about sorting out my own feelings as it's about sharing with them.

"It was vindicating to see him going through some of what he put me through, for sure. And I'm glad he won't be hunting me for the rest of my life, so that brought me closure in a few ways." I sigh, my giddiness wrestling with exhaustion after what has been a monumental day, what may be the hugest of my life. "But no matter what we did to him, no matter how just our revenge was, it still won't bring my family or friends back. It still won't take away my trauma or erase my scars. No matter what you or I ever do, it won't remove my darkness."

"Oh no, baby. Never try to remove your darkness," Brick leans over and kisses me on the forehead. "Your darkness is part of what makes you beautiful. It's electric. It gives you incredible depth and grit and rawness. It's what makes you *you.* Just like your gorgeous scars." He dips his head and kisses a couple of the raised marks on my shoulders. "And it's why you're going to take over the world one day. So channel every sliver of darkness within you, turn it into pure energy, and use it to set the world on fire."

Chapter Sixty-Eight

Angel

The next day

We're all seated around the dining table for breakfast. Normally there's a lot of chit-chat at the table as everyone plans their days, but today things are a little quieter. Somber's not quite the right word because there is an upbeat energy in the air... it's almost as if people are holding back, trying not to be too outwardly cheerful. Maybe everyone is still processing like I am.

Slade cooked for us as usual, but it's not our usual spread. Perhaps unsurprisingly, we're sticking to dry toast with butter and jam. I don't think any of us could stomach anything more after what transpired yesterday. Images of Brett Wolf eating his cousin's penis and his own tongue, and the smell of singed flesh are still etched into my mind, even after I scrubbed myself raw in the shower. I imagine the others feel similarly.

"Hey... so, I know we don't have boundaries, but can we make cannibalism a boundary? Even if we're making somebody else do it?" Aidan asks the table.

Slade gags. "Oh my god, yes can we please? I'm going to follow Brick's lead and go vegan for a while. I'm never going to look at meat the same way again. And seeing I'm the one who cooks around here, you're all coming along for the ride."

"I agree. Human meat is off the menu," says Roman, also gagging as he comments aloud. "Oh my god, I can't believe I'm even saying those words. I'm down for a vegan stint."

Aidan puts a hand across his forehead and shakes his head.

The rest of us half-gag, half-laugh. We're all on the same page about this.

"Okay, unanimous decision. No more of that," says Slade. "Lots of vegetables, grains and seeds on the cards for us until further notice."

Everyone laughs. Including me. Because it's funny and I feel happy.

Chapter Sixty-Nine

Aidan

"I'm glad you're okay." Angel gazes at me, her eyes intense and her brow furrowed.

"I feel like an idiot for letting him lure me there. It could have ruined everything. I just couldn't—." My voice trails off.

"What couldn't you?" she asks, placing her hand protectively on my shoulder.

"I couldn't bear the thought of you being taken by him. By him giving you more scars. Of him..." I pause and I can hear my voice wavering even though I try to hold it steady, "of him taking you from us."

Her hand squeezes my shoulder. "You bear so much responsibility. I can see it weighing you down," she says, running her hand down my arm. "It must be exhausting being the voice of reason all the time, when everyone just wants to go out and burn the world down. Feeling like you're responsible for everything."

I exhale deeply. "Yeah, I like that they always want to take action, to protect what's ours," I say, talking about the other guys. "But sometimes the way they go about it isn't in our best interests. I need to reel them back so we think things through. It's okay, I'm used to it now. It's not like it started with them."

"What do you mean?" She looks confused, which is fair. I am being cryptic.

"I'll tell you one day," I say, running a hand through my hair. "Now's not the time. Just know that I'm used to being the one who figures out what needs to happen next."

I don't want to go into it right now. She doesn't need to hear about my sad childhood. About how my parents couldn't care less about my siblings and me. I was second-oldest, but for whatever reason, I became the one who made sure everyone was okay all the time.

I protected them, and I protected myself. Made sure everyone got to the doctor for check-ups and when something was actually wrong, made sure we were all fed and clothed.

Forced my siblings to go to school when my parents couldn't have cared less whether they received an education or stayed holed up in their rooms playing video games or running around shoplifting and getting up to other mischief all day.

They were so wrapped up in their work and their social status, absorbed in their adult lives, full of parties and high society and all that crap, we were just a burden. I think they liked the idea of kids more than actually having them. Being able to say they had four children made them more normal, more palatable, in their social circles. But behind closed doors, there was very little love, very little affection.

My older brother had no idea what the hell was going on, and needed just as much guidance as the younger ones. And so the responsibility to raise my siblings fell to me. I was hardly equipped for the task, but hand on heart, I can say I truly did my best.

When my older brother took his own life while he was still a teenager, it shocked our family, but mainly me. I've always felt like I didn't do enough to guide him, to help him battle his demons and guide him through the dark times. Despite being younger, I very much fell into a parental role with him. But, being older, he had access to drugs and alcohol and sex and lots of people who didn't have his best interests at heart. He used all of those things to escape, to numb the pain. And I can't blame him for an instant.

I'll always wonder if I could have made one tiny change that could have prevented him from doing something so drastic, so final. If I could have noticed more signs, if I would have seen his last panicked text message sooner.

Inevitably, the rest of us grew up, and my remaining siblings came to rely on me less and less. We're still in contact, but I'm once again treated like a sibling, no longer responsible for their personal safety and helping to shape them into functioning adults.

But it's natural for me to assume that role, to take on responsibility for what really should be done by others. It's why I'm so protective of my brotherhood now, I suppose.

"And that's taxing on you," she says, as if she really sees me, as if she truly understands. "There must be so much going on inside your mind that you don't share. Like... deciding to try to rescue me by yourself."

"Ha. Yeah," my mouth tilts up on one side in what I hope is an adorable lopsided smirk. "That didn't work very well, did it, though? One concussion later for me, and those idiots all ended up saving you."

It felt like a repeat of all my past failures, the ones that I bury deep inside me. It was embarrassing, lying there, bound, not being able to free myself or help her. I felt useless, and I was full of fear that Brett Wolf would do something unfixable, irreparable, because

I wasn't there to save her. I didn't care what happened to me, but I was terrified of losing Angel, and I'm still torn up that I didn't get to be the one to save her.

"They're idiots for saving me?" She screws up her nose, and I melt a little at the sight of her adoring smattering of freckles moving on her face.

"Ha, no," I smirk. "They're heroes for saving you. Out of all people, I just thought it would be me who helped to free you, you know? Instead, I lay helpless, bound and gagged with a concussion and a splitting headache, while they rescued you."

"They do need you, you know," she whispers, her fingers trailing gently down the side of my face in front of my ear and down my jaw. Little tingles spread from her touch down my neck. "We all do."

"What did you say?" I ask, my voice husky, another little piece of me melting at her words. I heard her the first time, but I'm desperate to hear it again, her words soothing me in the most perfect way.

"I need you," she says again, tilting her head and pressing her lips to mine.

Chapter Seventy

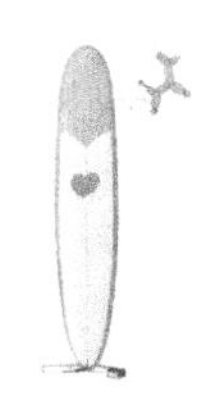

Brick

Angel pads down the wooden stairs to meet me in the basement. She looks around, and I can tell she's surprised by how quickly the room has returned to its normal state. No more garish carnival of terrors and accompanying cacophony. We're back to the clinical grey business you'd typically expect in a torture basement.

"Wow, you cleaned this quickly. I can't believe the transformation. You guys are amazing."

I shrug. "That entire setting was intended to be for a moment, for a very specific purpose. That moment has passed, and so we're back to business as usual. Everything in its place down here, you know."

She nods, chewing on her lower lip as she glances around. "Anything worth waiting for has a risk of being only temporary," she nods, as if convincing herself of something that seems to be weighing on her mind.

"I saw you looking at the rose on your hand a lot while everything was happening," I say, needing to bring it up. "At the corsage I gave you, I mean." I smile at her, and as the words leave my mouth, I'm sure it sounds like we're at junior prom and I'm seeking approval for my gift.

She laughs, a warm tinkle that echoes gently off the walls. "I've never had a corsage before. It's... cute." She wiggles her wrist to show it off. She went upstairs for a shower and she's put it back on afterwards. "I know it won't last forever and I want to make the most of it. It feels special, having an ornate arrangement adorning my wrist, like it gave me strength in battle or something."

"Cute? Do you really think that?" Cute isn't the word I wanted her to associate it with, although I like she mentions it giving her strength. "You don't really like it, do you?"

"No, I love it!" She explains. "I was actually thinking it would make a really cool tattoo."

I feel my eyes light up. "For real? You know I can do a mean tattoo. I have all the equipment."

"Really? Where?" She looks around the basement and sees that, as usual, everything is immaculately organized. There's definitely no tattoo equipment visible. I make sure I only bring it out when I'm using it. I can't stand unnecessary clutter.

"I keep it in one of the storage cupboards," I explain. "It's been a while since I last did one. I might be a bit rusty."

"I keep learning things about you, Brick. You're quite the enigma." She smiles at me. I love being thought of as an enigma.

"Yeah, I was thinking about going full-time with tattoos before I got into the torture and enforcement business. And then, you know, priorities." I shrug and gesture around the basement. "But I still have all the stuff! I'd love to tattoo you." I'm giddy with excitement at using my needles on her.

"Really? You'd do that for me?" She sounds excited, too, her eyes lighting up, her upper body getting fidgety at the prospect.

"Yeah, definitely," I nod. "If that tattoo would make you happy, of course I'd do it. And I think it's a good idea."

"Why's that? Because it will remind me of you?"

She totally gets me. "Well, that's a great reason. But I'm just so blown away by how you took control of things today. You barely needed us to take down Brett Wolf. You were the lead singer, and we were the backup dancers over there in the corner, just in case."

She laughs. "I still have a mental image of you dancing around in your ridiculous multi-colored sequin jacket with your clown makeup."

I grin. It was a departure from my usual 'uniform', but I know it was just perfect for the occasion.

"I did need to phone a friend when he literally had me backed up in the corner at the place he lured me to," she says, looking down, her voice low. "He would have killed me if you guys hadn't shown up."

"Maybe, although I actually think you would have figured a way out of it. You're quite the fighter," I smile at her. "But seriously. Your future tattoo should remind you that you are fierce, that you took your darkness, and you used it to overcome his evil. You are endlessly strong. He tried to break you, just like he used to when you were younger, over and over again. But you've never let him fully break you. You didn't let him even scratch the surface this time. You saw his words for what they were. Empty, cruel comments to get under your skin and make you feel weak, to distract you from your power. You maintained your control, you escaped from your restraints. And we don't even need to go into what you did in the basement, but it was fucking outstanding."

I think of Brett Wolf's skull bouncing along the ground, his eyes wide. I'm just so proud of her. From the look on her face, I'm guessing she's reliving it, too. Her expression is hard to pinpoint. Maybe a bit proud, but also a little haunted.

"I guess it was kind of cool, not that I plan on making a habit of it," she says. "He was truly a special case."

"So, a tattoo to commemorate your courage for the occasion? To being free of him and being able to move on now?"

She nods. "Well, let's make it happen then, Brick," she grins. "I'm game if you are."

I grin back. This is going to be fun.

Chapter Seventy-One

Angel

"You were such a bitch before." I narrow my eyes at Devon.

After some back and forth, we agreed to meet at a wine bar that's on somewhat neutral territory, and we've stepped outside for a cigarette.

So far, we haven't hurled insults or cut each other, so we're off to a reasonable start.

I was a little surprised when Devon reached out and said she wanted to meet, but the entire ordeal with Brett Wolf has given me a little perspective, and I'm willing to cut her some slack. She might be a bitch, but she's done nothing to truly hurt me. Rudeness seems too benign to warrant a full-blown feud, and I'm realizing we have a lot more to gain by partnering together.

Devon and I are standing in a back alleyway that runs along the side of the back entrance to the wine bar. We both lean against the brick wall, which is painted a very pale lemon cream color, our shoes crunching on the loose gravel underfoot. We're shaded by tall palm trees that sway gently in the breeze, and even though we're not directly by the ocean, the air still has a briny note to it.

The sky is a brilliant blue, with fluffy white clouds making pleasantly geometrical rolling shapes as far as the eye can see. Despite all the drama we've been experiencing, this really is a beautiful location.

"So were you. And I still am," she shrugs. "I have a feeling you are too, and that's fine. We just have much bigger fish to fry than being bitchy to each other. Consider this a truce, at least temporarily?"

I glance at her in an attempt to see if she's playing games, if she has some type of ulterior motive. But she seems genuine and I don't really see another option. "Deal."

We nod at each other in silent agreement.

"So I think we're aligned," she says, squinting at me as if trying to confirm we really are on the same page. "They need each other. They have no chance of taking control without leveraging each other's strengths."

"Right," I reply, nodding. "Alone, I don't think either group has the full set of skills needed and we risk losing the people we care about most if we let them continue along the way they've been going."

"I'm concerned they'll never listen to us, though," I sigh. "This is a lot for them, and we might be asking more than they're prepared to give."

I frown, trying to figure out how to approach my guys with our plan. As much as they care about me, I don't know how much they'll appreciate me meddling in their business, especially given how tense things have been between the two groups.

"Hell, I never thought I'd find myself saying this either, you know. But people can change their minds," she shrugs.

"Ditto. But here we are. So maybe you're right." She has a point. People evolve over time, people can change. Although I have a feeling that she and I are more open-minded and less stubborn than any of our guys.

She leans back against the wall, one foot propped up, and takes a drag from her cigarette, surveying me. She lets out a long exhale, plumes of smoke billowing from her mouth and nostrils. "You look worried still."

"I'm just still not sure how to convince them of this. All they do is complain about your guys." Some days I think if I hear about the 'snake guys' one more time, I'm going to scream. My men are always talking about what small fries they are, but they seem to take up a heck of a lot of real estate in each of their heads.

"Same, I'm super sick of hearing all about 'the Brixtons this, the Brixtons that'. But I'm sure you'll find a way. We both will. There's no doubt in my mind you can be quite persuasive." She smirks at me. "Clearly, they care about you. Just use what you have. Make sure there's something in it for you, too. That's what I do."

I peer at her. "You mean...?"

She smirks at me again and takes another drag on her cigarette and then stubs it out on the ground before turning and gesturing for us to head back inside. "You'll figure it out."

We return to the wine bar, where we sit back down at the bar-top and raise our champagne flutes. "Here's hoping we get this figured out and soon," I toast. "It's the only way we'll all get what we want."

"To getting what we want," she replies.

We clink our glasses together, solidifying our truce and our plan.

The guys would be pissed if they knew we were meeting like this. That we were forging a bond between rivals and planning for them to build an alliance. It's the last thing any of them would be in favor of.

But we can see that it truly might be the only way we can get them what they want.

What we all want.

Control of the islands, and to get rid of Tane Brown for good.

Chapter Seventy-Two

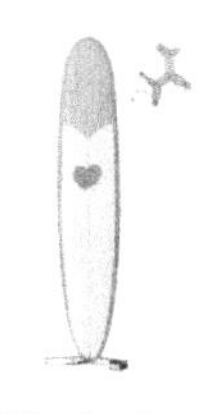

Brick

Angel watches me closely as I set up my tattoo equipment. I enjoy the attention of her gaze. It makes me feel a little giddy, giving me an opportunity to show off to her. These days, the thing that matters most to me is Angel's approval.

I bring out my custom-made tattoo bed, black leather with a Swarovski skull pattern weaving its way across the dark surface. It's one of my great pride and joys, other than my torture basement, of course.

And now Angel is rapidly approaching number one on that list. She's quickly becoming my pride and joy, too. And now I get to permanently decorate her gorgeous body.

"That's a nice chair," she says, circling it and taking in all its features. She runs a hand gently across the headrest, feeling the fabric against her fingers. "Is that real leather? It's so soft."

"Yep, I designed it myself," I grin and run my hand over it as well, enjoying the cool sensation. "Brought it over from the mainland when we moved. I couldn't let her go, she's my baby. Extendable headrest, hydraulic base, touch-sensor remote. Took me ages to find just the right specs."

"Talk dirty to me," she wiggles her eyebrows. "I've been wanting something like this for the salon for so long."

"Oh yeah? Like you want a combined hair salon and tattoo parlor?"

"Why not? A one-stop shop for making people feel their best, and bringing out the best in them."

"I love it," I grin. I love how we're always on the same page. She's creative, I'm creative. I mean, her creativity is usually about making people look and feel their best, and mine is about making them look and feel their worst... but we just get each other. Kindred spirits.

I place a sketchpad and pencils on the desk in front of me, alongside my tattoo guns, ink, needles and towels, along with a box of disposable gloves. I'm just as methodical when it comes to my tattoo work as I am when it comes to torture.

The difference with the tattooing is that I actually get to see my artwork live on with its human canvases, unlike my torture victims. I get a thrill from seeing their body art out in their day-to-day life, knowing I marked them up that way. So I like to make sure they heal properly so they look their best, and I have all the necessary bandages and ointment at the ready as well.

I'm so excited to tattoo Angel. I'm thrilled she liked the corsage I got her so much that she wants a permanent reminder of it. But more than that, I'm thrilled that she understood the meaning behind it, what drove me to get it for her on that day of all days. Because I meant every word I said.

I take hold of her hand, and anchor it still against the armrest as I sketch out the tattoo.

She jumps at the sensation of the cool pen on the back of her hand. "Are you ticklish, Angel?"

She laughs. "Maybe just a little. And the pen is cold and wet."

I grin back at her. "Hold still, or you'll end up with something you don't want."

I listen as she chats away about tattoos she's had done in the past. She tells a funny story about a friend who really did end up with a tattoo they didn't ask for after an awkward miscommunication with an artist.

"I promise that won't happen to you, Angel," I say, smiling at her.

"I know," she smiles at me through her long, thick eyelashes. "I trust you."

My heart melts a little. I can tell she means it, that she truly trusts me. And she knows what I'm capable of. Most people are terrified of me, whether just based on the way I look or actually because they know what I do for work. How I delight in cracking human bones and inflicting worlds of pain on people by the dozen. But not Angel. Here she sits, vulnerable and trusting of me. It's a rare feeling, and it makes me feel warm inside, which I'm not used to.

After a while of deep concentration, I complete the sketch on the back of her hand.

"What do you think?" I hold her by the wrist and tip her hand up so she can see the full design.

She tilts her hand back and forth so she can see all the angles. "Oh wow, Brick," she gasps, assessing every inch of the design. "You really are talented. I wouldn't change a thing. You've really thought about how this would look like as my hand moves, and it's just perfect. I can't wait to see what it looks like when it's done."

Angel always knows the right things to say to make a guy feel great.

The tattoo gun buzzes as I outline the rose on the back of her hand. As I glide the gun over the bonier parts of her hand, she grits her teeth, and a couple of times I hear a sharp intake of breath. But mostly, she just tilts her head back, closing her eyes and arching her back. I can tell she's enjoying the feel of the needle buzzing against her skin, finding pleasure in the pain.

I concentrate, biting my lower lip as I trace fine lines and add shading and other details. This tattoo has to be perfect, just like Angel. She deserves nothing but the best. She's going to take it with her everywhere she goes, and it needs to be as beautiful as she is inside and out. As the needle buzzes over her hand, where most people flinch, she watches with interest and a slight flush develops on face.

"You're enjoying the feeling, aren't you?" I ask her.

"Yeah," she bites her lower lip as she nods at me. "That's partly why I have so many tattoos," she says. "I enjoy the way they feel."

The entire process takes around three hours, but she never complains, just watches with interest, and frankly with what seems to be arousal. Which gets me going as well.

I've tattooed people who have shrieked and just about passed out, and sworn, and even hit me as I've worked on them. Everyone's response is unique. I've heard the same from friends of mine who do it professionally. But Angel is a true pro, taking it like a champ. Savoring it.

Once the tattoo is finally complete, I let her take a look. She tilts her hand back and forth again to see all the angles of the finished work. She gasps. "Oh, it's even more beautiful than I thought it would be. Thank you, Brick!"

She smiles at me and my heart melts a little more. Okay, and my dick gets a little hard as well.

I smile back at her as I gently cover it with a tattoo bandage. "Keep this on for at least two days, then you can remove it and start putting on this ointment a few times a day for a couple of weeks, just so it doesn't dry out."

"Yes, Doctor Brick," she grins at me. "You know I have hd tattoos before, right? I know the drill."

"Yeah, but I don't know what those lunatic artists you've been working with have advised you, do I?" I shrug. "There's so much conflicting aftercare information out there. I want to make sure you have the best advice directly from me." I smile at her.

"You're definitely the biggest lunatic that I've ever let tattoo me." She grins at me again through her lashes, raising her non-tattooed hand and running her fingers gently along my jaw. Jesus. The things this woman does to me just by being herself all the fucking time. The way she makes me feel so amazing. It's the little things, sometimes, that mean the most.

"So you really like the pain of being tattooed, huh?" I really am impressed by the way she handled the pain, and turned on by how much she seemed to enjoy it.

"Mmm yeah," she says, gesturing at her body, which is covered in them. "I guess you could say that."

"I know another place with more nerve endings." I bite my lower lip, trailing my eyes to her gorgeous mouth, down to her core, and then back up to meet her gaze.

"Oh yeah," she whispers. "Why don't you show me?"

My cock is rock hard at the thought of all of her nerve centers and what I want to do with them.

She locks eyes with me as I reach out three of my fingers and rub her pussy through her shorts. She arches her back some more and moans, grinding herself against my hand.

"Would you like me to continue?" I ask, continuing to rub her. "I think it would be better if you were wearing less clothing, though. Maybe none at all."

She nods at me, biting her lower lip. "Mmhmm," she moans.

I pull down her shorts and she lifts her hips so I can get them over her ass, and I slide them down her legs and toss them to the side. The scent of her arousal immediately fills the room. God, she's fucking fantastic.

"Your panties are soaking, Angel," I growl. "Being tattooed really does turn you on."

She gives me a sexy grin, her eyes half-lidded. "It helps when your tattoo artist is hot as fuck."

I involuntarily beam as I slide her panties off and throw them onto the ground near her shorts.

I yank her knees apart, spreading her thighs to reveal her slick folds, and run a finger up her slit. I pull it away, coated in her arousal, and press it to her lips. She takes my finger in her hand and pulls it to her mouth, licking off every drop of her juices. I groan as her tongue circles my finger, wrestling with it.

I return my hand between her legs and rub at her clit. She moans as I trace the distance from her entrance and back to her clit, and then massage it with more pressure and more speed. "Oh fuck, Brick!"

"Can I tattoo you somewhere more sensitive?" I ask, not wanting the tattoo session to end. I'm feeling spontaneous, and I hope she is, too. The things I want to do to her, this divine Valkyrie of mine.

"Yes," she gasps, as I continue to manipulate her clit with my fingers. She bucks her hips at me, and I increase the pace of my touch.

"Can I really tattoo you more, baby?" I hope she's not just teasing. I have plans for her if she's open to it.

"Yes," she gasps, rolling her hips and arching them toward my fingers. "You can."

"Do you trust me to do anything I want?" I slide two fingers inside her while continuing to manipulate her clit with my thumb, and she moans and bucks her hips even more wildly.

"I'm going to have to stop playing with your pussy for a moment," I say, "or your tattoo's going to be a series of squiggly lines, the way you're bucking your soaking cunt around all over my fingers."

She pouts as I pull my fingers out of her.

"Promise you won't stop for too long," she pants. "That felt too good to be the end of it."

"Oh, I promise, Angel," I smile at her. "I'll take good care of you and make sure you get exactly what you need."

She smiles back at me in anticipation.

I set up the gun again, this time with hot pink ink. This is going to be something small between us, to mark the occasion and to remind her of me.

I use my non-tattooing hand to pull her leg up and to the right, keeping her bare pussy exposed to me. She hisses as I tattoo a small pink heart on her inner thigh, and more arousal trickles out of her entrance.

Jesus. I need to be inside her as soon as possible. My cock is rock hard and ready to go, and I can see that she is, too. I place the tattoo gun carefully on the table beside the tattooing chair.

"You're a dirty girl, aren't you, Angel? Getting off on this pain. I can see how it turns you on and makes your cunt beg to be stuffed."

I slide two fingers inside her again, and she moans and grinds against the flat of my hand with her clit.

Using my now-free hand, I wipe off the tattoo with a cloth. "There you go. Now you'll always remember me. I've marked you with something special, something intimate, just for us."

"What about this, though?" She holds up her hand.

"That's a reminder of how powerful you are. Of what you were able to do that day. Of how you own your darkness." I point to her inner thigh. "Now this, on the other hand," I say, dipping my head to plant a kiss on her freshly tattooed skin. "This is a reminder of me, and how much I love your pussy. Of how you belong to me."

She smiles down at me, and the combination of her gorgeous face signaling approval, as well as the view of her soaking pussy and her new tattoo, are all enough to almost make me come in my pants.

I dip my head down and lap at her arousal, which is quickly becoming a puddle on my custom-made tattoo recliner. At this rate, I'm going to need a replacement, but as much as I love this chair, I'm not mad about it.

She squeezes her legs around my neck as I feast on her, wrapping my arms around her from underneath her thighs to hold her still, so she just has to sit there and take it. My tongue laps at her clit, twirling and flicking. I suck her clit into my mouth right as I slide two fingers inside of her and her hips fly into the air, an orgasm hitting her with force at my touch.

I hold my face to her pussy as she bucks, and I feel arousal coursing out of her, coating my mouth and my chin. I keep my tongue on her clit, lapping and sucking as she writhes against my face, still coming down from her peak, teasing her through her increased sensitivity.

"Fuck me," she begs, panting, trying to pull me up by my shoulders. "Please, I need you to bury your cock deep inside me."

I growl at the thought of slamming myself inside her, right to my hilt. I can't wait to feel her wet walls against my cock.

But first I want her mouth on me. "Suck my cock first, baby," I say, standing up and moving closer to her face. "I want your lips wrapped around me."

She licks her lips as she gazes at my cock. It's roughly at her eye level.

I grab a handful of her hair and pull her face down on it. She opens her mouth and takes it down into her throat, letting me slide it almost all the way in. I hear her saliva swish against my cock, a satisfyingly sloppy attempt at deep throating my shaft.

As I thrust my hips to sink my cock into her mouth over and over again, she grabs my balls in one hand and twirls them around, gently twisting and squeezing. I use my hold on her hair to raise and lower her head so that her mouth bobs up and down on my cock while she expertly sucks and licks at my shaft and tip.

"Fucking hell, Angel," I rasp. "Your mouth feels amazing on my cock. Those lips are insane."

She hums a response, causing vibrations from her mouth to ripple across my shaft and I groan, slamming her face onto my hardness.

"I need your pussy, baby," I growl. "You can do this again later, but I need to be inside you right now."

I pull her head away from my cock and she leans back in the chair. "Get on all fours and stick your ass in the air," I direct her, and she flips over, her creamy ass sticking up high to reveal her soaking pussy and her tiny asshole from behind. I use the hydraulic pump to get her to the perfect level, so her pussy is lined up with my cock. This chair has its advantages beyond convenience while tattooing, like a super advanced sex wedge guaranteeing nothing but perfect angles.

"Your cunt is so fucking wet," I growl as I look at it, in the air and glistening at me, inviting me to plunge myself deep inside her.

I smack her on her ass and her body trembles, a little arousal trickling out of her. I dip my finger into it and she gasps as I smear her juices across her back entrance.

"You like that, baby," I ask. "Does my little angel of death want me to stick my finger in her asshole?"

"Mmmhmm," she moans. "Please, I want to feel you inside both holes at once. Fill me up, daddy."

"That's my dirty fucking angel," I growl as I trace her cream around her puckered entrance. I spank her hard on one of her cheeks and she moans, sticking her ass up further in the air as if she wants me to do it again. "I'm going to fill you up and fuck you until you can't breathe, until you see stars."

She moans and I spank her again.

I work a finger inside her ass. She clenches tightly against me, and I thrust my finger in and out of her. She grinds her hips backward as if she wants my finger deeper inside.

"Please, baby. Harder. Faster. More," she begs.

"Good girl," I bend over her back and growl into her ear. "Begging for more like a dirty slut. Do you want my cock now, while I keep fingering your little asshole?"

"Yes, please. Fuck me," she moans.

"You're going to need to spread your thighs apart, baby. I need extra room. I'm bigger than my brothers," I growl, and she moans in response, obediently spreading her knees wide on the chair until they're almost falling off either side. "Good fucking girl," I groan as I look at her glistening pussy, bared to me and hungrily awaiting my engorged cock.

I line myself up with her entrance and slam my cock into her in one thrust, burying myself in her soaking cunt.

"Fuck!" she screams as I slam into her, driving my cock as deep as it can go, filling her up.

My piercing drags along her walls and she groans."Oh my fucking god, your piercing. It feels incredible. I want more. Harder!"

I hold her hips steady and I tease her with a few gentle, slow thrusts, pulling myself almost the full way out and then slowly gliding my entire length into her and burying myself to her hilt.

She tries to rock against me but I hold her still, controlling our movements.

I reach a hand around her waist, trailing it downward until I reach her clit and she gasps at my touch, angling her mound into my hand to increase the pressure. I stroke her pussy while I continue to thrust in and out of her.

"Oh fuck, I'm about to come," she moans, using her hips to back further onto my cock. "Brick, you feel so fucking good!"

"Good girl," I groan, my voice husky with desire. "Come for me, baby. Come all over my big hard cock."

Her body tenses, and I feel her pussy clench around my shaft as her hips buck and writhe in front of me. I hold them as still as possible, but she still manages to thrash around wildly on my cock as her orgasm takes over. Finally, it subsides, and she leans forward, panting.

"I want your ass, Angel," I growl, still hard and craving more of her. "Are you ready for that?"

I trail my finger back over her asshole, still slick with the lubrication of her arousal, and she moans softly.

"Fuck me in the ass, Brick," she moans. "I want it hard."

"Are you sure, baby? Because I won't be gentle."

"I'm very sure," she rasps. "Give it to me, baby."

I groan and slide out of her pussy and trail my cock up her taint, finding her back entrance. My cock is coated slick with her juices and I slide in the tip gently at first, but then keep going until I'm buried deep inside her tight little asshole.

"Fuck!" she gasps as I squeeze her by the hips. "That piercing again!" I hold her still once again as I thrust in and out of her.

"You're a good girl, taking my enormous cock deep in your ass after letting me fuck your pussy so hard," I grind out, and she moans in response, her voice husky and sexy as hell.

My thrusts intensify in their pace and intensity, and she cries out as I use my cock to rail her ass. She clenches against me as I reach down and squeeze her clit, and it sends me over the edge. I fill her up, releasing deep inside her ass, and she arches her back, grinding against me and clamping her ass on my cock as if she's trying to milk me of every last drop.

I pull out, and a combination of my cum and her arousal spills from her ass onto the chair. It's an expensive chair, custom-made and irreplaceable. But I don't fucking care. I hope it leaves a stain that will remind me of this moment forever. My angel of death, letting me tattoo her and then burying my cock in all three of her gorgeous holes. I will never ever forget this moment.

I flip her back over and lift up her bandaged hand, kissing it softly.

"Thank you for letting me mark you," I say. "I hope it's done you adequate justice. You're so beautiful, you know. And you deserve only the best."

Her eyes meet mine and she smiles, but I still detect a tinge of sadness in her joy. I know the last few days have been a lot, and while much of it has been positive, she has a myriad of emotions simmering just below the surface. While I'll do my best to distract her and ease her pain, I know it won't just go away overnight.

"Nobody has ever done anything like this for me before, Brick," she whispers, her eyes on the verge of tears as she admires the back of her hand once again. "Thank you."

"Anything for you," I whisper back, and kiss her hand again. I dip my head down and kiss her upper thigh again as well.

And I truly mean it.

I would do anything for this woman.

Anything at all.

Chapter Seventy-Three

Aidan

"For the fucking last time, leave us alone," I growl. "We have an arrangement. You're not meant to be slowing us down. You're fucking with our profits."

I'm beyond sick of these snake guys compromising our potential to grow as rapidly as possible. It's time to put a stop to it once and for all.

"You compromised the arrangement when you fucked with Devon," Zeke growls back, his eyes narrowing.

"We didn't *fuck with* Devon, *Zeke*." I can't help but spit out his name. He's so condescending, I can't stand him. "Angel was just being inquisitive. She didn't mean to blow up your relationship."

"You could never blow up our relationship," he scoffs. "That's the last thing I'm worried about. What we have is much too strong for the likes of you to have any impact on, no matter how hard you try to mess it up. But I don't believe a fucking word you say, bro. Like there wasn't an agenda letting her know about the debt repayment. Trying to pass it off as an innocent mistake. You're an absolute joke!"

"You're the jokes around here!" Slade snarls. "You won't even do your job properly. Making up stupid rules to get out of the actual work!"

"Because we won't murder people in cold blood or move hard drugs?" Skyler narrows his eyes at Slade. None of us like each other, but those two seem to have a particular dislike for each other. Then again, Slade has a particular dislike for lots of people, including Angel until very recently.

"Yeah, you're weak," sneers Slade. "You'll never be anything like us."

"You're the fucking weak ones. You'll do anything for money, no matter what it costs, if that makes sense. You're so fucking hungry for power you don't care about being human."

"Yeah? That's what you think? It's sure paying off for us. We've eclipsed you in, what... eighteen months?" I'm proud of what we've been able to accomplish in such a short time, and I don't mind rubbing it in. These guys have been so complacent, they've had a home-court advantage for so many years and have squandered it away. What a missed opportunity. I don't know that they're even smart enough to comprehend that, though, let alone regret it. They seem lazy, disorganized, the polar opposite of us.

"Sometimes power doesn't come from money," Skyler furrows his brow, his words coming out in a snarl.

"You're ridiculous," I smirk. "Your father would be ashamed of how you're butchering his legacy, Skyler."

Skyler's eyes darken, and he spits in my direction. "Don't you fucking dish out what you can't take."

I can't handle him spitting on me. In an uncharacteristically reactive and impulsive move, I throw a punch at Skyler and it glances off his jaw. He spins around and tries to upper-cut me but he partially misses. Still, his fist glances off my lip, splitting it and sending blood flying.

This only pisses me off more. I swing at him and connect with his jaw. His face jerks back hard and saliva flies from his mouth, my knuckles stinging at the impact. That was a good one.

He regains composure and punches me back, this time connecting with my jaw and sending my head flying back. My neck twinges as it bobs around in response to the impact like a crash test dummy. It's been a while since I fought like this. My adrenalin is racing, and I can only imagine this is how Brick feels like on the regular.

I see Slade beginning to circle Dom, his fists ready to fight. Skyler regains his fighting posture as well and moves closer to me. This could go on all day at this rate.

"Come on, Slade," I say, suddenly regaining my rationality. "This isn't going anywhere. It's not worth our time."

Slade spits at Dom, and Dom snarls. The glob of saliva barely misses him. And thankfully, it didn't make contact, or I think this entire fight would have just started up all over again.

"Slade! That's enough. Come on, let's go." I wipe my lip with the back of my hand and motion for the others to follow.

"You fucking started the fighting," snarls Slade, glaring at me.

"You're right, I did," I reply, glaring back at him. "And now I'm finishing it."

Chapter Seventy-Four

Roman

We pull up to a quiet road. A middle-aged man in overalls is walking toward his car, which is curbside a little further up the street. We've studied his routine, and know this is where he parks his car while he's at work. He finishes up this time of day like clockwork.

He doesn't notice as we pull to the side of the road and get out of our vehicle, or as we walk toward him purposefully, our pace faster than his as we gain on him. As he reaches for the handle on the driver's door, Brick taps him on the shoulder. He turns, surprised, and his eyes grow large as he sees two large men towering over him. He pays particular attention to Brick, who, as usual, is looking a little unhinged, his eyes wildly flitting around, taking in his surroundings and then honing in on the man.

"Hello, Billy," growls Brick.

"Who—who the fuck are you, and how do you know my name?" He tries to get into the car, but Brick grabs him by the back of his collar and holds him just out of reach of the car door. He's a fairly big guy, but Brick is enormous and visibly stronger.

"We're your worst nightmare, Billy. Avenging angels, if you will." Brick grins broadly at the man.

"What? Avenging for what? I don't get it." His eyes narrow and he shakes his head slightly. His confusion seems genuine. Maybe he has a lot of things that are worth avenging.

"Have you been to a club called *Temptation*, Billy?" asks Brick, his voice low and his words precise. "Think carefully before you answer, because we don't tolerate lying. We've cut men's tongues out for less. Literally just the other day we did that to someone, didn't we, Roman?"

I nod and shrug. "It's true. Although, to be fair, they did far worse than you did."

"It still could be a good option, though," says Brick, "depending on how you play your cards."

Billy's face grows ashen. "I—yes, I know the club you mean. I've been there once or twice." His gaze travels to the floor.

"That's our club, Billy," I say in a low tone. "We're the owners."

His face falls further. "Oh," he says, his voice low.

"Yeah, 'oh' is right, Billy. Do you really think we're going to tolerate a piece of shit like you coming into our club and roughing up our girls?"

"I don't know what you're talking about," says Billy, jutting his jaw out. His spooked eyes betray his attempt to feign ignorance.

I roll my eyes. "We have you on camera, Billy. It would be stupid of you to deny it when we can literally see you with your dick out."

"It wasn't me," he frowns, almost whiny in his denial. "You must have me mistaken for somebody else."

"Would you like to pull your dick out for comparison purposes? It's probably better if you just confess to what you did, because Brick has a very sharp knife in his pocket and he doesn't enjoy looking at other men's dicks."

Brick pulls the knife out of his pocket and flicks open the blade, grinning at Billy. "I've been wanting to test this out. Sharpened it just this morning."

If Billy could shrink into himself any further, he'd completely disappear. His eyes dart around, looking for an escape that doesn't come.

"The dancer you attacked. Melissa is her name. She identified you as well."

He narrows his eyes. "I don't know a Melissa. Dumb bitch probably made it up. Trying to get money off me or something."

Without hesitating, Brick swings his giant flat-knuckled fist at Billy and a cracking sound rings out as it crunches into the man's broad nose.

Billy groans and grabs at his face. "Jesus! Okay, okay. I might have gotten a little handsy. Meant nothing by it."

"We have a strict rule that anyone who hurts our staff gets a lifetime ban," I explain, shrugging. "And not just from the club. From the island."

He glares at me, blood gushing out of his nose, turning his lips a scarlet red. "Oh yeah? I've lived here my whole life, unlike you mainland fucks. You think you can kick me off my own island?"

"We don't just think we can," I growl. "We know we can."

"Would you like us to come and help you pack, or do you think you can get your own things together and get out of here in the next 24 hours?" Brick asks.

"You won't be able to find me," he says, his voice smug. "I know this island better than you. I have plenty of places to hide if I want to. My network is extensive."

"That's where you're wrong, Billy," I reply, my voice steady. "We know you live with your wife, Janice, over on Monterey Street. We know your children attend the local elementary and middle schools two blocks over."

"Yep," says Brick, nodding in agreement. "We also know you work at the auto parts store and your boss's name is..." Brick clicks his fingers, his eyes flitting up and to the side as he tries to recall the name. "Sam, that's it, Sam. He was very interested to hear that you're going to be visiting the mainland on some family business. He won't be expecting you around for a while. It was so nice of him to grant you an indefinite leave of absence under the circumstances."

"Wha—how?" I didn't think Billy's face could get any paler, but it does. His eyes flatten with defeat, his shoulders slumping in resignation.

"Billy, you underestimate us," I say, shrugging, my eyes locked on his. "We may not have grown up here, but we're like bacteria. Our networks have spread exponentially and we know everything there is to know about sorry little assholes like yourself who have nothing better to do than try to feel up and rape women who are trying to earn an honest day's pay. So unless you'd like Janice to receive photo evidence of you trying to shove your cock inside one of our dancers, and unless you'd like your kids to read about your rapist tendencies and other proclivities in the local papers, we suggest you get yourself to the mainland as soon as possible. Oh, and don't get any wise ideas. We'll be watching and waiting. And if you don't get out of here by this time tomorrow evening? We'll chop you into tiny little pieces and mail you to the mainland as a warning to anybody who wants to fuck with us. Do you understand?"

"Ye—yes," he stammers, nodding fast.

"We will be watching. No funny business, Billy."

"Okay, yes," he nods, his eyes like saucers. "I'll leave right away."

"Great. Now that wasn't so hard, was it Billy?" I smile at him, glad he finally understands the severity of the situation.

"No, it wasn't."

Brick says, "One more thing, Billy."

Billy turns to look at him and Brick grabs him by the shoulders. He rears his knee back and rams it forward, right into Billy's nuts. Billy groans as he crumples to the ground. "That was for Melissa."

Chapter Seventy-Five

Angel

"I want to pierce you," Brick growls.

"Oh yeah?" The combination of his husky voice and my imagination cause my pussy to clench. "You just tattooed me... twice, even... and now you want to pierce me, too?"

"Mmhmm." He bites his lower lip and his eyes trail down my body, stopping at my pussy. "Down there."

"Like... my pussy?"

"Yep. Clitoral hood. Vertical."

Slade coughs. "How long does that take to heal, Brick?"

He shrugs. "Something like six to eight weeks."

"We get a say before you do something extreme like that, bro," says Aidan. "If she's going to be out of commission while it heals, especially for that long, we get a say."

"There are other things we can do for that time."

"Hey! It's my body. I get a say as well." I laugh. Fucking idiots talking about putting holes and other things in my body like I'm not even there. I have heard having a piercing like that feels incredible, though. And with the amount of attention that part of my body has been getting lately, why not magnify the pleasure?

"I'd be keen," I say, winking at Brick. "But let's pick the right time. I feel like we have some things to get out of all of our systems before there's any downtime... there."

Four pairs of eyes explore my body with hunger. Fucking hell. Living with four hot men, you'd think I'd have enough, too much even. But every moment I spend with them, every time any of us are intimate, leaves me craving more. They're turning me into an insatiable sex fiend. Which they all seem to be totally fine with. Now that I think about it, so am I.

Brick scoops me up in his arms, one hand around my waist and the other under my knees. I wrap my arms around his neck and laugh. "Sorry, guys. I need to go show her why she needs one. Research," he adds. I giggle as he races out of the room with me and carries me up to his room.

He lays me down on the bed and carefully peels off my pants. He caresses my slit through my panties, and I can feel the material is getting soaked through.

"You're so wet, Angel, thinking about me piercing you. It's got you all hot and bothered, hasn't it, you dirty girl?" He grins down at me.

I smile up at him. "Maybe."

"Good. Would you like to hear about what it will feel like, while I'm doing it and after?"

"Mmhmm," I say, as he continues to stroke my pussy through my panties.

"I'm going to have to demonstrate," he says, sliding my panties off. He spreads my thighs apart so my legs are wide open, exposing my pussy.

He grabs a hand mirror from the dresser and holds it up to me with one hand. I watch as he strokes my slit up to my clit and back down, my pussy clenching as I watch him touch me in the reflection. He inserts a finger in my entrance, and when he removes it I watch some of my arousal trickle out onto the bedsheets.

"So when I pierce your clitoral hood," he points at it and then rubs it a little, "I'm going to do it vertically because that's meant to feel the best for you. That means I'm going to take this piece of skin that protects your gorgeous clit that I enjoy sucking on so much, and I'm going to stick a needle through it." He motions like he's piercing me, and I moan at the thought of him sticking a needle through one of my most intimate areas. "It's going to hurt a lot for just a moment, and I know you'll enjoy the pain. I want to look into your eyes as the needle passes through your flesh. Your clit will throb for a while, and it won't be comfortable. But in a month or two, it will heal completely. And then," he kisses my clit softly, "I'll be able to use my tongue to move the metal around, and it will pull on your clit and drag against it in the best way."

"Like your cock piercing drags along my walls?" I inhale deeply at the thought of the exquisite way his piercing feels when he's inside me.

"Exactly. And I will suck it into my mouth and tug on it until you scream." He sucks my clit into his mouth, simulating what he would do with the piercing. I moan as his teeth tug gently on my clit, causing ripples of pleasure to emanate down into my thighs and up into my belly. If it feels this good without the piercing, I can only imagine the sensations I'll feel when he tugs on that.

"Oh fuck, Brick," I moan as he flicks his tongue across my clit.

I pull my face away, replacing it with a finger and stroking languidly at her swollen nub. "And then do you know what I'll do?"

"No, what?"

He hooks his thumbs into his waistband and slides off his own pants. His cock is rock hard. He leans over me and lines it up with my entrance, and glides it into my wetness in one thrust.

"Then I'm going to get on top of you, just like this. And I'm going to slide my cock into your sweet cunt, making sure I press down on your clit so that your piercing drags against my skin, pulling back and forth, giving you pleasure. Do you want that?"

"Yes, I want that," I moan, arching my hips toward him, granting him deeper access to my pussy.

"I'll grab it with my teeth and tug on it until it hurts, until you beg me to stop because you don't think it can stretch any further." He reaches down and pinches my clit hard and I cry out, a ripple of pleasure and pain radiating down my inner thighs.

"And then," he growls, "you're going to flip over like a good girl and sit on my big, hard cock." He twists his hips so that we roll and he flips me onto him, my pussy still impaled on his iron-like hardness. "And then you're going to ride me and tilt your pelvis so that your piercing rubs against me until you can't bear it anymore."

I rock my hips, grinding against him. It stimulates my clit without the piercing and I moan. I can't even begin to fathom how much extra pleasure the piercing will add.

"So, you want me to do it, don't you, Angel?" he asks, his gaze locked on mine. "You want me to pierce your clit?"

"Yes," I gasp as he pulls me down hard onto his cock. "I want you to pierce my clit, Brick. And then I want you to fuck me like you hate me. But only if you promise to kiss it better when you make it hurt."

"I'll always kiss it better," he growls. "I'll always kiss every part of you better that I hurt. And I'll kiss the parts of you that other people hurt, too, to help you heal."

He dips his head and kisses me on my chest, right above my heart. And then he kisses me gently on the forehead. "I'm going to take away all your bad pain, my Angel. And then I'm definitely going to fuck you like I hate you, until your knees are weak. I can promise you that."

Chapter Seventy-Six

Angel

Later that day

"I want to go next," says Aidan, appearing in front of me, lining his cock up against my entrance.

There's no warning as he buries himself deep inside me with one thrust. I cry out as he fills me up while Brick watches. He groans. "Fuck, Angel. You're always so fucking wet for me. Always ready for me to fill you up."

I rake my nails down his back, scratching him. "Do you remember?" I whisper, thinking back to when we first met.

"I remember," he whispers back.

"The car."

He nods.

"I knew you'd put your nails on me this way," he says, adding more power to his thrust as I dig my nails in even harder.

For once, I want to mark *him*, mark all of them. Show the world they're mine.

He groans and buries his head in the curve of my neck and he nips at me playfully, and then sucks my flesh gently between his teeth. I guess he wants to mark me too, and that's totally fine with me. I'm proud to be his. Proud to be all of theirs.

"Do you want me to fuck you harder, baby?" he rasps as he rolls his hips and thrusts in and out of me.

I nod, breathless. "Mmhmm, yes! Harder, baby!"

He rails me, and I dig my nails deep into his back again, raking them down firmly and feeling his skin catch underneath the edges. He drives into me repeatedly, and the couch squeaks against the floor in response to the power of his thrusts as he impales me with his iron-hard cock over and over again.

As he slams into me, Brick appears beside me, and I turn my face toward him. He dips his head, bringing his mouth to mine and slipping his tongue inside. He crushes his lips against mine, muffling my cries as Aidan continues to plow into me.

"Have you ever fucked two guys at the same time before, Angel?" Aidan's breath is ragged, and his eyes bore into mine as he bites his bottom lip. His gaze trails over my body, watching my tongue wrestle with Brick's.

"No, but I've definitely fantasized about it," I pull my mouth away from Brick's to reply, a shiver of pleasure rushing through me at the thought. Who hasn't wanted to be railed by two hot men at the same time?

"You want to try it now?" Aidan rasps. "Brick's cock buried in your pussy while I fuck you in your tight little asshole?"

"Mmhmm," I moan, my pussy clenching at the thought of being double-penetrated by these two men.

"Good, because that's what we want, too," he growls. "Don't we, Brick?"

Brick nods enthusiastically, feasting on me with his gaze, reaching out to caress one of my breasts as he bites his lower lip.

"Have you two done this before?" I ask. I'm curious, not that it matters if they have or not. They're mine now, and that's what I'm focused on.

They glance at each other as I slide myself off Aidan's cock.

"Not quite like this," growls Brick. "And not with somebody as sexy as you."

"Are you ready for this, Angel?" Aidan asks.

"Yes," I moan.

"Are you sure you're okay?" Brick peers at me, wanting to be sure.

"Yes," I say, more firmly. "I want to do this. How many times do I have to say it?"

He laughs and puts his hands up in mock defense. "Okay, okay. We just want to make sure. This is kind of a big deal."

I nod. "That's fair. And I'm more than ready."

"Slide onto my cock," Brick says, and my pussy clenches as I look at his rock-hard cock, standing at attention, waiting for me to lower myself onto it. I eagerly move forward, straddling him and lining myself up over his tip. I reach down, grabbing his shaft and slowly lower myself onto him. I moan as he fills me up, stretching my walls. His cock is massive, and I'm a little grateful Aidan chose Brick to take my pussy this time, and let himself have my ass. Their cocks are both a decent length and gorgeous, but Brick's is more girthy, and while I'm sure I could get it all the way there, it would be a struggle to take all of him in my ass.

I lower my pussy onto Brick's hard cock, rocking my hips and squeezing myself around him. He groans, his eyes rolling back in his head as I grind against him.

"Fuck, your pussy feels so good wrapped around my cock," he growls. "But you need to wait so that you don't make me explode inside you before Aidan joins our fun." He holds my hips down firmly, stopping me from grinding on him.

I pout. "But your cock feels so good. I want to ride you."

"Be patient and you'll get a chance to ride two of us at the same time," he says, gesturing toward Aidan, who I can see is rock hard as well. "Isn't that what you want?"

I nod, closing my eyes as I think about how it's going to feel having both of them at once. It most certainly is what I want.

Brick rolls both of my nipples between his thumbs and forefingers, and I moan as a ripple of pleasure shoots from the center of my nipples down to my core. My pussy clenches around him involuntarily.

"Hey, I told you to wait," he says, his voice husky.

"You did that to me," I say, gesturing at my tits, which are still cupped by his powerful hands. "I can't help it."

He sucks one of my nipples into his mouth, tugging it gently between his teeth, and I involuntarily clench again. He gives me a warning look. "What? You did that again. It's all you," I laugh. He smacks me on my ass and grabs one of my cheeks hard.

"Stay still, you brat," he growls.

Aidan pops open a bottle of lube, and Brick lies down on his back, pulling my chest against his. I gasp as cold gel hits the top of the seam of my ass. It begins a slow descent, helped along by Aidan's fingers as he uses a finger to rub the lube over my asshole.

Brick reaches behind me and grasps my hair with one hand, pulling my mouth to his, while his other arm wraps tightly around my back. I swipe my tongue through his lips to meet his, and I moan as he sucks on the tip.

I gasp as Aidan slips a finger into my ass, enjoying the cool feeling of the lube.

"You okay, Angel?" asks Brick.

"Yeah, it's just been a while," I say. It didn't feel unpleasant, just something I'm not very used to, although I have had some action back there before. Never with two guys at once, though. This is new. A shiver of pleasure runs through me and I clench against Brick again.

"Watch it," he half-laughs, half-growls. "I told you to wait until he's inside you, too."

"Sorry," I say, not really sorry at all. "I was just imagining what it's going to feel like with my pussy clamped around your cock, and my ass around his, while you both fuck me."

This time I feel Brick's cock twitch inside me.

"Who's unable to control themselves now?" I wink at him and he narrows his eyes at me.

"I'm going in," says Aidan. "You sure you're ready for this?"

"I'm sure." I inhale deeply as he inserts the rest of his finger as far as it can go, and slowly slides it in and out. I feel my walls gripping his knuckle. "Jesus, you're tight back here," he says. "I can barely get one finger in and out, let alone my entire cock."

His finger manipulating the walls of my ass is sending many pleasurable and new sensations throughout my body and I keep clenching on Brick.

"Angel, I told you," Brick groans. "You need to stay still or I'm going to come before Aidan gets anywhere near you with his dick."

"I'm trying not to move," I gasp. "But he's doing things to me with his finger. I can't help it!"

Aidan laughs and leans forward, swiping the hair away from the side of my face and tugging my earlobe gently with his teeth. "You like me finger fucking your ass while Brick has his cock buried deep inside you, don't you, baby?"

"Yes," I moan, my breath quickening.

He slowly extracts his finger from my asshole, and I feel him line his cock up at my back entrance. "How about this?"

"Yes, please," I pant.

"Hold her still, Brick," says Aidan. "Otherwise she's going to bounce around on you and you'll come before I get anywhere near being inside her."

Brick pulls me to him, ensnaring me in his arms and immobilizing me. I enjoy the feeling of being restrained and being completely under their control.

"You doing okay, Angel?" he whispers. I nod, still panting, eager to feel Aidan's hardness inside me at the same time as Brick.

"I'm going to take things slow," growls Aidan, and I nod. "Just try to relax," he says, squeezing my shoulders from behind. "It'll be easier to move once I'm fully inside you."

He slides himself into me. The motion stings and stretches me, but it feels enjoyable as his cock makes its way into my asshole.

"Fuck! I can barely get in you!" he rasps, continuing to work his way in. "You've got a really tight ass. Did you know that?"

"Kiss me and relax your body," says Brick, pulling me to him. His tongue explores mine, distracting me, and I will my entire body to relax and become malleable.

Aidan seizes the moment and slides deeper into me, burying himself deep inside my asshole. I moan as I realize both guys are up to their hilts inside me, stuffing my body with their hard cocks.

I feel my entire body clench, my pussy and ass trapping their shafts, and they both groan under the vice-like grip my body is delivering.

"Jesus, Angel! How the fuck can your body be so tight?" grinds out Brick.

"You think her pussy's tight?" Aidan rasps through gritted teeth. "You should feel her ass. I think she's going to sever my dick in a minute."

It makes me laugh just a little, and that causes me to clench around them some more.

"Fuck!" yells Aidan. "You're so fucking tight. I can't even move! Stop laughing, it makes it worse!"

I pull myself together, taking a deep breath and willing my body to further relax.

"So, are you two going to fuck me or what?" I ask.

Brick's eyes burn dark with lust, and Aidan groans behind me.

"Alright, let's do this," grits out Brick.

They move their hips and quickly find their rhythm, synchronously stroking my pussy and my ass with their deliciously hard cocks.

I lean forward and my tongue swirls with Brick's. He moans as I wrap mine around his, wrestling for a deeper kiss. Aidan reaches around from behind and cups my breasts, letting his fingers trail around their outside curves and then down my back. As he continues thrusting his cock into my ass, he leans forward and kisses me on my upper back.

These two hot men, both inside me at the same time, have me so close to my peak, little bolts of electricity shooting around my entire body. I feel stuffed in a pleasurable way. It's an incredible sensation, like nothing I've ever felt before.

"I'm getting close," pants Brick. "She's fucking milking me."

"Same," grinds out Aidan as he continues to work his way in and out of my ass.

I tilt my hips ever so slightly so that my clit rubs against Brick. I cry out as the combination of their two cocks and the slightest pressure on my clit sends me over the edge, an orgasm ripping through me, my pussy and ass clamping down on both of them at once. My thighs tremble violently as my body seizes around the two cocks buried deep inside me, little fireworks going off in my head, my back arching against Aidan. "Brick, Aidan. Fuck!"

"Fuck!" Aidan cries out as he releases in my ass, and I rear back as I feel his seed shooting deep inside me. My body seizes against both of them, this time sending Brick over the edge, and he climaxes with a roar.

"Angel!" Brick groans as he spills inside me.

Both of their cocks twitch within me and I continue to clench down, milking them as my body trembles.

"Jesus fucking christ," rasps Aidan, kissing me on my back as he carefully slides out of me, his cock beginning to soften. "You're amazing. I really thought I was going to have no dick left after that."

I laugh.

Brick lowers me onto his chest and kisses me gently. "You really are incredible, Angel. I don't know how we got so lucky."

"I'm the one who got lucky," I say softly, wrapping my arms around him and laying my head on his shoulder while Aidan wraps his arms around me from behind.

We lay there for a while, slippery with a combination of my arousal and their cum and our combined sweat. I have never felt more attractive, more empowered and confident than I do right now, sandwiched between these two men.

A moment later, footsteps approach from the kitchen and Slade and Roman enter the room, returned from their outing.

"Well, what do we have here, Slade?" asks Roman rhetorically. "I don't want to jump to conclusions, but it looks a lot like some double penetration just went down. What do you think?"

"Yeah, that's what it looks like to me, too," says Slade, nodding and smirking at me as I lay book-ended by his two friends. "Next time I want to join in."

"Me too," says Roman. "Maybe all five of us can play." A devious grin breaks out across his face and despite having just orgasmed, my pussy twinges at the thought.

"How was it?" asks Slade, his gaze meeting mine. "Did you enjoy having Brick buried in your cunt while Aidan fucked you in the ass, you dirty girl?"

He and Roman are both visibly rock hard through their pants after seeing us like this, and thinking about what just took place.

"It was the fucking best," I say, feeling dreamy, as if I'm floating. "I can't wait to do it again."

The guys glance at each other and smile back at me.

I have the sense their plans for me have only just begun.

And I'm perfectly okay with that.

Chapter Seventy-Seven

Aidan

"Well, well, well. If it isn't the Lost Boys."

I wonder how many times we're going to do this, complain about our frustrations with each other without reaching any real resolution. We're just so different in our approaches to business, our philosophies generally opposed. I don't see room for compromise. But it also feels like we can't go on like this. It's too much of a distraction, probably for them, too.

I kneel, poised over Zeke, knife to his throat.

Rake has Roman in a headlock.

Brick is kneeling on Skyler's chest.

Dom has Slade in a choke hold.

This is a mess.

Zeke's eyes are locked with mine. He doesn't flinch or try to fight me, just stares at me. I have to give him some credit. Most guys would have pissed themselves in this situation. They usually do, turning into crying, whimpering little babies. But Zeke is holding his own. He'll die for his brothers if he has to.

"Just fucking do it, Aidan," he rolls his eyes. "What's the hold-up? Too chicken to slice me from ear to ear?"

"Don't tempt me," I growl.

"Let me guess," he says. "You're running through all the potential scenarios, trying to figure out whether killing me now or later is more beneficial? Assessing the risk?"

"I'm pretty sure it doesn't matter when I kill you, just that I do," I reply, matter-of-fact. He doesn't need to know that he read me accurately just now, articulating exactly what was going through my mind.

"You know I'm right, though," he says, his eyes seeing right through me. "You're paralyzed by analysis. I know you are, because I'm that way, too. Just ask any of my brothers." His eyes flick around to Skyler, Dom and Rake.

I glance down at him and arch an eyebrow. "I have a sharp knife pressed to your throat and you're trying to have a heart-to-heart with me to find all our common ground? That's cute."

He narrows his eyes at me. "You seem a bit more rational than, uh..." His eyes flick over toward the others. "I don't think I'd still be alive if your buddy Brick was the one with the knife."

I smirk. "Oh, he'd probably just knock you out and drag you back to his basement for his kind of fun. A spot of torture to pass the time." I shrug. "We might still decide to do that. We'll just have to see."

Zeke sighs and subtly shakes his head. It's like he's given up for now.

Keeping the knife to his throat, I glance at Brick and Roman.

Rake still has Roman in a headlock, and he's cackling as he messes up Roman's hair. "Take this, pretty boy!" he says as he tousles the top of his head. Roman writhes against Rake's forearm, but he refuses to let go. "You're lucky I don't have a pair of scissors or a razor blade!"

I snort. "Your boy's rearranging my brother's hair."

"Fucking idiot," Zeke shakes his head again casually, as if he doesn't have a knife pressed to his throat. The sharp blade nicks him and a little trickle of blood releases from his neck, but he doesn't seem to notice. "This is how he is unsupervised."

I glance at Brick and Skyler. They're wrestling each other, both full of energy. Skyler flipped Brick off him and now Brick is trying to flip him back over. Brick's clearly in peak wrestling phase. This has come after nunchucks, a flail, and most recently a spear. It feels like Skyler's getting off lightly with this one, the risk of grievous bodily harm still very much there, but reduced drastically without the industrial metals and spikes that Brick's recently been experimenting with.

"Wait!" Angel's voice rings out in the crisp evening air. The wrestling match pauses, everyone stopping momentarily.

"What the fuck are they doing here?" Slade growls, his voice projecting despite Dom still having his forearm wrapped tightly across his throat.

"Fucking hell," says Dom. "Women fuck up everything."

"Stop!" Devon runs to catch up with Angel and they stand in front of us, side-by-side, illuminated by the light overhead, casting shadows of both of them that make their legs appear extra long.

"You shouldn't be here," I yell. "And why are you together? That's weird!"

"He's right. Go home, both of you," calls Zeke, my knife still pressed to his throat.

"We're not going anywhere," yells Devon.

Angel clears her throat. "Don't you see what's happening here? You're tearing each other apart. You're doing exactly what Tane Brown wants you to do. You're doing his bidding and then cutting down anyone else who comes close to being as strong as you. All that does is make him stronger, and it thins the herd, just the way he wants it."

Devon takes her turn to speak. "Instead of fighting each other, what if you leveraged your respective strengths and joined forces? Then you might actually stand a chance of taking control of the island. But this?" she gestures at the eight of us poised to inflict grievous bodily harm on each other, maybe worse. "This is just Tane Brown getting his way. This is you getting in your own way. You may as well hand him the keys to the island and fly to the mainland with your tails tucked between your legs."

The eight of us guys look at each other. What nonsense are these women talking? Since when did they join forces and tell us what to do?

Angel nods. "She's right. So quit it. Stop this stupid fighting and call it a day."

"Since when did you two get along?" Slade yells. "This seems like bullshit to me. Stop trying to distract us when we're focusing on..." he looks around at everyone, "business."

"Since we agreed you were all acting like a bunch of idiots," says Devon, and Angel nods in agreement. "Since we could see that together you have so much potential, that you might actually stand a chance to get what you want. But instead, you're all about to sacrifice everything you've worked so hard for."

"You want us to work together with this bunch of Peter Pan man-children? That think they'll never get old because they have some fucking good energy from the island or whatever?" Slade scoffs.

"And you want us to work with this group of jackholes who came over from the mainland and started twirling their tiny dicks around, taking everything over in their sight and fucking us over in the process?" Skyler snarls. "I'd rather be a Peter Pan than a fucking boring wannabe big shot dude who wears suits every day and discusses stock market derivatives over breakfast."

"I care about you four very much," Angel indicates to me, Slade, Brick and Roman. "I admire your tenacity and ambition to grow your business. I don't think you're boring, you're just... focused. You're mature, but it's not like you're yelling at kids to get off your lawn." She pauses and glances at Slade. "I'm sure Slade would, if you had a lawn, but you know what I mean."

I glance at Slade and Roman and Brick, small smiles spreading across each of our faces. I know they're thinking the same as me, that it's nice to hear Angel sticking up for us, speaking to our character, especially among this group.

"And I love each of you," Devon glances at Skyler, Zeke, Rake and Dom. "Especially how you're all young souls, full of joy and mischief, even when fucked up shit is happening. I don't want to grow old before my time, and you keep me feeling young and satisfied."

Her four men grin at each other.

"Across this group, you have two strong women who love you," says Angel, her eyes narrowing at all eight of us. "So get the fuck over yourselves and your misplaced pride. Stop jockeying for position against each other. The energy is misplaced. You both have a legitimate and important place on this island, and with your combined skills, you actually stand a chance. You might still need help from others when it comes down to it, but the eight of you are exponentially more powerful than four and four separately. Or after the way you were going, like two and two."

They both roll their eyes at us.

"Jesus, they're like the twins in *The Shining* now. I preferred it when they hated each other," says Slade.

I snort at the mental image.

"Listen, I don't like it any more than the rest of you," I say, running my free hand through my hair. "But I think they're right."

"Me too," says Zeke, eyeing the blade in my hand still pressed to his flesh.

I roll my eyes. "For fuck's sake. You'd better know what you're talking about," I call out to Angel and Devon, and they return my gaze, motionless.

Moving my blade away from Zeke's throat, I stand and extend my forearm to him. He takes it and I help pull him up to his feet.

"You were never going to stab me, bro," he says, twisting to shift his back and shoulders into place.

"It was close," I shrug. "I would have if I needed to. You know how it goes."

"Yep," he says, nodding. "Sure do. So we're really partners now?" We stand side by side and survey the scene.

"I guess so," I reply. "Well, that sounds fucking weird, doesn't it?"

He smirks. "Yeah, really fucking weird. Like we're in a parallel universe or some shit. I never would have believed this would ever happen. Still kind of don't. But Devon and Angel sure are something special."

"They sure are," I sigh.

Rake gives Roman's hair one final tousle and then lets him out of his headlock. Roman raises himself up to full height and scowls at Rake. "No hard feelings, man. I'm sorry I fucked with your hair."

"All good, man," says Roman, smoothing his locks into place as much as he can without a mirror.

Dom begrudgingly releases Slade from his chokehold. He and Slade stand next to each other, both scowling.

"Oh my god, you have a grumpy one as well," I say to Zeke.

He laughs. "Yeah, he's our household curmudgeon."

Rake and Skyler help each other up. They're both covered in dirt after their wrestling scuffle. Skyler shakes his head at Brick. "You're one fucking weird dude, man. But you know how to fight. So I respect you."

Brick beams as if it's the nicest compliment he's ever received.

"Should we talk this through now?" Zeke asks, glancing at me. He looks exhausted.

"You know, it's been a big day," I say. "There's still a lot to process, to get our heads around. Why don't we call it a night and then regroup in the morning? We have a lot to discuss."

He nods and we head out. Ten people splitting into two groups of five, heading off in opposite directions.

"Am I still a distraction?" Angel asks Slade as we climb into our vehicle.

"Yes, a massive distraction. But you might have saved a few of us from serious injury tonight. Maybe even saved some lives. So, just this once, I'm going to let it slide," he replies.

Chapter Seventy-Eight

Slade

"But if we go into partnership with them, we lose some of our power. Plus, we'd lose our percentage of their take. It's been quite lucrative." I'm very concerned about the proposition to partner with the snakes. I don't feel comfortable needing to trust another group of people, particularly a group that we've had problems with since we moved to the island.

"That profit share was never intended to be permanent, you know that," says Aidan. "Besides, they've already paid off most of their debt. Taking down Tane would be worth so much more."

"It might also cost a lot more," Brick says, and Roman nods. They're both just as concerned as I am.

Aidan shrugs. "That's a risk I'm willing to take if it means getting him off our backs and taking more control."

"We'd have to split that power with them, though," I say. "Divide it amongst us. I don't think we should dilute our control."

"Nah, man, we need to collectively magnify our power," replies Aidan. "Otherwise, we don't have a shot of overthrowing Tane. He's just too strong. It's hard to say after everything we've been through, but we need them. From my point of view, there are no other options."

The three of us look at each other, then back at Aidan, and nod. We know that without a doubt, Aidan's run through many more scenarios than any of us could ever have considered. His logic is consistently sound, and we trust his judgement. Even when it makes us uncomfortable.

I guess that's part of what loyalty is about, believing that someone has your best interests at heart, even when their path to get there isn't what you might have chosen yourself.

Chapter Seventy-Nine

Angel

"I can't believe we got them to meet, here, on neutral ground." Devon gestures around the Airbnb we've rented for the night.

We both laugh, because the whole situation is just surreal.

I nod. "I know, right? The owners were really skeptical when we said what we wanted to use the space for. They made us give them a chunky deposit in case there's a brawl and the place gets destroyed. Nearly everyone on this island knows our guys don't get along."

Somehow, Devon and I have convinced the guys that they needed to meet and more formally align on some sort of truce. We truly believe that if they join forces, they'll be many steps closer to taking over control from Tane. Through our powers of persuasion combined, we're all in the same building, under one roof, and talking logistics for how the partnership will work in practice.

While things were a little tense at first, after a few tough conversations and cracking some beers open together over a meal, the guys seem to be finding they have more in common than they originally thought.

Not that they want to be best buddies suddenly or anything.

But they might be a wee bit less likely to shoot each other on sight if they end up in the same place at the same time.

They may even be capable of having a civil, amicable conversation.

We glance over at the men, all eight of them, and look back at each other.

"How'd you get yours to agree?" Devon arches an eyebrow.

"I took your advice and found a way to persuade them," I grin. "There was definitely something in it for me, too." I wink and wiggle my eyebrows, and she laughs.

"Nice," she smiles. "I'm glad I could be helpful." She looks across at the guys, who are deep in conversation. "You know, aside from all the craziness, and maybe even because of it, I feel like both of us really are living our best lives," she says, smiling in their direction.

"Most definitely because of it," I say, smiling at them as well. "I wouldn't have it any other way."

Chapter Eighty

Angel

I quietly close the front door behind me and walk outside. Because it's early, the air is crisp and refreshing, my favorite time to be outside on the island before the humidity and heat build, and before the island really wakes up.

I'm dressed simply in a cropped tank top and bike shorts, with sneakers with heels that are slightly raised. They're ideal for this type of activity, because I'm going to need comfortable footwear for what I have planned.

My vibrant purple hair cascades around my shoulders. Even though it's not sunny out yet, I wear a cap that matches the rest of my outfit and my headphones hold it down firmly in case there is an unforeseen gust of wind. I feel empowered and beautiful, like I can be unapologetically me now.

As I head out down the long driveway and onto the sidewalk, I turn right. My pace is brisk. I've always been a fast walker, and for me, walking is a source of joy. Not consistently being able to walk fast here is something I've had to get used to on the island, especially when I head over to the more populated beach areas where tourists are leisurely enjoying their vacation, wanting to take it slow as they travel on foot from point A to point B.

My naturally brisk pace means that this early hour is the perfect time for me to be taking a walk. It's a precious moment in the day before I'll need to regularly pause and wait for tourists as they dawdle and leisurely stroll along the pavement in the heat of the day. I have to remind myself that their pace is what's considered normal. That my almost breakneck walking speed is what's freakish and not in keeping with island time.

I don't really have a destination in mind. I just want to luxuriate in the fact that I'm able to be outside. My psycho stalker of more than half of my life is finally dead! I'm free, and I want to savor the ability to be in control of my life for once.

While I'm not sure exactly what's ahead, I have the opportunity to shape a beautiful life for myself. The guys seem to want me to stay, to consider me part of their chosen family now. While I have some lingering concerns, I am no longer afraid that they're going to kill me in the imminent future just for existing. Even Slade. Even though I witnessed Roman murder someone with a pair of my hairdressing shears.

I think by now they're all confident that I will not run to the police to snitch on Roman. There would be no benefit in me doing so, and our bond is too great now. I really have fallen for all four of them, and I see a future with them as long as they'll have me.

The air has a briny quality to it as I stalk along the pavement. I slip my headphones on and turn up a fast-paced house track that matches my walking speed. It's so energizing not having to worry about being terrorized by that psycho madman. Brett Wolf is gone for good, just a series of memories and the odd nightmare now.

I walk and enjoy the thumping music for what must be about an hour, just as an estimate. Every step I take is empowering, and I intend to enjoy every moment. It doesn't really matter how long I'm out for now, because there's no need to rush back and lock myself inside in case my stalker stumbles upon me.

After a while, I glance around and seem to be in a different neighborhood, a couple over from the compound. I don't recognize this part of town. What started off relatively industrial has gotten more sparse in terms of buildings. Things are more spaced out, a few abandoned vehicles here and there.

The energy has changed a little, although I can't put my finger on it. Maybe I shouldn't walk alone with my headphones blaring, but for the most part this island is meant to be pretty safe. Especially considering we've gotten rid of my life's primary threat. But I feel a little twinge of something in the nape of my neck and the pit of my stomach—I guess it could be a gut feeling, or maybe I'm just paranoid. I haven't been this far away from the guys since they took me captive. Maybe it's that.

I glance around and pull my headphones off my ears out of an abundance of caution. I hear nothing except for the tweeting sound of birds and the hum of traffic on the freeway off in the distance.

I continue to walk, placing my headphones back on, shrugging off the sense of unease. I get to not feel afraid now. He's gone, and I should be able to walk around wherever I want now. He doesn't get to keep his fear hold over me from beyond the grave. I crank the music back up and continue to walk.

That's when I feel the distinct rumble of an approaching vehicle nearby. I glance around again, and there's nobody else in sight. A large SUV makes its way slowly toward me from one end of the street. I look to see if there are any side alleys or other exits, just in case. I'm probably being silly, but it's always good to have a backup plan. In this case, there isn't one.

There's a chain fence topped with barbed wire to my left, about ten feet high, and even with my sensible sneakers, there's no way I'm scaling that. The other side of the road has an industrial building that spans the block. Signs prominently display 'Keep out' and 'Guard dogs, beware'.

The SUV continues to approach. It's probably nothing, just a coincidence a vehicle is in the neighborhood. It's weird I haven't encountered more people out and about on this refreshing morning. Everyone sleeping in is missing out on the beauty of this golden hour.

I'm sure I'm just still incredibly paranoid after all that's happened recently. Surely that's normal?. But I'm feeling afraid. I should have just stayed at home. But no, I should be able to be out here. Why am I like this?

The shiny white SUV rumbles up and pulls to a stop beside me. The windows are heavily tinted and I can't see inside, but then the windows roll down and I see three goon-like figures look out at me simultaneously. They're all large men, and they look tough. Why are they stopping beside me?

The one in the passenger seat smirks. "Need a ride, love?"

"No—no thank you," I say, quickly. "I'm just enjoying a walk. Thank you. Have a nice day." I continue walking and pick up the pace even from my normal rapid walk.

The SUV follows along beside me, keeping pace with me. "Oh, I should be more clear. We'd like to give you a ride, dear," the man says. "In fact, we insist on it."

My blood chills, and I feel goosebumps across my body.

Instinctively, I pivot and break out into an all-out run in the opposite direction, toward the compound. I've never been a super-fast runner, but I give it my all. My chest pounds and I gasp for air as I run back in the direction I came. I know the car is faster than me, but if I can just find an alleyway to shoot down, somewhere to at least hide while I figure out the next steps, then I should be able to get to freedom. The freedom that I have so desperately craved and finally thought I had in my grasp.

The road is uneven, little pieces of gravel and potholes in the sidewalk's asphalt. A couple of times I trip and once I awkwardly turn my ankle, but I keep going. I hear the

SUV turning around in the distance. It sounds like they're taking their time to do some type of three-point turn, not rushing to flip their vehicle around and pursue me. Maybe this will give me the break I need. Maybe this is my chance to get away or at least find a suitable hiding place while I figure out my next steps.

I should call the guys. I should use the phone they gave me to get their help. But I can't stop running or they'll almost certainly catch back up to me.

I reach into my fanny pack and pull out my phone. I try not to slow down as I open the display using Face ID and almost trip on a bump on the uneven sidewalk, but manage to rebalance myself at the last second. Relieved, I pull up my contacts and dial Slade, who shows up first on my recently called list.

I put the phone to my ear as I continue to race away from the SUV and toward the compound. By now, I can hear the vehicle rumbling toward me again, slowly now, as if taunting me. As if they know my heart is about to burst out of my chest and my running stamina is not that great and I'm feeling a searing pain in my shins. I'm not used to the pressure of my legs slamming down on the pavement with force. I may be a fast walker but definitely not used to urban running, or any running for that matter. I'm not built for this.

Slade answers on the second ring. "Angel, where are you?" He sounds confused. "Why are you calling... from the other side of the house?"

"I—," I pant, gasping for breath and struggling to get the words out. "I went for a walk."

"You left?" His confusion turns to concern. "We told you not to, Angel. It's dangerous."

My chest is searing as I struggle to breathe and talk. I can feel the SUV getting closer. "I— I needed to. I needed fresh air," I explain, my words coming out ragged. "He's dead. I thought it would be okay."

I need to stop for a second to gasp for air.

"Well, we can talk about that later, but are you okay?"

"No, there's... an SUV... following me. They insisted... I get in... their car." I keep moving, focusing carefully on the uneven sidewalk to avoid tripping again or twisting my ankle.

"What color is it, Angel?" Slade asks. "What type of SUV?"

I picture the vehicle with the windows rolled down and the goons looking out. "White with chrome wheels and tan upholstery, from what I could see."

"Which way did you go on your walk?" he asks.

By now, even though it's moving slowly, the SUV is almost right alongside me. Despite the heat I'm generating from my pace, I feel the shackles of my neck sticking up, icy goosebumps covering my body. I can almost feel the breath of the goons on me from the vehicle. I glance furtively left and right but still don't see any opportunity to dart away. Fuck.

"I... turned right.... out of the house. Kept walking... maybe an hour... I walk fast. Don't know.. this area. Industrial.... less populated."

"Okay, Angel," says Slade, his voice low. "Try to stay calm. Is there a way you can get off the road?"

"Don't... see... there are fences and buildings. Not any... alleys."

The SUV is fully alongside me now. The windows roll down again and I see the three goons all watching me. I gasp as the vehicle comes to a complete stop. The three men get out and approach me.

"They're... here. Can't... keep running." My chest is heaving, and I'm embarrassed as tears flow involuntarily from both of my eyes. This can't be happening. Just one walk, one taste of freedom, is all my soul craved. All I needed. It seemed like a small ask, inconsequential. But now I'm not so sure. What have I done?

The men flank me, and I know there's nowhere for me to run now. Especially after all the running I've already done. I'm exhausted.

"Hand us the phone," the guy from the passenger side of the vehicle says, extending his hand.

I comply, not seeing any other options than throwing it on the floor, which would seem to be counterproductive.

He takes it from me and puts it to his ear. "And who do I have the pleasure of speaking with today? One of the Brixtons, I presume?"

I can't hear Slade on the other end of the phone, but by the look on the goon's face, I am sure he's on the receiving end of a volley of expletives. He smirks. "Yes, we'll be taking Angel with us now. We'd like to negotiate a little redistribution of assets and control on this island. We will send further instructions. In the meantime, we're going to take her away, maybe have a little fun with her."

This time, I hear yelling from the other end of the line. I can't make out the words, but I know they're not polite. Suddenly, the noises stop and there's a feeling of calm.

I can almost imagine Aidan soothing Slade in the background, reminding him that responding in this way might cause these guys to hurt me more than they might already be planning to. Ice-cold fear grasps my heart, but there's also a sliver of warmness and familiarity as I see this scene playing out in my head. But just as quickly as it began, that thought is yanked away as the man growls into the phone.

"We will send further instructions. Do exactly what we say, or your precious girl dies." He ends the call and the three men circle me.

Then I feel a prick of pain in my neck from behind, and my vision blurs.

Fuck my life.

Not again.

Chapter Eighty-One

Roman

"She went for a fucking walk?" I rub my hand over my eyebrow and one of my eyes. "You have to be fucking kidding me."

"I guess she thought she was safe with her stalker gone," sighs Slade. "I don't think she realized the gravity of what living with us means. That it puts a target on her back from a range of other players trying to take over our turf."

"We need to save her and kill these fuckers," growls Brick, cracking his knuckles, his breathing audible and aggressive.

"Obviously, yes to all the above," says Aidan. I know what's coming. He's going to tell us we need to do it in a sensible way that keeps everyone as safe as possible. And then Brick and Slade will complain but eventually comply.

"Let's think this through first, not do anything rash that might compromise her safety."

Brick and Slade sigh simultaneously. Bingo. Not hard to psychoanalyze this little group. Or maybe it's just because we all know each other so well, we've fallen into these patterns.

"So what's the plan?" I ask.

"They said to await further instructions, so I think we should do that. It sounds like we were speaking with Swarenski's men, based on Angel's description of the SUV, as well as the brief exchange with one of the guys."

"They are all from here, right? Originals from the island?"

"Yeah," sighs Aidan, running his hand through his hair. "That's exactly right. And you know who knows them well?"

"Those fucking snakes," growls Slade.

"You're saying they might actually come in useful for something for once?" asks Brick, raising an eyebrow.

"That would be a fucking first. About time, though," Slade sneers.

"I think that's our best shot," nods Aidan. "Roman, would you like to do the honors, or should I?"

"I'll give Skyler a call," I reply, sighing. "I don't like the guy very much, but I think I can get through to him."

I dial his number, and he picks up on the third ring. "Roman?"

"Yeah, it's me, Roman." I take a deep breath and steel myself. I don't enjoy asking for favors. "Listen, we need your help."

"Oh you do, do you? That's interesting," says Skyler. "Keep talking."

Chapter Eighty-Two

Angel

Fuck. *Fuck!*

I wake up, and once again I'm not in the location I intended to be. I'm in a dark room, thankfully not shackled this time, but it's cold in here and I can't see shit.

The men on this island really can't seem to stop taking women hostage. Kidnapping them. Holding them captive. Just moving them around on a fucking whim, it seems!

My eyes adjust. It's cool in here, definitely air-conditioned. The room is fairly bland from what I can make out, empty. Four walls and no windows. I try to listen for anything helpful in figuring out where I am, but it's eerily silent.

I'm such an idiot for going for a walk, now that I think about it. So giddy that my psycho stalker was dead that I forgot who I was living with, and what the implications were of living with the Brixton men. They're powerful, successful, and there are other groups that covet their hold on this island. It was complete idiocy of me to forget that just because the man that taunted me for so long was dead, I still need to take safety precautions and not prance around like Miss fucking Independent. I could have taken a guard, but that just seemed so extra.

I just wanted a moment for myself, but now I see why that was a mistake.

A big one.

And now I may have to pay the ultimate price.

Chapter Eighty-Three

Roman

Skyler and I agree to regroup half an hour after the initial phone call. He committed to doing some research with his guys and to make some phone calls to figure out what we're really dealing with.

After almost exactly thirty minutes, my phone rings and it's him calling back. I answer on the first ring.

"Yep," I growl into the phone, eager to hear what progress he's made.

"Okay, here's the plan," says Skyler calmly. "Meet us around the corner of the Swarenski compound at 4 o'clock sharp. We're going in together. We know a weak point that should enable us to resolve this fairly quickly."

"You're sure? You think we can get her back this easily?"

"Listen, we have a history with these guys. We're prepared to leverage it to help you rescue your girl. I needed to call in a few favors, but seeing we're going into partnership consider this some type of olive branch."

"Alright," I growl. "But you better not fuck this up."

"Oh we won't," says Skyler. "We're more worried that you will."

Chapter Eighty-Four

Aidan

The eight of us guys stand over six of Swarenski's men. They're pitiful, kneeling down and flinching, protecting their heads and shoulders.

After Skyler gained us access to Swarenski's compound, we were able to pick off most of the guards one by one, and we ended up in the center of the building with these guys, who appear to be the strongest of the group.

"Why are you all cowering? What do you think we are, monsters?" Brick laughs like a maniac. He gestures to Dom. "Did you hear that, man? The sound of silence. They think we're monsters."

"I have no idea why they'd say that," says Dom, picking up one of the two branding irons that's been heating on the coals in front of us, and handing it to Brick. He holds the other one in his left hand.

"Now, how about you start telling us what we need to know." Brick smiles sweetly at the men.

He presses the branding iron into the hand that one man is holding on top of his head to protect his skull. There's a sizzling sound, a little billow of smoke emanating from the metal as it sears into the man's flesh. The man screams. "We're going to mark you all over. Nobody will accept you when we're done, so you may as well tell us what we want to know."

The man stays silent.

"Very well," says Brick. He shrugs, raises his gun and shoots the man in the back of the head.

The other men keep their heads lowered, but they flinch and adjust themselves awkwardly, probably wondering if Brick's about to completely lose it and travel down the line to dish out the same fate.

"This is your last chance, guys," Brick says, and Dom nods in agreement, the two enforcers doing their thing. "Let me help you help us. Tell us where she is."

They move in front of the second guy in the line. "Your turn, sweet pea! Tell us what you know."

The man whimpers as Slade joins Brick and Dom and touches the cold metal of the gun to the man's temple. "Clock's ticking. Tick-tock!"

The man cries out, "I don't know anything! I swear!" but his eyes betray him, darting to the man next to him.

"Maybe my friend Brick here can persuade you otherwise," Slade gestures at Brick, whose face is stony as he eyes up the man.

"I can be very persuasive when I want to be!" shouts Brick merrily.

He extends the branding iron and applies it to the man's cheek. The acrid scent of burning human flesh wafts through the room as the man screams in agony.

"You sound so pretty when you sing like that, dollface," says Brick in a sing-song voice, continuing to hold the iron against his flesh.

The man instinctively goes to grab the hot metal bar and rips his hands away at the agony caused by the molten heat. He whimpers more.

Despite the pain he's experiencing, his eyes point again to the man to his right, as if he's giving us a signal.

Slade moves on to the next man in the line, and Dom and Brick follow.

"What about you, sir? You've got some secrets you'd like to share?" asks Slade, getting into the enforcer role as well. "Information on our girl's whereabouts?"

This man stifles a whimper.

"It's okay to be scared, sweet cheeks," says Brick as he extends the red-hot poker until it's only a couple of inches from this man's eye. He flinches at the heat emanating from the hot metal.

"Start talking," growls Brick.

"I don't know anything," the guy says, his voice cracking.

"I have a real problem with lying," says Slade. "It's the one thing I can't let you off the hook for. I'd say 'you see' but that would be ironic, wouldn't it Brick?"

"Yep, a little too ironic." Brick grins as he stabs the branding iron into the man's eye socket. His eyeball sizzles and a satisfying pop rings out, and I can only assume the little explosion sound was from his eyeball disintegrating under the pressure and the heat.

The man screams and his body bucks as if he's having a seizure, his nerve endings firing all over his body, frantically trying to work out how to battle away this threat.

"Please, please stop!" he shrieks. "I'll tell you everything I know." He holds his hand over his eye and whimpers, fluid oozing to the floor into a puddle below him, a mixture of red and clear goo.

"That's more like it," croons Brick. "Tell us everything. No detail is too small."

The guy starts to speak, his voice coming out in a largely inaudible croak.

"Fucking snitch," the guy next to him interrupts, muttering under his breath.

"Silence!" yells Slade.

"Talk," growl Brick and Dom in unison.

The men refuse to talk. Something in the second man's tone has reminded the now one-eyed man that he made a vow, that there's a cause worth more than his own life.

"Fine, have it your way," sighs Slade, shooting them both between the eyes.

The row of dead men has no more tales to tell. We step over their lifeless bodies as we exit the room. Brick kicks one of them on the way out.

"We're going to get her back. If it's the last thing I ever do, I'm going to see to it that she's safe and away from these guys," huffs Slade.

"And then I'm going to torture them for taking her. I'm going to slice them into tiny little pieces one by one while the others watch," says Slade, his voice a little excited. "There's going to be a lot of basement time for me over the next week."

"I love the sentiment here, guys, but let's make sure we're focused on what needs to happen today, alright?" I need them to focus on the now, not what's happening afterward. We need to be completely focused on what it will take to get her back.

Skyler wasn't wrong. It only takes looking behind a couple more doors to find Angel locked away in a nearly empty room. Swarenski isn't far away, his primary goons no stronger than the six we just took out as they knelt pitifully on the floor.

"No more walks, Angel," Slade growls, wrapping his arms around her protectively after freeing her from captivity.

"No more walks. I get it now," she sighs, no doubt tired of being kidnapped countless times starting with Roman. She's so used to this by now, but I'm really hoping this is the last time.

We were four adversaries away from Tane Brown. Now we're three men away, and although the stakes exponentially increase each time we move up one position, it feels good.

Chapter Eighty-Five

Roman

"Well, we helped you save your woman," says Aidan to Zeke. "And now you've helped save ours. I think I'd call that even."

"I know we make fun of your moral code or whatever you want to call it," says Zeke. "I still don't agree with it, but I kind of understand it. It doesn't mean we'll ever have one, though. Let me make that clear. We'll go where the profits are to be made and where we can build the power."

"That's fine," says Aidan. "You guys do your thing. Hell, we've recently found we're willing to go way outside our boundaries. We'll do anything for Devon, anything to protect our queen." His face darkens as if he's recalling a very unpleasant memory.

"Oh, so you killed for her," nods Brick. "I know that look. The first time I killed someone, it was for a girl, too."

Zeke's face blanches slightly, like he's not proud of whatever happened. "I'm not going into details, but we did what we needed to do."

"Well, it's nice to know you're not a bunch of goody-two-shoes after all," shrugs Slade. "You just need a reason more compelling to you than money or power. We can get behind doing anything to support your woman. We feel the same way about Angel. We'd do anything for her."

Brick nods enthusiastically.

"When we heard you'd entered into this type of relationship, we thought you were copying us," says Skyler. "That because we had it you wanted it, too."

"Actually, it was Angel who saw what you had, the day that she and Devon first clashed and almost scratched each other's eyes out," shrugs Aidan. "I think it helped her to realize the possibilities. Things she might never have considered before."

"Damn, bro," says Rake. "We get credit for saving your girl, and now also for her being your girl. You're going to owe *us* now."

Chapter Eighty-Six

Angel

Roman knocks on my open door and pops his head into my room. "Angel, we all want to speak with you."

"Um, that sounds ominous." I squint at him. "Are you all still mad that I went for a walk and ended up being kidnapped?"

He shrugs. "It wasn't your best judgement, but we understand and none of us are mad. We're just glad you're back safely."

"Are you sure this isn't going to be about how you all want me to leave because your lives would be far more simple that way?" A frisson of concern shoots through my body, a little knot forming in my stomach. "That you're done with me?"

"No, no," he shakes his head quickly, trying to allay my concern. "It's nothing bad. In fact, we want to clear things up to make sure there's no doubt in your mind about how we all feel about you, individually and collectively."

"Oh, I see. Okay then." Finally, some clarity. Everything's been so organic until now, and I've been trying to go with the flow, to enjoy the moment as much as possible. But it has been hard, not knowing what's going to happen next, not knowing where I stand now that my psycho stalker is dead. I know they all care about me, and I know my relationship with them is strong in many ways, but I've always worried that I'm at risk of being discarded. And at this point, who am I without them? I've been strong, I've been independent, but they've woven themselves into the fabric of my being and I know I'd never be the same without the Brixtons in my life. So some clarity is welcome, even if this type of formal conversation about it is a bit intimidating.

"Meet us in the living room in half an hour, Angel."

"Okay. I'll see you soon."

He kisses me on the forehead and leaves.

I get ready, throwing on shorts and a tank and putting my hair up in a topknot. I put on some foundation and mascara and a slick of eyeliner and dab my lips with a shiny clear gloss. May as well look cute for this serious meeting.

When I get to the living room, they're all waiting for me. They look up as I enter, each of them smiling at me. The air is electric with a sense of expectation that I can't quite put my finger on. At least no-one is frowning or looking concerned. Maybe they do really want me here forever and this is just about logistics.

"Angel, come and take a seat," says Aidan, gesturing to a spot on the couch between him and Roman. I walk over and take a seat, enjoying the feeling of their strong thighs pressed against mine. Brick sits opposite us in the armchair, and Slade sits to the other side of Aidan.

"Listen, we realize that things have been a bit up in the air since… well, since the end of Brett Wolf."

Normally, a shiver would trickle down my spine at the sound of his name, but today I feel nothing. It's just a name now, an unpleasant memory and a sense of closure. I still have some work to do to fully process everything, but I know I'm on the right track.

"We want to let you know where things stand from our perspective, and how we want things to move forward from here."

"That sounds very formal," I say, half-joking.

"Well, here's the thing, Angel. We all care very much about you. We're all infatuated with you. I'll go so far as to say we are all completely in love with you. You've changed every one of our lives since you arrived at this house. We all want you to be here."

I look around at each of the guys and from the expressions in their eyes, I know this is true for all of them. Brick and Roman are nodding, and Slade's historically icy gaze has a surprising and comforting warmth to it, like at least part of him has thawed.

"So we wanted to talk through how this would work in practice. We don't want to set hard rules around who you spend time with and when. That's really not how we operate, and I think you know that."

I nod. I've never felt pressured to spend any time with one or more of them. It's just happened organically, and that's felt good to me.

"But," he says, putting a finger up, "you will belong to all four of us, and only us, if you choose to live under this roof. And we would commit ourselves only to you. You would be ours, Angel, and we would be yours. Do you understand?"

I'm breathless at the thought. These four incredibly hot, amazing men, wanting me. Wanting to be mine and mine alone. "I—yes, that's what I want too, very much." The words come out almost as a loud whisper, the loudest I can muster as I feel myself melting inside.

"It sounds like we should celebrate," grins Brick. "What do you all think?"

Slade grins, and it's even hotter than his resting Slade face, his mouth forming a half-smirk that I haven't seen before. Roman smiles at me, his eyes molten with desire, which takes me back to the time in his room where I dropped my towel and spent the night snuggled in his arms.

Aidan's gaze meets mine, and he doesn't need to say a word to communicate his desire. He places a hand on my thigh and my leg quivers at his touch. I can feel my panties getting saturated, arousal dripping from my core in anticipation of what's about to happen. He dips his head down and his mouth meets mine, the other men looking on as we engage in a passionate kiss, our tongues exploring each other, his hand purposefully trailing up my thigh, his fingers beginning to caress my folds through my clothing.

"We're all overdressed," says Brick. "It's time for a sexy party, and that requires no clothing on Angel."

I snort. Even comments like that couldn't kill the mood right now.

"Lift your arms up," directs Aidan, and I happily comply. He pulls off my shirt and bra, exposing my breasts, and my nipples immediately harden as I feel four pairs of eyes on them. He dips his head down and sucks one of my nipples into his mouth, caressing it with his tongue. I moan as the twirling of his tongue sends a lightning bolt from my nipple straight to my core.

Next thing I know, Slade is kneeling in front of me, and has taken my second nipple into his mouth and is sucking on it.

Aidan gently lifts me up by my hips as Slade continues to suck on my nipple, and slides my shorts and panties off in one movement, leaving me bare. Returning my ass to the couch, he presses his mouth to mine again, and I moan as he slides one of his fingers inside my pussy.

"Jesus, you're so fucking wet, Angel."

"How could I not be, in this situation?" I moan.

Slade looks up from my chest height and smiles at me. His hand is next to Aidan's, and he slides one of his fingers inside me as well. Both men have fingers inside me now, and I gasp as they move them in rhythm. I've never had two men fingering me at the same time before, and it's hot as fuck. I spread my thighs further apart to give them better access and I gasp as they both plunge their fingers in deeper, while Brick and Roman look on, their eyes dark with lust.

Brick moves over directly in front of me. "I need to taste you," he growls. "Do you mind?" He gestures to Aidan and Slade and they move to the side to give him access. He growls again as he presses my thighs apart, his eyes locked on my glistening folds. "Aidan was right. You are fucking soaking, Angel. I can't wait to taste how excited you are."

Grabbing me underneath my ass with his large, powerful hands, he pulls me to the edge of the couch, bringing me right up to his face. Then he dips his head and feasts on my pussy, his tongue exploring every part of me. I moan as he slides it inside me and tongue-fucks me, extracting my arousal and moaning as he savors the taste. Then he turns his attention to my clit, lapping at it while holding me still despite my hips feeling like they want to buck off the couch at his touch. When I'm at the edge of an orgasm, Brick abruptly pulls away.

"Ro, you want to do the honors?" he grins, and Roman wastes no time getting down on his knees in front of me and resuming where Brick left off. His tongue works expertly, too, and he slides two fingers inside me while he twirls it around my clit. In only a moment, I'm at the edge again, and this time I'm allowed to cross right over it, my hips bucking and writhing as my pussy clenches around Roman's fingers as he sucks my clit into his mouth and keeps it there while I come. My eyes roll back and I see stars as I ride the peak, and when the wave of pleasure finally subsides and I refocus my vision, I see the other three men looking on at my legs clamped around Roman's neck, his face still buried in my pussy.

"Mmm, good girl," says Aidan. "Now, sit down on me, Angel."

I turn around, my back to his chest, and straddle him. I lower myself onto his rock-hard cock and he groans.

"Fucking hell, baby," he growls in my ear. "Your tight pussy feels amazing wrapped around my hard cock. Did Roman and Brick make your pussy feel good?"

His husky voice causes my pussy to clench around him even tighter. "Mmhmm, real fucking good," I moan.

"Mind if I join you?" asks Slade.

I bite my bottom lip and beckon him over. "What do you have in mind? My pussy is... taken," I say, as I roll my hips on top of Aidan, grinding down on him.

"Not all of it is taken. And I want to taste you, too," says Slade, getting to his knees and spreading my legs further apart, causing me to sink down further onto Aidan's engorged cock.

He dips his head and licks the lengths of my folds, his deliciously long tongue twirling around my clit and then sucking it into his mouth. He flattens his tongue against my clit and begins lapping at it. My hips buck upward toward his face. I groan as he sucks my clit into his mouth again and lashes it with his tongue, his head bobbing up and down in rhythm with my hips.

"Hold her still," he says to Aidan. "Don't let her move for a moment. I want to torture her with my tongue while she can't move. I want to make her come all over your cock and my face."

"Okay, just keep your tongue away from my dick. She's the only one I want sucking it."

I moan and grind my pussy over Aidan's cock.

Aidan groans, "Oh yeah, baby. I'm so deep inside you." He leans forward and nips me on my upper back. I yelp and clench my pussy around him even tighter.

Aidan does as Slade instructed, grabbing my hips and stilling me so that the only movement is Slade's tongue lapping at my clit. I'm trapped, unable to move as his long tongue strokes against me, teasing me and whipping me into a frenzy. My clit is already sensitive from Brick and Roman's earlier attention, and I moan as he sucks it into his mouth and then nibbles on it, and my pussy seizes even more firmly around Aidan's cock.

He groans loudly. "Fuck. Your pussy is like a vice!". I may not be able to move my hips, but there's nothing stopping me from squeezing against Aidan's iron-hard shaft.

Although I just orgasmed from both Brick and Roman eating my pussy only moments before, my body is thoroughly enjoying Slade's follow-up and it doesn't take me long to get right back to the edge. My pussy clenches repeatedly around Aidan's cock as ribbons of pleasure roll outward from my clit and spread their tendrils throughout my body.

"Jesus, she's milking my cock, man. I don't know how long I can hold on. She's tight as fuck. I can barely move inside her."

He reaches around and cups my breasts, and I moan as he rolls my nipples between his thumbs and forefingers.

"You're so fucking beautiful when you come," says Aidan. "Isn't she, Slade?"

Slade nods, gazing up at me, my arousal slick on his mouth and chin. "Very."

"We're going to make you fall apart for us right here, right now. These are just a couple of the many orgasms you'll be having today. We fully intend to celebrate having you back, every inch of you."

Roman and Brick both surround us, so now I'm flanked by all four men. "Slade needs you, baby," says Aidan. "I do, too. But start off with him and come back to me. I want your ass."

Slade sits on the couch next to us, his rock-hard cock erect and welcoming. I slide myself gently off Aidan and turn to straddle Slade, then I slide my pussy down on Slade's large cock while the others watch.

He groans. "Fucking hell, you're so tight."

I roll my hips and gently slide myself up and down on him as he grabs my hips and helps to control my pace. My lips meet his and our tongues tangle in a passionate kiss as I continue to ride him.

I hear the cap of a lube bottle and my ass instinctively clenches in anticipation. I need to do the opposite, to relax. Because I don't know who intends on fucking my ass, but they're all pretty well endowed and the last thing I need is to tense myself up before they're inside me.

"Are you sure you're ready for this, Angel?" Aidan asks, his eyes dark with lust. "Because I have a feeling once we've had you this way we're going to want it all the time."

"Fuck yes, I want it like this," I moan.

I turn and watch as Aidan squeezes some lube from the tube and rubs it all over his cock. He spreads some onto two of his fingers and smears it over my tight hole, working it into my entrance.

"Hold her still," directs Aidan, and Slade tightens his grip on my hips so that I can't keep riding him. As much as I want to keep slamming myself down on him, I know I need to stop while Aidan also works his way inside me.

Aidan lines his cock up with my asshole and pushes himself in slowly. At first there's resistance and then the lube does its thing and he slides deep inside. I cry out as he buries me to his hilt. It was slippery, but he's still large, still filling up a place in my body that hasn't had a lot of attention before.

"Are you okay, Angel?" he whispers as he cups my breasts from behind, buried inside me.

"Yes, baby," I rasp.

He and Slade are both buried deep inside of me and I feel full, stuffed, and I can't wait to move with them.

I roll my hips, gently at first, while I get a feel for the best angle to accommodate both of their cocks. I tilt my hips and slide up and down and they both groan.

"We're going to fuck you now," says Aidan. "Let us take control."

I still myself, and they thrust into me. They're in sync, but the force is coming from my front and my back in a way that I'm not used to, so it feels unpredictable. I roll with their thrusts and moan as the pressure builds within me, the coil tightening in my core. Aidan reaches around my waist and flicks at my clit with his long, skilled fingers and I moan. My pussy and ass clench in response and they both groan again.

Aidan kisses me on my neck, nipping at me and I giggle, then lean forward and once again entangle my tongue with Slade's.

I've been so mesmerized by what's happening that I almost forgot about Brick and Roman. I glance over to the side. Brick is sitting on the couch, legs apart and cock out, stroking himself.

Roman stands just behind Aidan and gazes as Aidan and Slade bury their cocks deep inside me. He's erect and I can see a bead of pre-cum at his tip.

"Want me to get that for you?" I rasp, and he moves closer to us. His cock ends up being at the same height as my mouth and I lick the pre-cum off the tip.

"Get over here, Brick," I say, and he growls as he stands up and comes over to my other side, where I reach out and touch him with my hand, wrapping my palm around his shaft.

As I continue to ride Slade with my pussy and Aidan with my ass, I stroke my hand up and down Brick's shaft. He groans as I twirl my palm gently.

I slide my lips over Roman's hard cock and suck it into my mouth. He groans as I use my other hand to work his shaft as my tongue swirls around his tip. Continuing to stroke him, I turn my head over to Brick and take him in my mouth now.

"Fuck, Angel, your lips are so fucking perfect on my cock," he groans, thrusting himself into my mouth.

I turn my head again, alternating between him and Roman, continuing to use my hands on both. They roll their hips in rhythm with my hands, which are also in rhythm with the thrusts from both Aidan and Slade. I've never felt so full, so stuffed, so used in the best way. We're like an orchestra, moving together, nobody trying to overtake the other. It's selfless. They're all worshipping me and I am equally attending to each of them.

My body is electric, zaps firing all over me as all four men bury themselves in my holes, a plethora of sensations attacking me at the same time. It's sensory overload and my body tenses up. I can feel the pressure building from my core and radiating outward. My pussy and ass clench around Aidan and Slade and I grip Brick and Roman more tightly, moaning on Roman's cock as an orgasm shatters through my body, pleasure radiating all over me as I ride the wave. They all groan simultaneously and talk dirty as Slade and Aidan come inside me, releasing deep within me. Roman and Brick shoot their seed all over me, splattering my face and neck and chest.

I'm panting, covered in sweat, and they continue to ride out their respective orgasms, my body still wrapped around them all.

Brick leaves the room as Aidan pulls himself out of me and lifts me off Slade. He places me gently on the couch as Brick returns with a wet cloth and gently wipes me down. They all watch me, and they're all glowing like I know I am as well. That was an almost out-of-body experience and I couldn't imagine anything more perfect.

We sit there, together, all five of us, silently for a while. I'm snuggled up against Slade and Roman is on my other side, his hand stroking my thigh. Brick sits at my feet, his head on my leg.

"Let's get you to bed, Angel," says Aidan softly, after a while. He takes me by my hand and guides me to my bedroom, but he doesn't make a move to leave. "I want to lie with you tonight, if that's alright with you," he says.

"So do I," says Roman, his voice appearing from behind us.

I slip into bed and they each get in on either side. My back is to Aidan, and he snuggles up against me like the big spoon. Roman faces me and gently traces his finger along the side of my face, down my jaw.

"You're so perfect," he says. "I love you. We all love you."

Aidan squeezes his arms around me, his way of indicating he agrees.

"I love you too," I whisper. "Both of you. All four of you."

Aidan kisses me on the back of the head and I smile at Roman, my lids heavy in a relaxing and contented way, as I lay in their arms and we drift off to sleep.

Chapter Eighty-Seven

Angel

I look down at my hand, admiring Brick's literal handiwork, now that my tattoo is mostly healed. It's like he took the most beautiful rose and made it even more exquisite somehow. He's an enigma. This stone-cold killer who gets off on torturing people and knife play, but who would never eat an animal and draws the most delicate, intricate body art.

"Brick, thank you," I whisper. "It's the most beautiful tattoo I've ever seen. You're so talented. I can't believe I get to wear this on my hand forever."

"It was an honor to create a design on someone as breathtakingly gorgeous as you. And no matter what you decide to do, you'll have a memory of your strength that will be with you always. And maybe when you look at it, you'll think of me, too."

"Always, Brick," I whisper, slipping my hand into his.

He pulls me close and kisses my forehead. "My sweet Angel, my Valkyrie. I never, ever want to let you go."

I wrap my arms around him. I don't want to let him go either. I don't want to let any of them go. But I might have to.

Chapter Eighty-Eight

Angel

"We want to show you something, baby," says Brick, his eyes gleaming with excitement. "We picked it out just for you."

"Oh yeah? What is it?" I raise an eyebrow. I assume they've probably got me a nice dress or some sexy lingerie to wear for them.

"It's a bit of a drive away. Get ready and come with us."

I get dressed and pull my hair up in a ponytail. It feels like a casual but special occasion, having survived the events leading up to today, so I pull on a simple but elegant black romper that makes me feel cute and sexy. I apply a little tinted moisturizer, lengthen my lashes with mascara, and add a dab of bright pink lip gloss. On my feet I wear some stripy black sandals accented with silver, and I painted my toenails a vibrant pink hue. Assessing myself in the mirror, seeing the sparkle in my eyes, I can see that I look as happy as I feel. It has been a struggle to get to this point, but I've arrived and it feels really fucking good.

The guys all smile at me appreciatively as I descend the stairs. They're patiently waiting for me, nobody calling out to rush me, all perfectly content waiting to do whatever this is on my time.

We all head out of the compound and hop into the SUV. Aidan drives us carefully out of the industrial neighborhood, and onto the highway, where we continue to travel for about half an hour.

"Where are we going?" I ask, unfamiliar with the area we're passing through and seeing no sign of us taking an exit. "This is kinda far."

"It'll be worth it when you see it," says Slade. "Trust us."

I consider his words carefully and come to the conclusion that I really do trust them. It's a weird feeling. Trust. Doesn't feel familiar, but it also feels good with them.

After about five more minutes of driving, we take an exit into a neighborhood that seems to be a bustling combination of high-end apartment buildings and sprawling residential homes, boutique stores, and trendy restaurants and bars. We soon arrive at a standalone building with paper taped over the windows. It's painted cream with black accents, giving away no clue what's inside, although the color palate looks upscale.

Brick blindfolds me with a piece of black silk, and Slade and Roman each take one of my hands and lead me inside.

They carefully guide me several steps inside the entrance and get me to stop, and then they remove the blindfold and instruct me to open my eyes.

I look around the space and gasp as I take it all in.

It's the most beautiful hair salon I've ever seen.

At the entrance, there's an ornate marble desk with a state-of-the-art point-of-sale system to ring up happy clients. A discreet display stands behind it, featuring top-quality hair products that I've always fantasized about having in my salon.

The waiting room features a luxurious tufted couch that I can imagine clients relaxing on while they flick through the generous stack of attractively glossy magazines artfully stacked on the sleek glass coffee table that sits low in front of it.

The hair-washing stations are discreetly tucked away, and the recliners are gorgeously padded white leather armchairs with a massage function. Overhead, chandeliers scatter a warm, twinkling glow throughout the entire space.

Gold-framed mirrors line the walls, and each stylist station has a comfortable swivel chair for clients. Hairdryers and other tools hang on overhead hooks, out of the way and creating a hairstylist chic look.

"Oh my god," I gasp as I soak it all in. "This is the most beautiful hair salon I've ever seen. It's the salon of my dreams."

To the side is an area set up for tattoos. It's black and gold and gorgeous. I recognize the leather recliner from the house. "For me to do guest appearances now and then," Brick explains, beaming. When he was doing my tattoo, I didn't realize how carefully he was listening to what I was saying, how he must have been mentally taking notes that have manifested into noticeable touches throughout this space. My heart flutters as I realize how much he truly sees me, how much he cares. How much they all do.

"Wow, how did you find this place?" I ask. "It's amazing."

"We looked around until we found the place that was perfect for you," smiles Roman, his gaze warm and locked on mine.

"You—you really got this for me?" It doesn't feel real. I feel like the luckiest woman alive. And it's not because of this place. It's because of how these four men collectively make me feel. Seen. Heard. Truly cared for. Like I really belong.

"Yes, it's all yours," says Aidan, beaming at me. "Whether or not you stay with us, we want the best for you, always. Our queen deserves nothing but the best."

"Wow, I don't know what to say." I feel my eyes watering and I blink back the tears. Nobody has ever done anything like this for me. It's so thoughtful and generous. I didn't mind working out of my old salon in the strip mall. It had everything I needed, even though it was basic and not at all fancy. But this is the next level. Not because it clearly wasn't cheap, but because it represents me.

"Just say you want to be with us forever," says Brick, his eyes eager. Then he quickly looks down. "But only if that's true. I know we can't force you to stay. This has to be on your terms, and your terms alone."

Slade clears his throat. "Um, Angel, I have something for you," he says. He reaches behind his back to the counter behind him and retrieves a large bouquet of flowers. He hands them to me. My body stiffens and I resist the urge to squeeze my eyes shut as I remember the last one he gave to me.

"Again?" I say. "Didn't you hurt me enough last time you gave me flowers?" I feel my mouth tremble slightly as I speak. This moment means so much to me and I'm terrified that Slade is going to ruin it with one of his cruel barbed comments or another hateful gift.

"A lot has changed since then, Angel," he says softly. He looks down, but then steels himself and raises his gaze to mine. "I'm really sorry for how I treated you. That wasn't kind. You didn't deserve it, and it was more about myself than you. I want you to have these, to make amends for how I acted back then."

I take a deep breath, hoping this isn't a trick. Hoping it's nothing like last time.

Taking a closer look, the flowers are beautiful, including some I've never seen before. There are little yellow ones that I feel like I've seen growing on the side of the road, like wildflowers.

"Those are from the rue plant," he says, seeing me looking at them. "They symbolize regret and remorse. Seemed appropriate."

"They look too happy to represent something so dark," I say.

"Darkness can be deceiving. Darkness can be beautiful, too," says Brick.

"You're right. I've learned that from all of you," I reply, smiling at all four of them.

"So have I redeemed myself?" he asks, almost bracing himself at my potential response.

"Oh Slade, you'd already redeemed yourself," I say softly. "My guard was still a little up, just in case, because let's face it, you can be a bit unpredictable. Typical chef bullshit." The others snicker, and then Slade himself smirks. "But this is very sweet, thank you. I appreciate the gesture, and I'll gladly erase the first bouquet from my mind and replace it with this one."

His shoulders noticeably relax. "Thank goodness for that," he says. "I promise, I'll make it up to you for the rest of my life."

Chapter Eighty-Nine

Angel

"Now that you're free from Brett Wolf, but also from us, it's our life's work to make you never want to leave us. We will protect you at all costs, but not in a way that stifles you or pushes you away. We will adore you and treat you like a queen, because you are our queen. We will house you and feed you and spoil you, not because you're not capable of doing those things for yourself—because you are—but because we choose to do those things for you. We love you, Angel. We want you in our life, always. We need you. All of us need you. But it needs to be your choice to stay."

"Do you solemnly swear that each one of you will bury yourself deep inside my pussy and other holes upon request?" They all nod enthusiastically. Excellent.

"Will you grant me earth-shaking orgasms that rip through me and make my full body shudder and my toes curl?" They each nod some more.

"Will you tease me until I beg you to make me fall apart? Will you mark me as yours with bruises and welts and tattoos and piercings, in the perfect blend of pleasure and pain?" They nod again, and Brick gives me a double thumbs-up which makes me laugh. He liked that one a lot.

"And will you dominate me in the bedroom but always respect me, and remain faithful only to me? Even you, Roman? Are you capable of that?"

"Sure am," he smiles at me, and I can tell it's not his smooth player smile but that he genuinely means it.

"Sex aside, will you continue to embrace my darkness and encourage me to own the parts of myself that are emerging? To push my comfort zone and support me to be less beholden to false morals that people place upon themselves out of fear?"

"We one hundred percent will," says Aidan, the others nodding in agreement.

"Then I will happily remain committed to the four of you. As long as you uphold these vows, I am yours." I pause. "There are still many things about each other that we don't know. It hasn't been that long when you think about it. So I can't promise you forever. I know you want me to, but I can't. That would be foolish for me, for all of us."

I see their brows furrowing, concern palpable in their eyes.

"But I can promise that I will do everything I can to help you advance this empire. Our empire. One day, mark my words, we will overthrow Tane Brown and take control of these islands. People will say the Brixton name and shake in fear of our power, and Tane will seem like a tiny minnow. We will be the sharks. We will own these islands."

Relief washes over all of their faces. And respect. They can see that I truly want to support them in their quest, and they know I'm the right person to help them succeed.

"We got you something else," says Slade, glancing at the other guys.

"What? Besides the nicest hair salon that I've ever seen in my life?" They really are crazy. And crazy for me. I'm finally starting to believe it.

"Yeah, it turns out we enjoy spoiling the shit outta you, beautiful," says Aidan. "We think you're ready for it. And we will do everything to protect it as well as you."

Brick reaches into a cardboard box beside them I hadn't noticed before, and pulls out the most gorgeous black kitten I've ever seen. It has big blue eyes that dart about, assessing the environment for threats, food and things to play with.

"This is Brix," he says. "You can change his name if you like, but he answers to it already," he grins.

I smile as he hands the little squirming ball of fur to me. It looks deep into my eyes, assessing me, and then purrs. A low, soft purr of contentment as it snuggles into my arms.

"Hello baby!" I squeal, scratching him under his tiny chin with my forefinger, which only makes his purrs grow louder. "I like Brix," I smile at Brick and the others. "It suits him."

"Just like we suit you," he smiles back.

Chapter Ninety

Angel

"Brick, you are fearless. You fall down hard, and you fall down often, but only to get right back up. And you are quirky as hell and it's adorable." Brick lifts his shoulders back and pushes his chest out, puffing himself up so he's even bigger than usual. He beams.

"Aidan, you are resourceful and responsible. You lead us through the most fucked up situations with grit and calm, and you always follow through. You're also sexy as fuck," I say.

"Roman, you're a complete charmer. You make people feel like they're the only ones in your room. But under the surface, there's more to you. You are truly kind. You put people's needs above your own, you're supportive and you intervene when you see people being treated unfairly."

"And Slade. Slade, Slade, Slade." Everyone laughs, including me. "There's just so much to say about you, isn't there? About us?" He smirks and nods.

"You are a fucking fantastic cook. You're argumentative and bitingly sarcastic, but you're also extremely perceptive. You're highly attuned to the unsaid, the gently implied. You're more empathetic than most people probably realize. You just choose to be an asshole with the information you have at your resourceful fingertips." Everyone laughs again.

"All of you are protective of me. Some might say possessive." I glance at them and they smirk, a couple of them shrugging. No denying it.

"But truly, you set aside your own wants and needs to make sure I'm taken care of. You make me feel like your priority. You make sure I'm safe at all times, and that nobody can cause pain. Except for you in the bedroom, which is different." I wink, and they all grin. A couple of them start to look a little horny.

"And you're also all incredibly hot. I have never experienced any one man, let alone four, who has made me feel so beautiful, so confident, so sexy, simply by being myself. You make me less inhibited, more willing and adventurous about trying new things. You're sensitive to how I'm feeling, and you know just how to bring me pleasure."

"So you don't have any regrets?"

"None whatsoever. I wouldn't change a thing."

CHAPTER NINETY-ONE

Angel

Devon and I are furious. The guys got together to figure out next steps to take down Tane, but things got out of hand after what started out as a minor miscommunication, and they've all been bickering again. It's almost come to blows, and we're ready to intervene. This is nonsense.

"Stop all this talk about which group is right or wrong!" Devon cries out, as exasperated as I am. "You have to understand, everyone is morally gray to some extent. Some people are more obviously aligned with good or bad, but everyone has an element somewhere in between. In other words, nobody is truly all positive or negative, depending on the perspective you view them from. That goes for all of you, too!"

Devon eyes my guys. "You lot are willing to do whatever it takes to achieve your goals, even if it means hurting others in the process. That's why my guys have such a problem with you, because you'll go further than their boundaries allow to get what you want. But, from what I've seen, you also have a strong sense of loyalty and protectiveness towards those you care about, which is generally seen as a positive trait. That's something all eight of you have in common."

I double down. "All of you have complex histories that contribute to your moral grayness. Everyone here, including Devon and I, have made mistakes in the past and been forced into difficult situations where we've had to make tough decisions. In many cases, decisions we may not be proud of. Some of us are able to let it go, and the rest of us might dwell on those decisions for the rest of our lives. The decisions were still made, and we still have to live with the consequences."

I hand the figurative baton back to Devon. "Everybody here is complex. Nobody here can be totally categorized as good or bad. We all have flaws and have made questionable decisions, but every one of us also has redeeming qualities and I would go so far as to say we have all showed acts of kindness and heroism. So shut the fuck up trying to say this group is right or this group is wrong, or Angel and I will leave your dumb asses to fight in the playground while we go off and find some real men."

Everybody is silent. All eight men look sheepish, their eyes focused on the ground in front of them. They know they've fucked up.

"Well, fuck," says Aidan, running a hand through his hair. "I think they might have a point. We can agree to disagree on our approach, but one thing we can all agree on is that Tane Brown needs to be shut down, and he's the closest to evil anyone can get.

"Makes us all look like angels," says Skyler. He suddenly glances at Angel. "You know what I mean, not like a—."

I wave my hand and laugh. "I get it, I get it."

Chapter Ninety-Two

Angel

All ten of us stand on the beach, our surfboards at the ready as we gaze out at the gently rolling waves. Eight men and two women, two separate tight-knit groups now bound as one by our desire to take down Tane Brown and take over control of the islands.

The Brixtons, which now includes me and the cat, I guess. We didn't bring the cat. Maybe one day, judging by how courageous that little kitten already is.

And then Devon and the snakes.

I can barely believe we're in a truce with the fucking snakes, and we're about to join forces. This is wild, and none of us saw it coming until it hit us right between the eyes that there is no other way. But as difficult as it is to believe, and as challenging of a journey as it's been to get here, in this moment, it feels right.

As we wade into the water, we can feel the power of the waves beneath us, lifting us up and carrying us forward. Devon and I take the lead, carving a graceful path through the water as the men follow closely behind until we find a calm spot where we can turn and face the shore.

Looking around at this group, now sitting on our boards out in the ocean, I see strength, I see intelligence, and I see power in numbers. We're ready to make a plan to overthrow Tane Brown. And when the timing is right, we will strike. Together.

As the sun sets, the sky turns into a beautiful display of oranges, pinks and purples, casting a warm glow over the island in front of us. The temperature remains warm and inviting, and the sound of waves crashing on the shore provides a peaceful, relaxing soundtrack while we contemplate what's next.

This is a new era. This is the calm before the storm. And right now, there's no end in sight.

Also By

Blood and Sand (Dark Reverse Harem Romance)

- Sea of Snakes
- Sea of Sinners
- Sea of Rage
- Sea of Pain

Billionaire's Takeover Collection

- Irreversible Decision
- Compelling Proposal
- Love Merger
- The Billionaire's Takeover Collection (all 3 of the above!)

Novellas

- Love in a Seedy Motel Room

Sign up for my newsletter herefor the latest on new releases, promos, giveaways and events!

Join me on social media:

Facebook: @heidistarkauthor

Instagram: @heidistarkauthor

TikTok: @heidistark_author

Websitehttps://heidistarkauthor.com

About Heidi Stark

Heidi Stark is an indie dark romance author who grew up in New Zealand and now resides in the US.

She is inspired by the locations she visits on her travels, and the people she meets along the way.

When she's not writing, you can usually find her reading, listening to podcasts, or dreaming about her next book.

Learn more about Heidi Stark at her website. Sign up for exclusive content and her newsletter here.

You can also find out more about Heidi and her upcoming books on social media:

Facebook Page

Facebook Group

Instagram

TikTok

Made in the USA
Las Vegas, NV
27 March 2024

87866412R00267